Escape Velocity

ALSO BY CHARLES PORTIS

Norwood (1966)

True Grit (1968)

The Dog of the South (1979)

Masters of Atlantis (1985)

Gringos (1991)

Escape Velocity

A
CHARLES PORTIS
MISCELLANY

Edited and with an Introduction by
JAY JENNINGS

Cover Art and Illustrations by
MIKE REDDY

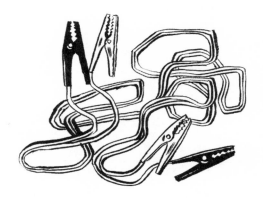

The Butler Center for Arkansas Studies
Central Arkansas Library System
100 Rock Street
BUTLER
CENTER   Little Rock, Arkansas 72201
BOOKS   www.butlercenter.org

First Printing, October 2, 2012

10 9 8 7 6 5 4 3 2 1

ISBN (13) 978-1-935106-50-0
ISBN (10) 1-935106-50-3

Project director: Rod Lorenzen
Copyeditor/proofreader: Ali Welky
Book designer: H. K. Stewart

Library of Congress Cataloging-in-Publication Data

Portis, Charles.
 [Selections. 2012]
 Escape velocity : a Charles Portis miscellany / edited and with an introduction by
Jay Jennings ; cover art and illustrations by Mike Reddy.
     p. cm.
 ISBN 978-1-935106-50-0 (hardcover : alk. paper)
 1. Portis, Charles--Appreciation. I. Jennings, Jay. II. Title.

 PS3566.O663A6 2012
 813'.54--dc23

                                      2012018195
Printed in Canada.

This book is printed on archival-quality paper that meets requirements of the
American National Standard for Information Sciences, Permanence of Paper, Printed
Library Materials, ANSI Z39.48-1984.

The publishing division of the Butler Center for Arkansas Studies was
made possible by the generosity of Dora Johnson Ragsdale and John
G. Ragsdale Jr.

Contents

Introduction

By Jay Jennings

I. What You Will Find Here

This collection began life as a fat folder in my file cabinet. For years, in haphazard fashion, I had torn out (or in later Internet times, printed out) every mention I saw of Charles Portis and placed it in the folder. A Page-a-Day calendar list of Garrison Keillor's five favorite funny novels, including *Masters of Atlantis*. A column by James Wolcott in *Vanity Fair* after the publication of *Gringos*. Too infrequently, a story by Portis himself, from the *Atlantic* or the *Oxford American*, would go into the file. I had a certain home-field advantage over other Portis aficionados (and they are legion) because I am from Little Rock. For example, I had written for and subscribed to the *Arkansas Times* (then a magazine, now a weekly paper) and therefore found in my mailbox in New York in 1991 a long piece by Portis about the Ouachita River, which meanders through the south Arkansas of his boyhood.

I had read *True Grit* sometime in my teens—it came out when I was ten and the John Wayne film the next year—but didn't recognize its greatness. Perhaps I didn't think then that a great book could come from our little outpost in Arkansas. The novels I borrowed indiscriminately from my mother's stash of Book-of-the-Month Club selections were set in glamorous locales: Arthur Hailey's *Hotel* (New Orleans), James Ramsey Ullman's *The Day on Fire* (Paris, haunted by an absinthe-drinking poet based on Rimbaud; Annie Dillard says this book made her want to be a writer), and Dostoevsky's *Crime and Punishment* (guess where).

The earliest inclusion in my Portis file was a 1984 story from the *New York Times*, a paper I read daily in a small apartment in Dallas where I was unhappily teaching high school. The story told of two bookstore employees in New York who were so smitten with Portis's five-year-old out-of-print novel *The Dog of the South* that they bought all 183 remaining hardcover copies (it had never appeared in paperback) and set them up as the sole window display in the Madison Avenue Bookshop. The books sold fast, to the curious and to those collared by the hand-selling bookstore staff (remember independent bookstores?), and the novel enjoyed a mini-revival. The *Times* writer contacted Portis in Little Rock, and Portis told the reporter he was "surprised and very pleased" by the attention. He also said, "I write in a little office without a phone behind a beer joint called Cash McCoo's." Because I was from Little Rock, just like the book's narrator Ray Midge, as I learned from the *Times* story, I knew the reporter had misheard the name of the beer joint, that it was actually Cash McCool's. For once, I felt superior to the *New York Times*. And because I knew exactly the building behind Cash McCool's, I could imagine Portis typing away in there and I could perhaps begin to imagine myself as a writer. Into a file it went.

And out I went to Half-Price Books, the rambling Dallas used bookstore where I spent most of my dateless weekends and where I easily found a copy of *The Dog of the South*, emblazoned on the top spine with a little Random House colophon, the scarlet stamp of the remainder. I tried the Sir Thomas Browne epigraph at the beginning ("the Tortile and tiring stroaks of Gnatworms") and didn't understand it but made a mental note to read Sir Thomas Browne since William Styron had also opened *Lie Down in Darkness* with a Browne epigraph. When I had imagined writing a book of my own, I thought it would probably start something like Styron's 119-word sentence that opens his first novel: "Riding down to Port Warwick from Richmond, the train begins to pick up speed on the outskirts of the city, past the tobacco factories with their ever-present haze of acrid, sweetish dust and..." When I read Portis's impeccable and economical first line about Midge's wife Norma running off with Guy Dupree, I was right into the story without any wind-up, and without the dangling modifier Styron threw in our face as evidence of his rule-breaking artistry.

Seven pages in, I learned that Ray Midge was twenty-six. I was twenty-six! And that he was planning to become a high-school teacher! (Don't do it, Ray!) But instead of the mopey, brokenhearted young adult I was, Ray was in pursuit. And the people he met. How they talked!

"Dix puts William Shakespeare in the shithouse."

"Your feet, I mean. They look odd the way you have them splayed out. They look like artificial feet."

"I can see at night. I can see stars down to the seventh magnitude."

What a story!, to quote Midge, who exclaims that more than once and ends up back in Little Rock with Norma, only to have her take off again. That seemed all too true to me.

A year later, in the fall of 1985, I too was back in Little Rock, driving a delivery truck, saving money for an eventual assault on New York and writing for the local alternative newspaper, *Spectrum*. In October, Knopf published *Masters of Atlantis*, Portis's first novel in six years, and I immediately bought a copy from WordsWorth Books in Little Rock (still there! Long live independent bookstores!). Screwing up my courage with the knowledge that I was also now a published writer (*Spectrum*) and perhaps more significantly that my mother, Portis's contemporary, was also from south Arkansas, I called him up (using my home-field advantage to get his number) and asked if he would sign my book. He agreed and invited me to meet him, not at Cash McCool's, but at another beer joint called the Town Pump (still there! Long live independent bars!). I don't remember anything about the meeting other than the fact that Portis did *not* wet down the four corners of his napkin before he lifted his beer and that he *did* treat me like a fellow writer. I moved to New York two months later, now knowing at least one novelist.

We corresponded sporadically over the years while I pursued a career as an editor and writer at various New York magazines and then eventually as a freelance writer in Brooklyn. Whenever I was in Little Rock visiting my parents, I would call him and we would go for a beer or have lunch. My file grew in fits and starts, with a great spasm after the publication of *Gringos* in 1991, and another after Ron Rosenbaum's essay in *Esquire* in 1998 ("Our Least-Known Great Novelist," page 337), which spurred Overlook Press to bring his books back into print. I wrote to him after his memoir "Combinations of Jacksons" appeared in the *Atlantic* in 1999, and when I next returned to Little Rock, I asked if that was perhaps part of a book-to-be. He answered no, it was a "one off," and I and others continued to wait for the next Portis book. He was still obscure to the public at large, but revered among writers. Once at a party in New York, I met novelist Jonathan Lethem and remarked that I'd seen where he had put *True Grit* on a list of novels overshadowed by films made from them (printed out from Salon.com, in my file). I then mentioned the idea that he was our greatest unknown novelist, and he quipped, "Yes, he's everybody's favorite least-known great novelist."

I moved back to Little Rock to work on a book of my own in 2007, my first, and began to see him more regularly, in the late afternoon at a bar near my house, the day-drinking prerogative of two freelance writers. My book, *Carry the Rock*, about a football season at Little Rock Central High School and the history of race relations in the city, came out in 2010, and I presented him with a copy of it at the bar one afternoon, along with an article from the *Wall Street Journal* that mentioned him—another for my file folder.

The article was a review of my book and it began:

> In August 1959, two years after Little Rock became a symbol for the ugly spectacle of resistance to school integration, a young staffer for the "Arkansas Gazette" named Charles Portis took a break from his regular beat to hold up a mirror to the media glare. He filed a report on the reporters themselves—"groups of wilted Dacron and damp mustaches"—who had converged from around the world to cover the crisis. In Mr. Portis's account, the members of the press come off as ignorant and self-righteous as the jeering mobs that had stained Little Rock's public image....
>
> Like Mr. Portis, Jay Jennings is a native son with deep roots in the area and an abiding love for the people and place.

What more could I hope for but to see those five words strung together: "Like Mr. Portis, Jay Jennings..."?

The Coen brothers' film of *True Grit*, released during the Christmas holidays of 2010, occasioned another round of Portis publicity and renewed interest in his work, and I spoke on a panel the next spring, along with two other Little Rock residents and fans, screenwriter Graham Gordy and magazine editor Kane Webb, at the Arkansas Literary Festival. I mentioned my fat folder and expressed the desire that somebody bring together all of Portis's miscellaneous works between covers so I wouldn't have to root through my folder every time I wanted to reread something. Gordy mentioned that he'd performed in Portis's play, *Delray's New Moon*, which had been staged at the Arkansas Repertory Theatre in 1996 and which had almost slipped my mind.

A few days later Rod Lorenzen, a former journalist and bookstore owner and now head of publishing at the Butler Center for Arkansas Studies (a department of the Central Arkansas Library System), called me and asked, "If I can get Portis to agree to do the kind of collection you mentioned, would you edit it?" I said sure. I had suggested the same thing to Portis a few years back, but he'd dismissed it with a wave of his hand, just as he had dismissed an idea I'd cooked up with Roy Blount Jr. to have a marathon reading of *Norwood* in New York on the book's fortieth anniversary. Lorenzen and Portis met for lunch and he now agreed to the project, warning that he'd be pretty hands-off about it.

I thought it would be easy, since I had my file, but once I began researching in earnest, I ran into some difficulties. The three pieces from the *Atlantic*, the two from the *Oxford American*, the one humor piece from the *New Yorker*, and the long travel story from the *Arkansas Times* were all at hand. On eBay, I found and bought a copy of the *Saturday Evening Post* from 1966 that contained his story about the country music scene in Nashville. The special collections department at the University of Arkansas gave me permission to reprint the interview from the *Gazette* Project with Roy Reed, which many Portis adepts had already found online. The one piece totally unknown to me previously was a nine-thousand-word story from a *Los Angeles Times* Sunday magazine in which Portis and his friend Andy Davis drove the length of Baja California. Though it was an early piece, all the elements were there: unpretentious diction, an expert ear for the spoken word, deep knowledge worn lightly, stoic acceptance of trying circumstances, skill with internal combustion engines, and more pure reading pleasure than I'd enjoyed in a long time. Unlike many of the other stories, it's been hard to come by and I'm thrilled to be able to make it more readily available here.

The other treat for Portis fans, published here for the first time, is his three-act play, *Delray's New Moon*. When I asked him about it, he wasn't sure where to find his copy or if he even still had one. Gordy hadn't kept his script, and another actor, Natalie Canerday, was certain she hadn't thrown it away but would have to dig it out from storage at her parents' house in a town an hour away. She also said they got standing ovations every night of its two-week run. Portis attended rehearsals and even did a "talkback" after one performance. Finally, I spoke with Judy Trice, a veteran of Little Rock stages, and she graciously provided her script and allowed me to copy it. The play is terrific to read—in places it's like taking the Ionesco exit off Interstate 30—but I also hope it will be produced again.

I knew from the start that I wanted to include a selection of Portis's newspaper work, and if the *L.A. Times* piece was a surprise, the newspaper reporting and writing (and he was highly proficient at both) was a revelation. During his short time at the *Commercial Appeal* in Memphis, he covered Elvis's mother's funeral (and gets a mention in Peter Guralnick's comprehensive biography of the King). At that time (1958), however, the action was clearly 120 miles west in Little Rock at the *Arkansas Gazette*, which had won two Pulitzers for its coverage of the integration crisis, and Portis soon sought and got a job there. When I Googled "wilted Dacron" from Eddie Dean's review of my book, hoping to find that *Gazette* column online somewhere so I could go to the date on the *Gazette* microfilm here in Little Rock, the review was the only item that came up. I contacted Dean, the co-author of Ralph Stanley's autobiography *Man of Constant Sorrow*, and found that he was also a Portis devotee. He had researched the young journalist's "Our Town" columns on *Gazette* microfilm at the Library of Congress on his own and was extremely helpful in pointing me to his favorite Portis stories there.

Finally, in his four years at the *Herald Tribune*, Portis showed himself to be a versatile and sometimes unparalleled journalist. (That period, and especially his time on the civil rights beat, is discussed in depth below.) To unearth his work there, I visited the New York Public Library, which has the paper on microfilm (as does the Library of Congress, but other copies of it are scarce), and the Dolph Briscoe Center for American History at the University of Texas at Austin, which had bought the paper's morgue and clip files. As I probed the envelopes at the Briscoe Center for lost Portis stories (the flaky, fifty-year-old newsprint fluttering onto my pants), I recognized in myself traits of the fastidious copyeditor Ray Midge as he plotted the trail of his wife and Guy Dupree through the locations on the receipts of his stolen American Express card. "I love nothing better than a job like that," he says. And I loved nothing better than this job, seeking and herding Charles Portis's stray words, collecting them here for other Portisites and soon-to-be Portisites.

II. Portis of Arkansas

The title of this collection, *Escape Velocity*, comes from a line spoken by Ray Midge in *The Dog of the South*: "A lot of people leave Arkansas and most of them come back sooner or later. They can't quite achieve escape velocity." It's one of my favorite Portis lines, and it's fairly representative. It's funny as hell (I won't drain the humor out of it by trying to explain why) and surprisingly poignant, and it's both specific and universal. It refers to the mysterious gravitational pull of the particular place called Arkansas, but you don't have to be from there to appreciate the hold that everyone's home has on them. Also, it's about wandering off and returning, a theme as old as the *Odyssey*.

It's tempting to extend the truth of the line to Portis himself. When he has allowed bios on his book jackets (the first editions of *The Dog of the South* and *Masters of Atlantis* had none), they have sketched his career thusly: Born and educated in Arkansas, he served in Korea as a marine and worked as a journalist in Memphis, Little Rock, New York, and London, where he was bureau chief of the *New York Herald Tribune*; he moved back to Arkansas in 1964, and except for road-trip research in Mexico and elsewhere, he's remained there ever since, working as a freelance writer. Tom Wolfe, his colleague at the *Herald Tribune* in the early 1960s, famously summed up Portis's return to Arkansas in a *New York* magazine story from 1972 (which later became the introduction to an influential collection called *The New Journalism*): "Portis quit cold one day; just like that, without a warning. He returned to the United States and moved into a fishing shack in Arkansas. In six months he wrote a beautiful little novel called *Norwood*. Then he wrote *True Grit*, which was a best seller. The reviews were terrific....He sold both books to the movies....He made a fortune....A *fishing* shack! In *Arkansas*! It was too goddamned perfect to be true, and yet there it was." Knowing Portis a bit as I do, I suspect that he gave appropriate notice to his employers and that the fishing shack was actually a cabin, but that's Tom Wolfe for you.

"In *Arkansas!*" Wolfe wrote, the assumption being that Arkansas was a kind of nowhere, and his italics *and* exclamation point are descendents of Mark Twain's tweaking of the state as full of "lunkheads" (in *Huckleberry Finn*) and of H. L. Mencken's hyperbolic decrying of its "miasmatic jungles." (A century or so later, the rise of Bill Clinton and Walmart will either refute or support those claims.) In any case, Portis set up his writing shop there, and if it wasn't exactly a jungle, it was a good place to go to work, far enough from both coasts as to be invisible to them. A writer in Arkansas, especially in 1964, could go peacefully about the daily grind of making perfect novels without the distracting noise emanating from literary fashion in Manhattan or the movie world in Hollywood. Portis produced five.

How perfect are they? Each fan has his or her own ranking, but unlike, say, Kingsley Amis or Robert Penn Warren, who produced one generally acknowledged great novel and many dismissible lesser works, Portis wrote at least one great novel, *True Grit*, and four maybe better ones. Ed Park's essay on Portis that originally appeared in the *Believer* magazine in 2003 and is included in the Appendix (along with tributes by other writers) sums it up this way: "He has written five remarkable, deeply entertaining novels (three of them masterpieces, though which three is up for debate)." The consistency of the quality of his work seems to me in line with Chekhov or Alice Munro, while the variety of Portis's subjects would require Chekhov to have ventured a play about, say, the California gold rush or Munro to have attempted to send one of her Ontarians into space. There's simply nothing like his oeuvre for its combination of excellence and heterogeneity.

Although he has lived 70 or so years in Arkansas, the state is not a fundamental part of the imaginative world of his novels in the way that Oxford is for Faulkner or Los Angeles for Chandler or Albany for William Kennedy. His first fictional creation, Norwood Pratt, lives in east Texas and merely passes through Arkansas—slamming on the brakes once, disastrously, to watch a possum climb through a fence—on his way to New York and back. (By far the most frequent response I've received when I tell people I'm from Arkansas is, "Oh, I've been through there.") Mattie Ross of *True Grit* fame is proudly from Yell County but lights out for the Territory on her revenge quest before coming home to spend her spinsterhood and eventually tell her tale. Ray Midge of *The Dog of the South* departs and returns to Little Rock but seems more a citizen of Phlegmatopia than anyplace else as he deliberately hunts his wife and her paramour through Texas and into Mexico. And the word "Arkansas" makes a lone appearance each in *Masters of Atlantis* ("Moaler was in his Arkansas duck blind") and *Gringos*, where Jimmy Burns IDs himself as being from the Arklatex, and even then from Louisiana. With each novel, Arkansas recedes.

If Arkansas has a claim on him, it is as the place where he learned to listen. In the interview with his former *Arkansas Gazette* colleague Roy Reed, in the Epilogue (page 285) here, Portis notes that, though his mother "liked writing and had a gift for it, but never the time to work at it much," his father's side of the family "were talkers rather than readers or writers. A lot of cigar smoke and laughing when my father and his brothers got together. Long anecdotes. The spoken word." (The interview also captures the voice of the low-key raconteur that readers of his novels will instantly recognize.) We read about his family in the one piece of direct memoir he has written so far, "Combinations of Jacksons." In it, he describes how his great-uncle Sat discoursed at length and "may well have been the last man in America who without being facetious called food 'vittles' ('victuals,' a perfectly good word, and correctly pronounced 'vittles,' but for some reason thought to be countrified and comical)." Portis's ear was honed in Arkansas while reading, too. He worked for the *Northwest Arkansas Times* when he was a journalism student at the University of Arkansas and edited dispatches from "lady stringers in Goshen and Elkins," he tells Reed, and his job "was to edit out all the life and charm from these homely reports. Some fine old country expression, or a nice turn of phrase—out they went." Ed Park suggests that he created the voice of Mattie Ross in "penance" for that act.

As far away as his imagination travels, Portis has stuck fast to Arkansas, where he has obviously paid careful heed to those not usually given close attention, whether they're passing through, native, or long deceased: salesmen, bar regulars, sixteenth-century explorers ("Those earnest enunciators who say 'bean' for 'been' should know that Hakluyt, the Oxford scholar, spelled it 'bin,' as did, off and on, the poet John Donne"), local historians, elderly people ("Don't you have any chirren to look after you?"), Confederate generals, random citizens ("We know a man in South Arkansas who says 'Pass those molasses' and 'These sure are good cheese'"), and cafe waitresses ("That woman that runs it, that was her sister that run it at night, and she got married and moved to Shreesport").

Norwood Pratt is not the most reliable guide to life, but he affirms one truth in the face of pretension, when his passenger to New York, Yvonne Phillips, claims New Orleans rather than Belzoni, Mississippi, as her home because, "If you live someplace a long time you can count it as your home." He counters, "Naw you can't....You could live in Hong Kong for seventy-five years and Belzoni would still be your home."

III. Portis as Journalist

As good as Portis's ear is, his eye is its equal. While it seems to have been keen from the start (the memories of his youth are evidence of that), journalism's charge to observe dispassionately no doubt honed his skill at finding the salient detail in a scene.

Over and over in the journalism—from his first job after graduation in Memphis to his dispatches from London—strikingly sharp and memorable details leap out, usually in the last few paragraphs of the story when the who, what, where, when, and why have been taken care of. In an otherwise ordinary report about a PR stunt, Portis notices that among the Memphis Jaycees costumed in Confederate uniforms is one who was "wearing a Harry Truman shirt and Japanese sandals." When he relates that Elvis Presley was "leaning on a windowsill" in the hallway of a hospital where the singer's mother would eventually die, we see instantly Elvis's trademark slouch.

As a columnist of the local scene for the *Arkansas Gazette*, he could indulge his eye more freely. There's the cluster of reporters in the heat of an Arkansas August with their "damp mustaches." At the *Herald Tribune*, even on deadline stories, he found the strange, novelistic detail amid the broader event. His story of an explosion at a New York Telephone Company building that killed 21 workers, mostly young women in an accounting office, closes with this: "A pair of high-heeled shoes stood upright in a bare spot where there must have been a desk. A disembodied desk phone was on the floor ringing, its little red extension light winking." His description of a Klan rally one night in Alabama, with two enormous flaming crosses, is more vivid for this observation: "There were a lot of bugs in the air, too, knocking against the crosses and falling into open collars." Perhaps he was remembering this scene less menacingly in *Norwood*, written just two years later, when the narrator comments that Norwood had lived in a tin-roof house in the middle of a Texas gas field with a "spectacular flare that burned all the time" and that "copper-green beetles the size of mice" came to die in it. "At night," he continues, "their little toasted corpses pankled down on the tin roof." Portis's journalism is rich with the kind of writing that presages the skill of the novelist.

It's easy to see why the *Herald Tribune*'s London bureau job might not have been such a plum assignment after the rush of the civil rights beat. Besides harboring a desire to write novels, he went from feverish reporting on the most pressing issues of the day to acting as bureaucratic overseer of the office in London (with those attendant frustrations) and covering things like former prime minister Harold Macmillan's seventieth birthday events. I've included only one piece from that time, a travel story to Wales and Ireland. After one year, he left the paper, and by 1967, it was out of business for good.

Despite his sometime (well, *frequent*) cutting comments about the profession, Portis was a skilled, diligent, and sometimes brilliant journalist, which I hope this selection of his best work will demonstrate. The failure of historians studying the civil rights era to acknowledge and draw upon Portis's work on the beat in the busy summer of 1963 is a mystery to me. His name is absent from David J. Garrow's *Bearing the Cross* (1986), Taylor Branch's *Parting the Waters* (1988) and *Pillar of Fire* (1998); Diane McWhorter's comprehensive history of Birmingham's troubles, *Carry Me Home* (2001); and perhaps most egregiously, from *The Race Beat: The Press, the Civil Rights Struggle, and the Awakening of a Nation* (2006), which won the Pulitzer Prize for history. Neither is he included in the two volumes of the Library of America's collections *Reporting Civil Rights* (2003), though one of his *Herald Tribune* colleagues, Robert J. Donovan, is.

Even at the time, however, his journalism was recognized for its excellence, and his account of two bombings in Birmingham that threatened to derail a desegregation agreement ("How the Night Exploded into Terror," page 43) was reprinted in the collection *Twentieth Century Reporting at Its Best* (1964), which praised it as a "crisp, tightly-written story." More impressive still is the deadline duress under which it—and an accompanying story about a Klan meeting—was produced.

On the evening of Saturday, May 11, 1963, Portis went to nearby Bessemer to cover a Ku Klux Klan rally. The animosity toward the press in Birmingham—and especially toward the New York and national press from the local authorities, including the police—was significant. Earlier that month, a *Life* reporter and his photographer, who captured with his camera demonstrators being pummeled by fire hoses, were arrested and had to flee the state after being bailed out, certain they could not get a fair trial. As tensions between the protesters and civic authorities rose, more press descended on Birmingham, including Portis, who had previously covered Martin Luther King Jr.'s jailing in Albany, Georgia. It looked as if King was making progress toward negotiating a kind of truce with the city business leaders to provide equal access to and opportunities for employment in downtown stores, but the Klan's meeting nearby was an ominous sign that the quietude might be ending.

Portis was aware of himself as a target for those local elements who despised the press. In a story filed earlier that day, he had written of a meeting Friday night in the county courthouse in which "angry white extremists" who opposed the businessmen's concessions "ejected" the newsmen. He added, with wry pride, "a reporter from the Herald Tribune, in particular, was booed." It must have taken no small amount of courage to then present himself at the Klan meeting the following night. Fortunately for him, the crowd there "was not rising to the rhetoric," as McWhorter writes, and when it ended at about 10:15 p.m., Portis headed back to the Tutwiler Hotel with some other reporters. Around midnight, he and the others heard the "dull whoomp" of an explosion—it was the same onomatopoeic word one of the girls in the New York Telephone explosion had used—and they rushed to the scene, the Gaston Motel four blocks away.

What followed was a full night of rioting, arson, and general civil unrest, unquelled until 6 a.m., by which time more than a thousand policemen and state troopers had brutally subdued the African American participants and spectators both. Portis himself, along with other reporters, had been in some peril from the fire, thrown bricks and bottles, and the reckless course of the city's armored police vehicle, which, he writes as he dips briefly into the first-person plural, "mounted the sidewalk once and made a headlong pass down it, sending about 50 of us spectators diving for the dirt."

The next day, no doubt on very little if any sleep, he produced a 1,900-word front-page story of that evening's chaos, one that manages not only to capture the scene with immediacy and concreteness but to give it context and lyricism. When he describes the attack of a Col. Lingo on some defenseless black bystanders, he takes the time to remind us that "Col. Lingo and his men had been chafing all week at the moderation and restraint of Chief Moore and his city police." When he notes that at dawn a police car is announcing for residents to "get off the God damn streets, get," he adds with subdued irony, "but someone put a stop to that, evidently because it was Sunday and Mother's Day."

Included with the long piece was Portis's sidebar about the Klan rally. Readers will recognize in it more clearly Portis the novelist, casting a gimlet eye on any organization or person that leans toward groupthink and messianism, much less notions of superiority underpinned by violence (see *Gringos*). His report portrays the gathering and its participants as tedious and shabby, reserving the unkindest cut for the visiting grand dragon of Mississippi in what is my favorite line of this collection: "Everyone drifted away and the grand dragon of Mississippi disappeared grandly into the Southern night, his car engine hitting on about three cylinders." For Portis, any man who can't even keep his car tuned is a man to be scorned indeed.

To my mind, Portis's complete coverage of that marathon evening is one of the great deadline reporting efforts of the civil rights era and maybe of the second half of the 20th century. Why has it, along with his other work of that time, gone unrecognized?

For one thing, his coverage of civil rights events was largely limited to that year; by November 1963, he had moved to England to be the paper's London man. So he lacked the length of time on the beat of other newsmen who made it their career, like Claude Sitton of the *New York Times* and the *Herald Tribune*'s own Donovan, who was based in Washington DC rather than on the front lines. Many of these reporters went on to write books about this pivotal time in American history while Portis left it behind to write novels.

Another reason might have been the dubiousness with which the tactics of the so-called New Journalism were viewed (though Hemingway had explored the more personal, "novelistic" style in his war dispatches decades before). The *Herald Tribune* was known as a writers' newspaper, and its marketing slogan at the time was "Who Says a Good Newspaper Has to Be Dull?" The answer for a few critics was, We do. Walker Gibson, for example, in his book *Tough, Sweet & Stuffy: An Essay on American Prose Styles* (1966), pointed to a Portis story about an earlier day's action in Alabama ("Birmingham's Trigger Tension," page 36) and accused the journalist, with horror, of employing *"the model of the novelist"* (italics in the original). Gibson favors Sitton's concurrent *New York Times* piece, which even he admits may be "a little dull, considering the circumstances."

Further, and perhaps ultimately more important, was the imminent demise of the *Herald Tribune*, which expired for good in its final incarnation after frequent starts, stops, and strikes in 1967. That abrupt ending left the work of Portis for the paper—not to mention that of other illustrious alumni like Dorothy Thompson, Dick Schaap, Red Smith, Lewis Lapham, Tom Wolfe, Virgil Thomson, Art Buchwald, and Jimmy Breslin—as an orphan of the eventual Internet age, consigned to microfilm, undigitized, and even so, the microfilm is rare. Some Internet billionaire would do literature, history, and journalism a great service by funding a project to convert the *Herald Tribune*'s microfilm to a searchable digital archive.

Finally and most obviously, a significant reason for the obscurity of Portis's journalism is the same one that caused his books to go out of print for a time: what some have called his reclusiveness, but as I prefer to think of it, a desire for privacy.

IV. What You Won't Find Here

I won't say very much about the topic of his aversion to publicity in general, which tends to make him sound like someone insistent on hiding his identity. On the spectrum of author privacy, he probably falls somewhere between Thomas Pynchon and Don DeLillo (with the late J. D. Salinger as the undefeated champion). He usually politely declines to speak to the press, but otherwise he seems to lead a fairly ordinary life, which includes having a beer at a local bar and visiting family and watching the Super Bowl and enjoying conversation with friends and going to the library and, the one extraordinary thing, laboring over his writing until he gets it perfect.

V. !

Gary Goldsmith, one of the Madison Avenue Bookshop employees behind that *Dog of the South* display, also told the *Times* reporter, "The book doesn't have a false note in it." The care with which Portis's sentences are constructed without having them come off as labored is a marvel, though he's quick to deny any overt struggle. In the *Gazette* Project interview, Portis says about his process, "I go pretty much by feel. People who know more about grammar than we know, well, aren't they pedants?"

There's a big difference between being a pedant (and he's created some of the most memorable pedants in American letters) and thinking carefully about what the right word is, or even what the right punctuation mark is. One of the joys of his writing is the attention he gives to the smallest details: a lawyer with an office in a hotel room next to his, he notes in "The Forgotten River" (page 110), had secured the sign on his door with a single, centered screw and had also added "bits of Scotch tape on the ends to keep it from tilting, perhaps demoralizing his customers." Similarly, he seems to be as minutely attentive to each stroke of the typewriter. When there's only one appropriate word to use, he will use it without hesitation; in "Your Action Line" (page 151), a "nacreous glaze" covers the facts collected by the "journalist ants" described. When there are no appropriate words, he will make them up, like the word "pankled" in the *Norwood* line mentioned above.

The same holds true for his consideration of punctuation. Behold the lowly but upright exclamation point! Cormac McCarthy recently declared that it has no place in literature (ditto the semicolon), but Portis's expertise argues for its retention. Two separate Portis fans I know who are wider, closer, and more astute readers than I, Little Rock lawyer Michelle Kaemmerling and author and humorist Joe Queenan—I name them because they deserve credit—independently commented to me about Portis's judicious and effective use of exclamation points. Midge upbraids himself for waking up too late with "What a piddler!" And Lamar Jimmerson in *Masters of Atlantis* fumes over the claims made by Churchward's *Lost Continent of Mu*: "What a hoax! Three hundred pages of sustained lying!" In "The Forgotten River," he notes the use of exclamation points in a historical source and riffs on their meaning:

xxii ESCAPE VELOCITY: A CHARLES PORTIS MISCELLANY

At another point [Dunbar] suddenly seems to remember that he is writing this report for Jefferson, the great democrat, and he praises the industry and sturdy independence of a man and his wife who had cleared a little two-acre farmstead in the woods...."How happy the contrast, when we compare the fortune of the new settler in the U.S. with the misery of the half-starving, oppressed, and degraded Peasant of Europe!!" Dunbar is not a man for exclamation marks, and when he gives us two of them here, we feel his discomfort with this kind of talk—however genuine the sentiment.

The larger point (!) is that Portis will use every tool in the box and for one purpose: to engage and entertain the reader. He rarely talks about the writing process, but he does repeat one piece of advice, or even exhortation, that he attributes to his editor at Knopf, Robert Gottlieb, and that earns its exclamation point: "Make them turn the page!"

VI. ?

What's left to say? Or, rather, there's much left to say (we haven't even gotten to cars or guns or the Civil War), but not by me, other than, Read this book. Those who know Portis's work well I hope will find much here they'd like to reread and some new Portis to enjoy. For those who don't know anything about him, they're likely to be as wowed by this collection as Austin Popper is by the display of simultaneous ambidextrous writing and calculation and conversation performed by Professor Cezar Golescu in *Masters of Atlantis*. As Popper says, "Oh boy, is he cooking now! How about this fellow?"

Little Rock, Arkansas
April 2012

One

SELECTED NEWSPAPER REPORTING AND WRITING

Memphis *Commercial Appeal*
1958

Portis's work in Memphis is of interest chiefly for his coverage of Elvis Presley's mother's illness and funeral. The first story, full of civic tomfoolery, already demonstrates his trademark wry humor and keen observation.

July 13, 1958

Yankees Taken as 'Renegades' 'Capture' Boat

The Rockport, Ind., Jaycee flatboat entered Memphis waters yesterday morning, and was duly captured by Memphis Jaycees after a few cap gun volleys and a lot of rebel-yelling.

The Memphians were aboard the Memphis Queen II, local excursion boat, which furnished a background of Southern music ("Dixie" played 42 times) for the battle.

The Yankees are making a voyage to publicize the Abraham Lincoln Sesquicentennial (150th birthday anniversary) to be celebrated next year in Kentucky, Indiana, and Illinois.

Lincoln once lived at Rockport and the Jaycees are re-enacting a flatboat trip he made when he was 19—except that Abe had to get down the river without screened-in quarters, two 35 horsepower outboard motors, and an LP gas lighting and refrigeration set-up.

The Memphis Jaycees, going along with the stunt, played the part of the renegades who attacked young Lincoln's boat and almost killed him. Taking a few historical liberties, they were dressed like Confederate soldiers, in Davy Crockett get-ups, and there was one wearing a Harry Truman shirt and Japanese sandals.

Included in the welcoming group of Jaycees and guests were the Jaycettes, dressed Southern belle fashion; Pete Sisson, president of the Memphis Jaycees; Stanley Dillard, city commissioner; Roy T. Combs, Indiana state auditor, and Miss Terry Lane, Miss Memphis of 1958.

Skipper of the Pride of Indiana is Frank Swallow, also president of the Rockport Junior Chamber of Commerce.

After a small but noisy parade downtown, the 10 bearded prisoners were taken to the Peabody for lunch and a kangaroo court trial presided over by Municipal Judge Beverly Boushe. They were found guilty of "being Yankees, a most heinous offense, spying on the city of Memphis, running whisky, and carrying concealed ideas."

The judge let them off by making them honorary Confederates. They were then presented miniature keys to the city by Sam Hollis, executive assistant to Mayor Orgill.

The flatboaters plan to cast off about 10 a.m. today, and hope to reach the next stop, Helena, Ark., by 5 p.m. tomorrow. They left Rockport July 4 and are scheduled to arrive at New Orleans Friday.

August 13, 1958

Elvis Visits Sick Mother; Granted Emergency Leave

Pvt. Elvis Presley made a rare flying trip here last night from Fort Hood, Texas, on an emergency leave to see his mother, Mrs. Vernon Presley, who is seriously ill at Methodist Hospital.

Her physician said last night she is suffering from "acute severe hepatitis with evidence of liver damage." Four specialists are aiding the family physician, but have not been able to pin down the cause of the illness.

"She improved somewhat today, and feels a little better," her doctor said last night, "but she is very sick." He did not list her condition as critical.

Elvis arrived here about 7 last night apparently on either a military or private plane. He said he would "rather not say how I came. I might want to come the same way again sometime."

The singer has flown only one other time in the last two years because his mother worries when he uses such methods of travel. His other flight was to return to Fort Hood after his two-week leave this summer.

He has a seven-day emergency leave and may get an extension, he said last night. It was granted after the family physician phoned Fort Hood.

When Elvis and his father entered Mrs. Presley's room last night, she was heard to say, "Oh, my son, my son," as they embraced.

When he came out he said, "Mama's not doing too well right now. Not well at all."

There were tears in his eyes as he spoke of his mother in a subdued tone. He was wearing his Army tropicals and looked drawn and haggard. Elvis gave waiting friends only a brief greeting as he strode to the sick room about 7:45.

"I nearly went crazy when I put her on the train down in Texas," he said. "She looked awful bad then."

Mrs. Presley was admitted to the hospital Saturday after returning from a visit with her son. No visitors are allowed except for the immediate family. The door is guarded by a police officer.

Elvis just completed advanced tank training at Fort Hood and is scheduled to go to Europe, "probably sometime in September," he said. He is in the 2nd Armored Division.

August 14, 1958

Mrs. Presley's Spirits Raised; Elvis Tells of His Devotion

Mrs. Vernon Presley was reported in better spirits yesterday in Methodist hospital after the Tuesday night arrival of her famous singer-son, Pvt. Elvis Aron Presley.

Mrs. Presley has been confined at the hospital since Saturday with an acute liver ailment—hepatitis. Her condition is still serious.

Elvis flew in Tuesday night on a seven-day emergency leave from Fort Hood, Texas.

Elvis and his father spent the day in Mrs. Presley's room yesterday, a routine he intends to follow for the rest of his leave. Flowers have been coming in steadily for Mrs. Presley from well-wishers all over the country, and Elvis said yesterday he was probably going to have to take some of them home.

The singer's flying trip here reflects a constant affection for his parents, noted and re-noted in news stories. A good part of the thick clipping file on Elvis at The Commercial Appeal is made up of stories dealing with the largesse he has showered on his parents.

When possible, he moves his family to wherever the exigencies of show business and the Army bring him. They stayed in Hollywood with him while he was making a picture, and just recently returned from a stay near him in Texas while he was undergoing training at Fort Hood.

"I just enjoy having my family around," he said yesterday in a hospital hallway interview. "I don't look at it as just a duty—something I ought to do. I love them and I like them and I like to have them around. They can't be replaced. They're all I've got in the world."

He said he didn't feel his closeness to his family unusual.

"Doesn't everybody feel the same way?" he asked.

While on the way up to the million-dollar bracket, Elvis shared his fortune by buying the family progressively larger and more expensive homes and, of course, cars. They now live at Graceland, a $100,000 mansion in Whitehaven, and have a garage full of Cadillacs.

Leaning on a windowsill in the hallway yesterday, he reflected moodily on the family's pre-Cadillac days: "I like to do what I can for my folks. We didn't have nothin' before, nothin' but a hard way to go."

About that time a small fat boy appeared and asked Elvis for an autograph. He grinned and ran his hand through the boy's hair and said in flawless diction, "You little rascal. You were standing there all that time and didn't say anything. Let me see that pencil."

He was talking to his public again. He was Elvis Presley again.

August 16, 1958

Elvis Presley Tells Mother, 'Goodby, Darling,' at Grave

Singer Elvis Presley, shaken and limp with grief, almost collapsed several times yesterday afternoon during the funeral services and burial of his mother.

After the brief graveside rites at Forest Hill, Elvis leaned on the casket and said, "Oh, God, everything I have is gone. Goodby, darling, goodby, goodby…"

Services for Mrs. Gladys Smith Presley were held at National Funeral Home before a crowd of about 700 persons. The group, mostly women and teenage girls, packed the chapel and overflowed into the hallways and outside parking lot.

Mrs. Presley, who was 42, was the wife of Vernon Presley. She died at 3:15 a.m. Thursday at Methodist Hospital after a heart attack brought on by acute hepatitis.

Most of the crowd at the service, and later at the cemetery, appeared more interested in the singer than the funeral.

The Rev. James E. Hamill, pastor of the First Assembly of God Church, officiated at the 30-minute service at the funeral home. He said:

"Women can succeed in most any field these days, but the most important job of all is being a good wife and a good mother. Mrs. Presley was such a woman.

"I would be foolish to tell this father and this son, 'Don't worry, don't grieve, don't be sorrowful.' Of course you will miss her. But I can say, with Paul, 'Sorrow not as those who have no hope.'"

Mr. Presley, his son and members of the family sat in a small room, closed off from the audience, at the front of the chapel. The room was heavily banked with flowers on all sides. Five uniformed policemen stood self-consciously on guard in the chapel during the service.

The Blackwood Brothers sang several hymns at the service including "Rock of Ages" and "Precious Memories."

Both Mr. Presley and Elvis were at the point of hysteria throughout the ceremony, and Elvis had to be helped in and out of the car at the cemetery.

The streets on the way to Forest Hill were lined with spectators watching the funeral procession, and a large group had gathered at the cemetery beforehand. The traffic and crowds were handled by about 80 officers, including city police, sheriff's deputies and state troopers.

There were about the same number at the cemetery as at the funeral home.

Mr. Presley stood by his son at the grave and said, "She's gone, she's not coming back, everything is gone now."

Police had set up ropes and formed a cordon near the grave to keep the crowd from intruding. Some spectators seemed to be honestly bereaved, but the majority craned their necks and chattered.

After everything was over and the policemen gone, the crowd milled around the grave awhile, some took flowers, and then drifted away.

Arkansas Gazette
1959–1960

After joining the *Gazette* early in 1959, Portis covered some of the political machinations in the aftermath of the integration crisis of 1957–58; one result of the turmoil was that the public schools were closed for the entire 1958–59 school year. By summer of 1959, Portis had been asked to take over the "Our Town" column, which ran on page one, column one of the B (local) section on weekdays and in a larger format on Sundays. The daily version featured the column's name and the writer's byline inside a picture of a downtown Little Rock street, and at all times, the columnist referred to the city as "Our Town" rather than "Little Rock."

Portis tells Roy Reed in the *Gazette* Project interview (Epilogue, page 285), "I thought I would do it well, but I could never—I don't know—get into a stride." It's true that many column inches were devoted to interviews with local "characters," like the woman who ran a bird hospital from her home, and mildly amusing squibs about city life, such as overheard malapropisms. On a number of occasions, however, Portis was able to let his imagination run and produced the kind of hilarious set pieces that would mark his later work in both fiction and nonfiction.

The occasion of the first piece below was the reopening of Little Rock's public schools in the late summer of 1959 and the gaggle of newsmen who once again, as in 1957, descended on Little Rock; Portis's eye and pen are rarely sharper, both here and later, than when he's applying it to his own kind: journalists. He also found a comfortable voice in "Our Town" when discussing language.

He filed his last column on October 9, 1960, then left for the *New York Herald Tribune*. Among those who stepped into that space after him was William Whitworth, who would later join him at the *Herald Tribune* before going on to write and edit for the *New Yorker* and, most notably, to become editor-in-chief at the *Atlantic*, where he would publish three of the pieces contained in this volume.

August 13, 1959

Biggest Spectacle

Among the spectacles at Our Town yesterday which brought in newsmen (and women) from all over the world, the one we would like to report on here is that of the news gatherers themselves.

They came early to Hall High School, about 100 [of] them, and stood around in little groups of wilted Dacron and damp mustaches, chattering and picking each others' brains.

The photographers diddled with their cameras and shot everything in sight. The reporters engaged in small talk, shop talk and speculation, occasionally taking notes on nothing.

We stood across the street from the School in the pine trees that come right up to the street, and someone wanted to know what kind of pines they were.

Somebody else said they were jack pines and we felt that was wrong but we didn't say anything. The tree man wrote in his pad, "jack pines."

A reporter from the London Daily Graphic told his colleague from the London Daily Mail that he had filed two pieces the day before—one on Cuba and one on Little Rock.

"They buried the Cuba story and ran only two inches on Little Rock," he said. "I guess I'm just not at the right place."

A man from Newsweek walked up to a group of prosperous-looking reporters, most of them from New York, and said, "I want to get with the high-priced help here and find out what's going on. What's the poop?"

There was no poop, just anecdotes about how it was when they were here last, in 1957.

As they watched the schoolchildren showing their identification cards to the police, one man in the group suggested that they needed a fresh-faced young reporter to sneak in with the students.

"Didn't you guys have some kid in blue jeans go in last time?" someone asked the man from Life.

"Hell, he's managing editor now," the Life man said.

We ambled over to another group where the man from Time was shedding his Robert Hall coat. (We glimpsed the label and note it here in the best traditions of that magazine.)

"Jeez it's hot here," he said.

We talked about the heat until a trim young blonde student got out of a car and started up the hill to the School. We stopped talking and watched her.

"Well, I'll say one thing," said Time, his eyes on the young lady. "You can grow that down here. She's a little Dresden doll."

As the morning wore on, the lack of rest room facilities presented a problem to the effete Eastern newsmen who couldn't see the forest at their backs for the trees. And they couldn't very well ask the police to let them go in the School.

Some made out all right, though. About a half-dozen newsmen, including CBS, AP, UPI and Gazette personnel, were spotted sitting in lawn chairs drinking buttermilk in the front yard of a house on the corner of H and McKinley Streets. They had flagged a milk delivery truck. Why buttermilk, the Lord knows.

Meanwhile, back in the jack pines, three reporters (New York Post, Minneapolis Star and Tribune and X) stood together talking it over.

"I can just see Time next week," said X, "'Integration came peacefully last week to modern, red brick Hall High School at Little Rock when three Negro children who had been denied an education for three years took the long walk...'" He trailed off here.

"I know this Time bit so well, man," he said.

We thought it a little windy for a Time lead but we didn't want to split hairs so we let it ride.

About that time three small T-shirted boys, 10 or 11, came rustling up through the woods, single file.

"We're surrounded," said New York Post, throwing up his hands in mock terror. "They're sending a midget army through the woods!"

When the boys emerged on the street a policeman told them they would have to leave.

As they filed out again, a reporter said to the last one, "You should have got you a press card, man."

Later in the day a Chicago Tribune reporter came up to the redoubtable Dr. Benjamin Fine [the education reporter for the New York Times who had become well known during the 1957 crisis—Ed.] and said, "Well look who's here. I thought you were safely ensconced in some college campus."

Dr. Fine explained that he was still a dean at Yeshiva University at Manhattan but that he also was writing a weekly education column for the North American Newspaper Alliance.

"I'm sort of ambivalent right now," he said, dean fashion.

About the middle of the day, some confusion set in as to where to go. We heard the Chicago Sun-Times man talking to Chicago on the phone:

"It's happening in too many places," he said. "You'll have to get somebody on rewrite to get the wire copy for the bones of the story because I'm going to have to be filled in."

It was a busy day for the press.

August 20, 1959

Remember?

Downtown the other day we saw a mother give her little girl what is sometimes called a good shaking and heard her say, "If you don't stop acting ugly I'm going to take you back to the car and wear you out."

We had not heard these expressions, "acting ugly," and "wear you out," in a long time, and it set us to thinking about Southernisms.

In a similar situation, we thought, the mother could have said, "When we get home I'm going to cut me a keen switch and stripe your legs good."

We thought of those two good adjectives, "tacky" and "ratty" that are being largely ignored these days.

"No, you're not going to wear that old tacky Captain Marvel T-shirt again today."

"Well, if you'd ever get up out of that ratty old chair long enough, I might get it fixed."

We thought of "cream" for ice cream and "wheel" for "bicycle."

"This is mighty good cream."

"Boy, hop on your wheel and go get me a can of Granger."

* * *

Then we thought of "shug" for "sugar" and "hun" for "honey," terms of endearment we are going to put back into action next chance we get.

This brought to mind "sugar" meaning hugs and kisses, which in turn took us back to the family reunion where a lot of this goes on.

"You better get on over here, Hun, and give yo' Aunt Dolly some sugar, 'cause if you don't I know somebody that will."

So you would march over and submit to a good wetting down, eyes, ears, nose, all over. "mmmmmmmmMMMMMMMuh," she would say. "I think I'll just take you home with me."

And more often than not, the ones who were the craziest about sugar were the ones who looked like aging toad frogs. But they were invariably the nicest ones, these affectionate ones.

How much more welcome were they than the uncle who enjoyed running his knuckles up the nape of your bristly neck, a trick which would make your eyes smart and which had something to do with a horse eating corn.

Then he might grab your foot and bend it back and say, "I can't let go till you say calf rope."

"Calf rope! Calf rope!"

But he wouldn't let go till he got ready. "What's that? I can't hear you. Snapping turtles don't let go till it thunders."

Later on, after he had nipped off your nose and thrown it away a couple of times, he would make an enclosure with his hands, and entice you to stick a finger in an opening he had provided.

When you did it he would drive his thumbnail into your finger and laugh. This had to do with a turkey or a banty rooster in a cage. He had an inexhaustible supply of these barnyard gags.

* * *

There were Presbyterians, Methodists and a sprinkling of Baptists at these get-togethers we attended, and when it came time to eat the honor of returning thanks usually fell to the windiest old man there.

He would send a long, thunderous blessing rambling up to the skies, and you would have thought that we had all just been delivered from the fiery furnace, instead of sitting down to eat some sweet potatoes with melted marshmallows on top.

After dinner the older men would sit on the porch and talk about church government and church politics and split doctrinal hairs, and one of them would tell about someone's daughter who had married a Catholic boy. Heads would shake.

Someone once said of the Germans and their love for theology that if they had a choice between Heaven and lectures on Heaven they would take the lectures every time.

That's the way we remember those old men: they would rather talk about it than go.

If you want to hear Southerners talk, and watch them, attend a gathering of a whole family of them. They're at their most Southern there where the conditions are optimum. And you can learn a right smart if you listen.

August 21, 1959

Scribe Scrubs

An Abilene, Tex., high school coach by the name of Chuck Moser was quoted by Jim Bailey in a Gazette article last week as saying:

"And kick off your bums—or rinky dinks or whatever you call them—in the springtime. Every squad has boys it shouldn't have. See if you can move these boys toward the school newspaper, the track team, or the basketball statistician's job. When you cut them in the middle of football season, it's a bad thing. They have friends on the squad. It hurts morale."

Moser, who has won 74 of 79 games in six years at Abilene, passed on this tip at the Arkansas High School Coaches Association clinic held at Our Town.

We stand in awe of Coach Moser's win record and we admire his Durocher-style candor, but his dismissal of the school newspaper as a harmless form of time-killing for rinky dinks strikes us as being a little cavalier.

We can see one of the rinky dinks now, a sullen lad with his pants at half mast on his behind, approaching the journalism instructor, a groveling Bob Cratchit sort of fellow.

"I come over from the practice field to see about knocking out a few editorials for you, Jack. Coach Moser said I didn't pack the gear to play on his team and he sent me over here to see you. What it is, I'm stupid and yellow and bad for morale."

"Glad to see you. You'll fit in fine here on the Eagle staff. Always happy to get one of Coach's culls. I only wish we could get more of the crumbs and scraps from the athletic table. It seems that this year all the bums are ignoring us for the band and the track team and the statisticians' jobs."

"Yeah. Well, I think I'd like to be editor, Dad."

"Good. Here, try on this green eyeshade and these sleeve protectors. Sometimes we lose our perspective and forget that the main thing we want to do here at A.H.S. is stay out of Chuck's hair so he can keep rolling up those victories. That's why we have all these peripheral activities like classes and the paper. The way I like to look at it is that we're all on the same team, and I like to think that back here behind the lines, so to speak, we are just as important in our way as our boys up there toting that spheroid. That's the way I like to look at it.

"Now if you'll excuse me I've got to run over to the gym and pick up Chuck's laundry. He's particular about his sweat socks and won't let anyone else on the faculty touch them. Just find you a typewriter anywhere and make yourself at home."

"Okay. I think I'll write a little something about school spirit."

"Great."

In the past, we have often been puzzled by Texas journalism. Not any more.

August 25, 1959

Dixieishness

We have a letter from a Little Rock man, a former Mississippian, with some comment on the remarks we made the other day on Southern expressions.

"Now, if you really need some material on Southern expressions, go down in Mississippi and attend a family reunion. Folks here in Arkansas are not quite as Southern as us folks down in Mississippi.

"For example: We say 'red bugs,' they say 'chiggers.' We say 'butter-beans,' they say 'lima beans.'"

Just about the last thing we want to be drawn into is defending Arkansas against Mississippi in a Southernness tournament. Still, you had better come up with something more substantial than red bugs and butter beans, Mr. Former Mississippian, if you want to defend your proposition.

When we last heard, they had not changed the name of the ball teams down at Fordyce to the Chiggers, and we never heard anybody south of the Arkansas River say "lima beans" for "butterbeans."

We know a man in South Arkansas who says "Pass those molasses" and "These sure are good cheese." You get much more Southern than that and you can't stand it, friend. Get past that point and you're not Southern anymore, you're sick.

February 3, 1960

Rare Specimen

Francis Irby Gwaltney, a commuter to Our Town from Conway and a rare specimen, an Arkansas novelist, said yesterday that he hopes to have the political novel he is working on completed and in the bookstores by November when the elections might help sales.

("Rare" is a judicious bluff here meaning that we don't know how many novelists there are in the state. We know of only one other, Wesley Ford Davis at the University. If there are others we'd like to know.)

The novel deals with contemporary Southern politics. "But I hasten to add," Gwaltney said, smiling, "that it is not laid in Arkansas."

Just what state it is may prove puzzling though, he said, since it is surrounded by Arkansas, Mississippi, Tennessee, Missouri, Oklahoma, Texas and Louisiana. "No, I never get around to giving it a name," he said.

Gwaltney is active executive secretary of the State History Commission—the state historian—with offices at the Old State House. When he's off duty he writes and he has four published novels to his credit.

Gwaltney's South is the changing South and Arkansas is a good vantage point to watch it from, he believes. "Things are boiling here," he said.

As for the supply of subject matter, he said he has enough novels in his head now to last him three lifetimes.

* * *

We asked about this business of breaking new ground, that is, of starting in writing about a people, a state, with almost no literary traditions. Any difficulty there?

"Well, my editor in New York sometimes questions my dialogue," Gwaltney said. "About the only South he knows is the literary South and I don't follow the line laid down by Faulkner and Caldwell. It's hard to convince him sometimes about things. My characters preach too much, he says. Well, that may be. But whatever weaknesses I have I do know how the people in Arkansas talk."

We asked him if he had any ideas on why a state like Mississippi, right next door, had produced so many fine writers and Arkansas so few.

"It's only a theory, and I guess a kind of left-handed compliment to Arkansas, but I think unhappiness probably has a lot to do with it," he said. "Same thing with Georgia. Unhappiness tends to produce writers, I think, and if you've ever traveled in those states maybe you've noticed that—I don't know—somber-chilling atmosphere. We've always been pretty happy here in Arkansas. I might say that I don't think unhappiness has been the motivating thing to me."

He shrugged. "It's just a theory, anyway."

* * *

Does he correspond or exchange ideas in any way with other Southern writers?

"Not if I can help it," he said. "There's no way in the world one writer can help another writer. That attitude has got me into a little trouble locally with writing groups. 'Gwaltney has staked out Arkansas as his personal domain,' they say. I don't know what they mean by 'staked out.' It's there for everybody."

We asked about Norman Mailer who served with Gwaltney in the same Army unit in the Pacific in World War II.

"We were once close friends," he said, "but we had an argument. I do say that I think Norman is one of the very finest novelists in America today. And that's covering a lot of ground."

Gwaltney's growing success seems to be reflected pretty well in the sales of his books. His first novel, "The Yeller-Headed Summer," sold 1,900 hard back copies and about 50,000 paperback; "The Day the Century Ended," 19,000 hardback and more than a million paperback; "A Moment of Warmth," 27,000 hardback and about 750,000 paperback, and "The Numbers of Our Days," which sold 29,000 hardback copies, is now going into print between paper covers.

* * *

Europe, Gwaltney said, is one of the best markets for his books, particularly England, Germany and the Scandinavian countries.

After his last novel was translated into Dutch, he said, the publisher over there wanted to change his name to "Franz Irby" because "Gwaltney" was so hard for them to pronounce. (It's pronounced "Galtney" here.) Gwaltney said he told him okay, on the condition that he get Queen Juliana to change the name of one of her unpronounceable daughters at the same time.

"That was kind of smart-alecky, I guess," he said.

His new novel is called "A Step in the River," a phrase he lifted from a sermon by his Methodist minister at Conway.

"I've forgotten the exact circumstances, but it was about taking one step in the river, the Jordan River. I wrote it down on the back of a church bulletin when I heard it."

Early on at the *Herald Tribune*, Portis demonstrated his versatility as a writer, excelling at the gimlet-eyed story on city eccentrics, the humorous first-person piece, and breaking-news reportage.

November 24, 1960

Court Rules: Lion Is a Wild Animal

A young Brooklyn longshoreman fought a spirited but losing battle in a Brooklyn courtroom yesterday for the right to keep a pet lion at his home.

After the drawn-out, somewhat tongue-in-cheek proceedings at Flatbush Magistrate's Court, Magistrate Matthew P. Fagan resolved the issue with a concise decision: "I take judicial notice that the lion is a wild animal. I find the defendant guilty."

The sentence was a $25 fine or ten days in jail. Anthony Ortolano, twenty-six, of 581 Carroll St., Brooklyn, the defendant, asked for ten days in which to raise the $25 and the magistrate granted the request, noting that Mr. Ortolano's care of the lion had been exemplary.

The specific charge was Section 197 of the city's Penal Law which makes harboring a wild animal capable of inflicting bodily harm a misdemeanor.

Mr. Ortolano's troubles with the law began Friday night when Patrolman Thomas Higgins and another officer stopped a car at Union St. and Seventh Ave. to check on the automobile registration. In the car were Mr. Ortolano, three other men and Cleo, a four-month-old male lion, three and a half feet tall and weighing 125 pounds. Mr. Ortolano has since corrected the name to Leo in light of the discovery made over the weekend.

Leo and Mr. Ortolano were hustled off to the Bergan St. police station, where they cooled their heels while a summons was issued. Leo was taken to the Brooklyn shelter of the American Society For the Prevention of Cruelty to Animals.

The trial began yesterday with Mr. Ortolano's attorney, William Kunstler of Manhattan, asking the judge if the lion could be brought in the courtroom as evidence that he was friendly and tame.

"Oh hell no," said Magistrate Fagan. "All these people in here would start running. And I wouldn't blame them." About 150 persons were in the room.

Then he turned to some officers and asked if they had their guns ready. "Don't bring him in under any circumstances," said the judge, "I will conduct this case outside."

The judge, attorneys, witnesses, defendant and newsmen repaired to an alley outside the court where Leo had been brought in an ASPCA panel truck. The flap was let down to expose the lion, which was beating his head against the wire netting.

The judge opened court in the alley and read the complaint. Mr. Ortolano allowed Leo to lick his fingers through the cage. Then a noisy group of students from nearby Erasmus Hall High School joined the spectators and Magistrate Fagan decided to take the trial back inside. "I'll take judicial note that I've seen the lion," he said.

The testimony of witnesses followed.

Patrolman Higgins told of the Friday night arrest. He said that Ortolano had told the police that he had bought the lion two weeks ago for $350 from an animal dealer.

Mr. Ortolano said he had a leash on the lion at the time of the arrest and that the windows of the car were up. He said he had a steel cage for Leo in the backyard at his home.

To prove that the animal was tame, said Mr. Kunstler, he would call as witnesses two animal experts.

The first was Mrs. Helen Martini, of 1026 Old Kingsbridge Road, the Bronx, who said she had been an animal trainer for twenty years.

Leo was not ferocious, but "very nervous," she said. But when she was cross-examined by Irving Singer, Assistant District Attorney, she conceded that the animal belonged in a zoo.

Next came Bob Dietc, a zoo-keeper at Fairlawn, N.J., who said that he had trained Leo himself and that he was safe. "He's only a baby, you could put him in your vest pocket," he said.

Asked if it wasn't true that the animal was unpredictable, Mr. Dietc said, "It's my opinion that all animals are unpredictable, from chickens to birds."

After the holidays the ASPCA will turn Leo over to Mr. Dietc who will keep him until he can sell him for Mr. Ortolano. Mr. Ortolano, who has been paying $3.15 a day for horsemeat for Leo, is busy getting together $25.

January 16, 1962

2 Men—1,700 Women, Peace Train to Capital

WASHINGTON

Twenty railroad coaches filled with women—tweedy, well-shod matrons for the most part—arrived here yesterday in a driving rainstorm to picket and demonstrate for peace in front of the White House.

Ink ran on their placards, their fur hats collapsed and hung limp over their ears, their tweeds constricted and steamed, but they marched on in the rain—for about an hour. There were 1,700 of them.

Most of them came from New York City, Westchester and Rockland counties, Long Island, and Fairfield County, Conn. They filled a chartered Pennsylvania railroad train that left New York about 8:30 a.m. with stops at Trenton, N.J. and Philadelphia to pick up more women.

The only men aboard were the conductors, the sandwich man, the engineer presumably, Abe Stafansky and myself.

Mr. Stafansky, a seventy-year-old butcher, saw something about the trip in a newspaper and decided to take the day off and come along.

"Fifty years I'm an American and I thought I'd like to see the White House," he said. First discovered just outside New York, the women threatened to throw him off, but they relented under Mr. Stafansky's charm.

Four reporters were thrown off before the train left the station. But it was through no lack of enterprise on their part, just a snafu in signals. They were at the front of the train where the policy at the moment was strictly no men. I was making my way forward and by the time I got to the front, we were speeding through New Jersey. (The women were sorry about leaving the others behind.)

The trip was first conceived at a meeting of women in New York last month. There is no formal organization, no officers, no dues, no rules. The women are just linked in their desire "to do something" for peace and disarmament.

Mrs. Ruth Chenven, of Manhattan, called the Pennsylvania Railroad and asked about chartering a train to Washington. Get 550 persons, she was told, and it could be done. The cost would be $12.50 per person round trip, including a box lunch.

The women called their friends, the friends called their friends, and the result was 1,300 women at Gate 12 in Pennsylvania Station yesterday.

The train started, then braked to a stop as shrieking late-comers from Roslyn, L.I., came running along the platform. They boarded and the trip resumed.

For the first two hours, women surged back and forth through the cars looking for seats. There were not enough. They made do with arm rests and took turns in the seats.

Mr. Stafansky and I did the best we could.

He found a seat and perused his "Morning Freiheit." I retired to the men's room—the only seat available—to eat my box lunch. Sanctuary there was brief. Within minutes the women were clattering at the door. Since it was a women's train they assumed (Why shouldn't they?) that both the men's and the ladies' rooms were at their disposal.

Mr. Stafansky showed me the article in the "Freiheit" saying that men, too, were permitted on the train. It was in Yiddish. He said he had called his boss and told him he was not feeling well, and could he take the day off?

Wouldn't it get him in trouble if it came out in a newspaper that he was not sick, but on a women's peace train to Washington?

"How could he know? My boss, he reads nothing. The stock market maybe. Put my name in the stock market, he might see it."

The women chattered and worked on their placards ("Peace is the only shelter," "No tests, East or West") and blew up white balloons inscribed "Peace or Perish." Others passed out tracts and booklets. One woman was collecting letters. "Any letters in here for the President?" she asked.

The majority of the women were thirty to fifty years old, almost all of them mothers, with a middle and upper middle-class background. But the rich were also represented, as were some humble homes in Brooklyn.

"Very few of these women ever dreamed they would be walking in a demonstration carrying signs," said Mrs. Ruth Gage-Colby of New York, one of the powers in the movement. "They went along leading their happy, secluded lives and suddenly they've been jolted by this thing, this spectre of the holocaust. Their children come home from school and ask about shelters, and 'Are we going to be burned up, mother?'"

Another marcher, Mrs. Valerie Delacorte, wife of Dell publisher George T. Delacorte, said, "I don't know whether what we're doing will have any effect or not. What can we do? Maybe the war will come but at least we protested, we cried out…"

The train arrived at 12:45 p.m. and the women took chartered buses to the White House. The President did not come out to greet them but at his press conference later, he said he had seen them.

"I recognized why they were here," he said. "There were a great number of them. It was in the rain. I understood what they were attempting to say and therefore I consider that their message was received."

After the march, the women gathered for a rally at the Metropolitan A.M.E. Church and then separated into small groups to call on their Congressmen.

One group paid a call at the Arms Control and Disarmament Agency where they were given an audience by the deputy director, Adrian Fisher. Others picketed the embassies of the nuclear powers—the Soviet Union, Great Britain and France. They left Washington at 5 p.m.

June 19–22, 1962

This four-part series ran on consecutive days at the top of the *Herald Tribune*'s local section.

Tuesday, June 19, 1962

Those Awkward Moments with a Room Full of Smoke

YONKERS, N.Y.

Tobacco is a dirty weed. I like it.
It satisfies no normal need. I like it.

Graham Lee Hemminger
(1896–1949)

A heavy calm lies over the Bates Memorial Medical Center, for it is mid-afternoon and rest period for those of us embarked on the Five-Day Plan to Stop Smoking.

This morning we drank a lot of fruit juice and water, did calisthenics and something called rhythmic breathing, had a vegetarian lunch and then went for a walk. Soon a nurse will come tapping on a door and we will file into a room to hear Dunbar W. Smith, M.D.

I smoke two packs of Camels a day and have no real desire to quit but J. Wayne McFarland, M.D., said, come on out anyway and we'll motivate you. (There's the call for the lecture.)…Just got back. Dr. Smith talked about chewing and digestion, using a big set of dentures to illustrate. (Said chew food thoroughly.)

Dr. McFarland and the Rev. E. J. Folkenberg, the originators of the Five-Day Plan are Seventh-Day Adventists, forbidden to smoke.

"We've had a lot of experience in helping people stop smoking in our church," said Mr. Folkenberg, "so we decided to give others the benefit of our experience." For the past two years they have traveled the country, giving their "group therapy" course, which involves no proselytizing for the church.

There are 12 of us enrolled in full-time, day and night courses here, for which the fee is $100, for room and board. Another 25 or so come out each night for the free session.

Art Rosenthal, who had the room next to mine, just came down the hall eating jelly candies from a bag and looking pained. A middle-aged man from Newfoundland, N.J., he said he smoked cigars during all his waking hours until Sunday night, when he checked in here. "I've got withdrawal pains," he said. "Headaches, perspiration."

Then Dr. McFarland looked in, and it was a little awkward because my room was full of smoke. "You ought to go get a prune to suck on to keep your blood sugar up," he chided.

The hospital, a former tuberculosis sanatorium, is located on a hilltop, and there are a lot of woods and birds. The Seventh-Day Adventists bought it last year and are now refurbishing it. It will be open soon as a center for general medical treatment.

The Adventists also discourage eating meat, which explains the vegetarian diet. (Mr. Folkenberg said it was part of the course, since eating meat causes a craving for tobacco.) For lunch there was corn, broccoli, a nut cup, scalloped potatoes and a round slice of some grayish material.

"How do you like the food?" asked Miss Rosalie Naderson, of Manhattan, who is the gamest and most cheerful one in our group. Miss Naderson applauds at all the lectures and films, and she jokes around a lot. I said it was fine, except for the gray object. She laughed and said it was soya cheese, and was very good with some of the no-meat gravy on it. The gravy helped some.

Upstairs there is a big display of vegetarian food, including cans of Nuttena, Nuttose and Vegeburgers.

Along with the physical regimen of deep breathing, exercises and drinking a great deal of water ("to flush the nicotine from the system") there is also a form of Coueism in the course. Instead of saying, "I will stop smoking," which shatters the will, if you do light up again, you repeat over and over again, "I choose not to smoke again." This is supposed to be more effective.

You also avoid smoking companions, and get up immediately after meals and go for walks to avoid the after-meal craving for a smoke. I don't have the motivation so far, but Dr. McFarland says I will after I see a terrifying film on lung cancer coming up tonight.

There are no ash trays at this place, and you have to sneak around putting out butts on window-sills or flushing them down the johns.

Wednesday, June 20, 1962

Half-Way: A Two-Pack Tribune Man Trying to Stop

YONKERS, N.Y.

Well, we're off coffee now, along with meat and cigarettes, and my head feels like a wheat gluten vegeburger, which was what we had for lunch yesterday.

It was smack in the middle of the Five-Day Plan to Stop Smoking, and a crucial day. Every one was drowsy and mopey. Every one except Miss Rosalie Naderson, who is still up to her old high jinks. During calisthenics, while doing a kind of side-way walk, she kept walking right out of the building. It was a joke.

Twelve of us are undergoing the course here at Bates Memorial Medical Center, a hilltop sanatorium owned by the Seventh-Day Adventist Church. Another 25 come out for each night session.

The Rev. E. J. Folkenberg and J. Wayne McFarland, M.D., have been conducting the therapy for about two years (with, they say, a success rate of 75 per cent), but this is the first time they've done it on a resident patient basis.

Mr. Folkenberg said yesterday that it may not be as effective as the outpatient method. "They may kick the habit here in these surroundings under a programmed routine, but I wonder if it will hold up when they return to work." Those who come to the night sessions have to fight it alone during the work day, and theirs is probably a more solid victory, he said.

"Won't it be all right just to smoke one, when it gets so terribly bad?" asked a woman at the Monday night meeting. "Well, we think it's better to stop completely," said Dr. McFarland. "It's rough, I know, but the main thing is to get through that first week."

Coffee is banned, he said, because it triggers an almost insatiable craving for nicotine with heavy smokers. For a substitute lift in the morning, he suggested a "cold mitten friction." You take a washcloth soaked with cold water and rub your arms and chest vigorously until the skin has turned pink. This increases blood circulation and approximates the effect of a cup of coffee, he said.

Several reported some success with it yesterday morning.

Mr. Folkenberg gave a persuasive talk on will power at the night session. If you keep on repeating, "I choose not to smoke again," he said, "and mean it," it will actually prepare the body for the change and make it easier on the nerves.

One man at the night session said he had fought it all day, but could not afford to have a fuzzy mind on his job, and was there anything to be done about it. No, said Dr. McFarland, but the fuzziness would pass in a few days. "Don't worry, you're going to make it."

I have more or less stopped smoking while here, rather than be a tempter. But I'm afraid I have been a nuisance in questioning others about their smoking habits.

"Will you please stop talking about cigarettes?" one woman told me yesterday. At any rate, no one has dropped out yet.

Thursday, June 21, 1962

Into the Stretch: Who'll Be the First to Puff? The Man from the Trib, of Course

YONKERS, N.Y.
Another day of lethargy in this bee-loud glade, trying to kick the smoking habit. It appears every one will make it but me.

I did, however, beat a kid at ping-pong three straight games. He had little short arms and all I had to do was tip the ball over the net out of his reach. So much for his nicotine-free lungs. After that I had a romp with a friendly dog named Shep, and batted a few skinners with the softball.

Let's see, what else: Kathleen Joyce, an English contralto, came in and favored us with some songs at the night therapy session. She sang "Danny Boy" and "D'ye Ken John Peel," and we all joined in on "When Irish Eyes Are Smiling."

In the morning she played the piano to give us the beat for our calisthenics. It was that song that goes "…this is the way we bake our bread, so early in the morning."

A dozen of us are enrolled here at Bates Memorial Medical Center, a Seventh-Day Adventist sanatorium, in the Five-Day Plan to Stop

Smoking. The course ends tonight and, despite my miserable failure, it has been of great help to the others.

Wesley Smith, a young man of 24 from Massachusetts, was smoking up to five packs a day when he came here. Tuesday he got by with a couple of drags, and yesterday he didn't smoke at all. He has put up a good fight, and he seemed to be coming out of the drowsiness yesterday, which means that the tough part is over.

Amanda Meiggs, an actress, was one of the lightest smokers of the group. She smoked only one pack a day but decided to take the course because she was having trouble with her throat. She stopped Sunday and has not weakened yet.

The craving, though, seems to be just as strong in light smokers as in heavy ones. Yesterday, she said, was her worst day.

"I'm absolutely dying for a cigarette, and I know you're sneaking out and smoking," she said.

What to do when the urge becomes irresistible? The Rev. E. J. Folkenberg, who is giving the therapy, along with J. Wayne McFarland, M.D., suggested the following:

1. Invoke your willpower by saying, "I choose not to smoke. I choose not to smoke."

2. Calm the nerves with a minute or so of steady rhythmic breathing.

3. If you're inside, go out and walk, and ask for divine aid.

4. Take out your watch, keep an eye on the second hand, and force yourself to go without smoking for two minutes.

By the time you've done all this, he said, the craving peak has been reached and is falling off. "And you should be able to manage it then."

The evening sessions are growing. About 40 persons came Tuesday night for the therapy.

At that session, Dr. McFarland asked for a show of hands of all those who no longer had a craving for tobacco.

No one moved.

Then the ebullient and ever-helpful Rosalie Naderson raised her hand and said she had whipped it. She stood and gave a moving testimonial to the efficacy of Dr. McFarland's methods.

"It's not so hard," she said. "After all, we were not born with cigarettes in our mouths."

Friday, June 22, 1962

As Confidently Predicted, He Puffed First

YONKERS, N.Y.

The how-to-stop-smoking course ended yesterday and the graduates were sent home with warnings ringing in their ears. Our ears, I should say, although I was the only one in our class of 12 who failed.

"All right, you've beaten the Number 2 health hazard in America, and now you're wide open for the Number 1 hazard—overweight," said Dr. Henry J. Johnson. "Food is going to taste a lot better to you now but you're just going to have to restrain yourself. If you don't, those pounds will creep up on you before you know it."

Dr. Johnson, medical director for the Life Extension Examiners in New York City, was a guest speaker for the occasion. Someone asked him what the Number 3 hazard was. He said he didn't know offhand.

He seemed to think that too much fuss is made over the act of quitting cigarettes. "I've had heart patients tell me, 'Well, Doc. I guess this means no more smoking.' I say, 'Yes, that's right,' and they stop, just like that. I did it myself."

Don't dwell on your addiction and don't pamper your weakness, he said, just stop smoking.

"We've helped you break away from smoking," said the Rev. E. J. Folkenberg, "but only for a short span of time. What are you going to do next week, or three months from now when the craving suddenly hits you? Well, we hope we've bolstered your will power enough to handle those situations. When will it be safe to take a drink, or start on coffee again? I don't know. That's one of the things each of you will have to work out in your own way."

Mr. Folkenberg and Dr. J. Wayne McFarland are administrators of the five-day course, which is sponsored by the Seventh-day Adventist Church. It was conducted at the Bates Memorial Medical Center, a sanatorium here that was recently taken over by the church.

Dr. McFarland advised us to increase our intake of vitamin B-1 and several other B vitamins, for their beneficial effect on the nerves. Wheat germ, he said, is a very good natural source of B-1.

Miss Rosalie Naderson, a classmate, said it had been her practice for some time to take a teaspoon of wheat germ oil daily. That, she said, is equivalent to five pounds of wheat germ, which sounded like a lot of wheat germ to me, but she stood by her figure.

Dr. McFarland also said that fear was not the best motive for kicking the habit, but that it had its value, like the use of a switch in disciplining a child.

"We've come in for a lot of criticism for showing this film One in 20,000 (a color picture showing a lung removal operation), and don't think we haven't given a lot of sober consideration to the criticism. But we're going to continue using it, and anything else we think will galvanize people to act."

A testimonial was given by Miss Esther Renner, a secretary from Des Moines, who took the course seven months ago. She had tried to stop smoking several times before, she said, but she had no luck until she undertook this plan.

Her fingernails were of some interest. Each one had a dark brown line across it, at about the seven-month growth point. The nails were dark brown above the line and pink below it.

Dr. McFarland called them "nicotine lines," and speculated that they marked the gradual exit of tobacco residue from her system.

At breakfast yesterday Miss Naderson said she rather regretted leaving the place. We were eating our wheat germ and other brown roughish things (even the sugar here has husks in it) and she was, in her manner, addressing us at large, as if we were all in a lifeboat together.

"This food is better than you get at the Waldorf," she said. "And do you know why?"

"No, why is it better, Rosalie?" I asked.

"Because it's prepared with love, that's why. And there's little enough love in the world as it is."

You can never get ahead of Miss Naderson.

October 4, 1962

The Shattered Scene of Blast

Dazed and disheveled young girls wandered about in the parking lot just behind the [New York Telephone Company] building, many crying, some near hysteria. Inside was the familiar New York disaster scene, police and priests and firemen and ankle-deep water, choking white smoke and Bellevue interns in yellow helmets placing mangled bodies in wire baskets.

A half-hour earlier some of the girls, 100 or more, were having lunch in the basement-level employees' cafeteria. The building is a long, low buff-brick structure with two floors above the basement. An oil-burning boiler stood in one corner of the basement, in a room adjoining the cafeteria.

Scarcely any one these days gives a thought to a boiler exploding, particularly in a new building, but suddenly at 12:07 p.m. this one went. It weighed at least a ton and it tore loose from its moorings and ripped across the cafeteria in a hellish explosion of steam.

"It was like a hurricane," said Miss Diane Gerstel, 22, who was there. "There was a terrible gush of steam. You couldn't see anything. I cried 'My God, what happened?'"

Mrs. Gloria Salour, 23, was there, too, and she thought a nuclear bomb had fallen. "The walls cracked, smoke came pouring through. I thought it was the end."

Directly above the boiler room, the blast punched through the concrete ceiling like a great fist, and flung girls and desks and filing cabinets all about the big accounting room on that floor.

Inside walls of cinder-block on both floors were shattered and buckled, but the outside wall near the boiler was not penetrated. Many of the outside windows were blown out and their metal frames twisted.

Some of the girls ran from the building, others helped drag or carry the injured out, and some climbed out the broken windows. Most of the dead were buried under the rubble near the boiler room or rather where the boiler room had once stood.

"They seemed to be coming out of every window and my son and I rushed across the street to help," said Francis Holland, 48, who lives in an apartment building at 502 W. 213th St., across the street from the telephone building.

"They were bloody and their clothes were torn and some of them had broken arms. It's about a six-foot jump from the windows to the sidewalk and we were grabbing them and getting them down."

The victims lay there on the sidewalk screaming with pain, he said, but so many others were coming through the windows that there was no time for first aid. Within minutes, ambulances arrived from Fordham and Jewish Memorial hospitals.

Mr. Holland, security guard at New York University, said the windows of his apartment were broken by the explosion.

Most of the injured were women, he said, but there were some men, too. Few of them appeared to be burned.

Except for the burning oil from the boiler, there was little fire. There wasn't much to burn among the plaster and concrete and metal office equipment, and the few small blazes that followed the explosion were quickly extinguished.

However, the ventilation system broke down. Both floors (they have low ceilings) and the basement were filled with smoke for more than an hour.

The girls at work on the top floor were knocked from their chairs and shaken up, but the blast did not penetrate through their floor. None of them was believed to be seriously injured.

The blast punched a bulge into the ceiling of the first floor, but did not quite break through into the second floor.

Considering the destruction, it would seem there must have been a terrific noise with the explosion, but there was disagreement over this.

Some of the girls said it was "tremendous" and "like an atom bomb" and others said it was "more of a muffled whoomp" and "like a garbage truck banging into a building."

Thousands of people gathered on the streets around the building, and police had to put up barricades to keep them back.

The neighborhood, near the very northern tip of Manhattan, is composed of five- and six-story apartment buildings and small stores. Inwood Park is four blocks west from the telephone building, and the IRT elevated tracks run just behind the building on 10th Ave.

There were many stories of heroic conduct. A girl on the first floor said her office was on the verge of panic when Miss Celeste Meola, a section supervisor, took firm command and led the girls in an orderly line downstairs through the smoke and outside.

No one knew what had happened immediately, and there was a great fear of fire after the explosion, but many of the young men being trained for executives remained in the building to help evacuate the injured.

About an hour after the explosion, a policeman with a bullhorn began to call for all the workers from the building to report to tables that were being set up in the parking lot. They wanted to find out who was there and who was missing.

The girls, crying, shaking, some with blood on their dresses, formed lines and had their names checked off at the tables. Bodies were still being uncovered and carried out.

Upstairs in the girls' long, wide-open accounting room, desks and cabinets lay toppled and covered with plaster under a pall of white smoke.

Papers and records littered the floor.

A pair of high-heeled shoes stood upright in a bare spot where there must have been a desk. A disembodied desk phone was on the floor ringing, its little red extension light winking. I wondered who was calling but I did not answer it.

New York Herald Tribune
1960–1964
Civil Rights Reporting

Portis's excellent civil rights coverage—and its neglect by subsequent histories of the time—is discussed thoroughly in the introduction.

May 8, 1963

Birmingham's Trigger Tension

BIRMINGHAM.

Three times during the day, waves of shouting, rock-throwing Negroes had poured into the downtown business district, to be scattered and driven back by battering streams of water from high-pressure fire hoses and the swinging of clubs of policemen and highway patrolmen.

Now the deserted streets were littered with sodden debris. Here in the shabby streets of the Negro section one of the decisive clashes in the Negro battle against segregation was taking place.

Last night a tense quiet settled over the riot-racked city after a day in which both sides altered their battle tactics.

The Negro crowds, who for days have hurled themselves against police barriers, divided into small, shifting bands, darted around the police and poured hundreds of separate patrols into the downtown business districts.

The police, who had crowded hundreds into the city's overflowing jails, abandoned efforts to arrest the demonstrators. They concentrated on herding the mobs back toward the 16th Street Baptist Church, headquarters for these unprecedented demonstrations.

By day's end, Alabama Gov. George Wallace had ordered some 250 state highway patrolmen in to aid beleaguered local police and had warned, at an opening session of the Legislature, that he would prosecute Negroes for murder if anyone died in the Birmingham riots.

The Rev. Martin Luther King Jr., a leader of the desegregation movement, said demonstrations would continue. Talks between the two sides will go on, he said, but "I wouldn't go to the point of saying this is the kind of negotiation we would like to see…"

And in battered downtown Birmingham, a store manager looked out on the now-silent street, shook his head and told a reporter:

"It can't keep building up….People can get to the boiling point."

The Negro drive had abandoned any pretensions of non-violence. The reaction of city officials had turned from determined resistance to harsh, personal hatred.

At the height of yesterday's violence, firemen turned the jet stream of a high-pressure hose on a tiny wooden shack in a parking lot. Inside was 56-year-old Mrs. Martha Jones, a Negro. Unable to escape, she was hit with gallons of water and flying shards of glass.

Another victim of one of these battering streams of water was the Rev. Fred Shuttlesworth, one of Dr. King's aides. Knocked flat by the jet stream he was taken away in an ambulance. "I been waitin' a week to see Shuttlesworth knocked down," said Commissioner Eugene ("Bull") Connor. "Too bad it wasn't a hearse."

The violence was between Negro crowds and law officers. White throngs on the downtown sidewalks watched or went about their business—but they did not take part.

What will happen if young, white roughnecks—who have been the storm troopers previously against Negro demonstrators—come on the Birmingham scene?

This possibility haunts responsible people. "I'm amazed that we've not had trouble," said Sheriff Melvin Bailey late yesterday.

The violence began around noon. About 500 Negro school children marched from the 16th Street church waving anti-segregation banners. Police shoved into the crowd, grabbed the banners, broke up the formation. But the police dogs that had been driven into previous Negro crowds were kept on their leashes. No one was arrested.

Milling around in a park across from the church were 1,000 Negro adults.

Suddenly, this crowd bolted toward the downtown area. Negroes surged into the street, and downtown Birmingham was a seething mass of demonstrators, spectators, marooned vehicles, and retreating, harried patrols of policemen.

The surge spent itself after half an hour and, in small groups, the Negroes began to drift back toward the church.

The crowd in the park grew and—as police cordoned off an eight-block area—an almost visible tension built up.

Four fire trucks lumbered up behind the lines of policemen.

Then, hundreds of Negroes, clapping, chanting, singing, suddenly reappeared in the downtown streets. They had apparently infiltrated; no mass movements had been seen.

The harassed police at the park listened to taunts from the Negro crowd: "Bring on the water…bring on the dogs."

The dogs—five of them—remained leashed, but firemen turned on their hoses, soaking the demonstrators. Rocks flew through the air in response.

It was while the turmoil was at its height that Gov. Wallace announced in Montgomery that he was sending in the state patrolmen.

Shortly thereafter, Negro leaders borrowed police megaphones and pleaded with the crowds to disperse before the city gave way to complete anarchy.

"Go home," they said. "You are not helping our cause."

And slowly the Negroes drifted away.

As dusk settled over the troubled city, some of the newly arrived state troopers were posted at traffic intersections in the downtown area while Negroes flocked into the 16th Street Baptist Church for a night mass meeting that overflowed into another church.

What had happened?

The Negro crowds had not followed the tidy plan mapped by their leadership, according to the Rev. Andrew Young, one of the Negro clergymen. The plan, he said, had called for no massive charges, but for small, orderly marches of placard-carrying demonstrators.

What was being done?

White and Negro leaders were meeting—the where and the who were not revealed—in hopes a compromise could be worked out. Dr. King had told a morning news conference that the Negroes would end their demonstrations when they had achieved four goals: better job opportunities, desegregation of all downtown public facilities, formation of a bi-racial committee to solve race problems, and dropping of charges against arrested demonstrators.

May 10, 1963

Birmingham Bargaining Before Watchful World

BIRMINGHAM.

A shroud of confusion hung over the battle for desegregation here last night as reports were circulated that peace was and was not imminent.

The Rev. Dr. Martin Luther King Jr., according to one report, said that a formula had been hammered out for settling the dispute. "The settlement has been sealed except for minor details," he was quoted as saying.

But Wyatt Tee Walker, Dr. King's executive secretary, said the story was "gravely in error," according to another report.

Earlier, Dr. King had said he was half way to victory and hoped to complete his bargain with the city's white leadership this morning.

"But if we can't reach an agreement," he said, "we will have no alternative but to resume large-scale demonstrations."

The bargaining was being carried on during the second 24-hour truce Dr. King had declared. He insisted it was the last one. He had set a deadline at 9 a.m. today (11 a.m. New York time), and said that if an agreement were not reached by then, 3,000 Negroes would gather at their churches for a mass march on the city.

The 11th-hour announcement by Dr. King came as the world watched Birmingham developments—called "ugly" by President Kennedy. The agreement—its details are to be told today—presumably made the mass march unnecessary.

Pressures had been building up on all sides. Dr. King has a firebrand element in his group that was growing increasingly impatient of the delays.

"We're getting tired of this," said the Rev. James Bevel, leader of the group's "angry young men." "We want freedom now," he added. Mr. Bevel is a field secretary in Dr. King's Southern Christian Leadership Conference.

The white business men who are meeting with the Negroes—and apparently acceding to their demands—are catching it from Gov. George C. Wallace, both city administrations and a large segment of the white population.

"We got the Negroes licked," said the outgoing Mayor, Arthur J. Hanes, who is still trying to hold the reins of government. "But the yellow-bellies and Quislings are down there now selling out our victory."

Even the new "moderate" Mayor, Albert Boutwell, who has an office in City Hall but no power yet, is backing away from the blue-ribbon merchants committee involved in the negotiations.

"The City of Birmingham, the municipal government nor I as new Mayor is a party to these negotiations," he said. He is being kept informed of what is going on at the meetings, he said, but he is not binding himself to any agreement reached at them.

The confusion at City Hall should be settled next week when the State Supreme Court is expected to pronounce just who is Mayor here.

Dr. King said earlier white leaders had agreed to two of his four demands—desegregation of lunch counters and all other facilities in downtown stores and upgrading the employment possibilities of Negroes in those stores.

The third demand—an amnesty for all demonstrators still in jail—is not in the merchants' power to grant, but Dr. King said he would be satisfied with a "strong recommendation" from them to that effect. The fourth demand is for setting-up of a bi-racial committee in this strife-torn city.

He is still unconcerned that neither of the city administrations has been consulted on the negotiations, believing that the white business leaders carry enough economic weight to put the agreement over at City Hall.

There are said to be 75 men in this group and they call themselves the Senior Citizens' Committee. It is an offshoot of the Chamber of Commerce.

The members of the committee had been invisible, nameless and unreachable until last night, when the chairman, Sidney W. Smyre, a realtor and former president of the Chamber of Commerce, identified himself as chairman of the group and issued a statement.

He said his committee "has had a number of meetings with responsible Negro leaders of the community and is still trying to work out agree-

ments which will assure us tranquility with some degree of permanence....We have made progress, and with the co-operation of all the
people, I believe we will be able to find the answers we must have."

As for the feasibility of desegregating lunch counters, Dr. King has
drawn support from a strange quarter—Safety Commission[er] Eugene
(Bull) Connor, policeman extraordinary.

Mr. Connor said he would not interfere if the merchants wanted to
permit Negroes at their lunch counters, and as for the city ordinances
against that practice, "they ain't worth the paper they're wrote on. The
Supreme Court has killed all them laws."

He had 1,200 policemen blocking off the Negro section of town from
the downtown business section yesterday and will have the same detail
on duty today.

His ever-growing force is made up of city and state police, sheriff's
deputies, game wardens, revenue agents and about 40 men in blue jeans
and khaki who look as though they might have been rounded up at the
bus station and deputized.

It turns out they are employees of the state Conservation
Department. All the lawmen wear helmets of various shapes and colors
and carry pistols and Louisville Slugger night sticks.

Col. T. B. Birdsong, Mississippi's state police director, was in town a
couple of days ago to offer help, but Mr. Connor said he had the situation
well in hand.

"I can have 2,000 men here in 15 minutes," he said. "I can get all
the men I need in Alabama." He said he particularly didn't want any
U.S. Marshals. "They don't know any more how to handle a crowd than
a snake knows about hips," he said.

It was suggested that a sticky situation might develop if the 19
out-of-town rabbis, who have come to help the Negro movement, are
used to lead the demonstrations. They have volunteered their services
to Dr. King.

"If them rabbis get in the way, we'll knock their asses down with the
hose like anybody else," said Mr. Connor.

The 68-year-old Mr. Connor does not like newsmen—he has been
burned so often in print—but he likes to talk, and an audience of five or
six is irresistible—to the great distress of Mr. Boutwell and some of the
"moderates."

Today should be the day of resolution, but then nearly everyone thought that the day before would be, too.

The city is bracing itself. As Mr. Abernathy said: "This is the largest non-violent army in the civil rights struggle." And according to Negro comedian Dick Gregory, who was bailed out of jail here yesterday, "the further you get away from that church, the less non-violent you get."

Mr. Gregory accused police of brutality. "I was whipped by five policemen," he told reporters. "They used billy clubs and hammers, and one guy had a sawed-off pool stick." A policeman called the charges "a wild story."

Asked about the food during his four days in jail, Mr. Gregory said at first it tasted like "garbage," but added: "After that, it's better than home cooking....Mama couldn't cook no better that third day, baby."

The rest of the world was watching Birmingham closely. European and Asian newspapers regarded the racial unrest as front-page news. Many have used dramatic pictures of demonstrators being attacked by police dogs and knocked down with fire hoses.

"Public opinion throughout the world repudiates this wave of racial violence in Alabama, at which state officials and Federal authorities snap their fingers," commented the Moscow newspaper Sovietskaya Rossiya.

The Italian Communist party organ L'Unita said the clashes "indicate that a revolution is already under way."

Financial support also was growing for the desegregation movement. The National Maritime Union said it had sent a check for $32,692 to Dr. King. The money was proceeds from a dinner the union held last October to honor its president, Joseph Curran.

The Women's Strike for Peace organization sent $575 to Dr. King's wife. The money was collected on a train carrying the women back to Philadelphia and New York from Washington, where they urged Congress to strengthen nuclear test ban negotiations.

In Toronto, members of a synagogue began a fund-raising drive and urged Prime Minister Lester B. Pearson to express "concern and distress" about Birmingham when he meets with President Kennedy this week end.

May 13, 1963

How the Night Exploded into Terror

BIRMINGHAM.

It was a hot night and down in the Negro section of town, around the A. G. Gaston Motel, the beer joints and barbecue stands were doing a good, loud Saturday night business. In a three-block area more than 1,000 Negroes were milling about.

Over at Bessemer, 12 miles away, the Ku Klux Klan was having an outdoor rally in the flickering light of two flaming 25-foot crosses. On hand were 200 hooded men, including the imperial wizard himself and a couple grand dragons and about 900 Klan supporters in mufti. There were a lot of bugs in the air, too, knocking against the crosses and falling into open collars.

For a month, through all the Negro demonstrations here, little was heard from the tough white element in the Birmingham area—very likely, the toughest in the South. Everyone wondered why, and then, Saturday night, the explosion came, literally.

Earlier in the day, the Rev. Wyatt Walker, Dr. Martin Luther King Jr.'s executive secretary, asked the police to place a watch on the Gaston Motel because some white men had been observed "casing it." At 7:30 p.m. a call came through the motel switchboard, warning that the motel would be bombed that night. It was a straight tip.

At 11:32 p.m. some night riders tossed two bombs from a car onto the front porch of the Rev. A. D. King's home in the suburb of Ensley. The front half of the house was ripped apart, but no one was injured. Mr. King is Martin Luther King's brother.

The night riders then sped four miles across town to the motel, head-quarters for the Negro leaders, and threw another bomb. It blasted a four-foot hole through the brick wall of one of the bedroom units. Three Negro women were sent tumbling—including one about 80 years old—but they were not seriously injured.

That did it. The Negroes in the area, many of them just leaving the beer joints at midnight closing, went into a frenzy of brick-throwing, knifing, burning and rioting that took four hours to stop, and then just short of gunfire. It was the worst night of terror in the South since the battle of Ole Miss. More than 25 people were injured and property damage was estimated at many thousands of dollars.

A few of us at the Tutwiler Hotel, four blocks away from the Negro motel, heard the midnight explosion—a dull whoomp—and got there a few minutes later. Only about 35 city policemen were on the scene, and they were standing in a small perimeter, arms over their heads, under a barrage of rocks and bottles from a mob of cursing and shouting Negroes closing in on them.

Mr. Walker—a Negro—was catching it from them, too, as he moved about with a bull horn pleading for calm.

"Please, please. Move back, move back. Throwing rocks won't help," he said. "This is no good. Please go home. It does no good to lose your heads."

"Tell it to Bull Connor," they shouted back to him. "This is what non-violence gets you."

Some of the rioters were attacking the police cars, smashing the windows with chunks of cinder blocks and cutting the tires with knives. One group kicked over a motorcycle and set it afire. Some others got around a paddy wagon and tried to upset it, but it was too heavy, so they battered the windows in.

Patrolman J. N. Spivey, alone and encircled in the mob, was stabbed in the shoulder and back. Capt. Glenn Evans and a deputy sheriff were kicked and punched pulling him free.

Help arrived soon in the form of a Negro civil defense unit with helmets and billy clubs, and more white police. These emergency Negro officers took just as much abuse and pummelling as the whites.

The city's armored car arrived shortly before 1 a.m. and its appearance provoked the mob anew.

"Let's get the tank," they yelled. "Bull, you —— ——, come on out of there." Public Safety Commissioner Bull Connor was not in the "tank" though this idea persisted throughout the night. (No one seemed to know where he was.)

The little white riot vehicle roared back and forth under a hail of rocks to scatter the crowd, and it mounted the sidewalk once and made a headlong pass down it, sending about 50 of us spectators diving for the dirt.

Some of the newsmen were hit with rocks and beer cans, but most of them quickly learned to stay away from such targets as the armored car and any large group of police.

Two blocks away, in a quiet zone, a gang of white boys were gathered on a corner throwing rocks and smashing the windows of Negro ambulances on their way to the motel. Police removed boys from the scene early, though, and no other whites appeared in the melee.

There came a frightening development at 1:10 a.m. That was when Col. Al Lingo, director of the Alabama Highway Patrol, arrived, itching for action. He and a lieutenant sprang from their car with 12-gauge pump shotguns at the ready, and moved toward the crowd.

"I'll stop those — —," he said.

"Wait, wait a minute now," said Birmingham Police Chief Jamie Moore, intercepting him. "You're just going to get somebody killed with those guns."

"I damn sure will if I have to," said Col. Lingo.

"I wish you'd get back in the car. I'd appreciate it."

"I'm not about to leave. Gov. Wallace sent me here."

In the end, he did go back to the car, jabbing a couple of Negroes with his gun on the way. But Col. Lingo would be heard from again before the night was over.

Chief Moore and his chief inspector, William J. Haley, used little rough stuff in trying to disperse the mob. The dogs and fire trucks were on hand but were never used.

Inspector Haley, his head protected only by a soft hat, moved fearlessly from one hot spot to another, taking punches and kicks and rocks, yet never losing his head.

The action took place on all four sides of the city block, bounded by 15th and 16th Sts., and Fifth and Sixth Aves. The motel is on Fifth Ave., between the two streets. It is a neighborhood of small grocery stores, taverns, frame shanties and churches.

The 16th St. Baptist Church, the starting point of all the recent demonstrations, is a block diagonally away from the motel at the corner of Sixth Ave. and 16th St. For a while it was thought the church was burning, but it turned out to be a taxicab that had been turned over and set afire in front of the church.

The Rev. A. D. King arrived at 1:45 a.m. and joined Mr. Walker and a number of other Negro leaders in trying to quell the riot with bull-horn pleas. Around 2 o'clock he climbed atop a parked car in the motel courtyard and gathered an audience of about 300 Negroes.

"We have been taught by our religion that we do not have to return evil for evil," he told them. "I must appeal to you to refuse any acts of retaliation for any acts of violence...We're not mad with a soul...my wife and five children are all right. Thank God we're all well and safe."

As he spoke and prayed, and as the gathering sang, "We Shall Overcome," a white grocery store was burning on the corner of 15th St. and Sixth Ave. Firemen trying to put it out were stoned by the mob. After a few minutes they retreated and the fire burned unchecked. The firemen pulled out so fast that they left a hose in the street, and it lay there burning in the no-man's land.

At 2:30, another grocery store directly across the street blazed up. Two frame houses on either side of the store caught fire, then a third, a two-story house. The rocks kept the firemen out, and it appeared the whole block would go.

"Let the whole — city burn, I don't give a God damn," said one of the rioters. "This'll show those white — —s."

"We have just spoken with the President's press secretary, Andrew Hatcher, and he asked you to return to your homes," announced one of the Negro leaders. "Please go to your homes. This is no answer."

At 3:05, with a police guard of about 75 men, the firemen returned to the blazing houses with two trucks and went to work again. The rocks and bricks were still flying, but a skirmish line of Negro leaders kept the rioters out of throwing range of the fire fighters.

In this scrap, Inspector Haley caught a brick on the forehead. With blood running down his face into his eyes, he stayed on the skirmish line calling, "Get back...get back, you must get back." He became so weak he had to be carried away.

An infuriated city policeman started toward the Negroes with a shotgun. When Mr. King tried to stop him, he knocked the minister out of the way with his gun. But a police lieutenant grabbed the angry patrolman and ordered him back. A few minutes later another policeman advanced on the mob and sighted his pistol across his left arm. Again the lieutenant stepped in and stopped him.

Soon there was left only a small pocket of rioters, young men in their teens and twenties, confined to 15th St. between Sixth and Seventh Aves. This group set fire to yet another grocery store at 15th St. and Seventh Ave. The blaze was nipped by Negro Civil Defense men.

It was pretty much all over at 3:40, when the state troopers began clubbing Negroes sitting on their porches. They had been sitting there watching all along, taking no part in the fight.

"Get in the house, God damn it, get, get," shouted the troopers, punching and pounding them with their nightsticks. And so the battle ended with the state policemen, who had played only a very minor role in the actual quelling of the riot, rapping old Negro men in rocking chairs.

Col. Lingo and his men had been chafing all week at the moderation and restraint of Chief Moore and his city police. "Moore is a Boy Scout," said Col. Lingo.

When daylight began to break at 4 o'clock, there were no Negroes in sight. The only sound to be heard was the screaming of sirens as more and more state troopers poured into the city, with their shotguns at ready and carbines with bayonets fixed.

The police, about 1,000 of them, cordoned off the troubled area around the motel from 14th to 17th Sts. and from First to Eighth Aves., allowing no one to leave or enter the area.

Shortly before 6 a.m. a state police sound vehicle cruised about downtown warning individual Negroes to "get off the God damn streets, get."

But someone put a stop to that, evidently because it was Sunday and Mother's Day.

After that the city was deathly silent, and no one was to be seen on the streets for several hours—until church time. It was a sparkling morning, and around the post office the air was fragrant with the scent of magnolia blossoms.

May 13, 1963

Klan Rally—Just Talk

BIRMINGHAM.
A Ku Klux Klan meeting, for all its cross-burning and hooded panoply, is a much duller affair than one might expect. The masked Klan rally in Bessemer Saturday night—just before the bombings in Birmingham— limped along for three hours of nothing but Kennedy jokes and invocations of Divine guidance.

It's hardly worth driving 12 miles and risking a clout on the head to hear President Kennedy and his brothers slandered, when you can get that on any street corner in Birmingham.

The rally was held in a well-kept little roadside park, a gift to the City of Bessemer from the Loyal Order of Moose. Moose Park, they call it. Two huge crosses were burned, one with an effigy of Martin Luther King on it. The crosses were some 25 feet high and about the heft of telephone poles.

There were 200 hooded and gowned men on hand and about 1,000 spectators in street dress. Entire families came, some with tow-headed kids that couldn't have been much more than 4 years old.

About 25 of the gowned Klansmen were in fancy red regalia—they were the dragons and kleagles. The other wore white. Their outfits are in three pieces—blouse, gown and pointed hood.

Some wore badly tailored cotton sheeting, but others had costumes of well-cut shiny nylon. Only a few concealed their faces. Most of them had their face flaps tied back.

"Klansmanship...Kennedy...niggers...Jews...the white man...Our Heavenly Father," these were the recurring words in all the speeches.

One or two spoke vaguely of bloodshed to come, but only in the sense of some unscheduled Armageddon.

A few references were made to the Birmingham situation. All were advised to cancel their charge plates and stop shopping at downtown stores there.

"We know who the men are who are selling out our country," said one dragon. "The K.B.I. (Klan Bureau of Investigation) has learned their names."

The imperial wizard of the Klan, Robert M. Shelton, presided and introduced the speakers as they appeared, one by one, on big flat truck trailer bed. [Mr. Shelton is a thin, intense man of about 40. An old friend of former Gov. John Patterson, he is a tire dealer from Tuscaloosa.]

Honored guests were the grand dragons of Georgia and Mississippi. [One of the favorite speakers was a man in red who warned of sickle-cell anemia, "a deadly organism lurking in all nigger blood."

"If so much as one drop of nigger blood gets in your baby's cereal," he said, "the baby will surely die in one year." He did not explain how he thought a negro would come to bleed in anyone's cereal.]

By 10:30 p.m. one of the crosses had collapsed and the other was just smoldering. Everyone drifted away and the grand dragon of Mississippi disappeared grandly into the Southern night, his car engine hitting on about three cylinders.

[Parts of the story enclosed in brackets appeared in a version distributed by the Herald Tribune News Service.—Ed.]

June 12, 1963

A Long Day of Defiance

TUSCALOOSA, Ala.
Down a path lined by steel-helmeted troopers and cleared by soldiers in battle dress, James A. Hood and Vivian Juanita Malone went to college yesterday.

They are both 20, they are both Negroes. They were both, for a day, in the center of the national stage as the President of the U. S. issued first a proclamation to "cease and desist" and then an order Federalizing the National Guard to stop the Governor of Alabama from keeping them out.

Together, they represent integration for an all-white state school system that has resisted integration longer than any other state in the union.

But as they walked into the red-brick registration building on the university campus, Gov. George C. Wallace—who backed down under the threat of a force greater than any he could muster—breathed defiance and told the world:

"We are winning this fight because we are awakening the people of the nation to the trend toward military dictatorship."

And then he quickly added, "We must have no violence today or any day."

That was the pattern of the hot, airless day: like a strange ballet, the forces on each side slowly took up their positions and slowly changed as strategy called forth counter-strategy. Seemingly, the only non-determined item was the fact that Miss Malone came to the campus yesterday morning in a black dress and yesterday afternoon went in to pay her $175 summer-term fee wearing a bright pink dress.

In a suddenly called national television and radio address last night, President Kennedy praised the students of the university—conspicuous by their silence, their restraint—and pointed out the lessons for every state made clear by posing the moral issue in Alabama as to "whether all Americans are going to be treated equally."

It was an epilogue to a moral drama.

The final act was set in motion at 1:34 p. m. when President Kennedy signed the executive order that brought the 15,000 troops and 2,000 air personnel of the Alabama National Guard under Federal jurisdiction.

The last time Alabama's crack 31st Infantry Division had been called up to national duty was in 1961—when Berlin was the crisis that called forth the headlines.

The President's order was transmitted immediately to Secretary of Defense Robert S. McNamara, and down the chain of command it went until Brig. Gen. Henry Graham, assistant commander of the 31st, marched to the doorway where Gov. Wallace stood—just as he had pledged in his last campaign—in the final effort to keep the Negro students out.

Dressed in fatigues, a Rebel flag patch on his shoulder, four tough special guardsmen flanking him, Gen. Graham said:

"I am Gen. Graham, and it is my sad duty to ask you to step aside, on order of the President of the U.S."

"General," the Governor said, reading from a crumpled piece of paper at a lectern set up just for the occasion, "I wish to make a statement first.

"But for the unwarranted Federalization of the National Guard, I would be your commander-in-chief. In fact, I am your commander-in-chief. I know this is a bitter pill to swallow for the National Guard of Alabama....

"We must have no violence...the Guardsmen are our brothers...God bless all the people of this state, white and black."

After a final vow to "continue this fight on the legal questions involved," the Governor got into his car and drove off in a roar of motorcycle police. Several students cheered.

And that was it.

Mr. Hood, who wants to study psychology, and Miss Malone, a business administration student, walked in minutes later with several Federal marshals and registered. A group of white students watched with no comment.

"This is our first and final news conference," Mr. Hood said afterward to part of the 400-man press corps that almost outmanned the 500-man state trooper contingent called up by the Governor. "We are very happy our registration has taken place without incident. We hope to get down to our purpose—study."

Both obviously looked forward to a procession before caps and gowns, not helmets and rifles.

So, too, did Deputy Attorney General Nicholas de B. Katzenbach, who directed the desegregation moves on the scene for the government, faced up to Gov. Wallace and his troopers in the morning and wore a broad grin and a ringlet of sweat beads as he came back at 5:17 p. m. for the final moves of the game. It was when Mr. Wallace saw 100 Federalized guardsmen—first of a contingent waiting a few blocks away on University Ave.—that he gave in.

Even when the day started, Mr. Wallace was under court order "not to interfere in any way" with the enrollment of the two Negroes. Under a carefully contrived technicality, he may not have done so, since he never actually confronted them.

In the early morning, before the two Negroes first came to the doorway of Foster Hall to register, President Kennedy issued a proclamation ordering the Governor to stop impeding the course decreed by the courts.

Ironically, it was countersigned by Secretary of State Dean Rusk, who must put the seal on all such proclamations, but who is particularly concerned at the propaganda picture the situation presents abroad.

The dramatic morning confrontation between state's rights and the Federal government took only 13 minutes.

It was 12:45 and the would-be students arrived in a three-car convoy. They had driven over earlier from Birmingham. Each had a $500 scholarship check from Negro organizations. Mr. Hood was prepared to pay his $280 to register in the college of arts and sciences, Miss Malone $205.20 to register for courses in the business school.

Around the building where the registration was to take place, a ring of state troopers stood in tight formation. Newsmen were clustered at the entrance, many of them wearing newspaper hats to ward off the sun. It was deadly hot.

A few students had been drifting in and out of the building all morning, but now none were to be seen.

Gov. Wallace was just inside the doorway, waiting, with a phalanx of state troopers behind him.

Deputy Attorney General Katzenbach, accompanied by U.S. Attorney Macon L. Weaver and U.S. Marshal Peyton Norville, both Southerners and graduates of the university here, got out of the lead car and walked the 20 or 30 steps to the entrance. Miss Malone and Mr. Hood remained in their car.

Gov. Wallace stepped forward to the lectern that had been set up and raised his hand to stop Mr. Katzenbach, actually touching Mr. Katzenbach's chest with his fingertips.

"I am here for the Attorney General of the U.S. and I have a proclamation here signed by the President of the U.S.," said Mr. Katzenbach. He then introduced Mr. Weaver and Mr. Norville, read the proclamation, explained that he was there to enforce a court order and asked the Governor to step aside and allow the Negro students to register.

Mr. Katzenbach said, "All they want is an education…"

"We don't need you here to make a speech," the Governor broke in. "Just make your statement."

Mr. Wallace then launched into his remarks, a five-page speech.

He used as his text the State's Rights Amendment of the Constitution—the 10th Amendment—and he spoke of "unwelcomed, unwanted, unwarranted and forced, indeed intrusion, upon the campus…by the might of the central government."

He concluded with a "solemn proclamation" saying: "Now, therefore I, George C. Wallace, Governor of the State of Alabama, have by my action raised issue between the central government and the sovereign State of Alabama…and do hereby denounce and forbid this illegal and unwarranted action by the central government."

"I take it from that statement that you are going to stand in the doorway," said Mr. Katzenbach.

The Governor, who had stepped back to block the double doorway with two troopers on either side, said simply, "I stand on my statement."

"Governor, I'm not interested in a show," said Mr. Katzenbach. "I don't know what the purpose of the show is. I'm here to enforce an order of the courts….These students have a right to be here….It is a simple problem. I ask you once more to step aside. It is your choice."

But the Governor had nothing more to say. Mr. Katzenbach asked him twice more to "step aside," and then said of the Negro students in his charge, "They will register today, they will go to school tomorrow and they will attend this summer session. They will remain on the campus."

And with that he, Mr. Weaver and Mr. Norville turned and went back to the car. The Governor had made his stand, and now the only thing to do was to bring in troops.

Miss Malone got out of the car, and three marshals escorted her to Mary Burke Hall, her dormitory, directly behind the auditorium. Mr. Hood was driven to his dorm, Palmer Hall, on the other side of the campus, a half-mile away. No troops were posted at the dorm entrances, and they had no trouble getting in.

The word "show" used by Mr. Katzenbach was a good choice. It was a well-staged pageant from start to finish.

Asked afterward if there was any plan to arrest the Governor, Edwin Guthman, Justice Department spokesman, said, "None whatsoever."

The troops will remain on the campus indefinitely, he said, but the Justice Department considers the campus under civil patrol. State troopers and Tuscaloosa police remained on duty at the university after the Governor left, and apparently will stay, with security under the dual control of Gen. Graham and Col. Al Lingo, head of the State Highway Patrol.

Personal guardians for Miss Malone and Mr. Hood will be the 30 U.S. marshals and border patrolmen brought in for the enrollment yesterday.

The president of the university, Dr. Frank A. Rose, was delighted with the way things turned out. "We could not have hoped for more exemplary conduct than that displayed by all those present for the crucial hours this morning and afternoon," he said. "We confidently expect that the University of Alabama soon will be able to return to normalcy, and we look forward to resuming fully our dedicated mission."

June 13, 1963

Murder in Mississippi

JACKSON, Miss.

Medgar W. Evers, the respected 37-year-old field director of the National Association for the Advancement of Colored People, was driving home.

He had been at one of those countless NAACP rallies he had attended during the nine years he led the crusade for civil rights in Mississippi.

It was shortly after midnight yesterday (about 2:30 a.m. New York time) when he got out of the station wagon in front of the house. He picked up a pile of NAACP sweatshirts, emblazoned "Jim Crow Must Go," and started into the house where his wife and three small children were waiting up for him.

He never made it. Lying in ambush, apparently in the fragrant honeysuckle bushes about 155 feet away, an assassin squeezed the trigger of a high-powered 30-30 rifle.

Mr. Evers, his white shirt forming an easy target in the porch light, was shot in the back. He died 50 minutes later in a hospital.

The rifle blast touched off a wave of shock across the nation. President Kennedy, who had made an appeal to the nation for an end to racial discrimination only a few hours before, was described as "appalled by the barbarity of this act."

Mississippi Gov. Ross Barnett, a staunch segregationist, called the killing of the Negro leader "a dastardly act."

Jackson Mayor Allen Thompson said the citizens were "dreadfully shocked, humiliated and sick at heart" and announced that the city was putting up a $5,000 reward for information leading to the arrest and conviction of those responsible.

The killing seemed to be the main conversational topic of everyone, from groups of idlers on Capitol Ave., the city's main street, to Southern belles in big white hats drinking iced tea in the dining room of the Heidelberg Hotel. Many feared it would trigger further violence.

A man in a beer joint at the edge of town seemed to represent the tougher elements of the city when he commented: "Maybe this will slow the niggers down."

In all, rewards totaling $21,000 were posted, including $10,000 from the NAACP, $5,000 from the city of Jackson, $50 from Jackson District Attorney Bill Waller, $1,000 from The Clarion Ledger and Jackson Daily News, and $5,000 from the United Steelworkers.

Shock and anger spread through Jackson's Negro district. At midday, 13 Negro ministers and a church layman staged a "mourning march" to the downtown area. They were arrested. A short time later Negro youths started a march to protest the slaying and 146 were arrested immediately by no less than 200 officers of the law.

Attorney General Robert F. Kennedy offered the full services of the FBI to track down the killer, but by nightfall about the only solid clue was the murder rifle, which was found in the bushes not far from Mr. Evers' house. A friend of the NAACP leader said he saw a "tall white man" running through a lot near the scene of the killing. Investigators also had a report that three men ran from the scene immediately after the shooting.

Threats and violence were not new to Mr. Evers, who has been in the forefront of the long drive for integration in Mississippi—a drive that has resulted in 804 arrests, including yesterday's, since May 28.

Only two weeks ago, a soft-drink bottle filled with gasoline was tossed into the carport next to Mr. Evers' house. It did not explode.

In an interview last summer with a CBS television reporter, Mr. Evers was asked about threats. This was his answer:

"I've had a number of threatening calls—people calling me saying they were going to kill me, saying they were going to blow my home up and saying that I only had a few hours to live.

"I remember distinctly one individual calling with a pistol on the other end, and he hit the cylinder and, of course you could hear that it was a revolver. He said, 'This is for you.' And I said, 'Well, whenever my time comes, I'm ready.'

"And, well, we get such pranks pretty frequently. But that does not deter us from our goal of first-class citizenship and getting more people registered to vote and doing the things here that a democracy certainly is supposed to espouse and provide for its citizenry."

Early yesterday the bullet which fatally wounded Mr. Evers smashed through a window pane, pierced a wall and hit the refrigerator in the kitchen. It bounced off the refrigerator onto a counter near the sink and rolled under a watermelon.

A trail of blood in the driveway showed that Mr. Evers staggered 30 feet through a carport and alongside a bed of red petunias before he fell by the back steps.

His wife, Myrlie, and the three children, aged three to nine, rushed out to him. Mrs. Evers became hysterical. The children were crying and pleading with their father to "get up."

Neighbors quickly picked up Mr. Evers, put him in his own station wagon, and raced off to the hospital. Houston Wells, one of the neighbors, said:

"On the way to the hospital he said, 'turn me loose.' He said that a number of times. That's all he said."

At last night's rally, several ministers called upon the Negro community of Jackson to boycott downtown stores for 30 days and to wear black for 30 days in mourning for Mr. Evers.

And another mass meeting was called for 10 this morning at the church—meaning more demonstrations.

Mrs. Evers, the Negro leader's widow, addressed the meeting briefly and tearfully. "I come to you tonight with a broken heart," she said. "But I come to make a plea that all of you here will be able to draw some of his strength, some of his courage. Nothing can bring him back, but this cause can live on."

June 14, 1963

Fires of Hate in Jackson

JACKSON, Miss.
Things are ripe here for another Birmingham riot. A Negro woman stood on her front porch yesterday afternoon and simply screamed and cried in the summer afternoon, expressing the angry frustration of Jackson Negroes.

The police are tired and equally frustrated, but they seemed to draw some relief yesterday by clubbing a Negro girl on the head and a white "nigger lover."

The trouble, of course, runs deep, but now it is at the boiling point and has been since the ambush-slaying Wednesday of Medgar Evers, 37-year-old Mississippi field secretary for the National Association for the Advancement of Colored People. And it is getting worse.

At 12:20 p.m. yesterday, 80 young Negroes and four whites emerged from the Pearl Street A.M.E. Church and marched in a column of twos for one block, down Rose St. to Deer Park St. A good many of them were waving small American flags. Police stopped them at the intersection.

"Everybody stop. This is a police order," Deputy Chief J. L. Ray told them through a bull-horn.

He told them to disperse or they would be arrested. They stopped, but refused to disperse and police began to herd them into paddy-wagons and trucks, snatching the flags angrily from their hands. Some of the youngsters threw the flags on the pavement in disgust rather than let the police take them.

More and more police began to arrive, and in a few minutes there were about 125 on the scene, the city police in blue, the deputy sheriffs in brown, all with helmets.

While the Negroes were being hustled into the trucks, a large number of Negro bystanders began to chant, "We want freedom, we want freedom, we want freedom." Most of them were on the porch of a frame house at 608 Rose St., and among them were two white men, John R. Salter, 29, who teaches at a Negro college here, and the Rev. Ralph Edward King Jr., 27, Methodist chaplain at the college.

Chief Ray told the group to stop chanting or he would arrest them for disturbing the peace. They refused, and about 25 police charged the porch, swinging billy clubs. Two policemen grabbed Mr. Salter and held him while another beat him on the head. Another one knocked down a 15-year-old Negro girl, Carol Myles, and three more jumped her brother, 17-year-old Tommy Earl Myles, and slugged him.

The crowd scattered, and there being no one else to threaten, the police turned on a group of newsmen. A deputy sheriff shoved one reporter to the ground and raised his club and shook it at another one and said, "Get back before I bust your head open."

The Jackson police do not like to have people taking notes when they are going about their business.

Mr. Salter, his head bleeding, was hustled away by two policemen, and Mr. King shouted angrily at the milling policemen from the porch. "What's wrong with you cops! You beat a woman on her own front porch...she's lying in here bleeding. I know you're white and how you feel, but will you please call an ambulance?"

Eventually an ambulance came. Mr. King is a native of Vicksburg, Miss., and is chaplain at Tougaloo Southern Christian College where Mr. Salter is assistant professor of social sciences. Mr. Salter is from Flagstaff, Ariz.

A half dozen or more barking police dogs were brought to the scene, but it was all over before they could be used. When the dust had settled, the Negro woman stood on her porch and screamed hysterically at the police. Words failed her.

"I don't know what's going to happen," said Mrs. Ruby Hurley, southeast field secretary for the NAACP, who has taken over the operation here since Mr. Evers' death. "Washington needs to do something before another outbreak. I can't think of another instance in NAACP experience when things have been so dangerous."

She and the rest of the leaders are trying to channel the Negro anger into controlled demonstrations, she said, "But these young people are getting harder and harder to hold down. Just the presence of Federal troops nearby would be a help. The Federal presence in the South has a strong psychological effect."

"Some people are ready to shoot, they're going around buying guns," said the Rev. G. R. Haughton, Negro minister of the Pearl Street Church. "We're trying to keep them under control, but I just don't know."

City police, deputies, state detectives and FBI men are still working around the clock in the search for the killer of Mr. Evers. A suspect was questioned yesterday, but was cleared after the questioning. Rewards for the identity of the killer now stand at $22,350.

Later in the afternoon, 11 Negro ministers called on Mayor Allen Thompson to ask for bread, and he gave them velvet-wrapped stone. They gathered in the handsome white antebellum City Hall and had a friendly but profitless discussion.

"We want peace, too, and we love the city of Jackson," said the Rev. R. L. T. Smith. "You don't love it any more than we do, Mayor. All we want is a fair chance before the courts, a fair chance for jobs, just a fair chance. We just want what every other American has, that's all."

They had eight requests, involving the desegregation of public facilities and downtown eating places and establishment of a bi-racial committee.

But, as he has done in the past, the congenial Mr. Thompson turned them down with a smile. He did renew his offer to accept Negro applicants for the police force, but the Negroes did not consider this much of a trade.

As for the police clubbing, the Mayor said he was already investigating and that "if the reports were true," the guilty policemen would be disciplined. "There will be no police brutality in Jackson," he said. "I can assure you of that."

The Mayor knew most of the Negro preachers well enough to call them by their first names, and he seemed to be on particularly friendly terms with the older ones. He agreed with them that Jackson had reached its exploding point, and he pleaded with them to "calm your people down."

The demonstrations are dangerous and in the end futile, he told them. "They're not going to get anywhere, and we're going to see that they don't get anywhere."

There were handshakes all around—all the amenities were observed—and the ministers left to take the sad news back to their people.

A funeral for Mr. Evers will be held at 11 a.m. tomorrow at the Negro Masonic Temple here on, of all things, Lynch St. The NAACP headquarters are also in the temple building. Mr. Evers' body will be on view at Collins Funeral Home tonight. Many prominent civil rights figures in the country are expected to attend the service.

August 29, 1963

Rolling Down From N.Y.: Hopes, Fears and Holiday

WASHINGTON.
William Penn, an exuberant young man in beret and wrap-around sun glasses, sneaked on Bus 10 twice in the confusion, but was caught both times and ejected.

"Look lady, I've been with the cause all the way," he said. "Now how about a seat?"

"I don't want to tell you again, Penn," said George Johnson, 30-year-old trail boss of CORE's 24-bus convoy to Washington. "You're supposed to be on Bus 6: now get on it and stay on it."

It was 2 a. m. at the staging area, 125th St. and Seventh Ave., and Mr. Johnson already had his hands full with a hundred other problems. One group was complaining about having to ride on a school bus. A French TV crew had no tickets and wanted to get on Bus 10. Many youngsters were running around swapping tickets to be near friends.

Mr. Johnson finally threw up his hands. "All right. All right. I've had it. Get on your buses and stay there. No more switching. We're leaving."

Departure time was set for 2:30 a. m. We left at 3:40. Just before pulling out, however, the 34-year-old unemployed Mr. Penn came swinging aboard again, this time with a No. 10 ticket. "I got this cat to switch with me," he explained. "I told him No. 6 was air-conditioned."

Mr. Johnson was too tired to argue.

Everyone wanted to get on No. 10 because it was a prestige bus. Mr. Johnson was on it as captain and so were such other CORE luminaries as Omar Ahmed and Jim Peck.

The rest—there were 49 of us, including 27 whites—were a mixed bag of earnest young ideologues, middle-aged women and teen-agers. Mr. Penn was in a holiday mood. He wanted to sing and crack jokes.

No one else did, however. As soon as we passed through the Lincoln Tunnel nearly everyone went to sleep. Occasionally there was muttering in the back of the bus—"Make Penn get in his seat," or "Shut up, Penn."

At five we stopped for a break at a Cranbury, N.J., bus terminal. It was a mob scene, hundreds of buses.

"I hope this march will put the fear of God in our Congressmen," said Mr. Johnson, sipping coffee from a paper cup. "But you just can't put any faith in white men."

At a near-by table a 15-year-old Negro boy named Bill Swinton was having coffee with his "Big Brother," Marvin Holmes, a 39-year-old white man. As a Big Brother, Mr. Holmes spends much of his free time taking Bill to ball games and shows. Bill is an orphan who lives with his aunt in the Bronx. A few weeks ago Mr. Holmes asked Bill if he wouldn't like to go to the big march.

Back on the Jersey Turnpike at 5:55, this time with the three French TV men aboard. They had been following in a car. Dawn was breaking, but there is really nothing to see on that featureless super highway. Just fog hanging in the low places of the meadows.

An hour and a half later we stopped at New Castle, Del., at a place called "Clemente's—largest bus stop in the world." I don't know how they figure that. The place at Cranbury looked bigger. More coffee.

"Lord, I hope we don't have any trouble down there," said Dorothy Jones, a middle-aged Negro woman from Manhattan. "That would just maybe show that we're not ready for responsibilities. But you know, I think we are. We're ready to give something to this country, and we want to give."

Did she have any trouble getting the day off?

"Oh no. Good old Mayor Wagner. I work at the city Personnel Department." Mrs. Jones' seat-mate on the bus was Mrs. Ruby Borges, her supervisor in the department. Also a Negro, Mrs. Borges was one of three people aboard who could speak French well enough to be interviewed by the TV men.

Ready to go again at 8:30. "Penn! Where's Penn?" A search was instituted. After most of the buses had left, he finally showed.

"We've been waiting for you for 20 minutes," said Mr. Johnson, furious.

"I've been in the bathroom."

He tried once again to start to sing, but no one was very interested. They wanted to talk.

"A Chinese-African alliance seems to me the most obvious thing in the world," said Mr. Ahmed.

"If we cannot solve this domestic race problem, we, as a nation, cannot survive," said Mr. Johnson.

"You'll have to define your term," said E. F. Karman, a 35-year-old white Peace Corps member, who is leaving for Nigeria soon. "Do you mean that in the context of 1870 or 1910 or what?"

"Well, if it comes to that, I'll take Chinese imperialism before Western imperialism," said 19-year-old Wayne Kinsler, one of the Negro sit-ins arrested last week at City Hall.

This time it was Mr. Penn who went to sleep.

Through the Baltimore area there were groups of Negroes on the sidewalks waving at us. One girl had a sign saying, "You tell 'em."

Same thing in Washington, the sidewalks were lined with wavers.

We crossed the city limits at 10:30. One of the first things to come into view was the Washington Monument. "One of these days, we're going to change that to the Booker T. Washington Monument," said Mr. Johnson.

The Washington police were terrific. The city was alive with buses, but it took just 20 minutes to pilot us in to our parking place on Independence Ave. and 17th St.

We had been on the road seven hours and ten minutes and the bus tachometer said we had gone just 221 miles from that dark Harlem street corner. Everyone was rumpled and sticky and had grainy eyes. But spirits picked up immediately as soon as we piled out on the grassy mall.

The buoyant Mr. Penn stepped out ahead of everyone and Mr. Johnson had to call him back. "We are in this town to do some marching," said Mr. Penn. "I'd say, let's go to it."

New York Herald Tribune
1960–1964
London Bureau

Portis talks about his stint as the London bureau chief in his interview with Roy Reed, included here in the Epilogue. While there, he covered Britain's reaction to John F. Kennedy's assassination, the opening of John Osborne's controversial play *Look Back in Anger*, and the continuing conflict in Cyprus. He also profiled a self-proclaimed witch who carries a jackdaw named Hotfoot Jackson on her shoulder ("She told how he would dance to radio music. A comic bird"). He left the paper in November of 1964 and returned to Arkansas to write fiction. As the travel story below shows, he was never more comfortable than when he was on the move and observing other people on the move.

August 23, 1964

An American on Dylan's Trail

HOLYHEAD, Wales.
The misty green island of Anglesey in North Wales is not the easiest place in the world to get to. It is a long way from London and you can't arrive there by mistake. Consider then how disappointing it is to drive day and night over narrow mountain roads sustained only by cigarettes and Radio Caroline to find that other Americans have beaten you to the place.

At Holyhead, the end of the line, there was an entire family at the Esso station gassing up their car. What business did they have here? Truly, the Yank tourist is everywhere under foot. In a pub called the Dublin

Packet there were two more, two college boys, drinking Welsh ale and interfering with a dart game.

"You're not trying to hit the middle then?"

"Nah, not the middle," said a fat man, and he went on to explain that complicated game.

The pub was crowded with beefy longshoremen in boots and sweaters but it was curiously quiet. When strangers are about it is always the same. At Laugharne ("Larn") in South Wales, Dylan Thomas's village, one enters the pub on the cove there and the old regulars are sitting around laughing and needling each other.

It is impossible to understand them, their English, but the sound effects are a joy. Then you hear someone order in an American twang, and it turns out to be you, and a dead silence falls. It is as though the Sundance Kid had just walked through the swinging doors. After a while the talk starts again, but very low, and the fun is over until you leave.

Polite, helpful to a fault, the Welsh are nevertheless not to be drawn into familiar conversations with strangers. The exception too often turns out to be the town bore. He wants to talk about Goldwater because he thinks you want to talk about Goldwater. It is a hard topic to choke off.

Well, I don't think he'll be elected anyway, he is told.

"Aye, that's what they said about Hitler."

Goldwater's not that bad. He's not Hitler.

"I'm thinking they said the same about Hitler."

They didn't say he wasn't Hitler, did they?

"They said he was not a dangerous man. Chamberlain said it, they all said it. You must read your history."

Holyhead is the jumping-off place for Ireland. Irish sixpences and shillings turn up in your change there. The mail boat, a comfortable old tub called the Princess Maud, runs twice a day to Dublin and costs $6.86 one way, second class. The crossing takes three and a half hours and it raises a terrific Celtic thirst. They drink Guinness stout on that boat like condemned men.

"I served with Her Majesty's forces for 27 years," said one big fellow doing a fair imitation of Victor McLaglen *[British actor and Oscar nominee for* The Quiet Man—*Ed.]*. "I was a sergeant in the Irish Guards but I was mustered out of the Indian Army as a major. I'm the chalk man in a turf parlor now and I make plenty, don't worry about that. Chalkie, they call me."

Are the Irish the best of the guards regiments? he was asked.

"I will have to confess they are, my good friend. Mind you, I'm not saying the Welsh don't have more V.C.s [*Victoria Crosses, a British military honor—Ed.*] than we do."

There was an American girl on the Maud, a political science major from Chicago, who was making a lone junket around Europe on the backroads and staying at youth hostels for 50 cents a night. She too wanted to talk about Goldwater and, surprise, she was *for* him. "Goldwater is a respectable conservative and I would like to get that across to the Europeans I meet along the way," she said. She is in for some long talks.

On arrival in the Irish Republic she was annoyed because no one would stamp her passport, and she wanted it as a souvenir. The traffic is so heavy between Britain and Ireland that they don't bother on either side to check passports. The once-hated Englishman can even vote in Ireland and vice versa.

Dublin was alive with Americans, the richer ones there for the horse show. Not a hotel room was to be had, nor a car to be rented. A cab driver pointed out Trinity College and the windowless Bank of Ireland, then fell into a morose silence. The gentle Liffey was running Kodachrome green.

Rebellious American actor Sterling Hayden, said the Dublin Sunday Independent, was wandering bearded and unrecognized down around Cork with a rucksack on his back. At James Joyce's Martello Tower there were no pilgrims, no Americans, no one. In an alley off O'Connell St. a crowd gathered to watch a man bind himself in straitjacket and chains, then wriggle free.

"Please bear in mind, ladies and gentlemen, that I am a man of 56 years of age," he said. "You would pay two shillings to see this in performance anywhere in the free world. All I ask is your very close attention and one small silver six pence."

The boat back to Holyhead, for no apparent reason, was loaded with family groups. Boisterous children were everywhere, running and skidding on the deck, which was wet with Guinness'. Rule: The Irish are kinder to their children than the English and take no disciplinary action until the nippers really get out of hand. Then they swat the daylights out of them. The English tend to treat their children like simple-minded little soldiers who need constant correction. Rule 2: Irish girls are livelier and more fun but the English and Welsh girls are better looking.

Britain has no fairer scenery than coastal Wales and the mountains of the north. The 13th-century castle at Caernarvon is itself worth the trip. The beaches, especially the one at Borth, are fine, but the sea is like ice. Impatient, must-get-there tourists shouldn't bother because Welsh roads are narrow and positively medieval in some villages. It takes twice as long to drive 10 miles as it would in the United States. There are no motels to speak of but there are a good many hotels. In summer months reservations are absolutely necessary in Britain and Ireland though there are plenty of "bed and breakfast" places—boarding houses—good for an overnight stay.

I went to one in Dublin and when the landlady said it would be one pound ten ($4.20) for the night I said I had been told it was only a pound. She was redheaded and she almost hit the ceiling.

"Are you English?"

"American."

"Oh…very well then, a pound."

Two

TRAVELS

That New Sound from Nashville

The cover story of the *Saturday Evening Post* from February 12, 1966, featured a photograph of Roger Miller. Portis, the contributors' page states, "has written a comic novel that will be published this year by Simon & Schuster"; portions of that novel, *Norwood*, about the travels and travails of the would-be country star Norwood Pratt, were published in two installments in the *Post* in June and July of 1966.

Nashville, the Athens of the South, is home to Vanderbilt University, Fisk University and at least half a dozen other colleges, as well as a symphony orchestra, a concrete replica of the Parthenon and a downtown beer joint called Tootsie's Orchid Lounge. Tootsie's is where the country-music people hang out—those who don't object to beer joints. It has a very active jukebox and shaky tables, and there are 8-by-10 glossies all over the wall and a clutter of small-bore merchandise behind the counter—stuff like gum, beef sticks and headache powder. The hostess is Tootsie Bess, a motherly, aproned woman who doesn't mind noise or a certain amount of rowdiness, but whose good nature has its limits. One night a drunk song-writer addressed Maggie, the cook, as "nigger," and Tootsie threw him out and banned him. She has three cigar boxes full of I.O.U.'s.

On Saturday nights, performers on the Grand Ole Opry step out the stage door and cross an alley and go in the back door of Tootsie's to get aholt of themselves between sets with some refreshing suds. Songwriters—"cleffers," as the trade mags say—sit around and chat and wait for artistic revelations. Deals are closed there. New, strange guitar licks are conceived.

Roger Miller (*King of the Road*), the antic poet who was too far out to have any success on the Opry itself, was singing and clowning in Tootsie's back room years ago, for free. "He wrote *Dang Me* right here in this booth," says Tootsie. But his rates are stiffer now. He just did a special for NBC-TV and is talking with them about starring in a series next year. "Yeah, Roger's doing all right," says a Nashville business associate. "He was in here the other day with a quarter of a million dollars in his pocket. It was two checks."

Tootsie's is like a thousand other beer joints in the South with such names as Junior's Dew Drop Inn and Pearl's Howdy Club, and a certain type of country boy feels right at home there, whether he has $250,000 in his pocket or just came in on the bus from Plain Dealing, La., with a guitar across his back and white cotton socks rolled down in little cylinders atop his grease-resistant work shoes. And a song in his heart about teardrops, adultery, diesel trucks.

This is the *milieu* of commercial country music, the Southern honky-tonk. Sometimes it's called "hillbilly music," which is only half accurate, because the southern lowlanders have contributed just as much as the hill folks, perhaps more; and sometimes "country and western," which is misleading because such of it as reflects the culture west of Abilene, Tex., tends to be pretty thin stuff. "Southern white working-class music" would never do as a tag, but that's what it is.

By any name, country music is prospering, and so is Nashville's recording industry, which now does a brisk non-country trade. Perry Como, hitless for almost two years, packed a carpetbag recently and went to Nashville and came back with a hit single, *Dream On, Little Dreamer*, by two country-music writers, and a hit album, *The Scene Changes*. The golf was good too, he says. Both RCA Victor and Columbia have built big new studios there in the past year, and all sorts of unlikely people—Al Hirt, Ann-Margret—are going there to record. Elvis Presley always has.

It is odd in a way that the country-music business should have settled in Nashville, instead of in a rougher, rawer town like, say, Shreveport. (Shreveport does have a lesser version of the Opry called "The Louisiana Hayride.") Nashville is an old town (1780), a state capital, a college town, and a headquarters town for southern churches.

There are some 200,000 people in the city proper. It is a pleasant, green, genteel, residential place on the banks of the Cumberland River in the rolling hills of middle Tennessee. Nashville once had poets like Sidney Lanier and Allen Tate, and now it has Ernest Tubb and doesn't quite know what to do with him, except ignore him. Few country singers manage to get themselves taken seriously in Nashville. Eddy Arnold is a big community man, and he is being discussed as a Democratic nominee for governor next year. Roy Acuff ran for governor as a Republican, unsuccessfully. But generally, the Athenians of the South go one way, and the country-music people another. Less than 10 percent of the Opry audiences come from the Nashville area. Middle-class Nashvillians, anxious lest they be mistaken for rubes, are quick to inform the visitor that they have never attended the show. It is not for them, this hoedown. They long for road-company presentations of socko Broadway comedies. Even radio station WSM, which carries the Opry, is not really a country-music station. "Oh, no," says Ott Devine, WSM's Opry manager. "Except for the Opry and a few record shows we're a *good* music station."

But settle there the business has, and it now brings in some $60 million a year to the town. From the Opry it has grown into a complex of 10 recording studios, 26 record companies, and a colony of 700 cleffers, 265 music publishers, and 1,000 union musicians, about half of whom can read music with some facility. Nashville has replaced Chicago as the country's third-busiest recording center, after New York and Hollywood, and is probably ahead of Hollywood, says RCA Victor vice president Steve Sholes, "in the production of successful single records." The main reason is that it has developed its own style, what outsiders call "The Nashville Sound." Nobody wants to define it, but it amounts to country music with a dash of Tin Pan Alley, in the form of noncountry instruments like drums and trombones.

The music, in its present form, is not really very old. It is a blend of British balladry, American folk songs, 19th-century Protestant hymns, Negro blues and gospel songs, southern-white themes and, now, a touch of northern pop. There were important pioneers in the early 1920's such as Vernon Dalhart ("If I had the wings of an angel...") but for most practical purposes the music dates from 1927 when Jimmie Rodgers made his first record (Victor) for a goldback $20 bill.

Rodgers was The Blue Yodeler, The Singing Brakeman. He was a consumptive drifter from Meridian, Miss., who, in a span of six years, established commercial country music as a distinct new form. He was not quite 36 years old when he coughed himself to death in a New York hotel room in 1933. At the end he was so wasted and weakened with tuberculosis that he had to lie on a cot while recording at Victor's 24th Street studio in New York. He left a legacy of 112 songs, many of them classics like *My Carolina Sunshine Gal*, *I'm in the Jailhouse Now*, and

> *I'm goin' to town, honey,*
> *What you want me to bring you back?*
> *Bring me a pint of booze*
> *And a John B. Stetson hat....*

With a strong assist from The Carter Family (*Wildwood Flower*, *Wabash Cannon Ball*) Rodgers set the pattern for the music, and the Grand Ole Opry formalized it and gave it a home. The Opry is the mother church. Actually this show predates Rodgers's recording career by two years, but in the beginning it was only a fiddler's show, and it wasn't until later that it took on its present form as a singin' and pickin' jamboree.

* * *

In the 1930's the music remained pretty well localized in the South and Midwest, except for the hemispheric exposure it was given by the Mexican-border radio stations, beaming it out at 200,000 tube-shattering watts, the hillbilly songs sandwiched in between harangues from jackleg preachers and pitches for towels and chickens. ("Send your card or letter to *Baby Chicks*! That's *Baby Chicks*! Sorry, no guarantee of sex, breed or color.")

But it didn't get off the ground nationally until World War II, when the northern boys and city boys got strong doses of it in barracks and on decks and in southern camp towns. For those in uniform there was no escape from *Smoke on the Water* and *Pistol Packin' Mama* and *Detour* and *There's a Star-Spangled Banner Wavin' Somewhere*. Some of the city boys developed a tolerance for it, a few even came to like it. In 1944 the USO polled GI's in Europe to determine the most popular singer and, lo, Roy Acuff's name led all the rest. It was much the same in Korea. There were few rifle companies in that war without a wind-up record player and a well-worn 78 rpm record of Hank Williams's *Lovesick Blues*. The Chinese even used the music in an attempt to make the American troops homesick, or maybe it was their idea of torture. For whatever reason, they set up giant speakers and boomed ditties like *You Are My Sunshine* across the valleys in the long watches of the night.

The music soon went into eclipse again, as it had done after World War II, and it wasn't until the late 1950's that it began making its present comeback—this time with The Nashville Sound.

A White Sport Coat and Pink Carnation
I'm all dressed up for the dance....

The boom started just a few years after country music was laid low by rock 'n' roll. "Elvis made *Heartbreak Hotel* in whenever it was, 'Fifty-something [January, 1956], and all those rock songs came along and country music took a nose dive like nobody's business," says Buddy Killen, executive vice president of a Nashville publishing house called Tree Music. "Things began to look up when Ferlin Husky made one called *Gone*. I think that was the first big one with the new sound. It had the beat and the piano and Jourdanaires. That's the thing now, the beat. It used to be the song."

Others cite Marty Robbins's *A White Sport Coat* or Sonny James's *Young Love* as the breakthrough tunes. All three records had a country flavor, but they weren't *too* country; they were country-pop hybrids that sold well in both markets. They had The Nashville Sound.

They don't call it that in Nashville, of course. They call it "uptown country," as opposed to "hard country," which is the traditional hillbilly music that is still big on the Opry and on five a.m. snuff shows. Hillbilly is characterized by a squonking fiddle introduction, a funereal steel guitar and an overall whiney, draggy sound that has never set well with urban ears.

The masterminds of The Nashville Sound have abandoned all that. They have smoothed out many of the rough edges likely to offend. They use sophisticated new chord progressions and, while the guitar remains the primary accompaniment—lead, rhythm, steel, 12-string—they have added piano, drums and choral voices, and anything that strikes their fancy—vibes, tenor sax, harpsichord, trombone. The prejudice against non-string instruments has largely gone by the way. Even the Opry now permits drums on the stage, though it is still holding the line against brass and woodwinds.

So popular is the new sound that the number of country-music radio stations has increased from 81 to 200-plus in the past four years, and that includes several 50,000-watt heavyweights in places like Los Angeles (KGBS) and Chicago (WJJD). Even New York City—where there are restaurants for Polynesians, northern *and* southern Italians, northern *and* southern Chinese, Moors, Scandinavians, Lithuanians and Romanians, but where you can't buy a decent plate of turnip greens, purple-hull peas and fried okra—even that market has been opened up. Since last September, WJRZ in Newark, a former pop station, has been beaming Lefty Frizzell and Ferlin Husky across the Hudson all day and all night, and it has increased its audience 1,000 percent.

"This music has a new acceptance and a new dignity," says Harry Reith, the general manager of WJRZ. "It's not, you know, the old hillbilly stuff, the nasal voices, those guitars thumping and all. Our mail response has been fantastic."

Few people can agree on precisely what The Nashville Sound is, but there is pretty general agreement as to who the masterminds are— namely, Chet Atkins, Victor's Artist and Repertoire man in Nashville; Owen Bradley, A-and-R man there for Decca; and Don Law, A-and-R man for Columbia. The A-and-R man is the guiding hand in record production. He matches the song with the singer and directs recording sessions—so far as anyone can be said to "direct" a session in Nashville. He picks the recordings to be released and the ones to be shelved. He puts albums together.

Chet Atkins, who may be the best guitarist in the country, is a quiet, introspective man who sits tieless in a plush executive office on Nashville's Music Row and reflects on such things as posture as a key to character. "Look at me," he says, as though trying to puzzle out how he got the job. "All I really am is a hunched-over guitar player."

Questions about The Nashville Sound seem to bore him. He shrugs and says it is not much more than a gimmicky tag. "You can get the same sound with country records made in Hollywood," he says. "You can get it anywhere with these same musicians, boys from this part of the country. They're country boys, poor boys from the farm. The music they play has honesty. It has the same quality as Ray Charles. Soul. If you have it, it comes out in your music. That's all it is."

A few years back Atkins was playing in an after-hours club in Nashville called the Carousel, and some say this was the origin of the sound. The band was made up of Atkins, Grady Martin and Hank Garland on guitars, Floyd Cramer on piano, Buddy Harman on drums and Bob Moore on upright bass. These are the musicians seen over and over again at the recording sessions.

The tinkly, gospel-rock piano work of Cramer is one of the most distinctive things about the new sound, that and the smooth choral backing of the Anita Kerr Singers and the Jourdanaires. Nashville A-and-R men are not as much inclined to electronic trickery (echo chambers, etc.) as their rocker counterparts in Detroit and Hollywood, but in the current spirit of *anything goes*, they are moving in that direction. Already they do quite a bit of overdubbing, and if a sideman gets carried away and hits a crazy lick or makes a weird noise, it's usually left in. A lot of the unidentifiable noises are produced by Pete Drake on his steel guitar. He can make it *gronk* like a tuba if gronks are called for, and he can make it sound like someone talking underwater if this need arises.

Atkins, of course, is a soloist, but he occasionally does some personal overdubbing. That is, he will take a taped song and superimpose his own guitar runs on it to beef up the thin spots. Cramer and Drake are soloists too, but they are also among the busiest sidemen in town. The money is good, $61 for a three-hour session, double that for the leader, and they have no objection to playing nameless on someone else's record. There are about 100 sidemen in Nashville who work with some regularity at the studios, says Musicians' Local 257, and about 35 of them make from $20,000 to $80,000 a year.

Decca's Owen Bradley, another guitarist-executive, also flounders a bit in trying to define the Sound. "I've been asked what it is a thousand times and I've given a thousand different answers. And I think I've been right every time." He peers over his glasses at a clock that tells him what time it is in Hollywood and New York and smokes a cigarette in a holder and carries on a long-distance phone conversation and a personal chat, all at once. "A few years ago we were forced to take a second look at some of these songs. They were better than we thought. This *Sound* business, all it boils down to is an approach. It's the spontaneity of certain musicians here getting together and making up an arrangement on the spot. The A-and-R men are just some kind of referees."

Music Row, where the business is concentrated, runs for three or four parallel blocks on 16th and 17th avenues in a going-to-seed residential section about five minutes from downtown Nashville. A Nashville record-ing session is a very casual affair. There are no arrangers, no producers and no written music, except once in a while a lead sheet, and the singer has probably brought that along for the words, not the music. Usually no one has rehearsed except the singer. At the start of the session he goes through the song once, or just plays a demo (demonstration record) for the sidemen. If the A-and-R man is an accomplished musician like Atkins, he may have some definite ideas about how it should be done. If not, he, the singer and the sidemen simply work it out as they go along, and stop when everybody is more or less pleased. They know one another well and they anticipate one another's moves. Everybody is free to offer suggestions and there is a lot of fast infield chatter.

"Hey, Pig, why don't you do that twice?"

"Brighten it just a hair, Jerry."

"And right there, more ching-ching-ching."

"We're all lollygagging, come on, punch it up."

"You got any squirrels out at your place?"

"I ain't seen a squirrel this year. Plenty of hicker nuts but no squirrels."

"Bear with me, chillun, I'm 'on sing this lover if it takes all night."

There is not much written music to be seen in Nashville, except for what is embroidered on clothes, but pianists and bass players are fre-quently seen reading from scraps of paper on which series of numbers have been scribbled. The numbers are code—each of them represents the bass note of the chord in one bar of music. Some musicians are so deft at it that they can jot the note numbers down after listening to a demo once.

"If we gave even the most mediocre written musical test, I doubt very much if half our members could pass it," says George W. Cooper, president of Local 257. "But that's not to say they aren't good musicians. We've got some of the best." "Oh, they read music all right," Atkins says. "But they read it with their ears instead of their eyes."

Atkins is an artist and he naturally takes his own guitar work seriously. The same goes for Bill Monroe, the father of bluegrass picking, and his protégés, Flatt and Scruggs. For the most part though, to ask serious ques-tions about country music—apart from what it's doing in the charts—is to draw blank looks. The songs have been scorned and ridiculed so long by outsiders that the performers themselves have come to place little value on them. A good many of the singers, one gathers, would turn to pop music tomorrow morning if they could change their accents and get booked in Las Vegas. They yearn to see their records in the pop charts, where the money is. At the same time they must not *seem* to be wanting this; they must be careful not to alienate their country fans, who are a jealous lot.

The situation makes for curious ideas of loyalty.

* * *

Wesley Rose, who runs the town's largest publishing house, Acuff-Rose, is known as a passionate advocate of pure country music. "I've been fighting this battle for years," he says. "I tell my boys to keep their eyes off the pop market and concentrate on making good country songs. If they're good enough they'll make their way anywhere." A few days later one finds Rose directing Roy Orbison, a rock-pop singer, in a recording session. Orbison was one of the rockers with Sun Records in Memphis in the 1950's who dealt country music such a terrible blow.

Or take Audrey Williams, who is the handsome platinum-blonde widow of Hank Williams, probably the most legendary figure country music has produced. Audrey Williams is something of a celebrity herself, having been the provocation for so many of Hank's famous laments. She now directs an operation called Audrey Williams Enterprises, which involves a small movie company, a record label and the management of her singer-son, Hank Jr. She is not without sentiment. She keeps in her garage the 1952 blue Cadillac convertible that Hank died in on New Year's Day, 1953. But when Sam Katzman made a movie based on Hank's life (*Your Cheatin' Heart*), she agreed with the boys from the Coast that Hank's twangy, countrified singing should not be used on the sound track. The much blander voice of Hank Jr., then 15, was used instead, along with new arrangements and instrumentation. Of course it was Hank, not Hank Jr., who sold all those records, but Mrs. Williams does not see the point of the objection. "We thought it would reach more people this way," she says. "A lot of people don't like that old fiddle-and-steel-guitar sound. I believe in progress."

Then there's Buck Owens (*I've Got a Tiger by the Tail*) who has the Buck Owens Pledge to Country Music. It's in scroll form, and free copies are available, suitable for framing. "I shall sing no song that is not a country song," it goes, and "I shall make no record that is not a country record," and so on. Fair enough, except that one of Buck's latest releases, a big seller, is an instrumental called *Buckaroo* that you can do the Watusi to.

It is probably foolish to pursue this sort of thing, and it is certainly unrewarding—like trying to get a triangulation fix on Roger Miller, the biggest thing out of Nashville since Hank Williams. "Oh yeah, we still think of Roger as a country singer," says Buddy Killen, Miller's publisher in Nashville. "No, no, Roger's not a country singer, not anymore," says Don Williams, Miller's agent. "I don't know just what I am," says Miller, rehearsing for a television show in New York. "I like to entertain everybody. Scooby doo."

> I see you going down the street in your big Cadillac,
> You got girls in the front and got girls in the back,
> Yeah, and way in the back you got money in a sack,
> Both hands on the wheel and your shoulders rared back,
> ...I wish I had your good luck charm and you had a do-wacka-do wacka-do.

To many people the most interesting thing, the *only* interesting thing about the business is the money—the idea of all them old country boys being in the chips, driving Cadillacs with six-shooter door handles and wearing outrageous, glittering Western suits, designed by Nudie of Hollywood. Country singers are growing weary of this image, if not weary enough to stop making money.

"I guess you're going to write another one of those articles about how we're all a bunch of rich idiots," said Faron Young, the Singing Sheriff. "Rhinestones on our clothes and all that." "Well, a lot of you are idiots, Faron, remember that," said Jan Crutchfield, an irreverent cleffer. The former movie lawman was not amused. "Not all of us, neighbor. Not by a long shot."

The big money is in personal performances—state fairs, coliseum shows, one-night stands in tank towns. Young Johnny Cash grosses around $500,000 a year on personals alone. He, Roger Miller and Buck Owens are the superstars, and they get $2,500 and up for a single show, against a percentage of the gate, usually half. Porter Wagoner, The Thin Man from West Plains, gets $1,400 and up for a show, and Ernest Tubb (*I'm Walking the Floor Over You*) gets upwards of $1,000. Tubb and his

Texas Troubadours are on the road some 200 days a year, traveling as much as 500 miles a day. Tubb has been at this grind since 1933, and you can see it in his seamed, exhausted face. "Just to look at him you wouldn't think Ernie was only twenty-eight years old, would you?" says Miller, with a straight face. "That's what the road'll do for you." But Tubb's schedule is not unusually rigorous. Some of them are on the road 300 days a year.

A lot of them also have to rush back from the man-wrecker road to meet their Opry commitments, or to tape their syndicated television shows. This is the new mark of prestige, the syndicated television show. Flatt and Scruggs have one, and so have the Wilburn Brothers and Leroy Van Dyke. Carl Smith has a network show on Canadian television. Porter Wagoner's show, sponsored by a purgative called Black-Draught, is probably the most successful. It is shown in 80 "markets," and claims an audience of 20 million people. This is about the same size as Jimmy Dean's ABC network audience.

For most country singers there is not much money in records. "Country records are like salt and pepper in the grocery store," says Owen Bradley. "The turnover is not big but it's steady." This reassuring salt metaphor (sometimes flour) is often heard in Nashville.

Eddy Arnold (*Bouquet of Roses*), most durable of the country crooners, has had 56 top-10 records since 1948, which makes him far and away the leader over a period of years. He, Miller, Cash or Owens could make a handsome living on record sales alone, but not many could.

In fact, a record can make the top five in the country charts and not sell more than 15,000 copies. At a wholesale price of 50 cents per record the company gross on a 15,000 seller would be $7,500. Take at least $700 off the top for the cost of the recording session ($850 if choral voices are used, $1,200 with strings) and that leaves $6,800. The singer would then get about four percent of that or a $272 check for his "hit."

And that's all he'd get. Jukebox operators, who buy most of the country singles, pay no royalties to anybody because of a curious interpretation of the copyright law, and radio stations pay no royalties to the "artist" or singer. The stations do, however, pay royalties to the publisher and composer. So almost every singer and picker in Nashville seems to be a music "publisher" these days. The word actually is a misnomer, a holdover from the days when sheet music was a substantial part of the business. Acuff-Rose still prints sale copies of its songs, and Tree Music contracts out the printing of Roger Miller's songs, but few others print anything. If you went to a small "publisher" and tried to buy a sheet copy of something like *You Broke My Heart, So Now I'm Going to Break Your Jaw*, the chances of getting it would be slim, unless you had a subpoena.

* * *

These days the "publisher" is really a talent scout and a copyright agent. He seeks out songs, copyrights them and peddles them, usually on demo tapes, to the singers and the record companies. For this service B.M.I. (Broadcast Music, Inc.) pays him four cents per radio play (the composer gets 2.5 cents). The composer and publisher get a penny apiece for each record sold.

At one time, in true folk tradition, just about every country singer wrote his own songs. Most of the classics are productions of the singer-writer: Jimmie Rodgers's Blue Yodel series, Roy Acuff's *Great Speckled Bird*, Jimmie Davis's *You Are My Sunshine*, Hank Williams's *Cold, Cold Heart*. The singer-writer is still very much around—Roger Miller sings only his own material—but in recent years there has been a proliferation of nonperforming writers. It is a precarious trade.

Miller himself first made his reputation as a writer. "The Opry never figured me for much of a singer," he says. In 1958 he wrote a string of country hits such as *Half a Mind* (Ernest Tubb), *Invitation to the Blues* (Ray Price) and *Billy Bayou* (Jim Reeves). "I was a great big success; the only thing was, I wasn't making any money."

Writer Jan Crutchfield explains about that kind of success: "I wrote one in 1961 with two other guys that was in the charts 26 weeks. It was called *The Outsider*. Bill Phillips cut it. You know what my royalty check was? Thirty-three dollars. Yeah. I looked at that check and I thought, 'Yeah, a few more hits like this and I'm going back to gospel singing.'" Crutchfield's third of the royalty represented a sale of about 10,000 copies. Nevertheless, with a few really big sellers and a small catalog of standards, a writer can retire young.

Crutchfield and collaborator Fred Burch, both thirtyish and Kentuckians, are two comers, part of Nashville's new wave. They wrote *Dream On, Little Dreamer*, which Perry Como recorded and which shows signs of becoming a standard, and they have had a number of moderate successes. Crutchfield is a tall, thin, moustachioed country hipster who used to share a boardinghouse room with Roger Miller. Burch is an admirer of author Terry Southern, and he has an upper-middle-class, tousled, campus air. He once planned to attend the New School for Social Research in New York, and is writing a novel about the Nashville scene. Together he and Crutchfield write rock songs, pop songs, uptown country and hard country. At taping sessions, Crutchfield does the singing—now he's Fats Domino, now T. Texas Tyler—and Burch sits in the control room and makes suggestions and laughs at the songs and Crutchfield's antics. In two hours, with four pickup sidemen, they get eight songs on tape.

Afterward they sit in an office at Cedarwood Publishing and decide on the disposition of their newly minted tunes. One is called *Push My Love Button*. It breaks Crutchfield up. "That is one more raunchy song, ain't it? Yessir, that goes to Ann-Margret." Ann-Margret? Does she sing? "Hell, naw," says somebody, "but she makes records." Other people have drifted in, bookers and secretaries, to listen and offer advice. "Do me a favor, Crutch, and pitch that one to Lefty Frizzell....Now that's a George Morgan song if I ever heard one. Or Buck Owens. Buck's would sell more, but I kinda like to hear George do it...."

Detour, there's a muddy road ahead.
Detour, paid no mind to what it said,
Detour, all these bitter things I find,
Should have read
That Detour sign.

Nashville is not a closed shop anymore, but, say Burch and Crutchfield, it's still much safer not to stray too far from the mainstream of traditional country music. "Look at Roger Miller," says Crutchfield. "He's a genius and he was knocking around here for years and couldn't get anywhere. They didn't even know what he was trying to do."

Miller's career is a good measure of what the Grand Ole Opry is all about. In the bad old rock-'n'-roll days, the Opry stood firm when other hillbilly shows around the South were giving way. The Opry came through it and the others only managed to lose both audiences. But this same conservatism led it to overlook Miller.

The pay is bad on this show and the working conditions are primitive, but a country singer will do anything—lose money, drive a log truck up from Moultrie, Ga.—to get on it. A few years ago a singer named

Stonewall Jackson did that—parked his log truck outside the WSM building, went in, sang a song and won a spot on the show. The Opry's pay scale starts at 10 dollars, and nobody, big star or jug blower, is paid much more than $60 for a Saturday night's performance.

Many singers have a deep loyalty to the Opry. Roy Acuff, the King of Country Music (Dizzy Dean gave him the title), has been a regular since 1938. He certainly doesn't need the billing or the money, and he couldn't be dragged off the show. "I never thought the Opry needed me." he says. "I need the Opry. I still get a little shaky every time I go out on that stage."

Every Saturday night in the cold and heat, people line up for blocks outside the ratty old Opry auditorium and wait patiently for three hours to get inside, where they will sit on hard church pews for five more hours of Hank Snow and Stringbean and Wilma Lee and Stony. Surprisingly, most of the people who come are not from the South but from Indiana, Illinois and Ohio. Family groups prevail—grim, watchful guys who you know are not going to clap, their subdued wives and small kids, who will be asleep on the pews, mouths open, before it's all over. Along the wait- ing route there are souvenir shops that sell Kitty Wells cookbooks. A man out front with a big card in his hat sells chicken cacklers, little oral noisemakers. People are afraid it's a trick, that the cackler won't work when they get it home, but they are even more afraid to try it out there on the sidewalk and have 3,000 people watch them make hen noises. "I sell more than you would think," says the cackler salesman.

Backstage, there is a lot of socializing and a lot of coming and going to Tootsie's. There are two bare dressing rooms, but nobody seems to dress in them, because they are always open. Jim and Jesse, a new bluegrass team, are in one of them, jamming. Over there is Porter Wagoner, resplen- dent in a purple brocade creation, signing a popcorn box for an autograph hunter who got past the guard. Pretty Loretta Lynn (*Blue Kentucky Girl*) is sitting on a bench telling a stranger about her recent European trip. "Put in your article about how bad the toilet paper is over there," she says. "I wish you could see it, hun, you wouldn't believe it." A chubby woman comes by and says, "Loretta, have y'all eat up all them butter beans?" Loretta says, "Girl, what are you talking about? I put up fifteen quarts last Saturday. Come on out to the house and get you some." Married at 14, now a 31-year-old grandmother, Loretta can sing like nobody's business.

While the show is going on, wives, girl friends, children wander idly back and forth across the stage. The announcer, Grant Turner, looks around to see if the singer he is announcing is actually there. If not, he brings on another one. The show runs in 30-minute segments and for radio purposes it must run on time. Somehow it does. No one is even sure who is going to be on the show until Thursday or Friday. "But that's the Opry," says manager Devine. "If we produced it we'd kill it."

Hank Williams, who couldn't stay sober, was dropped by the Opry in August 1952, for missing shows, and banished to The Louisiana Hayride in Shreveport, whence he came. He was making $200,000 a year, and people like Tony Bennett had begun to record his songs. If ever a country singer didn't need the Opry, it was Hank Williams. And yet for the next five months, the last five months of his life, he was on the phone to Nashville almost every day trying to get back on the show.

"If you were an opera singer, you'd want to sing at the Met, wouldn't you?" said Carleton Haney, a promoter who books Coliseum shows. "Look, there's what?—four billion people on earth, and only forty-eight of them can be on the Opry. Think about that."

> Cigareetes and whusky
> And wild, wild women,
> They'll drive you crazy,
> They'll drive you insane....

The legend is that the country singer is a hell of a fellow. Big spender, big drinker, a poolroom fantasy come true. It is based largely on the life of Hank Williams and, to a lesser extent, that of Jimmie Rodgers. Rodgers set the style—sudden fame and riches, a short, tragic life—and Williams fulfilled it.

Rodgers's influence on the music was all-pervasive in the 1930's. Young Clarence (Hank) Snow heard his records in remote Nova Scotia and marveled, and left the farm to sing and yodel like Jimmie, so far as he could. Down in Texas and Oklahoma, Ernest Tubb and Gene Autry were doing it. Of this lot the widow Rodgers pronounced Tubb the champ, and she presented him with one of Jimmie's fancy guitars, one that said THANKS on the back in mother-of-pearl. It remains an object of veneration in the country-music world, and Tubb plays it only on special occasions.

Rodgers was known to take a drink, and because of his tuberculosis he came to rely on drugs, but his excesses were as nothing compared to those of Hank Williams. Hank had troubles. Thin and sickly, he too had a legitimate need for drugs. He suffered chronic bouts of pain from a spinal injury. He was an alcoholic, the kind who can get drunk in 20 minutes; and, beset by chippies, his home life was often rancorous and stormy.

No one since Rodgers had shown more talent in the field. If it took him longer than a half hour to write a song, he said, he threw it away. He was known for his generosity, and for his black, bitter moods. "Y'all don't worry," he would tell his audiences, "cause it ain't gonna be all right nohow."

In 1952, as his drinking grew worse, he was fired by the Opry and divorced by his beloved Audrey. He went to Louisiana and married a pretty young divorcée ("To spite Audrey," he said) named Billie Jean Jones Eshliman, who, as it turned out, wasn't quite divorced. He married her once in a more or less private ceremony, again on the stage at a matinee show in New Orleans, and yet again on the night show, for those who had missed the matinee. He picked up a paroled forger who treated him for his alcoholism at $300 a week. This was H. R. (Toby) Marshall, "B.A., M.A., D.S.C., Doctor of Science and Psychology and Alcoholic Therapist"—who later admitted he had never got beyond high school. "Doctor" Marshall administered, among other things, chloral hydrate, a knockout potion he was fond of.

Hank was desperately trying to get hold of himself, and, right at the end, on Jan. 1, 1953, he got a bit of hope. The Opry finally gave in to his pleading and agreed to give him another try, in February. That day, with this happy news, he left Knoxville, Tenn., in the Cadillac with an 18-year-old chauffeur, Charles Carr, for a show in Canton, Ohio. Before leaving Knoxville he managed to get two shots of chloral hydrate. He stretched out on the back seat and Carr drove.

At Rutledge, Tenn., a policeman stopped the car for speeding. He wrote out a ticket and peered through the window at the form in the back. "That guy looks dead," he said. Carr explained about the sedation, paid a $25 fine and drove on. But by the time he got to Oak Hill, W. Va., he sensed something was wrong. He touched Hank, found him cold and drove him to a local hospital, where he was pronounced dead. Hank was

29. A coroner's jury declared he had died of "a severe heart condition and hemorrhage."

More than 20,000 people came to the funeral in Montgomery, Ala., including all the Opry luminaries. Red Foley sang *Peace in the Valley*, and "Doctor" Marshall presented the widow Billie Jean with a bill for $736.39 for his therapy services, possibly on the basis that he had stopped Hank's drinking. Billie Jean suggested there was more to Hank's death than met the eye. "I will never accept the report that my husband died of a heart attack," she said. Later she and Marshall both testified at a legislative committee hearing in Oklahoma on narcotics traffic, but nothing came of it as far as shedding light on Hank's death was concerned. Probably he did die of a heart attack. This was a clinical detail. He knew and his friends knew that he was running out of time. "I just don't like this way of living," he sang, and, "I'll never get out of this world alive...."

Disaster and sudden death have come to be a part of the country-music scene. In 1960 the unlucky Billie Jean was widowed once again by a country singer when her third husband, Johnny Horton (*Battle of New Orleans*), was killed in a car wreck. In March, 1963, Opry stars Patsy Cline, Hawkshaw Hawkins and Cowboy Copas were killed in a plane crash near Camden, Tenn.

Two days after that accident, singer Jack Anglin (of the Johnny and Jack team) was killed in a smash-up while driving to Patsy Cline's funeral. The venerable Texas Ruby was next; she died in a house-trailer fire. In August, 1964, Gentleman Jim Reeves, a crooner whose posthumous releases still appear in the charts, was killed in a plane crash just outside Nashville, along with his accompanist.

"We were burying 'em around here like animals for a while," Roy Acuff recalls. "I don't even like to talk about it." Last July Acuff, who wrote *The Wreck on the Highway*, and guitarist Shot Jackson were badly injured in a wreck on the highway near Sparta, Tenn. Acuff, who is back on his feet now, had every sizable bone in the right side of his body broken. He thinks he and all the other singers who haven't been killed yet are lucky and ahead of the odds, when their mileage, often mileage under pressure, is considered. Since the late 1930's he has traveled about 100,000 miles a year. "But I'm thinking about cutting down."

It's not an easy life at all. There's fame in it, of a sort, and money, and that keeps a lot of them going. But there's some deeper feeling too that keeps them out on the road, with a night here and a night there and a long drive in between, singing their songs, some trash, some gold, about hearts and wrecks and teardrops. They can't talk about those things, so they sing them.

An Auto Odyssey through Darkest Baja

This story appeared in the *Home* magazine of the Sunday *Los Angeles Times* on February 26, 1967. In the same issue was "A Man's Best Friend Is His Hog," an excerpt from Hunter S. Thompson's new book, *Hell's Angels*.

The idea was to get something sturdy and fairly reliable for a drive down the Baja California peninsula. Something cheap, too, expendable. Something you wouldn't mind banging up, or even abandoning if it came to that. The best thing is a jeep or a Scout or some other four-wheel-drive vehicle but for a one-shot trip a standard pickup truck is good enough.

I found what I was looking for on a Santa Monica car lot. It was a rat-colored 1952 half-ton Studebaker pickup. Just the thing. It had character and looked eager to please. It had big tires too, snappy 9.00/15 Cadillac whitewalls, a bonus in appearance, traction and height. There was a black diamond painted on the tailgate.

A crew-cut salesman spotted me and came over and said a man and his wife from Big Bear sure were interested in that truck and they were expected in momentarily. He looked at his watch. I got in the cab and turned the wheel and messed around with the pedals.

"It's got overdrive and 40 pounds of oil pressure," he said. "I didn't believe that oil pressure myself at first. Both those spotlights work."

I couldn't find the starter.

"It's under the clutch," he said.

It wouldn't start.

"We'll have to get that battery charged up for you," he said. "Kids come around at night and turn those spotlights on." He called for a boy to bring over a booster battery. "I believe if you drive this little truck you'll buy it. And I'll tell you something else. You're going to be happy with your gas mileage. Surprised. You've got your little Champion Six going for you and then your overdrive cutting in at about 35."

* * *

We got it started and I drove it around town. The clutch chattered a little and the shock absorbers were busted but there seemed to be no serious organic ailments. He had $495 on the windshield and we closed out at $375. That still sounds like too much but even now, after what happened, I'm not kicking about the price. It was in the back of my mind that I could sell that piece of iron for about $600 in Mexico. Pay for the trip. I did feel bad about getting in ahead of the Big Bear folks. They must have had an accident or a death in the family as they did not show.

I bought two new tires and put shocks on the truck and had it serviced and tuned up, new plugs and everything, and altogether sank another $50 in it. Then for $20 more I joined the Automobile Club of Southern California so I could get a big map of Baja and a detailed driver's log. This is a fine map (although it doesn't show elevation), and the log is good too, but I believe the best mile-by-mile guide for the Baja run is the *Lower California Guidebook* by Peter Gerhard and Howard E. Gulick (the Arthur H. Clark Co., Glendale, California).

* * *

I didn't know this fact at the time because it's hard to get any straight, first-hand dope about Baja in Los Angeles. A woman at the Mexican Government Tourist Office gave me a *turista* card, said the road was very bad and sent me to the Auto Club for any further information. A girl there gave me the map and log and her best wishes, but no, she didn't know how I could get in touch with anybody who had made the drive. People I knew said, "Why don't you fly down like Eisenhower?" and "Did they ever find those people that were lost down there?"

At the Mayan temple that is the Los Angeles Public Library I read the works of such veteran Baja desert rats as Erle Stanley Gardner and Joseph Wood Krutch. I pored over the Auto Club map and log, which carries a list of exactly 100 items of equipment to be taken on the drive—things like spare axles and leaf springs and a short-wave radio. And a calendar. Probably so you can note the passing seasons while you're trying to change an axle down there on the Vizcaino Desert. "Confound this list!" I exclaimed, after calculating the expense, and went out and bought a few things you would take on an ordinary camping trip, plus some gaso-line cans and water cans. (A small roll of baling wire was the lifesaver.)

I am not a hunter or a fisherman or an adventurer, nor do I have any particular affection for Mexico or the beauties of the desert, but I do like maps and I had long been curious about that empty brown peninsula. It snakes down through almost 10 degrees of latitude from Tijuana to the Tropic of Cancer. It is 800 miles long (more than 1,000 by road) and ranges in width from 150 miles at its bulging midriff to about 30 miles at the Bay of La Paz.

People live there of course, and by choice, but then people will live anywhere, even in New York City and Presidio County, Texas. The 800,000 inhabitants of Baja are not enough to clutter up the landscape. Most of them are concentrated in and around the northern border towns of Mexicali, the capital (200,000), and Tijuana (250,000), with a sprin-kling of farmers and fishermen and billy goat ranchers and cattlemen scattered all down the line.

The Spaniards first saw Baja in 1533 when an expedition sent out by Cortez sailed into the Bay of La Paz. A number of abortive attempts were made to colonize the place but no Europeans were hardy enough to stick it out until the Jesuits came in 1697. The Indians then living there (esti-mates of their number range from 12,000 to 70,000) were possibly the most primitive of any in the New World. They slept naked on the ground and wandered aimlessly about eating worms and roots and the lice from one another's hair. When the Jesuits came they found "not a hut, nor an earthen jar, nor an instrument of metal, nor a piece of cloth."

* * *

In 1768 Fra Junipero Serra and his Franciscans replaced the Jesuits, who had fallen from favor in Madrid, and the Franciscans in turn were replaced by the Dominicans in 1773, with Serra going on to bigger things as a missionary to the upper desert of Alta California, now a fruited plain governed by Ronald Reagan.

American forces seized Baja and held it throughout the Mexican War, but the treaty negotiators at Guadalupe Hidalgo gave it back to Mexico in a fit of indifference. Five years later, in 1853, a 29-year-old Tennessee *filibustero* named William Walker sailed into La Paz with 45 men, captured the town and the governor without firing a shot and pro-claimed "the Republic of Lower California." The central government of

Mexico did not offer much resistance, but the United States, then trying to swing the Gadsden Purchase, disapproved of Walker's adventure and forced him to abandon his new republic after seven months by blocking shipments of men and supplies. (Walker later became president of Nicaragua. In 1860 he was executed by a firing squad in Honduras.)

This then was the place that Andy Davis and I set out for last July 15 [1966—Ed.] in the gray truck that we had come to call, in our humorous way, "the Diamondback Rattler." Andy is a friend from college days at State U., a fellow Arkie exiled in California and a pretty fair hand with a crescent wrench. He got clear to go right at the last minute, and a good thing too.

* * *

We entered the freeway off Sunset in Los Angeles at 6:30 a.m. hoping to beat the rush-hour traffic, since I had no U.S. insurance on the truck. (I did have Mexican liability insurance. Not having it can lead to trouble, like jail.) The freeway was busy even at that hour but we were aggressive, if slow, and held our own. We hadn't quite got to City Hall when the front wheels started shimmying. A sudden, terrible vision appeared of Andy's wife driving out to pick us up at about the Disneyland exit. Then we found that the shimmy started at 48 m.p.h. and went away at 56 m.p.h., so we were okay as long as we kept the speed above the critical point.

We had about 600 pounds of gear in the back, the heavy stuff being four 5-gallon cans of gasoline, three 5-gallon cans of water, three 1-gallon water bags, one 2-gallon can of motor oil and a sack of spuds. The tires were aired up hard and tight and there was not much sag. At San Diego we bought some ice and piddled around, then crossed the border at Tijuana and drove through town resisting shouts on all sides from auto upholsterers and hawkers of religious statuary.

The road is paved for about 140 miles south of Tijuana and it is a pretty drive in the mountains and coastal stretches around Ensenada. This is a port city of about 35,000 people and the last town of any size before jumping off into the interior. We had a mechanic there check the shimmy and he said the trouble was a warped wheel. If we drove 3,000 kilometers at 50 m.p.h. the vibration would cause the front end utterly to collapse. He seemed sure of those exact figures. We could have put the spare on but for some reason we didn't do anything.

A few miles south of Ensenada there is a roadside stop where a uniformed officer checks tourist cards. The card is all that is necessary for driving in Baja. In mainland Mexico a *turista* windshield sticker is required, and a much closer check is kept on vehicles. Some idlers were hanging around the guard shack and when it became known that our destination was La Paz, one of them divined my plan and said the truck ought to bring about $750 down there. Wasn't that illegal, bringing a vehicle into Mexico and selling it? This got a big laugh from everyone except the officer.

We stopped for the day not far from Ensenada on a high bluff called Punta Banda overlooking the sea. Beautiful prospect. The two-burner gasoline stove worked okay and we had bacon and eggs and potatoes cut up with the peelings left on and fried with onions. The bargain Japanese canteen cups were a mistake. The metal was some Oriental alloy that had the property of staying 38 degrees hotter than the coffee therein. Fried your lips.

July 16. Odometer read 247 miles from Los Angeles. A cold white fog blew in during the night. Hated to get out of those sleeping bags. We couldn't see the sea. We had a leisurely breakfast of eggs and corned beef hash and were on the road at 8 a.m. This pace didn't last long. We told ourselves we were not going to rush, but before the day was out we were leaning forward on the seat just trying to get miles behind us. At a store called El Palomar we gassed up. The Rattler was getting 17 miles per gallon. Also bought some 2-inch Rocket Boy firecrackers from Macao. ("Light Fuse. Retire Quickly.") Some surfers from San Diego stopped by in a Volkswagen truck and asked if we had a firing pin for a .22 pistol. Sorry.

We left the pavement at Arroyo Seco and the gravel surface wasn't too bad for the first 15 miles or so, then it got murderous. The road was built up about 3 feet above the desert floor and drainage had made corduroy of it. We drove the ditches mostly where it was not so rough, although much dustier. Red dust. Several times we had to stop when it enveloped us. We picked up a hitch-hiker named Miguel. He refused to understand my Spanish even after I had treated him to a pack of Dentyne. A lug nut worked loose and rattled like crazy in the hub cap. Put it back on and discovered five others loose.

It was siesta time at San Quintin Bay but we woke up the owner of a little resort there and bought two cans of beer. We drove around the bay and ran into some more surfers. They were in a Volkswagen car and a Nissan Patrol, a kind of Japanese jeep, and had driven down from La Jolla. The Nissan owner, a four-wheel-drive snob, said they were turning back here, and intimated that we would be wise to do the same with our clunker. We showed them our tailgate.

We had hoped to make El Rosario that day but at 7 p.m. we gave up and pulled over near a rocky beach for the night. The desert—sand, cactus—runs to the very edge of the sea here. You expect a fall line and a marginal strip of something or other, but the desert simply stops and the water begins. For miles up and down the coast big breakers were crashing. There was nothing else to see. We built a fire of driftwood and had a big feed—bacon, potatoes and two cans of black-eyed peas. We had passed up lunch, and continued to do so. It would waste valuable driving time. The surf here was violent and as it retreated through the rocks it made a weird grinding noise that kept us awake for some time.

July 17. Mile 401. Off at 7 a.m. in a mighty burst of Studebaker power. Too much; the vacuum hose to the windshield wiper popped loose. Got it back on, then saw that one of the arms from the little motor had fallen off. Could have fixed it easily with a piece of wire but kept putting it off. *Mañana*. We had used the wipers to clear dust away.

* * *

El Rosario has 400 people and a green jail, and the weekly bus going south turns around here. Ditto the telephone line and mail service. We stopped for gasoline and children stood in doorways to watch us. South of town we saw our first Auto Club road sign. The American club posted the entire route with metal signs a few years ago, but few are left and most of those have been shot up so as to be unreadable. Probably by Americans as it does not seem likely that Mexicans would waste expensive .38 and .45 cartridges on such mean foolishness. Mean because it's so easy to get off the main road—Mexico 1—even with a good map and a compass and a close mileage check.

We met two big trucks hauling slabs of marble or onyx and pulled over out of the ruts to let them by. They stopped to pass the time of day, as is the custom, and we had our question ready.

"*El camino a San Agustin es malo?*"

A gringo-sounding Mexican at the wheel said, "Yeah, it's *malo* as far as you're going."

We kept foolishly asking that question, hoping someone, even if he was lying, would say the road got a little better. It got very hot that day but we had no way of knowing the temperature since our thermometer was no good. It would register 50 degrees one minute and 130 the next. At mid-afternoon the needle in the amp meter stopped moving. We pulled up short thinking the fan belt had broken. It was okay but the distributor wires were loose and the screws that held the top on the voltage regulator had shaken out. The top was just hanging on. Andy messed around with things and eventually got some movement out of the needle and wired the top back on.

We started climbing a range of burnt red mountains on a roadbed of sharp rocks. On the harder pulls—some stretches appeared to be 45 degrees—the engine began to miss and sputter. Too hot? Water in the gasoline? Bad points? The spark plugs were new. By getting running starts we rammed that poor old truck up and over each crest. The Cadillac tires never bargained for this but they held up.

On the downgrade the engine smoothed out and it was running like a sewing machine when we reached San Agustin. This was a forlorn hut right out on the desert with a windmill, not moving, and seven or eight guys sitting around drinking tepid Modelo beer from a kerosene refrigerator. One played a guitar and sang. We got some water for the radiator out of their storage tank. The water is no good to drink, they said.

A cloud of dust in the distance drew closer and soon an air-conditioned Jeep Wagoneer pulled in bearing a San Diego dentist, his wife and eight-year-old son. "La Paz or Bust," said a little sign on the window. "We're going all the way to Cabo San Lucas," said the boy, which news the Mexicans received with equanimity. The dentist said he too had had trouble with things shaking loose, and had had one flat. When driving in sand, he said, he let some air out of his tires for better flotation. He had a spark plug device that used engine compression to pump them back up. Nifty.

A few miles below San Agustin we saw our first palm tree, in a low wash where there was some underground water near the surface. There was a house nearby in some shade, and a very hospitable woman who let us draw some water from her well. "*Es muy bueno,*" she said, and she was right, it was sweet, cool water. Such ground water as exists in Baja is often brackish or alkaline to the taste. We drove on and began to look for a place to stop but this was flat desert with no natural features that would make one place better than another so we finally just stopped. In 11 hours driving we had made 98 miles.

* * *

After supper we broke the code of the desert by needlessly hacking open a barrel cactus. The hide was thick and bristly and it took about five minutes with a sharp machete to get to the middle. Bulletin: There's no water in those things. Not in this one anyway, just a damp core that could have done little more than infuriate a thirsty man. It was too hot that night to get inside the sleeping bags so we lay on top of them under the wide and starry sky. Then some bats came around and I zipped up and sweated. Andy's concern was for snakes. We never saw one.

July 18. Mile 499. Corned beef hash with Tabasco for breakfast. We had other things but Andy kept wanting to eat that stuff, going on about what a hearty dish it was. The next settlement down the line was Punta Prieta, once a gold mining center, now a handful of huts on either side of a dry wash. The gasoline man was David Ramirez. He siphoned it out of a 55-gallon drum and we filtered it through a chamois skin. We told him about the sputtering and he removed the points from the distributor and filed them with an emery cloth. Still no good. He took off the carburetor and cleaned it. Not much better but we decided to press on for Santa Rosalillita, of the three L's, a fishing camp on the coast. You don't have that trapped feeling on blue water. Ramirez had worked on the truck for about two hours but said there was no charge. Maybe a pack of cigarettes. We gave him some smokes and had to force money on him.

On the way to the coast we saw a lot of ground squirrels, or anyway some kind of speedy rodents with tucked-up white tails, and hundreds of quail, the gray kind with crested heads. And a sand-colored bobcat, who stopped in the road for a moment to see what was coming, then fled. The Rattler choked and popped on the hills but made it in.

There was rejoicing in the fishing camp. The supply truck from Tijuana had arrived just ahead of us. It was a week late and the fishermen—there were some 30 or 40—were out of gasoline and cigarettes and down to short rations. Now the smoking lamp was lit and a blue haze hung about. A young abalone diver named Chito was the mechanic of this lash-up and he was under our hood in a flash filing the points, resetting the timing and blowing through the gas line. A solemn little shirtless boy held Chito's cigarette while he worked, between drags. He held it still and was careful not to get his thumb and finger on the mouth part. Chito declared that the spring was bad in the spark advance. He found a similar one, cut it for length and put it in. That didn't do it either. Chito gave up. Must be the *puntas*, he said.

* * *

What to do? There was an old 1-ton Studebaker truck in camp that might have some usable points in it but the owner was gone and would not be back for a day or two. Pete, the skipper of a launch, said he would be going to Ensenada in about a week and we could ride up on the boat with him, get the points and come back with him. Thanksgiving in La Paz. Or we could try to make it down the coast to Guerrero Negro where there was a big salt works and probably some repair facilities. Scammon's Lagoon was down that way too, where the California gray whale breeds and calves. We didn't want to miss that. This seemed the best course.

We had to cross a deep gully getting out of the camp and it took about 20 running starts before we finally got up the other side, to loud cheers from the *pescadores*. (Let me say emphatically that the Champion Six, power-wise, was equal to any grade we met with; it was just that the firing system was on the blink.) Another young diver named Adam Garcia hitched a ride with us. His family lived down the coast.

About two miles from camp we hit some deep sand and in getting out of it we let the engine stall and die. Now it wouldn't even start. Well, that was it. Garcia asked if we wanted to sell the truck. No, not quite yet. He continued on by foot. It was growing dark. After some cussing and some recriminations we decided we would walk back to the camp in the morning and see about the points in the derelict truck. Sufficient unto the day was the evil thereof. But was it the points? So many hands, including our own, had been in that distributor. Maybe the coil. A cold wind was blowing from the sea and we took all the gear out of the back of the truck and slept in there under the tarp.

July 18. Mile 597. Just before setting off on the hike we had a last-minute go at the starter. The engine caught the first time. Hurrah for the bonnie blue flag! We loaded quickly and took off once more for Guerrero Negro. In about a half-hour we came to the Garcia fishing camp on a wide sandy beach. The main business here was catching *cahuamas*, big sea turtles, for canning. Garcia was surprised to see us. He rounded up a brother or a cousin who was something of a *mecanico*.

They found an old, rusty, six-volt coil in a shed and Andy went to work with them on the Rattler while I had coffee with Garica's mother, who spoke very good English. "You'll be okay when you get to Guerrero," she said. "They have everything there." We sat at a table in her dark kitchen, earth floor. A timid teenage girl poured the coffee and two men stood in the doorway blocking the light. I sat there like a boob for some time smoking and drinking their coffee before it occurred to me to offer the cigarettes. Nobody asked for one, and they had been out of smokes for 10 days, I learned.

Señora Garcia said the market for canned turtle meat was not so good. Did I think the people in the States would like it? It added a nice touch to many different dishes. I said it might go over in Southern California, which came out like—those nuts will buy anything—although I don't think she took it that way. I hope not.

The change of coils was an improvement, temporary at least, and Andy got the voltage regulator perking again. The points in it had been sticking too. We left the Garcias some stuff and struck out once more for Guerrero.

* * *

Almost immediately we got lost trying to thread our way through a maze of ruts down the coast. We kept bearing right, seaward, which was a good plan except that it didn't work. Twice we had to double back; one road led to a deserted beach and stopped, and another took us into some impassably deep sand. The spare tire fell off but we didn't know it for a while, with all the other noise, until the spare carrier started dragging and making a terrific racket. We wired the carrier back up under the bed and backtracked again until, very luckily, we found the tire.

Soon we were traveling inland, southeast, you couldn't fool the compass, but there was no way to get off that road. At Rancho Mezquital a couple of cowboys in leather chaps told us we had left the coastal road far behind but that we could still reach Guerrero by taking a certain right turn down the way. Good. Now we were out on the Vizcaino Desert, driving and driving and not getting anywhere. The road was not so bad here, smooth sand ruts. We rode up high on the sides to keep from dragging center.

This was no open desert but a thickly growing forest of cardon and cirio. The cardon cactus, with its right-angle traffic cop limbs, is like the giant saguaro of Arizona, although there is said to be some small difference. The cirio (candle) looks like a big, gray, bristly carrot growing upside down, with a yellow flower on top. It grows in Baja and in one spot in Sonora and no place else on earth. Naturalist Joseph Wood Krutch calls it the boojum tree.

We came to a village and an old man there said it was El Arco. This could not be because El Arco was way below Guerrero, almost 50 miles, and we got out the map and showed the old timer how he was wrong. He insisted that he knew the name of his home town. Again we had missed the cutoff. It was not in the cards for us to see the fabled Guerrero or Scammon's Lagoon.

The store in El Arco was out of gasoline. This village, too, was once a gold mining center, with more than a thousand workers, but the mines closed after a long strike and perhaps 100 people live there now. All of them were indoors on this day except for two little girls who were wiping the dust off the storekeeper's Chevrolet pickup. He gave us a pan of water to wash up with, and offered $10 for the radio that was slung under the dash in the Rattler. I said okay and he and a pal went to work. Those two should enter a Motorola removal derby. They had it out in about a minute, antenna and all. Parked beside the store was the dustiest 1965 Ford Mustang in the world. The foolhardy owner was taking it to La Paz and got this far before busting up the radiator. He had hitched a ride back to Tijuana to get a new radiator, the store-keeper said, and was now gone two weeks.

We camped that night south of El Arco beside the biggest cactus we had ever seen, a cardon with 12 spires, nine of them 30 to 40 feet high.

* * *

July 20. Mile 792. Up at 5:15, before sunrise, some quick hash and coffee, then onward across the Vizcaino. The road was rocky, something like a dry creek bed, and we soon lost high gear—that is, we couldn't shift into high. We drove in second much of the time anyway but this was a nuisance. At 11:30 a.m. we reached San Ignacio, which is a true, classic oasis. You come over a hill after hours of desert driving and there it is below, two limpid ponds fed by springs, a large grove of date palms and a shady little town square. Some 900 people live there. On the square is a whitewashed stone church that has walls 4-feet thick. It was built by the Dominicans in 1786.

We asked around and located a garage. It was run by one Frank Fischer, an elderly gent who said he had been in Baja since 1910, when, as an engineer on a German freighter, he had jumped ship in Santa Rosalia. "It was the second mate," he said. "I didn't like the S.B."

He called in the house for his son, a man about 40, and set him to work on the Rattler while he, the elder Fischer, told us a few things. He had been to the United States once, in San Diego, in 1917, but had found no reason since to return. American and Mexican beer did not compare with European beer because the water in the Western Hemisphere has saltpeter in it. Mexicans did not know how to fix roads. He looked over our 9mm. pistol. "German?" No, Spanish. He handed it back. "Then it's no good." The United States had been wrong everywhere since 1945 and was decidedly wrong in Vietnam.

"The U.S.A. is no good splitting these countries up," he said. "Germany, Korea, Vietnam. All those boys getting killed are poor boys, they are not rich men's boys."

We agreed that the draft was not fair.

"Look at goddam L.B.J. Johnson," he said. "His sons are not over there."

We said we didn't know the President had any sons.

"He has two sons hidden there on the ranch. He's keeping them out of the war."

* * *

He said he kept abreast of these things from a German newspaper he subscribed to. We argued with him a little about Vietnam, then decided to let it ride, remembering the Mojo proverb—*man with faltering '52 Studebaker not wise to antagonize mecanico in middle of Baja.* (And yet the Mojos—squat, hairless, loyal—were foolish in many ways and the tribe was no more.) The young Fischer said a small flange had fallen off the gearshift column. He fixed it and put a new spring in the voltage regulator. That, he said, would correct our electrical trouble. Could be, but Mexican mechanics seemed to be spring happy. The charge was only $4. Did they want pesos or dollars? "Dollars," said the old man.

At a roadside stop called the Oasis we bought all the gasoline in stock, about 12 gallons, and had a shower and a change of clothes. We were filthy. The owner of the place had magazine pictures of John F. Kennedy and Lopez Mateos [*president of Mexico 1958–64—Ed.*] tacked up all over the walls. As I was shaking the dust out of a shirt he said, "*Mucha tierra,*" then asked what *tierra* was in *Ingles*. He had a tablet in which he entered English words that came in handy with the gringos passing through.

"Tierra es dirt."

"Dort?"

"No, *dirt*."

"Si, dort."

"Dirt!"

"Dort!"

"Okay."

On the road again, high gear working, amp meter showing charge. Below an extinct volcano called Las Tres Virgenes we ran into a roadblock. A 2-ton grocery truck coming north on the one-way shelf road had a flat, right rear, and the driver and his partner were repairing it there with a cold patch. They had no spare. The truck was built for dual wheels but like most big trucks in Baja this one was running with single wheels because of the narrow ruts.

A '58 Ford car going South had tried to drive around the truck but had slipped sideways down the hill and bogged in the sand. So now everything was blocked. Another car, a '58 Mercury and two pickups were also ahead of us. The cars and pickups were all together, a convoy from Tijuana to La Paz. When Mexicans deliver cars down the peninsula they usually travel in a pack, with a truck or two along to carry gasoline and other gear. It would be hard to make it with a loaded car, the clearance would be so low.

The repair took about two hours and a good part of the time was spent pumping up that big 9.00/20 12-ply tire. The driver had the stamina of a horse. He wore an Afrika Korps cap and had a bandanna tied around his forehead. Andy pitched in and helped pump while the convoy drivers and I sat in the skimpy shade of mesquite bush and passed around a water bag and smoked Domino cigarettes. It must have been 120 out in the sun.

Late that afternoon we reached the Sea of Cortes, or, as current maps insist on calling it, the Gulf of California. No cold blue Pacific breakers crashing here. The water was green and very salty and warm, almost 80 degrees, and still as a lake. A slight lapping along the black gravel beach was the only movement. It is not always like that, we were told. Treacherous winds come up often on the Gulf, and from time to time a big blow called a *chubasco*.

* * *

We breezed into Santa Rosalia (pop. 5,361) on a strip of blacktop at 40 and 50 m.p.h., just flying. The shimmy was gone. This is the first real town you hit after leaving Ensenada and we cruised around a while taking in the sights—the new police building, a pastel blue church made of galvanized iron. Santa Rosalia is a copper town; the mines are nearby and the smelting and shipping is done here. A French company used to run it (they brought that odd church over in sections) but it has been a Mexican operation since the early 1950s.

At the Hotel Central we had fried shrimps, caught that afternoon, and a salad, paying no heed to guidebooks warnings against eating fresh vegetables in Baja. A truck driver from Tijuana who was a little tight on beer joined us. He was on his way home from La Paz. We struck him as a couple of good sports, he said, and he believed he would turn his truck around and go to La Paz with us.

"I know many beautiful ladies in La Paz," he said. "Many." He elaborated. Two pals came and dragged him back to the truck. You can take the boy out of Tijuana but can you take the Tijuana out of the boy?

A young married couple from Santa Monica named Bob and Judy (Dick and Jane had just left) were also stopping at the Central. They had sailed down the Gulf in an 18-foot catamaran. Or rather they had sailed as far as the Bay of Luis Gonzaga, about 300 miles up the coast, where the fiber-glass cat had cracked up on some rocks. They hitched a ride in the rest of the way with their cat loaded on top of a truck carrying 1,000 gallons of lard. It took five days; the truck had six flats and broke an axle. But they made it. Things have a way of working out in Baja. Santa Rosalia was the nearest place they could get fiber-glass repairs.

Crime fans will remember Billy Cook, the desperado with the bad eye and the tattoo "Hard Luck" on his knuckles who murdered six people in 1951, including an entire family, and movie fans will remember the Edmund O'Brien film, "The Hitch-hiker," about Billy's auto flight down the desert with two hostages, but who remembers that right here near the Central was where Billy was tracked down and nailed by Tijuana Police Chief Kraus Morales? That evening we sat outside and listened to the local mariachi band. Bob and Judy had been planning to sail around the tip of the peninsula and back up the Pacific coast. They were making a film of the journey. But now maybe they would sell the cat in La Paz if they could get a good price. Bob said I might get as much as $1,000 for the truck there. The band played until well after midnight.

July 21. Mile 919. Up early and down the street to the Tokio Cafe for Spam and eggs. A big gringo in a cowboy hat who looked and sounded like Lee Marvin, the actor, flagged us over to his table. He said his name was Jim Smith and he lived in San Ignacio.

"I saw you guys there yesterday at Fischer's," he said. "I didn't stop because I don't get along with the old man. I guess he told you all that crap about jumping ship."

* * *

We said he had, whereupon Smith gave us his version of the Mexican advent of Frank Fischer. Without prejudice, it was even harder to believe. I won't repeat it, just as Sherlock Holmes would not tell about his case concerning the Giant Rat of Sumatra. (He said the world was not ready for it.)

Smith said he had been in Baja on and off since 1953. He had been a cop in Lubbock, Texas where he missed capturing Billy Cook by minutes, and in Los Angeles, where a motorcycle accident had banged him up and provided him with a pension, which he didn't think was big enough. Now at 35 he was "guide, hunter, pilot, boat skipper, writer and freeloader." He had ridden the length of Baja on muleback, a five-month trip, and it had once taken him six weeks to deliver a truck to La Paz; he had to replace the engine and differential on the way.

He said he was related to President Johnson ("I'm kin to half the folks in Texas") and then went on to attack him with great passion, exceeding even Frank Fischer on this score. But from a different angle.

"That's why I'm down here, to get away from that crap. I'm making my last stand here. You know what they're trying to do now? Boy, the Great Society. They're trying to send some of those Peace Corps punks down to Ignacio for training. Well, you can take the word back, Shriver better not send any of those —————— beatnik —————s around my place or somebody is liable to get his head blown off."

Song: *I Left My Head in San Ignacio*. Smith said his first wife had remarried, a man named John Smith, and that he, Jim Smith, was now engaged to a wealthy, 31-year-old Mexican widow. ("They got this priest checking up on me.") He expressed contempt for most writers about Baja (he likes Antonio de Fierro Blanco's novel, *The Journey of the Flame*) and for all dudes and tourists, but he likes to talk, too, so he has to make do with what comes along.

* * *

We all went down to the waterfront (where there was a rusty, half-sunken ship) and watched Bob work on his catamaran. It was blue and looked sturdy enough. There was no shelter on it except for what shade the sail provided. Judy, a pretty blonde, was a game girl. We got a mechanic there to check out the Rattler. He wore his cap sideways like Cantinflas, not for any antic effect, as he was very gloomy, but for some practical reason of his own. He put on a new voltage regulator. It didn't do much good but, like hypochondriacs, we no longer expected results, we just wanted attention.

Smith said Mexican mechanics were ingenious. He said one down below La Paz had managed to break an anvil. How much did he think the truck would bring? "You might get $500," he said. "Studebaker parts are hard to get. They like Chevys." Smith himself had a Volks camper and renovated weapons carrier with high clearance. "You could sling a cat under that baby," he said.

The guidebooks dismiss Santa Rosalia as a boring mill town but we hated to leave. Down the line we ran into some long stretches of deep sand and drove across them as fast as we could, using some principle of momentum I don't fully understand—as though you could catch the sand napping. We got stuck a couple of times but rocked free without too much trouble. With four-wheel drive these places would be a breeze.

Mulege was the next settlement and it looked like something out of Central America, with its little river, date palms and thatched roofs. There are several expensive resort hotels here to accommodate American fishermen who fly down in their own planes. The place also seemed to mark the end of the hospitality belt. Behind us we had met with nothing but a ready generosity; now when we asked directions we got grudging, mumbled answers. The same with the Yanks, no more wilderness camaraderie. We had supper that night at one of the hotels, *La Serenidad*, and our table was next to one at which two American couples were sitting. An uncomfortable hush prevailed. Nobody spoke to anybody. Maybe we just wanted them to ask about our trip.

* * *

It was the off-season and there were no other guests. The manager said 42 planes had come in on Memorial Day. His big problem, he said, was getting good help and supplies. "For days now I have been out of Cointreau." Roughing it at *La Serenidad*. We left and did some night driving for the first time, and played around with the spotlights. But we couldn't distinguish the little potholes from the big ones, the axle busters, because of headlight shadows, and we gave it up after a while. My air mat had blown away and I folded up the tarp and used it for a pad. We heard a coyote yipping and howling that night but he was not close by.

July 22. Mile 985. Up at 5:30 anticipating the drive on the ledge of terror above the Bay of Conception. An American in Santa Rosalia had described it in fearful terms. "All I can say is, don't look down," he said. This was misleading. It was a one-way shelf road above the water and if we had met another vehicle it would have been inconvenient, but there was plenty of room for anything short of a Greyhound bus. The water in the bay was so clear that we could see big fish lolling around from 200 feet up on the cliff. There were good white beaches along here too, and lots of pelicans.

We stopped for a swim with the mask and snorkel and tried out our Hawaiian sling. This was a fish spear (really a frog gig) with a loop of rubber wired to the end of the handle. When you grasp the handle up near the business end you have a cocked missile. Catamaran Bob told us how to make it. We got two gray fish about as big as your hand and grazed some bigger ones, fat groupers, but before we had mastered the use of the thing we had broken three of the four tines on rocks. The fish were plentiful and multi-colored. It was like swimming in an aquarium. The pelicans had better luck. They dive-bombed all around us with heavy splashes and scored almost every time.

After leaving the bay the road got worse and worse and the terrain took on a sinister aspect. Big volcanic slabs of rusty brown rock we had not seen before. It was the hottest day so far. Andy started belching, more than seemed necessary, and blamed it on the heat. I said that didn't make any sense. He said it made as much sense as my wearing that stupid cowboy hat all the time. Then there was a dispute about who was responsible for the chocolate mess in the glove compartment. Leaving those Hydrox cookies loose in there. Over the door there was a strip of metal that pulled out about four hairs every time you put your head against it. It had been a small joke; now we beat on it with fists and wrenches. We were having trouble again shifting into high gear and we argued about whose was the better shifting action—his double-clutching maneuver with a brief pause in neutral, or my fast jamming move.

He must have been right because I was driving when it went completely out of whack, just limp. It wouldn't shift into anything. We stopped and investigated. There were four empty bolt holes on the shift column. We walked back down the road almost a mile looking for we didn't know what, found nothing and came back.

The silence there—after the hot engine had stopped contracting and popping—was total. No birds, no insect noises, no wind, nothing. All you could hear was the blood humming in your ears. Andy checked the column closer and decided there was no piece missing, only the bolts. He ran wire through the four holes joining whatever parts they were together, then crawled underneath with a 10-inch Crescent wrench and tightened up some boss nut that held the entire truck together. He knew his stuff; we had gears again.

Not far from there in a dry wash we came upon the carcass of a pony, dried, perfectly preserved, as in a museum. It was standing upright, or rather hanging. Someone had taken thick strands of hair from his mane and tail and tied them to the branches of a mesquite tree. Whether before or after death we could not tell.

* * *

Soon we were climbing a range called Sierra de la Giganta. The road goes right over the top and on the steep switchbacks the engine started missing again. At each new level we stopped to regroup and plan the running start for the next stretch. Sometimes there was a choice of roads, a short steep one or a long, not-so-steep one. The way we were gunning the truck in low it's a wonder we didn't throw a rod. On one long grade near the very top going about 3 m.p.h. in low, engine shrieking, the Rattler coughed and misfired completely and we were almost in a dead stall when Andy bailed out and began to push. If he hadn't I believe the truck would still be there. The reduced load and added thrust of one manpower just got us over.

That afternoon we descended into a deep canyon and entered Comondu, a strange place indeed. It is an oasis of springs and date palms on a narrow canyon floor, bounded by towering cliffs. Hidden, isolated, it is the Shangrai-La of Baja. About 700 people live there and they have the power to cloud men's minds. At least I find no entry for the place in our notebook, except for arrival and departure times. Of course we were already loopy from the heat.

Just before sundown we hit gravel. It was a head-rattling washboard road but nonetheless gravel, two lanes wide, the work of some official road gang up from La Paz. Andy scented victory. He took the wheel and drove like a madman, jaw set, eyes hooded. We bounced and skittered all over the road at speeds approaching 35 m.p.h. and such was the racket that we didn't talk again—we couldn't—until 11 p.m. when we reached the pavement and I finally got him to stop. I was glad I didn't have to use the pistol. We flaked out in the ditch, spent.

* * *

July 23. Mile 1,170. A long pull at the water bag, no hash, and off at 7 a.m. The pavement was good and a little after 9:00, at mile 1,268, we rolled into La Paz. We were very proud of the Rattler.

La Paz (Pop. 34,000) is situated on a pale green bay, and oddly, for a Gulf-side town, faces west. For 400 years it was one of the world's great pearl fisheries but there has not been much pearling in recent years. The locals say their Japanese competitors put "something" in their water before World War II and ruined the oyster beds. The town now caters largely to Americans who fly down to catch marlin and sailfish and such.

(The richer anglers go to Punta Palmilla, down on the Cape, where there is an exclusive luxury hotel suitable for high-level, right-wing plotting.) In La Paz there is a pretty drive along the bay called El Malecon. The bay is shallow but there is a channel that permits sizeable ships to come in and tie up at a T-head pier. A big new ferry shuttles back and forth to Mazatlan on the mainland.

We checked in at the Perla Hotel and had breakfast in the outdoor café. Our hands were swollen from gripping the wheel. Fat fingers. Nobody from the local paper came around to interview us, but we were joined for coffee by a thin American lad from San Francisco named Gregory. He wore a Bob Dylan cap and sported a ban-the-bomb button and one with *Huelga!* (Strike!) on it.

He said he had been there two months working at the John F. Kennedy Bi-lingual Library. But the library business was a drag and the fish cannery workers were afraid to organize and he was anxious to go home and get back in the vineyards with the National Farm Workers' Association. He said he didn't know Jim Smith.

"The thing is, nobody reads books here," he said. "You just sit there all day. All they read is schlock stuff like the Police Gazette and Bugs Bunny and those photo-novels."

Andy and I discussed going fishing. Or skin-diving. Or maybe driving down to the Cape, to the very tip of Baja. We still had half a roll of wire left. But a tropical lassitude had set in and we didn't want to do anything.

That night we ate at one of the fancier hotels, Los Cocos, in a grove of coconut palms on the bay. The dining area was outdoors, paper lanterns and all. Aeronaves pilots frolicked in the pool with stewardesses. A good many Americans were there, all of whom seemed to be talking fishing except us and two men in the bar who were still mad about Truman firing MacArthur. One said, "You can have Nimitz. MacArthur won that war. He was the finest soldier that ever put a foot in a boot."

Later we went to a nitery outside town called *Ranchita*, sharing a cab with a talkative sport from Las Vegas and his silent, unhappy girlfriend. They had flown down that afternoon. "I didn't realize it was so *far*," he said. "I thought we'd *never* get here." We let that one slide, with difficulty.

* * *

The *Ranchita* had colored lights and a cornet player with a sharp Latin attack but everybody seemed to be down in the dumps. Surely they weren't all worrying about Mac. Then a tall drunk fell on the dance floor, right on his chin, and this brought what Franklin W. Dixon, author of the Hardy Boys books, would have called whoops of laughter. Jim Smith had told us he once had a difference of opinion in the *Ranchita* with "Duke Morrison." Who? "Duke Morrison. You know him as John Wayne." He said he didn't come off badly either.

July 24. Andy had to get back to Los Angeles and he caught the morning plane. I stuck around to see about the Rattler. A customs agent said yes, he understood I wasn't trying to profiteer, and yes, vehicles were needed there, but the law was the law. It would not be possible to sell the truck. Then I would give it away, perhaps to an orphanage. Was there one in town? Yes, but that too was prohibited, unless the arrangement was handled through customs.

Word got around that the truck was for sale. For the next two days prospective buyers came to my table at the *Perla* where I sat drinking coffee and reading the Warren Report amidst a swarm of small, barefooted Chiclets salesmen. But I couldn't close a deal the way I had worked it out. On the third day a cab driver came over. His card identified him as Abrahan Wong V., Taxi No. 17 (English Spoken). I couldn't figure out the name; was there a country club anywhere in the world that would accept this man? I told him the truck had overdrive and 40 pounds of oil pressure. Both spotlights worked. It had used only one quart of oil on the drive from L.A., which was true.

Yes, yes, he could see, the truck was *bonita*. He had once owned a Studebaker Commander himself. Very good car. He had broken his arm and nose in it. He showed me the place on his nose. How much was I asking?

How much would he give? He thought for a minute and said $300. I said okay. Like a fool, too fast. He smelled a rat and started backing off.

"Have you got tlikslik?"

"What?"

"Tlikslik. Tlikslik." He mimed a piece of paper.

The pink slip, the title. I said "no" because I had only recently bought the truck myself but I had the temporary thing and the bill of sale. It was clear.

"Must have tlikslik," said Abrahan Wong V.

That afternoon I made a deal with the owner of a sport fishing boat. I would sell him everything on the truck—gas cans, water cans, a 3-ton jack, crowder peas, Mazola, two spare tires—the lot—for $200, and give him the truck free, if he could get an okay from customs. Done, he said. Except. Wait a minute. He was a little strapped right now. He would give me $100 now and mail the other $100 later. Oh, but he would send it very soon. All but weeping, I let the Rattler go for five $20 bills.

On the $51.25 flight back to Los Angeles they served a good baked chicken lunch. A man across the aisle asked if I had been down on the Cape and I said no. "You missed the best part," he said. The peninsula looked more barren and forbidding from the air than at truck level, and if I had flown it first I'm not sure I would have gone overland. Jim Smith said a woman in San Francisco once told him she was planning to make the Baja run, and what should she do for preparation? He told her to pack a lunch.

The Forgotten River

This story appeared in the September 1991 issue of the *Arkansas Times*, which was then a monthly magazine and is now a weekly newspaper, based in Little Rock. Dee Brown, the historian and writer (*Bury My Heart at Wounded Knee*) from south Arkansas who inspired this trip, died in 2002 at age 94.

The forest rangers at Mena were all very nice but they could tell me only approximately where the Ouachita River began. It rose somewhere out there in the woods, they said, above the little bridge at Eagleton, where I would find the first Ouachita River road sign. I wanted to see the very origin and so I floundered about between Rich Mountain and Black Fork Mountain with further inquiries.

Through that forested valley runs Highway 270, as well as the Kansas City Southern Railway, and the headwaters of the Ouachita, at an elevation of 1,600 feet above sea level. The two mountains rise another thousand feet or so from the valley floor. A sign warns hikers about the presence of black bears.

Nearby, right on the Oklahoma line, there is a log cabin beer joint, which might have once served the Dalton Brothers; Bill, Grat, Emmett, and Bob. It was dark inside, like a cave, with a very low ceiling. The girl behind the bar knew nothing, which was all right. You don't expect young people to know river lore.

Then a young man sitting far back in the gloom—the only customer—told me just how I should go. I was to enter the woods at the start of the Black Fork Mountain hiking trail. When I reached the river, here a small watercourse—"so narrow you can straddle it"—I was to walk upstream for about a mile, and there I would find

three or four trickling threads of water coming together to form the
Ouachita River.

This would have to do, though I had hoped for a spring, a well-de-
fined source. Probably I didn't walk the full mile. I followed the dimin-
ishing rivulet up to the point where it was no wider than my three fingers,
and declared victory. After all, it was much the same as spring water, cold
and clear. I drank some of it. From here it flows 610 miles, generally
southeast, to Jonesville, La., where it joins other streams to form the
Black River.

I grew up in south Arkansas and thought of the Ouachita only in
local terms, certainly not as an outlet to the sea. It was a place to swim
and fish. I knew you could take a boat down it from the Highway 82
bridge near Crossett to Monroe, La., because I had done it once with a
friend, Johnny Titus. It was shady a good bit of the way and we had the
river pretty much to ourselves. The keeper at the old Felsenthal lock was
annoyed at having to get up from his dinner table to lock through two
boys in a small outboard rig.

But I knew no river lore, less than the Oklahoma barmaid, and it
came as a great surprise to me lately when I learned that there was regular steamboat service on this modest green river, as late as the 1930s, and
as far up as Camden. I am not speaking of modern replicas or party
barges, rented out for brief excursions, but of genuine working steamboats, with big paddle wheels at the rear, carrying bales of cotton down
to New Orleans and bringing bananas and sacks of sugar back upstream,
along with paying passengers.

There were two vessels, the *Ouachita* and the *City of Camden*, and
they ran on about a two-week cycle—New Orleans-Camden-New
Orleans, with stops along the way. The round-trip fare, including a bed
and all meals, was $50. Traditional steamboat decorum was imposed,
with the men required to wear coats in the dining room. At night, after
supper was cleared, the waiters doubled as musicians for a dance.

It was Dee Brown of Little Rock, the author of *Bury My Heart at
Wounded Knee*, who told me about this, and how as a teen-aged boy
in the late 1920s he took the *Ouachita* from New Orleans to Camden.
He had a summer job at a filling station between Stephens and
Camden, and had often watched the steamer tie up and unload. "'I've
got to ride that boat,' I kept telling myself." He saved up a bit more

than $50 for the adventure—"an enormous sum in those days"—but then thought better of this extravagance. He would keep half of it back. "So I made a reservation for the other end and hitch-hiked down to New Orleans. Hitch-hiking was easy and safe then, and faster than the boat."

His timing was good, which kept expenses down. He paid a dollar for a night's lodging at a boarding house near the French Quarter. The trip back was a delight, as Mr. Brown remembers, a leisurely voyage of five or six days. He got full value for his $25. The big splashing wheel pushed the steamer up the Mississippi, the Red, the Black, and at last into the Ouachita at Jonesville, with the two walls of the forest closing in a bit more day by day.

There were fine breakfasts of ham and eggs, when ham was real ham, with grits and hot biscuits. At lunch one day he found a split avocado on his plate, or "alligator pear," as it was called on the menu. "I had never seen one before. I wouldn't eat it." Young Mr. Brown was traveling light and so had to borrow a coat from a waiter at each meal before he could be seated. He had a tiny sleeping cabin to himself with a bunk bed and a single hook on the wall for his wardrobe.

He enjoyed the nightly dances, though he had to sit them out as a wallflower because he didn't know how to dance. Townsfolk along the way came on board just for the dance, and among them were young Delta sports sneaking drinks of corn whiskey and ginger jake. These were Prohibition days. A young girl from New Orleans, traveling with her family, offered to teach Dee Brown how to dance. "I wanted to dance with her, too, sure, but I just couldn't bring myself to do it." This family, he recalls, who had never seen any high ground, marveled over the puny hillocks of the upper river. He remembers an Arkansas woman vowing never again to eat sugar, after seeing the deckhands, dripping with sweat, taking naps on the deck-loaded sacks of sugar.

* * *

Dee Brown, then, got me interested, and so in late May and early June [of 1991—Ed.] I drove down the Ouachita valley to take a look at things.

The Ouachita National Forest, where the river rises, is still a dark green wilderness, if not quite the forest primeval that DeSoto saw when he came crashing through these woods 450 years ago, with some 600 soldiers, 223 horses, a herd of hogs, and a pack of bloodhounds. He was looking for another Peru, out of which he had taken a fortune in gold, more than enough to pay, from his own pocket, for this very costly expedition. As it turned out, there was no gold or silver here in "Florida." What he found was catfish.

"There was a fish which they [the Indians] called Bagres: the third part of it was head, and it had on both sides the gilles, and along the sides great pricks like very sharp aules [awls]; those of this kind that were in lakes were as big as pikes: and in the River, there were some of an hundred, and of an hundred and fiftie pounds weight, and many of them were taken with the hooke…"

This comes from a report written by one of DeSoto's Portuguese officers, who identifies himself only as "A Gentleman of Elvas" (the town of Elvas, in Portugal). The Portuguese version was published in 1557, and was rendered into this King James English by Richard Hakluyt, and published in London in 1609, under the misleading title of "Virginia Richly Valued." Hakluyt was promoting English exploration and settlement in the New World, and any news at all from that quarter was grist for his mill. There is not one word about Virginia in the text, and a more accurate title would be "Florida Poorly Valued." By Spanish reckoning, the continent belonged to Spain, being a gift from Pope Alexander VI, himself a Spaniard, and all that country lying east and north of New Spain (Mexico) was regarded more or less as Florida.

Elvas tells of seeing "…many Beares, and Lyons, Wolves, Deere, Dogges, Cattes, Martens [minks] and Conies [rabbits]. There be many wild Hennes as big as Turkies, Partridges small like those of Africa, Cranee, Duckes, Pigeons, Thrushes and Sparrows…There are Gosse Hawks, Falcons…and all Fowles of prey that are in Spaine…"

He spoke too of "small chestnuts" [chinquapins] and of "many Walnut trees bearing soft shelled Walnuts in fashion like bullets," which could only have been pecans. Some of his "Plummes and Prunes" were very likely muscadines and persimmons. There is no mention in his bestiary of buffalo, or bison, then roaming the country from coast to coast. DeSoto's men knew about these "hunch-backed cattle," as they had traded with the Indians for their hides, which made good bedding, but they had no luck in hunting them and there is some question whether they ever saw one on the hoof. There is only one passing, inconclusive mention of a hunt. It is a wonder, perhaps, that they saw any wild creatures, who must have heard this band approaching from some distance away, clanking, snorting, grunting, barking.

The forest has changed; it is no longer a virgin stand of timber with a high canopy and an uncluttered, parklike floor, on which horses could move about. The Beares and Deere still thrive, but the Lyons are gone, or so believes Larry Hedrick, of the National Forest's Game and Wildlife Division. "We do get occasional 'sightings,' but there is just no good evidence of free-living, free-ranging cougars out there. Of course, they are reclusive, like bobcats. We're overrun with bobcats, but you don't see them." As for the native red wolves, they have mated with intruding, wily, trickster coyotes to form a curious hybrid pack. The chinquapin, sweetest of nuts, has disappeared too, in my lifetime, or it is almost gone, a victim of the chestnut blight.

Yet even with change the forest remains an impressive tract of mountain greenery, bigger, at 2,500 square miles, than the state of Delaware, and the river that flows out of it is one of the prettiest in the country.

Early trappers and market hunters paddled their canoes up it, far past Camden, the present head of navigation, past the bluff where the Caddo enters at Arkadelphia, past "the hot springs," and on to the hills not far from the present town of Mena. This upper stretch is still navigable by canoe, in season, in the familiar pattern of a fast-flowing stream: shoal water followed by a pool followed by a shoal. For some reason, however, it has not caught on well with recreational floaters, slaves of fashion that they are. On a warm day in late spring, with plenty of water running, when there must have been war parties of canoes colliding at every bend of the Buffalo River, I saw not a single floater on the Ouachita between Ink and Oden, nor a bank fisherman nor a swimmer.

The parks and campgrounds were spruced up for the summer season. The state roadways were clean, too. Where was all the litter that people complain about in letters to newspapers? Also, where was the old rural shabbiness?

The farmhouses on Highways 270 and 88 were well-kept, in fine trim, the mobile homes neatly skirted. Around them were shade trees, ornamental shrubs, flower beds and well-tended lawns. Not what we used to call landscaping in the Arkansas countryside, when the custom was to level every living thing around your house for about a 50-yard radius. We were the original clear-cutters, and this dead-zone tradition lives on in east Arkansas, where you can see a new brick house plopped down in the middle of a muddy soybean field, without so much as a crabapple tree or a petunia out front—as though people who farm in a big way couldn't be bothered with mere horticulture.

The new attention to lawn care can be attributed, I think, to the invention and spread of the riding mower. Cutting the grass is no longer seen as a chore, as men don't outgrow their boyhood love for dodging about in midget cars with tiny steering wheels. I believe this also accounts for the popularity of golf. Take away the little motorized carts and the links would be largely deserted.

It may be that outlanders have brought in new ideas about some of these things, along with their comfortable retirement incomes. You hear a lot of non-Arkansas voices these days in the Ouachitas. At Lum and Abner's Jot-em-Down Store in Pine Ridge, I was greeted by a nice lady from some northern clime who never in her life said, "Well, I swan!" much less, "Ay grannies!" At another store, in neighboring Polk County, there were flat white wicks for sale, for kerosene lamps, but I found no country store so humble or remote that it didn't offer a selection of video cassettes. In the towns there are signs of a modest prosperity, such as new police cars (big Chevrolet Caprices, mostly) and new Masonic halls, Moose lodges, and American Legion huts. All these brotherhoods seem to have hired the same architect, a grim man, who likes to build on defensive, bunker principles. His signature is the blank wall. The new clubhouses, with few exceptions, are long, low buff-brick structures with no windows.

There is no longer much agriculture in this country, in the strict sense of field crops. The old straggling hillside corn patches are now pastures where polled Hereford and Angus cattle graze. A lot of fat healthy saddle horses are running about too. The long metal chicken sheds appear to be mostly abandoned, or in use for storage of those big cylindrical rolls of hay. The vegetable gardens are still deadly serious, with rows of pole beans and squash 90 feet long.

Mount Ida is where the hexagonal quartz crystals are found, with their radiant powers. Just north of town the mountain stream loses its "rolling impetuosity" as Dunbar would put it, and begins to spread and go still and blue as it is penned up by the hand of man. Here, for some 50 miles, the river loses its identity in a chain of dams and lakes—

Ouachita, with a shoreline of almost a thousand miles, and the older and smaller Hamilton and Catherine. All are associated with Hot Springs, though the city itself is not on the river.

For William Dunbar and his expedition up the Ouachita, from October, 1804, to January, 1805, it was a nine-mile hike from the river bank to the valley of "the boiling springs," which is now Central Avenue downtown. Dunbar was an immigrant from Scotland who had done well in America. He owned a plantation near Natchez and had a good education. He knew how to do things, which made him a man after President Thomas Jefferson's heart. Jefferson and the U.S. Congress had just paid Napoleon $15 million for the entire western drainage of the Mississippi River—the Louisiana Purchase—and exploring parties were being organized to look over the new territory. Dunbar was sent up the Ouachita. He went in an unwieldy barge 50 feet long, with a Dr. George Hunter of Philadelphia, a guide, three of Dunbar's slaves, and a rowing

party of 14 soldiers from the New Orleans garrison. It was a small, regional version of the Lewis and Clark expedition up the Missouri, and
on to the Pacific.

Surprisingly little was known at that late date of the country between
the Mississippi and the Shining Mountains, or the Stony Mountains, as
the Rockies were then called. Jefferson, perhaps the best-informed man
of the country, thought there still might be mastodons or mammoths
grazing to the west. They would be much bigger than the tropical ele-
phants. Jefferson wanted our New World animals to be the biggest. In
the same spirit, Robert Livingston, negotiating in Paris for the purchase
of La Louisiane, told the treasury minister that, anyway, the French would
never be able to sell their goods here, such as Cognac, because
Americans preferred Kentucky peach brandy, "which, with age, is superior to the best brandy of France." It was truly morning in America.

The cynical Napoleon, 33-year-old First Consul, may or may not
have believed it. On first meeting Livingston, at a reception, he took a
playful line with the presumptions of the new nation.

"You have been in Europe before, Monsieur Livingston?"

"No, my General."

"You have come to a very corrupt world." Then, to Talleyrand,
"Explain to Monsieur Livingston that the old world is very corrupt. You
know something about that, don't you, Monsieur Talleyrand?"

The Anglo-Americans were slow to learn from the Indians and the
French that canoes were the thing. Dunbar's monster barge, designed by
Dr. Hunter, drew two feet of water and had an external keel. Over and
over again the soldiers had to jump into the cold water with a rope and
drag the thing off snags and over sandbars and shoals. At Fort Miro, or the
Washita Post (Monroe, La.), they changed to a lighter boat and the going
was faster, but they still had to manhandle it over the rougher shoals. One,
north of the Caddo, had a straight vertical drop of four-and-a-half feet.

Dunbar remarks on the beauty of the river and how it was clear and
drinkable along the entire course, unlike the Red and the "Arcansa,"
which were always muddy, "being charged with red terrene matter." The
trees on the banks—willow, black oak, packawn [pecan], hickory, and
elm—were not so grand or lofty as those along the Mississippi, but had
their own charm and "appear to bear a kind of proportion to the magnitude of their own river."

The Ouachita wasn't completely unknown. It was late fall and the bears were fat with oil and their furs were prime. Dunbar met hunters along the way "who count much of their profits from the oil drawn from the Bear's fat, which at New Orleans is always of ready sale, and is much esteemed for its wholesomeness in cooking, being preferred to butter or hog's lard; it is found to keep longer than any other oil of the same nature, without turning rancid…"

He comments on the indolence of the white settlers—"always a consequence of the Indian mode of life"—and tells us that the young army officer in command at Fort Miro, a Lieutenant Bowmar, while capable enough, lacked "the polite manners of a gentleman." At another point he suddenly seems to remember that he is writing this report for Jefferson, the great democrat, and he praises the industry and sturdy independence of a man and his wife who had cleared a little two-acre farmstead in the woods. They had corn for bread, plenty of venison, bear oil, fish and fowl for the taking, and there were hides and wild honey to sell for cash. Their prospects were indeed bright, and he stops just short of having them reading a bit of John Locke or Rousseau by firelight, before turning in.

"How happy the contrast, when we compare the fortune of the new settler in the U.S. with the misery of the half-starving, oppressed, and degraded Peasant of Europe!!" Dunbar is not a man for exclamation marks, and when he gives us two of them here, we feel his discomfort with this kind of talk—however genuine the sentiment.

They found two abandoned log huts at the base of Hot Springs Mountain, where the smoking waters poured forth to form a creek. The sick from Natchez were already coming here to soak their bones. Dunbar examined the rocks and vegetation. Dr. Hunter, of whom Dunbar speaks in a guarded way as "a professed chemist," conducted experiments with his pans and beakers. Dunbar determined the latitude with his sextant. (Is there anyone today living between Natchez and Hot Springs who could do that—go off into the forest and calculate the angular distance of his position in degrees and minutes from the equator?) He measured the temperature of the springs and pools, and his readings of 132 to 150 degrees F. tally pretty well with the current reading at the source of 145.8 degrees. So we can't blame a badly defective thermometer when he tells us that the air temperature fell to 6 degrees on January 2, 1805, as they were camped on the river bank in 13 inches of snow. They ate well, bagging turkeys and deer at will. They shot one young bear. But, as with DeSoto's men, they had no luck with the buffalo. On two occasions in south Arkansas these beasts were "shot at and grievously wounded, with blood streaming from their sides." The soldiers couldn't bring them down, however, and couldn't or wouldn't track them down. Soldiers perhaps lack the patience to be good hunters.

Elvas puts it this way: "The Indians want no fleshmeat; for they kill with their arrowes many deere, hennes, conies and other wild fowle: for they are very cunning at it: which skills the Christians [Spaniards] had not: and though they had it, they had no leasure to use it: for most of the time they spent in travel, and durst not presume to straggle aside…"

Dunbar doesn't identify his weapons, other than to call them "rifles," which suggests they weren't smoothbore muskets. It is possible his party was fitted out, as were Lewis and Clark, with the army's new 1803 model rifle, a flintlock of .54 caliber. DeSoto's troops had a few firearms, of a kind known as the arquebus, a primitive matchlock shoulder weapon firing a .65 to .75 caliber ball, and using a smoldering wick called a match or matchcord to ignite the powder charge. These pieces were cumbersome, inaccurate, with a much shorter range than the crossbow, which was DeSoto's primary weapon, together with swords and lances. The thundersticks weren't even of much help in terrifying the natives, who, as one account has it, "not only had held no fear of the arquebuses but had scorned and ridiculed them…" In the end the survivors of the expedition melted down the useless guns to make nails for their escape boats.

Was DeSoto at Hot Springs? Here is the brief passage, again from Elvas, that is the basis of this belief: "The Governor [DeSoto] rested a moneth more in the Province of Cayas. In which time the horses fattened more than in other places in a longer time, with the great plentie of Maiz [corn, planted by the Indians] and the leaves thereof, which I think the best that hath been seene, and they drank of a lake of very hot water, and somewhat brackish, and they drank so much, that it swelled in their bellies when they brought them from the watering."

There are three accounts of the expedition written by participants. The one from Elvas is the longest, at 179 pages, and there are short, brisk, official reports from Hernandez de Biedma, the king's factor, and Rodrigo Ranjel, DeSoto's private secretary. Some 50 years after the event, one Garcilaso de la Vega completed a fourth account, a long, literary book, which he claimed was based on interviews with a knight and two soldiers who accompanied DeSoto. This work is held to be the least reliable.

In only one of the four—Elvas—can I find mention of geothermal water, warm or hot, and his water is somewhat brackish. The Hot Springs water is not at all brackish, and contains no particular belly-swelling agents. The "lake" comes from the Portuguese word "lagoa," which can mean anything from a small lake to a puddle.

The U.S. DeSoto Expedition Commission cites a mention of "hot streams" from Ranjel—"from the missing parts of his diary." It is still missing from the only published Ranjel account I could find. This commission, a blue ribbon government panel, of which Col. John R. Fordyce of Arkansas was vice chairman, delivered its report in 1939, on the 400th anniversary of DeSoto's landing at Tampa Bay. Colonel Fordyce and his colleagues made an exhaustive effort to map out DeSoto's wanderings, from vague topographical clues and the rough estimates of distances and directions given by Elvas and the others. (Coronado, then exploring to the west, was better organized; he had a man designated to count off the paces of each day's march.)

The DeSoto distances are given as so many days' journey, or so many leagues, when given at all. But what was a day's march? What league were they using? With eight to choose from, the commission members finally settled on the Spanish judicial league of 2.634 miles, not to be confused with the ordinary Spanish league of 4.214 miles or the Portuguese league of 3.84 miles. The report is an impressive work of scholarship, conjecture, and divination.

But if not Hot Springs, where was this Province of Cayas? It is pretty well established that the Spaniards were in the central part of the country at that time, and nowhere else in the region (except at nearby Caddo Gap) are there springs of warm water coming from the earth, fresh or brackish. Anyhow, I like to think that DeSoto was here in 1541, and I like to think that Shakespeare, still working in London in 1609, picked up the little Elvas-Hakluyt book and read about the hot lake, and about Camden and Calion, and the earlier crossing of the Great River near Helena. It is just the kind of chronicle he quarried for his plots and characters, and DeSoto, a brutal, devout, heroic man brought low, is certainly of Shakespearean stature. But, bad luck, there is no play, with a scene at the Camden winter quarters, and, in another part of the forest, at Smackover Creek, where willows still grow aslant the brook.

(A note here on Hakluyt's English: Those earnest enunciators who say "bean" for "been" should know that Hakluyt, the Oxford scholar, spelled it "bin," as did, off and on, the poet John Donne.)

Below Lake Catherine the Ouachita runs free again, for a while. The momentum is less, the river having already dropped from 1,600 feet to 315 feet at Malvern, and the rate of fall is leveling off fast. But there is still shoaling, as you can see from the Interstate 30 bridge near the Malvern exit. Above and below the bridge the water breaks on shelving rock, and we can imagine the trouble Dunbar had in dragging a heavy boat over it.

Sturdy bricks are made at Malvern, 200 million of them each year, and in the adjoining and older community of Rockport, there is a white frame church, the Rockport United Methodist Church, with a sign proclaiming it to be the "Oldest Church West of the Mississippi/ Est. 1809/ Elmo A. Thomason, Pastor." Oldest Protestant church, I gather, is the meaning, but on the day I stopped, the Rev. Mr. Thomason was not around to clarify the point. Yellow ribbons girdled the shade trees around the church—none of your latter-day Wesleyan revisionists at Rockport. Little Rock did well enough in welcoming home the troops from Desert Storm, but I noticed that the small towns in Arkansas and Louisiana, more directly affected by the call-up of Reserve and National Guard units, did much better. They were more exuberant, more lavish with their ribbons and banners.

At Arkadelphia (Blakleytown, until 1838) we know we are out of the hills when we see the statue of a Confederate soldier on the courthouse lawn, and an African Methodist Episcopal Church, and a snarling yellow Ag-Cat cropduster dipping low over a rice field—irrigated from the Ouachita. The Ag-Cat is an excellent workhorse, but the bulging cockpit canopy is ugly and the plane just doesn't have the pleasing lines of the old Stearman.

The Caddo enters the Ouachita here, and at one time you could freely drive to a bluff overlooking the confluence. No more; you are now confronted by a locked gate. Arkadelphia had irregular steamboat service from 1825 until the 1870s, when the Iron Mountain Railroad came through, and even after that a few boats came up from time to time. One, in 1912, reportedly took on a load of 2,000 bales of cotton. But commercial navigation this high on the river was always seasonal and chancy.

Highway 7 south of town becomes a shady corridor of tall, skinny pines. Below Sparkman ("Welcome to Sparkman/ A Good Town/ Raiders are Winners") there is a turn-off to Tate's Bluff, where the Little Missouri joins the Ouachita. A low concrete bridge, which washes out now and then, spans the river. I ran into my first floaters here, two young men in a canoe, who had made their way some 30 miles down the Little Missouri. "We only had to drag once." Did they ever float the Ouachita? "Not this far down. There's just not enough current. Too much paddling." Did they know of any songs about the Ouachita? Well, no. They tried hard, too, to think of a song. Everybody was very obliging.

Camden, head of navigation, has the feel of a river town, though you can no longer get a catfish lunch downtown, or any kind of plate lunch. Along the bar pits middle-aged black women are fishing with cane poles. They stand very still watching their corks. They are all bundled up against the heat and the mosquitoes, and their broad-brimmed straw hats are well cinched down with colorful sashes.

Between the railroad track and the river there is a big metal building with the hopeful words, "Port of Camden," painted on it. But where are the tugs and barges? It seems there are none. According to Mrs. Eunice Platt, there hasn't been a commercial run up this far since December 1989, when four barges, pushed two at a time, came from Monroe to get a load of gravel for rockless Louisiana. Mrs. Platt, of Camden, is the executive director of the Ouachita River Valley Association, and a tireless worker in promoting navigation improvements on the upper Ouachita.

The situation, as I understand it, is this: The old dams and locks, completed in 1926, provided a six-and-a-half-foot channel from the Black River to Camden. The new system was finished in 1985 and provides a nine-foot channel with new dams and locks at Calion and Felsenthal in Arkansas, and Columbia and Jonesville in Louisiana. The locks will accommodate four standard barges tied two abreast ahead of a tugboat. Some of the bends in the river, however, are so tight that these four-barge units can't negotiate them. The shorter, two-barge units, are said not to be commercially feasible. To remedy this, Mrs. Platt and the Corps of Engineers want to lop off some of the meanders, most of them in Arkansas.

"They say we're trying to make a muddy ditch out of the river," she said. "Well, that's just not true. We're talking about a total of 14 bend widenings and eight cutoffs, out of what, more than 300 bends in the river? We're talking about a total of 341 acres of land. That's all that will be used. I'm trying to help the river, not hurt it. I'm an environmentalist too. I'm just as much an environmentalist as Richard Mason is."

Mr. Mason, of El Dorado, co-chairman of the Businessmen's Coalition to Save the Ouachita, agrees with the numbers but thinks they are misleading. He said, "Some of those cutoffs are huge and will really take in as many as seven smaller bends. Look, every conservation and wildlife group in the state is against this thing—every single one." He also thinks it's a waste of money. "An obvious pork barrel proposition, nothing else. You could make that river as straight as an arrow and no-body would use it." It is much cheaper, he claims, to haul goods by truck from Crossett to Greenville, Miss., or from Camden to Pine Bluff, on the Arkansas, and offload on barges there, than to ship down the Ouachita. As for the El Dorado petroleum products, there are existing pipelines. "You can't ship cheaper than a pipeline."

The cutoff project is now hanging fire, pending acquisition of the 341 acres, which the five affected counties in Arkansas must pay for. In Louisiana, the state government must pay. I came away with the impression that Mrs. Platt is right about the predicted damage to the river being exaggerated, and that Mr. Mason is right when he says that the prospects for high-volume barge traffic are not very good. *[The project was not completed.—Ed.]*

* * *

When Dunbar came through here in 1804 he noted the presence of a trail through the woods: "…the road of the Cadadoquis Indian Nation [Caddo] leading to the Arcansa Nation; a little beyond this is the Ecor a Fabri [Fabri's Cliffs] 80 to 100 feet high: it is reported that a line of de-markation run between the french and spanish provinces, when the for-mer possessed Louisiana, crossed the river at this place; and it is said that Fabri, a french-man and perhaps the supposed Engineer deposited lead near the cliff in the direction of the line…The additional rapidity of the current indicates that we are ascending into a higher country. The water of the river now becomes extremely clear and is equal to any in its very agreeable taste as to drinking water…The general breadth of the river today has been about 80 yards."

The Ouachita remains about the same width but the bluff is not half that high today, having been trimmed down over the years by railroads and other developers.

Again, the question arises: Was DeSoto here? The DeSoto Commission thought so, tracking the expedition south along the Little Missouri and the Ouachita, as the Spaniards made their way back toward the Great River in late 1541. Camden, or perhaps Calion, says the report, was very probably the Autiamque of Elvas, or Utiangue, as Garcilaso has it. Here is Elvas:

"The next day they came to Autiamque. They found much Maiz laid up in store, and French beanes [?] and walnuts, and prunes, great store of all sorts. They took some Indians which were gathering together the stuffe which their wives had hidden. This was a Champion countrie, and well inhabited. The Governor [DeSoto] lodged in the best part of the towne, and commanded presently to make a fense of timber round about the Campe distant from the houses, that the Indians might not hurt them without by fire...hard by this town passed a River, that came out of the Province of Cayas..."

So far, so good. The puzzling part comes next. Elvas tells us that they spent the winter at Autiamque, three months in all, with plenty of food. The Indians showed them how to snare rabbits, both cottontails and another breed which were "as big as great Hares, longer, and having greater loines." These may have been swamp rabbits, whose loines are great indeed.

They passed the winter there resting and trapping rabbits "which until that time they knew not how to catch...The Indians taught them how to take them: which was, with great springes, which lifted their feete from the ground: and the snare was made with a strong string, whereunto was fastened a knot of cane, which ran close about the neck of the conie, because they should not gnaw the string. They took many in the fields of Maiz, especiallie when it freezed or snowed. The Christians staied there one whole moneth so inclosed with snow, that they went not out of towne..."

Snowbound in Camden for a month? Or Calion? Garcilaso puts it at six months:

"There was much snow that year in this province, and for a month and a half they were unable to venture into the countryside because of the extensive amount that had fallen. Nevertheless, with the great luxury of firewood and provisions, they passed the best of all winters they experienced in Florida, and they themselves confessed that they could not have been more comfortable in the dwellings of their families in Spain…"

DeSoto left Autiamque-Camden in March of 1542, moving down the Ouachita, and after 10 days' journey, which would put him somewhere in Louisiana, "there fell out such weather, that foure daies he could not travell for snow…" Snowbound in Louisiana in March?

An exceptionally severe winter. Either the geography is all wrong or the weather, over 450 years, has changed. Knowing nothing about changing weather patterns, but, being a journalist and thus having no scruples about commenting on the matter, I think they may well have changed. It was, after all, not quite 200 years ago when Dunbar and his men were besieged with snow and ice near Hot Springs, with temperatures in the single digits.

Two months after leaving Camden, somewhere on the Great River in the Ferriday-Natchez area, Hernando DeSoto died on May 21, 1542, of malaria or fatigue or despair. The soldiers hid the body so the Indians couldn't see that this Childe of the Sunne (as he had introduced himself) was mortal, and then they placed it in a hollow live-oak log, or in a shroud weighted with sand (the accounts differ), and by night rowed it out into the Mississippi, at a place where it was 19 fathoms or 114 feet deep. "…They lowered him in the center of the river, and commending his soul to God, watched him sink at once to its depths."

I asked about local historians and was directed to a lawyer, Col. John Norman Warnock, U.S. Army, Retired, who is almost 80 years old. He lives south of Camden in the community of Elliott and kindly agreed to see me. His house had recently burned, he told me over the telephone, and he was now living and working in a trailer.

I took this to mean a mobile home, but it was in fact a trailer, a blue and white 28-footer that you could hook up to your stretched black Cadillac limousine, if you had one, and be off with in short order, with a good laugh for everybody left behind. The Colonel has two of these extra long Cadillacs, a 1974 and a 1979 model. The battery and the alternator—"that big, $180 alternator"—had been stolen from the '74, and one tire was flat, but the '79 was running fine.

"I buy them from a man in Dallas," he said. "I like the protection and comfort of a big car."

The trailer was parked in the shade of big pinoak trees. Two shaggy little Pomeranian dogs yapped at me. There were eight Rhode Island Red hens in the yard. They were older chickens, laying hens who no longer laid eggs, but who were still proving useful in their retirement years. "Look. See how they peck at everything that moves? They keep this yard completely free of ticks."

The Colonel, who retired from the army in 1965, is a small, dapper man with soft white hair. He reminded me of Lew Ayres, the actor. He wore a tan cord suit, tan shirt, and tan bow tie. His manner was quiet, polite, very Southern. The trailer was packed to the roof with boxes, files, books, clothes, leaving only a tiny space at one end for his office. His secretary, a young lady, was typing away at something. She sat at a little shelf-like table similar to the ones used by flight engineers on the smaller Boeings. The Colonel graciously gave me the only other seat, a stool, and he stood as we talked about the Ouachita. I believe there would have been more room in one of the Cadillacs, as there was no more than 18 inches of space between us.

His family, he said, both the Warnocks and the Moons, had been in Ouachita County since the 1830s, and an enormous amount of valuable documents and memorabilia had been lost in the house fire. Did he plan to rebuild? He said he didn't know, hinting at certain dark obstacles, "You lend people money, and they won't pay you back."

He, too, like Dee Brown, rode the steamboat *Ouachita* in the 1920s, and he remembers how it would stop to pick up driftwood for the boiler furnace. It got stuck on a sandbar once, and by the time it reached Camden all the bananas had turned brown. "They sold them for 25 cents—a stalk! The boys around here got sick stuffing themselves with soft bananas."

As he recalls, this last gasp of steamboat service came in right after the locks and dams were built in 1926. "That was old Captain Cooley [L.V. Cooley] who started it, and I believe it all died with him too, around 1934 or '35. It was quite a thing, the band playing, the dancing at night on the river. All this was cotton country then. Gins everywhere. A lot of cotton was shipped out of here. Now it's all in pine trees."

Colonel Warnock himself brought a boat up to Camden from New Orleans at the end of World War II. He bought it in Germany, a 40-foot cruiser with a steel hull, and had it shipped to New Orleans on the deck of a merchant vessel. "It drew three feet of water, about the same as the steamboats. I came up in June and had no trouble at all." The "liquor" discharge from the local paper mill damaged the hull, he claims, and some years back he sent it to Louisiana for repairs. It remains there, beached, in some sort of legal limbo "at a Lebanese-Italian boat-yard in Morgan City."

I asked him why Camden did not make more of its history. There is, for example, no DeSoto Street.

"No, they don't make much of anything around here. You try to put on some Civil War thing and nobody's interested. Why, there were more Civil War battles fought around here than around Natchez. Small ones, yes, but still."

The oil country begins a few miles south at Louann. There are strip-per wells along the highway. The horsehead pumping units bow and rise ever so slowly as they pull up four or five barrels of crude a day. "The strippers have become drippers," I was told in Smackover. Here in a downtown park, a metal plaque states that "...the French settlers called this area 'Sumac Couvert.' This was anglicized to 'Smackover' by later English settlers..." Covered with sumac? Sumac bower? Sumac shelter?

Perhaps, but I suspect Dunbar is more likely correct. He made this entry for November 20, 1804: "At 7 1/2 a.m. passed a creek which forms a deep ravine in the high lands and has been called 'Chemin Couvert.'" This was Smackover Creek, where it enters the Ouachita from a deep cut. Dunbar was dealing with hunters, guides, settlers, soldiers, and such maps as there were, and he very probably got the name right, "Chemin Couvert," covered way, which was soon corrupted into Smackover. Upstream from the creek he tells of seeing an alligator "which surprised us much at this late season and so far north."

* * *

I paid $1.23 a gallon for regular gasoline at El Dorado, the oil city, more than at any other place along the way. On the other hand, my motel room cost only $21, and, a bonus, a man was practicing law in the next room. Two strange law offices in one day. This one, an ordinary motel room, had the lawyer's shingle fastened to the door, just above the number, with a single screw in the middle. There were bits of Scotch tape on the ends to keep it from tilting, perhaps demoralizing his customers. I was all set if I woke up in the night with a start and the urgent feeling that I should dictate a codicil to my will. Against that piece of luck, however, I had to weigh this: The cafe I like in El Dorado was no longer serving an evening meal. The new, shorter serving hours were explained to me this way: "That woman that runs it, that was her sister that run it at night, and she got married and moved to Shreesport."

El Dorado, of course, is not on the river, but is close enough, and the town had steamboat service in the 19th century by way of the Champagnolle Landing. At Calion I looked over the first of the four new dams on the river, this one named for the late H. K. Thatcher, who worked for many years as a lobbyist and gadfly for the project. It is a mighty work of concrete and steel. On the far side, the Calhoun County side, high water was streaming unchecked over the low part of the dam. No one was about. No boats were in view. The lock water appeared stagnant, as though it had been standing undisturbed for some time. A dead

and bloated buffalo fish with a cloudy eye lay washing about in the debris.
The river looked almost as wide as the Arkansas at Little Rock.

Because of the high water, the ferry at Moro Bay wasn't running. I
was to be denied another ferry ride south of Columbia, La., for the same
reason. The Arkansas Highway Department has only two other ferries
left in operation, at Spring Bank on the Red, and at Bull Shoals Lake.
Here in the backwater at Moro Bay, I saw a moccasin about two feet
long. He was swimming toward me and then stopped when he saw me,
undulating in place, but not showing much fear.

The Saline River now comes in from the east to meet the
Ouachita and form a kind of overflow swamp known locally as the
Marie Saline. It is not named for a lady, as we used to think. Dunbar
explains: "Between 11 and 12 o'clock passed on the right the 'marais
de la Saline' (Salt-lick marsh). There is here a small marshy lake, but
it is not intended by its name to convey any idea of a property of brack-
ishness in the lake or marsh, but merely that it is contiguous to some
of the licks." It was the same for the Saline River, then going by the
name of "the grand bayou de la Saline (Salt-lick Creek)…" Hunters,
Dunbar says, took their boats some 300 river miles up the Saline, and
"all agree that none of the springs which feed this Creek are salt; it
has obtained its name from many buffalo salt licks which have been
discovered near to the Creek."

Here, where the river crosses into Louisiana, is the lowest point in
Arkansas, with the state Geology Commission giving it as 55 feet above
sea level and the Corps of Engineers at 43.8 feet. This water has fallen
1,550 feet since it left Polk County, and it still has a long way to go before
reaching the Gulf of Mexico, and only another 50 feet to fall. All this
low country is now the Felsenthal National Wildlife Refuge, a swampy
wilderness much like that of the White River Refuge, but with not quite
so much hardwood timber.

West of Crossett near the Highway 82 bridge there is a new slack-
water harbor, ready for business, with a wharf on concrete pilings and
a new and empty warehouse. Again, no one was about. There were
no boats. I drove the back roads above the Felsenthal Dam. Always
at some point I would run into a body of water and have to turn
around. These are deep woods. I saw a house on stilts near the river,
not a hunting lodge but a home, with clothes on a line and broken

toys in the yard. There was no power line, and no telephone line, television antenna, satellite dish, or mail box. Getting your news by barge might not be so bad.

I detected no immediate cultural change as I entered Louisiana, perhaps a bit more clear-cutting of timber, but not much more than I saw in the Huttig area. At Sterlington I did find an industry that uses the river for shipping, the Angus Chemical Co., which has little docks and terminal pipes projecting out from the river bank. But much of this plant was destroyed by an explosion and fire in May, in which nine workers were killed and more than a hundred injured.

All along the lower river I stopped in towns and asked about the tonnage shipped on the river. The current tonnage, I thought, when compared to the tonnage of bygone years and the projected tonnage of the future, would give us all something to mull over. At city halls and chambers of commerce I would be shown into the office of a very courteous if puzzled man. He would tap a pencil on the desk. "Yes. Let's see now. The tonnage. Brenda, why don't you get Charles some coffee." Brenda would later be sent here and there in search of an elusive folder that just might contain some river matter. Long after it became clear that no one knew or cared about the tonnage, I asked about the tonnage. I didn't care either, but I felt a nagging dreary duty to come up with some figures.

Monroe is the biggest city on the Ouachita, with a population, including West Monroe, of 65,000. The river splits the two towns. There is a high bridge on Interstate 20, and three older bridges that can be raised or pivoted on turntables to allow river traffic to pass. But days go by at a time with no call to raise or swing the bridges, I was told by Bruce Fleming, planning director for Monroe, and there is no "Port of Monroe," as such, though the city does own an excursion boat, the *Twin City Queen*, which it rents out to clubs.

It was getting through to me that people living on the Ouachita no longer see their river as a highway, in any important commercial sense. It is just there, every day, a pretty stream of water, handy for recreation, useful in dry years for irrigation, inconveniently overflowing every spring.

Somewhere along here in the pecan groves on Bayou DeSiard I stopped talking about tonnage and started asking people how they pronounced "bayou." It came out "by-yoo" and "by-oo," about half and half, with an occasional "bya." We said "byo" in southeast Arkansas, or "bya."

In defending this usage, I pointed out to a woman in Monroe that Hank Williams says "byo" in his song "Jambalaya." Yes, she said, but Hank was forcing a cheap rhyme with "me-o-my-o." I countered by informing her that Arkansas Post (1686, Tonti) is older than New Orleans (1718, Bienville). She didn't believe me. Nor did she believe me when I informed her that "bayou" is not a French word.

It is a Choctaw word, "bayuk," which the French explorers adopted for use in the Mississippi valley, calling any sizeable stream entering one of the bigger rivers a "bayou." But then it seems they left it behind when they returned home. The word is not listed in Cassell's or Heath's French dictionaries, so I suppose it is actually Choctaw-French-American. The Corps of Engineers could not give me an official definition of a bayou, or of a creek or a river. I would have expected these officers—soldiers, engineers, bureaucrats, all tidy men—to have had some strict system of classification and nomenclature, but not so. In this matter they defer to local tradition. If the people of north Arkansas want to call their fast-flowing, whitewater, mountain stream a bayou, the Illinois Bayou, say, then a bayou it is, and there is no objection from the Corps.

South of Monroe the river was out of its banks, lapping at the highway in places and pushing into the cotton and soybean fields. As it draws closer to the Mississippi, it joins a tangle of rivers and bayous that are flowing more or less parallel here on the alluvial plain, and sprawling in wide meanders. Roads and ferries were closed and I had to make detours. Highway builders in Louisiana work on the Jeffersonian assumption that west (and east) is the proper direction of travel. There are fine east-west interstate highways, but traveling north and south is slow going. But then road building is an expensive business here, with so much fill dirt being required for the elevated and literal high ways.

I stopped at Columbia to pay a call on former Governor John McKeithen of Louisiana. He lives on a farm here and keeps an office downtown. Something of the squire in these parts, he is perhaps the most notable figure living on the bank of the Ouachita. But he was out of town.

More failures: I couldn't track down a commercial fisherman, and there are a few left, from Calion on down, netting catfish, buffalo and drum, in descending order of value. I turned up no song about the Ouachita, and it is certainly as deserving as the Wabash or the Swanee or the Red. I did find two poems celebrating it, both written in the 19th century, by Albert Pike and a George P. Smoote. I showed them to a woman who is a judge of such things, and she read them unmoved.

"Welcome to Jonesville/ Where the Four Rivers Meet." It is the end of the line, Jonesville, population 2,620, some 30 miles by road and bridge from Natchez. Jonesville makes the further claim of being DeSoto's ancient Indian town of Anilco, at the mouth of the Anilco or Ouachita River. No one knows if these Indians were the same as the "Ouasitas," a small Caddoan tribe first mentioned by Tonti in 1690. They moved west in the 18th century and were absorbed by the Natchitoch Indians.

I stood behind the grain elevators of the Bunge Corporation and watched the Ouachita, still greenish, for all the flooding as it poured into the Tensas (pronounced Tensaw), and where they both suddenly became the Black River. The fourth river, called the Little River, enters the flow a bit farther down. A half-mile upstream from the mouth of the Ouachita the Bunge Corp. has a dock and a big blower pipe, where barges are loaded with soybeans and other grain. Here at last was a volume shipper.

"Oh, yes, we use the Ouachita all the time," the manager told me. "That last half-mile of it, anyway."

Motel Life, Lower Reaches

This story appeared in the *Oxford American* magazine in the January/February 2003 issue. In April 2010, the magazine presented Charles Portis with an award for Lifetime Achievement in Southern Literature.

MOTEL #1

Back when Roger Miller was King of the Road, in the 1960s, he sang of rooms to let ("no phone, no pool, no pets") for four bits, or fifty cents. I can't beat that price, but I did once in those days come across a cabin that went for three dollars. It was in the long, slender highway town of Truth or Consequences, New Mexico.

That cute and unwieldy name, by the way, was taken in 1950 from the name of a quiz/comedy radio show, and has stuck, against long odds. The show was okay, as I recall, a cut or two above the general run of broadcast ephemera, with some funny 1949 moments. But why re-name your town for it? And by now, a half-century later, you would think the townsfolk must surely have repented their whim and gone back to the old name, solid and descriptive, of Hot Springs. But no, and worse, the current New Mexico highway maps no longer offer both names, with the old one in parentheses, as an option, for the comfort of those travelers who wince and hesitate over saying, "Truth or Consequences." Everyone must now say the whole awkward business.

I was driving across the state at the time, very fast. There were signs along the approaches to town advertising cheaper and cheaper motel rooms. The tone was shrill, desperate, that of an off-season price war. It was a buyer's market. I began to note the rates and the little extras I could expect for my money. Always in a hurry then, once committed to a road, I stopped only for fuel, snake exhibits, and automobile museums, but I had to pause here, track down the cheapest of these cheap motels, and see it. I would confront the owner and call his bluff.

There were boasts of being AIR COOLED (not quite the same as being air-conditioned) and of PHONE IN EVERY ROOM, KITCHENETTES, LOW WEEKLY RATES, CHILDREN FREE, PETS OK, VIBRO BEDS, PLENTY OF HOT WATER, MINIATURE GOLF, KIDDIE POOL, FREE COFFEE, FREE TV, FREE SOUVNIERS. (Along Arkansas roads there are five or six ways of spelling *souvenirs*, and every single one of them is wrong. The sign painters in New Mexico do a little better with that tricky word, but not much better.) The signs said SALESMEN WELCOME and SNOWBIRDS WELCOME and TRUCKS WELCOME/BOBTAILS ONLY—meaning just the tractors themselves; their long semi-trailers would not be welcome. And there were the usual claims, often exaggerated, of having CLEAN ROOMS or NEW ROOMS or CLEAN NEW ROOMS or ALL NEW CLEAN MODERN ROOMS.

I decided not to consider the frills. How could you reckon in cash the delight value of a miniature golf course with its little plaster windmills, tiny waterfalls, and bearded elves perched impudently on plaster toadstools? I would go for price alone, the very lowest advertised price, which turned out to be three dollars. It was a come-on, I knew, a lowball offer. Sorry, I would be told, but the last of those special rooms had just been taken; the only ones left would be the much nicer $6.50 suites. I would let the owner know what I thought of his sharp practice, but not really expecting him to writhe in shame.

The three-dollar place was an old "tourist court," a horseshoe arrangement of ramshackle cabins, all joined together by narrow carports. The ports were designed to harbor, snugly, small Ford sedans of 1930s Clyde Barrow vintage, each one with a canvas water bag ("SATURATE BEFORE USING") hanging from the front bumper, for the crossing of the Great American Desert.

But there were no cars here at all, and no one in the office. I gave the desk bell my customary one ding, not a loutish three or four. An old lady, clearly the owner, perhaps a widow, came up through parted curtains from her cluttered female nest in the rear. She was happy to see me. I asked about a three-dollar room, for one person, one night. She said yes, certainly, all her cabins went for three dollars, and there were *vacancies*.

This, without bothering to crane her neck about and peer over my shoulder, by way of giving my car out there the once-over. Desk clerks do that when I ask for a single, to see if I am trying to conceal a family. These clerks are trained in their motel academies to watch for furtive movement in the back seats of cars, for the hairy domes of human heads, those of wives, tykes, and grannies left crouching low in idling Plymouths.

This old lady had come up in a gentler school. She was honest and her signs were honest and her lodgers were presumed to be more or less honest. She had caught me up short and rattled me. Who was bluffing now? I couldn't just leave, nor, worse, give her three dollars and *then* leave, compounding the insult to her and her yellowish cabins. I paid up and stayed the night, her only guest.

My cabin had a swamp cooler, an evaporative cooling machine that is usually quite effective in that arid country. A true air conditioner (brutal compressor) uses much more electricity than a swamp cooler (small water pump, small fan). But then the cooler does consume water, and the economy of nature is such—no free lunch—that the thing works well only in a region where the humidity is low—under forty per cent, say. Where water is scarce, that is, and thus expensive.

It was dry enough here, but my cooler was defective and did nothing more than stir the hot air a bit.

I looked the room over for redeeming touches. It wasn't so bad, beaten down with use and everything gone brown with age, but honorably so, not disgusting, shabby but clean, a dry decay.

The bedding may have been original stock. That central crater in the mattress hadn't been wallowed out overnight, but rather by a long series of jumbo salesmen, snorting and thrashing about in troubled sleep. A feeble guest would have trouble getting out of the mattress. He would cry out, feebly, for a helping hand, and nobody in earshot. The small lamp on the bedside table was good, much better for reading than the lighting systems in expensive motels, with their diffused gloom. Motel decorators, who obviously don't read in bed, are all too fond of giant lampshades, a prevailing murk, and lamp switches that are hard to find and reach. The bath towels were clean but threadbare, and much too short to use as wraparound sarongs while shaving. The few visible insects were dead or torpid. There were no bathroom accretions of soft green or black matter. The lavatory mirror was freckled and had taken on a soft sepia tint. Mineral deposits clogged the shower head, making for a lop-sided spraying pattern, but the H and C knobs had not been playfully re-versed, nor did they turn the wrong way. There were sash windows you could actually raise, after giving them a few sharp blows with the heels of your hands, to break loose the ancient paint. Here again the feeble guest, seeking a breath of air, would struggle and whimper.

I had paid more and seen worse—murkier and more oppressive rooms, certainly, with that dense black motel murk hanging about in all the corners, impossible to dispel and conducive to so many suicides along our highways, I had seen worse rooms, if not thinner and shorter towels. There was plenty of hot water. I had the privacy of a cabin, and indeed not a single neighbor. What I had was a cottage, and a steal at three dollars.

Early the next morning the lady came tapping at my door. She had a pot of coffee for me on a tray with some buttered toast and a little china jug of honey. It was that unprecedented gesture, I think, and the grace note of the honey—no sealed packet of "Mixed Fruit" generic jelly—that made the place stick in my head so, and not the price at all. I like to think the old cabins lasted out the good old lady's widowhood. It must have been a close-run finish. And it comes to me now, late, a faint voice, saying the price was really two dollars.

MOTEL #2

A few years later. This one was in the Texas border town of Laredo, across the Rio Grande from Nuevo Laredo, in Mexico. You expect it to be the other way around, with the older, primary Laredo on the Mexico side, and so it was in origin (1755) when the north bank of the river *was* Mexico—or, actually, New Spain then. You might also expect the Rio Grande here to be a mighty stream, so far down on its 1,900-mile run to the Gulf, but it's more like a weed-strangled municipal drainage ditch than a Great River.

I was driving up out of deeper Mexico. On the U.S. side of the bridge I was greeted, if that's the word, by a suspicious INS agent in a glass sen-try booth. He asked me a few questions and directed me at once to the customs inspection shed. No doubt I made a good fit for one of his Detain profiles. *Lone white dishevelled Arkansas male in four-wheel-drive pickup with winch. Subject admits to extensive travel in rural interior of Mexico. Tells lame story re purpose of trip.*

The big shed was open along the sides but still very hot. I had to unload all my baggage from the truck, everything moveable, and spread it out on an extended table. A customs agent went first to the opened suitcase, so inviting, the bared intimacy of it. He made a long business of inspecting my paltry wardrobe, lifting articles of clothing one by one with the deliberation of a shopper. Then he moved leisurely along to the loose gear—fuel cans, water jugs, cans of oil, cans of quack chemical engine remedies, tools, books. These things, too, he picked up one by one, and as he turned them over in his hands he appeared to be muttering words of inventory, thus—*lantern, bottle jack, scissors jack, some sort of dried gourd here....*He lifted the books and read the titles to catch their heft and flavor, but made no critical comment.

Another agent was going over the truck itself with a flashlight, a small hammer, and a dental inspection mirror, with the little angled head. He rolled himself underneath, belly up, on a mechanic's creeper, and peered into crevices and felt about in them. He made delicate, cache-detecting taps on body panels with the toy hammer. The searches are necessary, granted. I knew I had no contraband but the agents didn't know. Still, the innocent—blameless in this matter, at least—grow impatient. At last, after a whispered conference, the two men gave up and said I could go. I had looked so promising, then let them down. Not that I was cleared, exactly, just sullenly dismissed for lack of evidence, and left to load everything up again.

I drove into Laredo for a bit and stopped at what, in my road stupor, I took to be a chain motel in the middling price range. I was wrong. The national chain had depreciated this one out and dumped it on the local market. An older couple I will call Mom and Dad had picked it up.

In the office lobby there were two women seated at a low table, drinking iced tea and having a chat. One was Mom. I asked about a room. The women looked me over. I was a mess, dead on my feet. For a night and the best part of a day I had been driving hard, without sleeping, bathing, or shaving. My khakis, heavy with sweat, were clinging to my flesh here and there.

Mom said, "We don't take no show people here."

"Show people?"

The other woman explained the situation. "It's a carnival come to town down there. We were just now talking about it."

So, this was just more of the Welcome Home party. First the fun in the customs shed and now I was accused of being in show business. I told Mom that I was no such romantic figure as a carnival worker, but only a road-weary traveler. Did she have a room or not?

She relented, though still perhaps suspecting me of running a Ferris wheel or a rat stall. This being the one where you put your money down, gaping rube that you are, and watch a white rat race about on an enclosed table top. The rat eventually darts into one of several numbered holes, but not your numbered hole. Or maybe she really didn't care and was only showing off a little before her friend, who could now spread the word about Mom's high social standards as an innkeeper.

She had given way pretty fast. It might well be that Mom enjoyed nothing more in life than filling her rooms with jolly roustabouts ("My boys") and the more tattoos the better.

The room was okay, which is to say it was pretty far along on the way down but not yet squalid, just acceptable. A sharp distinction for those of us in the know. We can tell at a glance, from the doorway. The swimming pool was nearby, too. Just the thing in this heat. I took a shower and put on some trunks.

It was a big pool from a more expansive motel era, with a deep end that was deep, but with a derelict look overall. No one was about. The chain-link fencing sagged, and there were rips and gashes in the wire. The non-sparkling water was of a cloudy green hue and perfectly still. Floating leaves and styrofoam cups bobbed not at all. A Sargasso calm. Perhaps the pump was broken. No diving board, of course, the diving board lawyers having seen to that, even then. Only the stanchions remained, the chrome-steel pipes rooted in concrete.

I made a ground-level entry dive and swam one lap. The water had a prickly, tingling feel. It stung my eyes. The pool chemicals gone bad, I thought.

Now here came Dad at a limping trot, shouting at me, "Hey, get out of there! Can't you read?" I was already climbing out when he started this, and he was still telling me to get out of the pool when I was standing there safe ashore, upright and dripping, before his eyes. Once a tape got rolling in Dad's head, it wasn't going to be cut short by any external event.

He looked around, baffled, then saw that his DANGER/KEEP OUT/NO SWIMMING sign had fallen from the wire fence. He picked it up and showed it to me. Electricity, it seems, was leaking into the pool water from corroded wires and terminals near the underwater lamps. I asked Dad why he didn't drain the dangerous electrified pool. Because, he said, it was only the great lateral pressure of all that water that kept the thing from collapsing in on itself, and he didn't want to lose his pool. He pointed out cracks and bulges in the retaining walls.

I said I had suspected toxic chemicals and wouldn't have thought of electricity coursing through a swimming pool. As for that, Dad said, his chemicals had gone sour, too, under the beating sun, and what with the stagnation…but they didn't account for the prickle, only for the sting and the unnatural greenness and the sharp metallic taste of the water.

Wasn't there a lawsuit here? I could hire one of the diving-board lawyers, preferably one in cowboy boots. Into the mixed bag of damages we could throw the pain I had suffered from Mom's suggestion, before a witness, that I was in show business. We would pick Mom and Dad clean, seize everything, and kick them out of the motel, destitute, into the streets of Laredo. Then it occurred to me that Mom's lawyer might have some boots of his own, made of animal skins even more exotic, costly, and menacing than those sported by my man. What if he put me in a line-up parade before the jury, full face and profile views, with some carnival guys trucked in from the midway? How would I fare? I saw, too, that on the witness stand, under oath, I would have to admit that I had actually felt better, perked up a little, after my dip in Dad's electro-chemical vat. Best maybe just to let this slide.

That evening after a nap, I tried to make long-distance call from my room. I was expecting a check in the mail. Like a carnival guy, I had no fixed abode then (had Mom sensed this?) and was using the home of my father and mother in Little Rock as a mail drop. The bedside telephone had the full array of buttons. Some, however, were dummies. Pressing 8, the long-distance one, got me nowhere. I couldn't even get the desk.

I walked up to the office, where Mom informed me with relish that she and Dad were no longer set up for long-distance service. It was nothing but trouble. People were always using it. Local calls only. But couldn't

I make the call here, now, on that office phone, under her gaze and supervision? A brief one? My credit-card billing for the room was still open, and she could add to it whatever she liked in the way of fees, for the call and her inconvenience. I wouldn't be calling Shanghai, only Little Rock.

"We're not set up for that. There's a pay phone out there."

I had no American money in my pockets. Mom, living here in a border town where the banks readily exchanged pesos and dollars, didn't see how she could possibly give me a handful of quarters and dimes for my Mexican currency. She shrank from handling the alien notes. The republic of Mexico was a half-hour stroll from here and for Mom it was *terra incognita* and would on principle remain so.

Back to my room where I rooted about in luggage and found a few coins, enough to spring open a circuit at the pay phone and gain the ear of an operator. She dialed the number in Little Rock. Home is the place where, when you have to call it collect, they have to accept the charges. My mother answered. The operator told her that this was a collect call from her first-born son Charles, in Laredo, Texas. Would she accept the charges? My mother, not always attentive, said, "I'm sorry, he's not here, he's down in Mexico somewhere," and hung up, before I could gather my wits and shout to her.

The close of a long day. I meant to ask Dad about the curious slashes in his pool fence. Berserk vandals with chain saws? Environmental zealots with axes? In Laredo? But I kept forgetting, and at dawn, still ignorant on that point, and not much worse for the wear, I was off and away again in my white Chevrolet truck. And I saw on further reflection that Mom had been right to place me in a pariah caste. It was just one she didn't know about, that of the untouchable wretches called freelance writers.

MOTEL #3

Now to the more recent past and a place in southern New Mexico, bright land of bargain motels and fair dealing, where I was doing some research on Pancho Villa's 1916 raid across the border. My room was in a motel I will call the Ominato Inn, not quite a dump, with a *weekly rate* of $130 flat, no surcharges. The price quoted was what you paid, with no tourist penalties, bed taxes, bathroom duties, or other shakedown fees

piled on, such as to make a joke of the nominal price. There should have
been a pair of signs out front, flashing back and forth:

NOT QUITE A DUMP   AT DUMP PRICES

Or no, they weren't needed. By late afternoon, almost every day, the
parking lot was filled with a motley fleet of cars, vans, trucks, and mo-
torcycles, giving the appearance of a police impound yard. Far too many
of these vehicles had weak batteries.

It was in the Ominato that I came to know celebrity, two onerous
weeks of it, as "that guy in number twelve with the great jumper cables."
The first to seek my help was an old man I will call Mr. Sherman Lee
Purifoy. He was a retired policeman, a widower, from southern Illinois,
of that region near the confluence of the Ohio and the Mississippi. Year
after year he came here to stay the winter months, in the Ominato, and
in the same, much-prized room, number three, the only one with a kitch-
enette. The Purifoy Room, but without a plaque.

I had just checked in when he accosted me in the sandy courtyard,
which was the desert floor itself, unpaved. His battery was dead. Could
I give him a jump? His car looked like other cars, but it was one I had
never heard of, a Mercury Topaz. When I mentioned this, intending no
slight, that the Topaz was a new one on me, he took offense. He took
me to be suggesting that he was the kind of man who would drive a
freakish, not to say ludicrous car. As though I had accused him, say, of
wearing sandals. The Topaz happened to be a very good ottamobile, he
said, and for my information there were plenty of Topazes out there on
the highways, giving good service every day. And any car at all could
have a bad battery.

Except mine. With my hot battery and my two-gauge, all-copper
cables I soon had his Topaz humming away again. Santiago—let us call
him that—had come by to watch. He was the assistant motel manager,
electrician, and handyman. He admired the heaviness of my cables,
their professional girth. And those fierce, spring-loaded clamps! Such
teeth! People who needed cables usually didn't have them, he said, or
they had the cheap, skinny kind that couldn't carry enough amps to do
the job. Mine were the best he had ever seen, and he had seen a few.
Already I was basking.

From there the word went around, down the road, even, into a motor home park, to which I felt no ties of loyalty. I was on call night and day with my cables. I feared the knock on the door. I found myself lingering, to the point of loitering, in places away from the Ominato and the room I had paid for. Celebrity turned out to be disappointing, but it was hard to say no when you had been given the power to raise the dead.

And Mr. Purifoy was okay, if a little too much underfoot, a great accoster, and something of a tar baby, with time on his hands. He caught me going out and coming in, and, on occasion, he would catch me in an ambush at some unlikely place miles away—once, in the lobby of a county courthouse.

One afternoon he stopped me cold in my tracks and said, "Just look around. Half the people in this motel are criminals."

"That's a lot of criminals, Mr. Purifoy."

"At least half. I'm not even counting some of the dopers in that."

I looked around. Mr. Purifoy, I thought, must have lumped in with his bad boys, willy-nilly, all the scruffier transients who stopped here, and so had arrived at his high estimate of the criminal density. Drifters as such were guilty, of drifting. My guess was that on a given night at the Ominato no more than ten per cent of the lodgers were genuine felons on the lam, some with their molls. Of the rest, only about two per cent would be British journalists named Clive, Colin, or Fiona, scribbling notes and getting things wrong for their journey books about the real America, that old and elusive theme.

Another time he asked me what my business was here in New Mexico. Against my better judgement I told him. He didn't think much of the Pancho Villa project, taking it to be one of glamorizing a thug and serial rapist. He said I could expect no help from him in working this thing up, whatever it was, nor, when it was done, would there be any use asking him to look it over, as he had better things to do.

Another time he told me that he never bothered to turn off his television at night, his sleep being fitful. He would doze for an hour or so, wake, and watch "the TV" for an hour or so. It didn't matter what—golf highlights of 1971, the giant termite mounds on the African *veld*. There was no roaming about through the channels. But what a lot of people didn't know was this: *You can do other things while watching the TV*. Little mindless chores. Sometimes he polished his shoes. And so he drowsed and woke through the long night, drifting in and out of alternating dreams.

Then daybreak at last, always a joy, when he could pop out of his box and go into the world again. A third hallucination, perhaps, though with its sunny radiance much brighter than the others. Better still, in this one was a blue Mercury Topaz.

He rose early and drove to a McDonald's restaurant for a breakfast of biscuits and gravy, many free refills of coffee, and for a long visit with his retirement cronies. It was a gathering place. Some weeks back he had taken the trouble to write down a good recipe for "thickening gravy"— milk gravy. He gave it to one of the girls at McDonald's but suspected that she and her bosses had never even so much as tried it. They were still dishing out the same old stuff.

There were other cronies who preferred Wendy's restaurant, but Mr. Purifoy said he wouldn't be going back to that place any time soon. Some woman was always there in the mornings, reading things out loud from a newspaper to her husband, who was neither blind nor illiterate. Humorous snippets mostly, but longer pieces, too. How could you think straight or talk to your friends with this woman droning on like that? Well, you couldn't, and she never let up. She kept finding nuggets, as she thought, here and there in the low-grade ore of the newspapers.

As a gentleman, in his way, Mr. Purifoy could hardly scold the woman herself, directly, but neither was he one to shirk a clear social duty. He said he took the husband aside and spoke firmly to him about this nuisance. With no effect. The poor man was henpecked, his spirit broken years ago. He had shamefully admitted he could do nothing to stop his wife from reading things out loud to him, in private or public. Mr. Purifoy said one day that quiet bird would club her to death. One AP snippet too many.

The least of our criminals was probably Lash LaRue. With his black boots, jeans, shirt, and hat, he reminded me of the old black-clad movie cowboy of that name, who popped revolvers out of the hands of saloon louts with his bullwhip. But this younger Lash had no whip, and the sinister outfit was only a costume.

Santiago brought him to my door one morning. Lash said he had left the headlights of his truck burning all night, and his "battery"— singular—was down. It was a big Ford pickup a year or two old, with a diesel V-8 engine and a Louisiana license plate. Lash spoke of it as "my truck," and he did possess the truck but I don't believe he owned the truck. First, he couldn't find the hood-latch release, then he had trouble working it. With the hood up at last, he was struck dumb by what must have been his first sight of the monster engine. He was a calf looking at a new gate. I, too, was impressed. It was a beautifully organized work of industrial art, filling and overflowing the engine bay.

His plump young female companion (Brandi? Autumn?) lurked and pouted in the doorway of their room. They were running away to California, that must be it. They had stolen her Daddy's newish truck, his treasure, and left him back in Opelousas, to putt around in Lash's little Dodge Omni.

I pointed out the two big batteries up front, wired in series, one on either side of the radiator. More amazement from Lash. "*Two* batteries!"

Diesels with their high compression are by nature hard to crank, thus the booster. I wanted to walk away. These peculiar engines make me uneasy. Hard to start when cold, and then, once going, they sound like machines trying to rip themselves apart in a furious suicidal clatter. So much for my ignorance. They manage to clatter away like that for years on end.

No matter, I still don't like them, and already I had lost face with Mr. Purifoy in failing to jump-start a diesel motor home owned by one of his cronies, in the nearby park. My excuse, plausible enough, was that the man's battery cells were so absolutely stone dead as to be no longer conductive.

I told Lash it wasn't going to work, that I couldn't pump enough amps through all the batteries and circuitry to turn over that diesel crankshaft. He said maybe then we could push-start the truck, and he must have known better, the transmission was automatic. But he was going into a panic. Brandi said maybe we could tie a rope from my bumper to theirs and pull-start the truck. She had not moved from the shadowy doorway. Preserving her lily pallor? Those white cheeks would pink up pretty fast in the desert sun.

Lash ignored her and was now begging. Please, couldn't we at least *try* a jump-start? With those deluxe cables he had heard so much about?

A shrewd appeal to my pride. Well, why not humor him? It wouldn't take long to go through the motions. I broke out the cables yet again and hooked them up. I started my engine, leaving it to run for a bit and do some charging. Then I climbed up into the truck cab and turned the starter key one notch over to light the glow-plug. This is a little Zoroastrian fire prayer ritual, which must be observed. After what I judged to be the proper interval, I turned the key all the way over to en-gage the starter motor, expecting to hear nothing, or at most a click. But the starter *did* spin, and then we had compression-ignition. The infernal oil-burning machine had come alive and was clanging away on its own.

Lash was so crazed with relief that he offered to pay me. He and Brandi lost no time in fleeing the Ominato. She waved bye-bye from the cab and told me not to worry, that they would take care to park the truck on a slope tonight when they stopped. She still thought you could roll-start the thing. I noticed some stenciled words in white on the tailgate: LICENSED AND BONDED. Licensed as what? Who would license Lash and what body of underwriters would stand good for his handiwork? California can always use one more Lash and one more Brandi, and I wished the young lovebirds well, but no, that big fine work truck didn't belong to Lash LaRue.

My Saturday afternoon loitering place was a small bar in a small American Legion post. It was like some forgotten outpost where the sol-diers had grown old waiting for the relief column. Here I drank and brooded with others of this lost platoon, who had their own reasons for not going home. There was a pool table, always in use, and a juke box, not much played, though it had a good repertoire of older stuff. No din, that was what we wanted, but now and then out of the blue we would hear "You Win Again" from Hank Williams, or Fats Domino singing,

> You broke
> My hort,
> When you said
> We'll port
> Ain't that a shame.

One Saturday Mr. Purifoy appeared there, to my surprise. He was AA, or as he liked to call it, ND. The letters stood for Nameless Drunks, his jocular cacophemism for Alcoholics Anonymous. Saying the words always made him laugh.

He said he had seen my car out front and just thought he would drop in for a minute. He had some news. But I wasn't to hear it until he had gone through a long and disruptive business of settling in. It took him some little time to get seated properly, then clear away his bar space and give his order: "JUST A GLASS OF ICE TEA FOR ME, PLEASE." A general rebuke but no one was put to shame or flight. He went on to tell the bartender, who hadn't asked, that his health, on the whole, overall, for his age, was pretty good, "except for all these blood sores on my arms." They weren't as bad as their name. He pushed back his sleeves to show us some subcutaneous splotches, like red bruises.

The news was that he had bought a new battery—but we could look at it later. He could show me the expensive new 72-month battery later, in the Topaz. Then, by way of throwing out a conversational tidbit for the bar at large, he said that over in neighboring Arizona there happened to be certain chapters of Alcoholics Anonymous which allowed you to drink two cans of beer every day. What they called a maintenance dose.

Our fellow Legionnaires scoffed. Baloney, they said, and worse, but wanting to hear a little more. I was sitting between Mr. Purifoy and a hard, sun-dried little man called Vic, a pygmy sea lawyer, bald, yet still with scarcely any forehead at all. Possibly an old brig rat. Vic, like so many others, had come to the desert to make a clean end to his life, to shrink further here and indeed to waste away by degrees from evaporation until he vanished. He said he was from Montana—we were all carpetbaggers—but he told anecdotes in the dramatic New York City manner. With the injured tone, that is, and exuberant gestures and that fast delivery in the historic present tense ("So then this creep, can you believe it, he turns around and says to me...").

Vic wondered if it might not be possible under the Arizona indulgence to count malt liquor, a stronger brew, as a kind of beer. And if the ration were stated simply as "two cans of beer," not further qualified, then why couldn't you just buy the bigger cans, huge ones, even, which would require the use of both hands to lift from the bar?

He and some others challenged Mr. Purifoy and pressed him hard to give the precise locations of the renegade AA groups. Mr. Purifoy couldn't remember offhand. Globe, maybe, was one of the places. You can't remember everything. Some fellow from Arizona was telling him about this, and he would know, wouldn't he? The man was from Arizona and an honorable lodge brother in good standing who drove a good car and made a pretty good living as a professional square-dance caller and who stood to gain nothing at all by telling a gratuitous lie about the two cans of beer. Could any one here dispute that? No? Then maybe some people should just shut up for a change and then maybe talk about something they did know something about for a change. How would that do? He finished his tea and left.

Later, there was a commotion, a diversion, at the pool table. One of the players fell unconscious to the floor—of a diabetic fit, it was said. He was a fairly young man, the very last one of our crew you would expect to keel over. Someone called for an ambulance. Everyone, Vic included, jumped up to offer help, with an alacrity that wouldn't be seen in a public bar. But how to help, exactly? Some said it was the head that must be elevated in these cases, and others the feet. The feet, I thought, but wasn't sure. The poor fellow was tilted first one way and then the other.

He soon came around, despite our efforts, and was shooting pool again when the ambulance arrived, flashing, shrieking, and setting all the neighborhood dogs barking. A welcome diversion for them, too. But the young man refused to be examined or wired up to any diagnostic machine or hauled away to a hospital—and he certainly wasn't going to sign his name to no paper on no clipboard. Forget it, he said, a false alarm.

There were angry words with the two paramedics. The senior one, the driver, was a heavy and hairy young man (Bull?) with nothing much of the nurse about him. He looked like the senior bouncer in a very big highway honky tonk, the bouncer of last resort. He dug in. Someone here, he said, and make no mistake, was going to sign this trip log and take responsibility for this deadhead run. It was a hard job he had, one demanding a healing touch of sorts and the driving skill of a stock-car racer, along with the brass and belligerence of a debt collector. The row was still going on when I left for the day, with the yard dogs still raving and foaming. I don't know how it came out, but I would have bet on the big medico-bouncer.

MOTEL #4

I left the Ominato for good the next morning, rising earlier than Mr. Purifoy himself, our early bird. The Topaz was in place. No one at all was stirring. Criminals become criminals so they can sleep late. All their cars here would be at least a quart low on oil. I virtuously checked mine, then slammed the hood down with no consideration for their rest. And in motel life at the low end, you don't bother to say good-bye. It isn't done, you must keep a certain churlish distance, unless you're young and still human like Brandi and haven't yet learned the ropes. One day you just steal away and your disappearance is little noted if at all.

I drove up to Truth or Consequences on a whim, going out of my way, for a look around. I could find no trace of the old yellow cabins, nor even locate the site. Things disappear, too, utterly. The hot springs downtown were still flowing hot, or warm. The name of the place still grated, but less so now, burnished as it was a little by time and the friction of use. Some of the locals had taken to calling it "T or C." No improvement there, the cute made cuter.

That evening I stopped at a small motel called the Desert View—the real name this time. My room was a bit small but clean, new, modern, all those things, with a gleaming white bathroom. The bed was flat and firm. Over the headboard there were two good reading lamps mounted on pivots. I had air conditioning, cable television, a refrigerator, and a microwave oven. It was a quiet place with few guests, none of sly or rat-like appearance. I could park directly in front of my door. The nightly rate was twenty-five dollars flat, no surcharges. Allowing for inflation, this was little more than I had paid for the old cabin.

The Desert View was, in short, something pretty close to that ideal in my head of the cheap and shipshape roadside dormitory, what I kept looking for all those years. Now, after finding it, I was confused. This place was too good to be true. I sat on the firm edge of the firm bed, very still, wary, taking stock. Something felt wrong. Everything, more or less, but something bizarre in particular that I couldn't put my finger on. Then it came to me—the very *carpet* was clean. *Motel carpet!* What was going on here? I didn't get it. Who were these Desert View people? Where was the catch? I cleared out of there at dawn and still don't know.

Three

SHORT STORIES

Your Action Line

(YOUR ACTION LINE SOLVES PROBLEMS, ANSWERS QUESTIONS, CUTS RED TAPE, STANDS UP FOR RIGHTS. YOUR ACTION LINE WANTS TO HELP!)

Q—I have a 1966 Roosevelt dime that has turned brown. A guy in the office told me it was worth $750 and I now have it hidden in a pretty good place. Where can I sell it?

A—Benny Mann of Benny's Stamp and Coin Nook informs Action Line that the "1966 Brown" is not as valuable as many people seem to think. In fact, he tells us that some shops and restaurants will not even accept it at face value. But if you take your dime by the Coin Nook, in the Lark Avenue Arcade, Benny will be glad to examine it under his Numismascope and give you a free appraisal.

Q—Last May I ordered a four-record album called "Boogie Hits of the Sixties" from Birtco Sales in Nome, N.J. They cashed my check fast enough, but I got no records. I tried to call the place and the operator said the phone had been disconnected. I wrote and threatened legal action and they finally sent me a one-record album of Hawaiian music. Now they won't even answer my letters.

A—Your boogie tunes are on the way. Action Line tracked down the president of Birtco, Al Birt, to Grand Bahama Island, where he moved after the settlement of the Birtco bankruptcy case (the company's inventory and good will are going to Zodiac Studios, of Nash, N.J.), and Mr. Birt explained that your misorder was probably attributable to an "anarchy" condition in the shipping room. Zodiac has knocked the bugs out of the system, he assures Action Line, and all orders will be processed within seven months or he'll "know the reason why!"

Q—We have just moved into the Scales Estates. The house is O.K., but we can't get a television picture at all, and we can't pick up anything on our radio except for American Legion baseball games and rodeo news. We can't even tell where these broadcasts are coming from, what town or what state, because the announcers never say.

A—Developer Zane Scales tells Action Line that part of the Scales Estates lies on top of the old Gumbo No. 2 mercury mine. This cinnabar deposit, in combination with the 30-story, all-aluminum Zane Scales Building, makes for a "bimetallic wave-inversion squeeze," he says, and that sometimes causes freakish reception. Scales hastens to add that the condition is nothing to worry about, and that only about 400 houses are affected.

Q—There is a beer joint called Hester's Red Door Lounge in the 9300 block of Lark Avenue. It doesn't look like much from the outside, but I have heard some very curious and interesting discussions there at the bar. I am told that you can send off somewhere and get transcripts of what is said there and who said it. I can't stop at the lounge every day, you see, and even when I do I forget most of the stuff as soon as I leave.

A—Only weekly summaries of the conversation at the Red Door Lounge are available at this time. Send one dollar and a stamped, self-addressed envelope to Box 202, Five Points Station, and ask for Hester's White Letter. Hester Willis tells Action Line that complete daily transcripts (Hester's Red Letter) have been discontinued because of soaring stenographic and printing costs. Many subscribers actually prefer the summary, she says, particularly during football season, when there is necessarily a lot of repetitive matter. Hester hastened to assure Action Line that all the major points of all the discussions are included in the White Letter, as well as many of the humorous sallies. Sorry, no names. The speaking parties cannot be identified beyond such tags as "fat lawyer," "the old guy from Texarkana," and "retired nurse."

Q—Can you put me in touch with a Japanese napkin-folding club?
A—Not with a club as such, but you might try calling Meg Sparks at 696-2440. Meg holds a brown belt in the sushi school of folding, and she takes a few students along as her time permits. Beginner napkin kits ($15.95) are available at the International House of Napkins, on Victory Street, across from Barling Park.

Q—What happened with the Salute to Youth thing this year? We drove out there Saturday night and the place was dark. If they are going to cancel these things at the last minute, the least they can do is let somebody know about it. We had a busload of very disappointed kids, some of them crying.
A—Drove out where? The Salute to Youth rally was held Saturday night at Five Points Stadium, where it has always been held. The program lasted seven hours and the stadium lights could be seen for thirteen miles. There were eighty-one marching bands in attendance, and when they played the finale the ground shook and windows were broken almost a mile away in the Town and Country Shopping Center.

Q—I joined the Apollo Health Spa on June 21st, signing a thirty-year contract. It was their "Let's Get Acquainted" deal. I have attended four sessions at the place and I am not satisfied with either their beef-up program or their weight-loss program, which seem to be identical, by the way. The equipment is mostly just elastic straps that you pull. No matter how early you get there, the lead shoes are always in use. I want out, but they say they will have to "spank" me if I don't meet all the terms of the contract. Those people are not from around here and I don't know what they mean exactly, whether it is just their way of talking or what. That's all they will say.

A—Action Line will say it once again: Never sign any document until you have read it carefully! Don't be pushed! So much for the scolding. You will be interested to learn that the Attorney General's office is currently investigating a number of spanking threats alleged to have been made by the sales staff at Apollo. Ron Rambo, the Apollo Spa's prexy and a former Mr. Arizona, tells Action Line that he, too, is looking into the matter and that he has his eye on "one or two bad apples." As for the equipment, he says your cut-rate membership plan does not entitle you to the use of the Hell Boots, the Rambo Bars, the Olympic Tubs, or the Squirrel Cage except by appointment.

Q—Help! I live on Railroad Street and I have been driving to work for many years by way of Lark Avenue. Now they have put up a "NO LEFT TURN" sign at the intersection of Railroad and Lark and I have to turn right and go all the way to the airport before I can make a U-turn and double back. This means I have to get up in the dark every morning to allow for the long drive.

A—You don't say where you work. If it's downtown, then why not forget Lark and stay on Railroad until you reach Gully, which has a protected left turn. You may not know it, but Gully is now one-way going east all the way to Five Points, where you can take the dogleg around Barling Park (watch for slowpokes in the old people's crossing) and onto Victory. Bear right over the viaduct to twenty-seventh and then hang a left at the second stoplight and go four blocks to the dead end at Lagrange. Take Lagrange as far as the zoo (stay in the right lane), and from there it's a straight shot to the Hopper Expressway and the Rotifer Bridge.

Q—My science teacher told me to write a paper on the "detective ants" of Ceylon, and I can't find out anything about these ants. Don't tell me to go to the library, because I've already been there.

A—There are no ants in Ceylon. Your teacher may be thinking of the "journalist ants" of central Burma. These bright-red insects grow to a maximum length of one-quarter inch, and they are tireless workers, scurrying about on the forest floor and gathering tiny facts, which they store in their abdominal sacs. When the sacs are filled, they coat these facts with a kind of nacreous glaze and exchange them for bits of yellow wax manufactured by the smaller and slower "wax ants." The journalist ants burrow extensive tunnels and galleries beneath Burmese villages, and the villagers, reclining at night on their straw mats, can often hear a steady hum from the earth. This hum is believed to be the ants sifting fine particles of information with their feelers in the dark. Diminutive grunts can sometimes be heard, too, but these are thought to come not from the journalist ants but from their albino slaves, the "butting dwarf ants," who spend their entire lives tamping wax into tiny storage chambers with their heads.

The New Yorker, December 12, 1977

Nights Can Turn Cool in Viborra

"What were those dull bonks I heard this morning?"

Jason and Mopsy had just come down to breakfast, and I threw up my hands in mock dismay as she put that old, old question to me.

"Why, Mopsy, don't tell me you haven't read my travel articles! Shame on you! Those were the famous thudding church bells of Viborra! 'Thunk, thunk, thunk,' they say. 'Welcome, Mopsy! Welcome to Viborra!'"

The poor girl went pink and the dining hall of the Pan-Lupus Hotel erupted into good-natured laughter. The diners laughed and the waiters laughed and so did Ugo, the jolly old elf at the buffet table, who was sprinkling a bit of this and a bit of that into his tangy and oh so scrumptious herring paste—a Viborran delight called *huegma*.

Nonresonant church bells? Freshly pounded *huegma* smeared on warm buns straight from the oven? Romantic moonlight rides in circular boats not much bigger than tubs. The gaiety of an open-air market with unfamiliar vegetables on display—so knobby and streaky? Narrow cobbled streets? Bargain belts—and purses too? Great fun at breakfast?

Well, yes, and these are just a few of the joys awaiting the traveler who finds his way to this lovely old colonial city nestled in a sapphire cove under a cerulean sky on the Sea of Tessa—known locally as Da Magro, or "the Burning Sea."

We had arrived the night before on a high-wing Tessair Fokker—I and my new chums, Jason and Mopsy Crimm. With my port-of-entry know-how I soon had us cleared through customs—a painless business on the whole. The Crimms were dazzled by my moves as I pushed in ahead of others, jumping this line and that one. With a wave and a knowing wink I steered them quickly through all the control points. There was one awkward moment, when the Propriety Officer caught sight of Jason's hideous jogging shoes. But then the officer—doing a priceless double-take—recognized my distinctive turquoise velveteen smoking jacket (so loose and comfy on long flights), and the poor man was all but speechless.

"Chick Jardine!" he sputtered. "Winner of five gold Doobie Awards for travel writing! How I envy your powers of description, sir!"

After that, as you can imagine, the city was ours.

This brings me, however, to my one teeny caveat for you folks planning your first trip to Viborra. Be advised that the Ministry of Fitness and Propriety maintains a Vigilance Desk at the airport. If the duty officer there perceives you to be a lout, rich or poor, he will assign you to the Morono Palace, a magnificent hotel for louts on the eastern beach, or mud flats, just across the Bal River from Viborra proper, regardless of any previous arrangement you have made. As a registered lout (stamped thus on your visa in luminescent orange ink—LOUT), you will be somewhat restricted in your movements, to the eastern beach and to the markets, bars, and shops around the Arch of Nimmo, or the Plaza of Louts. You will also be fitted with and made to wear an orange plastic wristband for ready identification.

But not to worry. The guests at the Morono Palace have loads of fun in their own way, and prices are considerably cheaper in that district— particularly on belts, yo-yos, fishnet tank tops, heavy woolen shower curtains, and tortoise-shell flashlights. You can even watch these unique torches being made in ancient workshops, where the delicate craft of shell-routing is jealously guarded and passed on from father to son. And the central dining hall at the Morono is a show in itself, with its famous rude waiters cavorting comically about in striped jerseys as they insult the guests, and with its Morono Mega-Spread, a free-for-all salad bar 188 feet long. Then, blazing and blaring atop the Palace, there is the legendary Club Nimmo, reputed to be the world's loudest nightclub, with music and hilarity and flashing lights twenty-four hours a day.

"No, no," I said to Mopsy, as I caught her making a move toward the bud vase on our breakfast table. "Smell, but don't touch. That delicate white blossom is not so innocent as it appears. That, my dear, is an *artu* flower from the volcanic highlands, and it exudes a toxic alkaline resin that can blister the fingers. A defense mechanism, you see."

It was all coming back to me, remarkably enough—a torrent of Viborran memories and lore, on this, my first visit to the old city in many years. I thought how lucky the Crimms were to have scraped acquaintance with me, for I seldom reveal my identity to ordinary people on my jaunts around the world, knowing and hating the fuss that always follows. My helpful tips to less experienced travelers are strictly confined to my prizewinning magazine articles and my widely syndicated newspaper column, and when I hear star-struck people murmuring around me (they having spotted my trademark turquoise jacket), I go all deaf and ignorant.

But then, how natural it is that celebrities should gravitate to one another. In our chat on the Fokker it came out that Jason and Mopsy, far from being ordinary, had appeared on the covers of nine popular financial magazines in the past year, posed in front of their restored Victorian house, with expensive new silvery cars parked in the driveway. Mopsy showed me the most recent cover, and an amusing photo it was, too. Jason, his arms straining under the load, is standing behind a red wheelbarrow that is filled and indeed spilling over with documents representing his sensible budgets, wise investments, and long-range tax-planning strategies. At his side is our little gamine, Mopsy, with a sheaf of CDs and tax-free municipal bonds spread fanwise and peeping out ever so coyly from her bodice. She confided to me, with pardonable pride, that of all the grinning young couples ever to appear on the covers of these magazines in front of their restored Victorian houses, she and Jason were judged to have the least-blemished shutters and the most beautifully complacent grins.

People who matter, then, people worth knowing, and the feeling was mutual, to put it mildly. Can you picture the scene at the airport when the officer spilled the beans—that I was award-winning syndicated columnist Chick Jardine? The Crimms were addled with delight!

It also turned out that none of us was paying for anything. Plane fare, hotel rooms, meals—all free. I never pay, on principle, as a guest of the world, and the ever-calculating Crimms, who read forty-one financial newsletters each month, had managed to get in on the ground floor of something called the Ponzi Travelbirds, through which society, as Early Birds, they will enjoy free travel for life, at the expense of all Late Birds joining the club. Need I say it? My kind of folks!

* * *

After breakfast we were off for a day of adventure under the azure vault of the sky, with yours truly acting as cicerone. We clambered up the winding stone staircase to the topmost battlement of the old fortress known as the Castle of Abomination. We made our way down narrow cobbled streets to the Thieves' Market, and we took a bus ride to the Crispo Lupus Windmill Plantation. There is little to see on that barren hilltop—a tangle of copper wire and seven or eight rusting steel towers with broken windmill sails. Not one watt of electricity was ever generated by the project. But I knew this little excursion would be a treat for the Crimms. Back home they could entertain their friends with the story of how they had ridden on a ramshackle bus in a tropical country—*with pigs and chickens aboard!*

We inspected the bushes at the National Arboretum, running mostly to prickly, grayish xerophytic scrub. We toured the Arses Lupus Mask and Wig Factory downtown. We admired the slavering ferocity of the women gnawing on leather (to soften it) at the Arses Lupus Belt and Purse Co-op. We descended (watch your head!) into the dark, dripping dungeons of Melanoma Prison, now a horror museum complete with shackled skeletons artfully laid out on straw. In the lower, blacker depths of that infamous hole you will need a candle, on sale at the reception desk for fifty pilmiras. Luckily, I had my own penlight, and the alert Crimms neatly got around the fee by exchanging some little foil-wrapped bricklets of butter (lifted from the hotel buffet) for their candles.

Then once again out into the shimmering light of day, and under a sky of that heartbreaking shade of delft blue you will find nowhere else in the world, we took a pleasant stroll along the bayfront promenade. We ate flavored ices and watched the children clubbing rat fish in the shallows.

Jason was fascinated by the Viborran coins, light as fine pastry. (Even the money is fun in Viborra!) I explained that they are minted from a curious alloy of chalk and aluminum, or actually baked, on greased sheets, in government kilns, and that, unlike all other coins in the world, they float. The 500-pilmira pieces are particularly buoyant, and these huge gray discs are used to stuff life jackets.

Pilmira coins have a dusty surface somewhat like that of a butterfly's wing. This creepy feeling or quality of dry slipperiness is held in great esteem by Viborrans, and they have a word for it—*rhampa*, which translates not only as "free of asperities" but also as "charm," "magic," "felicity," "a leap of the heart," "brutal cunning," "inner certitude," or "a sudden white spikiness, as of a yawning cat's mouth," according to context. If you wish to say "Thank you" or "Is it not so?" or "Beat it!" or "The bill, please," you can never go far wrong with the all-purpose phrase "*Ar rhampa palayot*," delivered with a servile bob of the head.

"Our free tub ride!" Mopsy cried out, as she looked at her watch. "It's almost noon! Are we far from the tub docks?"

Not far, I assured her, and cautioned her against using such derisory terms as "tub" and "bucket" around the fishermen. These proud fellows do not laugh at jokes about their small leather coracles—called *moas.* Mopsy had her coupon ready. Through clever booking—all their trips are planned in detail a year in advance—the Crimms had received from Tessair a free bottle of skin lotion and a book of valuable coupons, one of which entitled them to a free *moa* ride in Viborra Bay on any weekday before noon, between April 20 and December 5.

Hearty singing told us that the fishing fleet was coming in—and with a good catch! The little round vessels, painted in soft pastel colors and decorated with painted human eyes, gyrated and jostled against one another like bumper cars at the fair as the men struggled to bring them in against the current. Steering a *moa*, or indeed making it go at all, in a particular direction is a difficult art to master.

And noon is not, perhaps, the best time of day to take a *moa* out into the Burning Sea. The sun at meridian is a fearful thing in Viborra. We paddled frantically and our goatskin craft kept spinning around and around in place. There was no breeze. Stinging sweat blurred our vision. (But nights can turn cool in Viborra, so be sure to pack a sweater or light wrap.) Still, you must make the effort, because the only proper way to see the Melanoma Memorial is from the sea.

This is a colossal equestrian statue of the late President Eutropio Melanoma, rising up against a cobalt sky at the end of a long mole, or breakwater. Fabricated of ferro-concrete on site, and standing as high as a nine-story building, it commemorates the long rule (more than forty years) of the beloved old President. It is a robust, lumpy work (what one art critic has called "the apotheosis of portland cement"), and a grand tribute to the man's political genius and "The Year of the Edict"—1949—which is sometimes called "The Year of Decision." The horse is rearing up in a fine capriole, and the presidential sword (giver of victory) is pointed out to sea. A black rubber raven (bird of prophecy) is perched on his shoulder.

The old President was elected over and over again by acclamation and is still fondly remembered here for his disheveled hair and clothing, for his dramatic and alternating acts of mercy and cruelty, and for the mischievous teasing of his ministers, some of whom he made give their reports while running alongside his moving Packard, with the window glass only partly rolled down. He also undertook to teach lawyers humility, giving his Supreme Court justices the choice of working for three months of the year in the nitrate mines or serving for three months on road-repair crews, wearing red vests and flagging traffic.

At the Café Tessa, a waterfront bar where dissident jugglers and poets meet to grumble and conspire, you will hear that it was the old man's simple tastes in food and his modest pleasures that most endeared him to his people. One of his favorite amusements was to prowl stealthily about the grounds of the presidential mansion with a garden hose, squirting water on cats and servants, and taking gopher colonies by surprise with sudden inundations of their little underground apartments. At night, after a light supper of a single warmed-over bean cake, he liked to retire to the ballroom for an hour or so of running his fist up and down the white keys of a piano.

Something of a prodigy, Melanoma consolidated his power early on, as quite a young man, by disposing of all likely claimants to the office of chief executive. His father and his infant sons he garroted personally. With his brothers, uncles, and nephews, for whom he felt less natural affection, he was more severe, condemning each of them to a protracted, popeyed death in leather harness, dragging ore carts out of the nitrate pits. But he had overlooked someone in his planning, and so the Melanoma era came to an appalling, not to say sizzling, end in 1979, when his only legitimate daughter, Arses Melanoma Lupus, plunged a white-hot poker into the sunken belly of the ascetic old man. The puncture was mortal. Arses's husband, Crispo Lupus, then succeeded to the presidency, after a brief scuffle with guards on the veranda of the mansion.

Elderly firebrand poets at the Café Tessa, whose subsidies were sharply cut back by the new administration, will tell you that Crispo Lupus lacks *rhampa* and a masterly hand; that he neglects his duties; that he is not a man of bold strokes, of deeds you could sing. They say he does nothing but fool about with his hunting birds, leaving the much feared Arses in full and very active command at the mansion. Under the Lupus regime, the poets say, the people of Viborra have actually become shorter and uglier, and everybody's hair has gone all gummy. Whatever the truth of the matter, it is certain that Lupus has never captured the hearts of his countrymen in the way that Melanoma did with his Edict of 1949, by which decree the listings in the telephone directory were alphabetized.

* * *

Anyone can direct you to the Café Tessa, which is situated near the base of the natural rock pinnacle known as the Needle of Desolation, and just around the corner from another downtown landmark, the Arses Lupus Black Pavilion, or the Dark Hall of the People. This very modern structure, with lots and lots of darkish glass, is something of a barren shaft itself, rising up in bleak splendor under the gentian bowl of the sky. The thing fairly takes your breath away, and in Chick Jardine's humble opinion there is nothing in New York to touch it for sharp angularity of line and blankness of aspect.

It is here, in the spacious atrium of the Hall, that Carnival season begins each year with the auction of public offices and preferments. Nimmo Lupus, the playboy son of Crispo and the imperious Arses, presides over the bidding in the red silk robes of Grand Chamberlain, to which is affixed the golden sunburst badge of Inspector of Libraries. He is usually accompanied on these state occasions by his youngest son, Bungo Lupus, a cute toddler, who, all decked out in a little policeman's uniform, sits dozing on his father's knee. One frequent bidder told me that he took the limp Bungo at first for a dummy! The poets say that Bungo has the same weak eyes as Nimmo.

So—Carnival in Viborra. Should you go? Yes, but be prepared for something a little different. The revels in Viborra proper are nothing at all like those in Rio and New Orleans. There are no gala parades or balls. The people simply go out at night wearing dog masks or dog helmets and mill about in darkness and eerie silence. They take measured steps and move in slow tidal fashion up and down the narrow cobbled streets. Now and then they stop and look at one another, nose to nose, without speaking, rather like dogs, for some little time. And when the shuffling stops— such stillness! The ceremony, it seems, is not an ancient one, but I have been unable to find out when or how it started, or just what the point of it is. The Long March of the Dogs, they call it, though there is no canine friskiness about the thing; it is really more like a shambling procession of cattle. Bring comfortable walking shoes. Leave your dog helmets and dog masks at home, as they will only be confiscated at the airport. Only those made in Viborra (with longish snouts) and certified by the Central Committee can be worn in the March.

Things are livelier, of course, across the Bal in transpontine Viborra, where, every night at midnight, there is the celebrated Stampede of the Drunks, around and around the Plaza of Louts. It is not for everyone, this stumbling, boisterous race, but to say you have run with the international drunks on the River Bal—well, take it straight from Chick Jardine, few travel claims confer more prestige these days. Your application for the Stampede of the Drunks, with passport-grade photo and $200 entry fee, must be made to the Central Committee six months in advance.

All other events are open to the public. Everyone (with orange bracelet) can join in the frolic around the fountain and in the reflecting pool and along the narrow cobbled streets radiating out from the Nimmo Arch. Wear casual clothes. Beware the melon ambush. Take care when rounding corners or you are likely to have a watermelon or some rotten and unfamiliar vegetable smashed down on your head—with what seems to me unnecessary force. Stay well clear of those roving gangs of hooded urchins who call themselves the Red Ants; they will seize you and gag you and truss you up and scrawl Red Ant slogans across your belly and then toss you about on a stretched bull hide. Keep a sharp lookout for boulders and burning tires rolling down the hillside streets. There is a certain amount of capering around bonfires. After the first night the streets are littered with putrefying vegetable fragments. There are one or two deaths each night and a good deal of broken glass.

In recent years the season has been spoiled a bit by nightly typhoons, which are sometimes followed by predawn tsunamis. The poets claim that something has gone wrong with the prevailing winds, and they blame the unholy Arses and her practices in necromancy. Despite this, the merrymakers still come in swarms, and I must caution you that there is a lot of shameless overbooking in Viborra during Carnival. You may be forced to double up in your hotel room with unsavory strangers, and sleep in shifts. "Hot bunking," as we call it in the trade. Three years ago,

I am informed, the Morono Palace was so jam-packed with louts that the hotel itself subsided eight and a half inches into the mud.

* * *

Poor Mopsy was ready to drop. It was just after one in the morning and we were weary and stuffed. We were fairly waterlogged with oysters. But we still had a gratis supper coming, and the dining hall at the Pan-Lupus didn't open until 2:00 A.M. (Note well: It is not fashionable to sup in Viborra before about 2:30 A.M. This by way of showing you do not have to rise early.)

What to do? Fighting off sleep, and determined not to be done out of any meal that was due us, we gave each other playful slaps and dashed cold water in our faces. We went to the bar to kill some time and found it filled with English travel writers in suede shoes and speckled green suits. What a scene! They were laughing and scribbling and asking how to spell "ogive" and brazenly cribbing long passages of architectural arcana from their John Ruskin handbooks, which are issued with their union cards.

"Look, that sod Jardine is here too!" one of them shouted. Then he and the others came crowding around, seething with bitter envy of me and my *Chick's Wheel of Adjectives*, a handy rotating cardboard device, which, at $24.95, was such a super hit with the travel journalists at our winter conference in Macao. Mopsy feared for my safety as the chaps bumped up against me and heaped childish ridicule on my cluster of lapel pins, tokens of numerous professional honors. A serene and scornful smile soon sent them reeling back in confusion.

We left them there, stewing in resentment and muttering over their pink gins, and at two on the dot we were standing first in line outside the dining-hall doors. From campaniles all over town the bells of Viborra were striking the hour, with paired thuds and thumps of slightly different pitch. I was explaining how these strange dead bells are cast from a curious alloy of pumice and zinc when Mopsy silenced me with a raised hand.

"No—listen," she said. "Those—bells. They seem somehow to know we're off tomorrow on the morning Fokker. They seem to be—saying something."

"But I don't understand," said Jason. "How do you mean, Mopsy? Just what is it they—seem to say?"

"Those—sounds on the wind. Can't you hear? 'Come back!' they seem to say. 'Come back, Mopsy! Come back, Jason! Come back, Chick! Come back to the sparkling shores of the Burning Sea! Come back in time to a more gracious and all but forgotten way of life in the enchanting old city of Viborra nestled snugly in a sapphire cove 'neath the vast rotunda of an indigo sky!'"

The Atlantic, December 1992

I Don't Talk Service No More

Once you slip past that nurses' station in the east wing of D-3, you can get into the library at night easy enough if you have the keys. They keep the phone locked up in a desk drawer there but if you have the keys you can get it out and make all the long-distance calls you want to for free, and smoke all the cigarettes you want to, as long as you open a window and don't let the smoke pile up so thick inside that it sets off the smoke alarm. You don't want to set that thing to chirping. The library is a small room. There are three walls of paperback westerns and one wall of windows and one desk.

I called up Neap down in Orange, Texas, and he said, "I live in a bog now." I hadn't seen him in forty-odd years and I woke him up in the middle of the night and that was the first thing out of his mouth. "My house is sinking. I live in a bog now." I told him I had been thinking about the Fox Company Raid and thought I would give him a ring. We called it the Fox Company Raid, but it wasn't a company raid or even a platoon raid, it was just a squad of us, with three or four extra guys carrying pump shotguns for trench work. Neap said he didn't remember me. Then he said he did remember me, but not very well. He said, "I don't talk service no more."

We had been in reserve and had gone back up on the line to relieve some kind of pacifist division. Those boys had something like "Live and Let Live" on their shoulder patches. When they went out on patrol at night, they faked it. They would go out about a hundred yards and lie down in the paddies, and doze off, too, like some of the night nurses on D-3. When they came back, they would say they had been all the way over to the Chinese outposts but had failed to engage the enemy. They failed night after night. Right behind the line the mortar guys sat around in their mortar pits and played cards all day. I don't believe they even had aiming stakes set up around their pits. They hated to fire those tubes because the Chinese would fire right back.

It was a different story when we took over. The first thing we did was go all the way over to the Chinese main line. On the first dark night we left our trenches and crossed the paddies and slipped past their outposts and went up the mountainside and crawled into their trench line before they knew what was up. We shot up the place pretty good and blew two bunkers, or tried to, and got out of there fast with three live prisoners. One was a young officer. Those trenches had a sour smell. There was a lot of noise. The Chinese fired off yellow flares and red flares, and they hollered and sprayed pistol bullets with their burp guns and threw those wooden potato-masher grenades with the cast-iron heads. The air was damp and some of them didn't go off. Their fuses weren't very good. Their grenade fuses would sputter and go out. We were in and out of there before they knew what had hit them. It could happen to anybody. They were good soldiers and just happened to get caught by surprise, by sixteen boys from Fox Company. You think of Chinese soldiers as boiling all around you like fire ants, but once you get into their trench line, not even the Chinese army can put up a front wider than one man.

Neap said, "I don't talk service no more," but he didn't hang up on me. Sometimes they do, it being so late at night when I call. Mostly they're glad to hear from me and we'll sit in the dark and talk service for a long time. I sit here in the dark at the library desk smoking my Camels and I think they sit in the dark too, on the edges of their beds with their bare feet on the floor.

I told Neap service was the only thing I did talk, and that I had the keys now and was talking service coast to coast every night. He said his house was in bad shape. His wife had something wrong with her too. I didn't care about that stuff. His wife wasn't on the Fox Company Raid. I didn't care whether his house was level or not but you like to be polite and I asked him if his house was sinking even all around. He said no, it was settling bad at the back, to where they couldn't get through the back door, and the front was all lifted up in the air, to where they had to use a little stepladder to get up on their front porch.

You were supposed to get a week of meritorious R and R in Hong Kong if you brought in a live prisoner. We dragged three live prisoners all the way back from the Chinese main line of resistance and one was

an officer and I never got one day of R and R in Hong Kong. Sergeant
Zim was the only one who ever did get it that I know of. On the regular
kind of R and R you went to Kyoto, which was all right, but it wasn't
meritorious R and R. I asked Neap if he knew of anyone besides Zim
who got meritorious R and R in Hong Kong. He said he didn't even
know Zim got it.

He asked me if I was in a nut ward. I asked him how many guys he
could name who went on the Fox Company Raid, not counting him and
me and Zim. All he could come up with was Dill, Vick, Bogue, Ball, and
Sipe. I gave him eight more names real fast, and the towns and states
they came from. "Now who's the nut? Who's soft in the head now, Neap?
Who knows more about the Fox Company Raid, you or me?" I didn't say
that to him because you try to be polite when you can. I didn't have to
say it. You could tell I had rattled him pretty good, the way I whipped off
all those names.

He asked me how much disability money I was drawing down. I told
him and he said it was a hell of a note that guys in the nut ward were
drawing down more money than he was on Social Security. I told him
Dill was dead, and Gott. He said yeah, but Dill was on Okinawa in 1945,
in the other war, and was older than us. He told me a little story about
Dill. I had heard it before. Dill was talking to the captain outside the
command-post bunker, telling him about the time on Okinawa he had
guided a flamethrower tank across open ground, to burn a Jap field gun
out of a cave. Dill said, "They was a whole bunch of far come out of
that thang in a hurry, Skipper." Neap laughed over the phone. He said,
"I still laugh every time I think about that. 'They was a whoooole bunch
of far come out of that thang in a hurry, Skipper.' The way he said it,
you know, Dill."

Neap thought I must be having a lot of trouble tracking people down.
I haven't had any trouble to speak of. Except for me and Foy and Rust,
who are far from home, and Sipe, who is a fugitive from justice, everybody else went back home and stayed there. They left home just that
one time. Neap was surprised to hear that Sipe was on the lam, at his
age. How fast could Sipe be moving these days, at his age? Neap said it
was Dill and Sipe who grabbed those prisoners and that Zim had nothing
to do with it. I told him Zim had something to do with getting us over
there and back. He said yeah, Zim was all right, but he didn't do no more

in that stinking trench line than we did, and so how come he got meritorious R and R in Hong Kong and we didn't? I couldn't answer that question. I can't find anyone who knows the answer to that. I told him I hadn't called up Zim yet, over in Niles, Michigan. I wanted to have the squad pretty much accounted for before I made my report to him. Neap said, "Tell Zim I'm living on a mud flat." I told him he was the last one I had to call up before Zim. I put Neap at the bottom of my list because I couldn't remember much about him.

I can still see the faces of those boys who went on the Fox Company Raid, except that Neap's face is not very clear to me. It drifts just out of range. He said he could feel his house going down while we were talking there on the phone. He said his house was going down fast now, and with him and his wife in it. It sounded to me like the Neaps were going all the way down.

He asked me how it was here. He wanted to know how it was in this place and I told him it wasn't so bad. It's not so bad here if you have the keys. For a long time I didn't have the keys.

The Atlantic, May 1996

The Wind Bloweth Where It Listeth

The editors are spiking most of my copy now, unread. One has de-scribed it as "hopeless crap." My master's degree means nothing to this pack of half-wits at the *Blade*. My job is hanging by a thread. But Frankie, an assistant city editor, is not such a bad boss and it was she who, out of the blue, gave me this choice assignment. I was startled. A last chance to make good?

Frankie said, "Get some bright quotes for a change, okay? Or make some up. Not so much of your dreary exposition. Not so many clauses. Get to the point at once. And keep it short for a change, okay? Now, buzz on out to the new Pecking Center on Warehouse Road, near the Loopdale Cutoff. Scoot. Take the brown Gremlin. But check the water in the radiator!"

An introductory word or two on the subject at hand will not be out of place before we come to the exciting work now going forward inside the new Hazel Perkins Jenkins Pecking Center at 75002 Warehouse Road, near the Loopdale Cutoff.

Readers of the *Blade* will recall an old theory/prophecy that went as follows: a hundred monkeys pecking away at random on a hundred typewriters will eventually reproduce the complete works of William Shakespeare. The terms may be a little dated, what with the typewriters, and that modest round number, meant to suggest something like "many," or even "infinite." And one monkey, of course, would suffice, given enough time and an immortal monkey. In any case, the chance duplication would require the monkeys—let us say a brigade of mon-keys—to peck out 38 excellent plays and some 160 poems of one met-rical beat or another.

Is the musty old prophecy at last being fulfilled? We now have mil-lions of monkeys pecking away more or less at random, day and night, on millions of personal computer keyboards. We have "word processors," the Internet, e-mail, and "the information explosion." Futurists at our leading universities tell us the day is at hand when, out of this maelstrom of words, a glorious literature must emerge, and indeed flourish. So far, however, as of today, Tuesday, September 14, late afternoon, the tally still seems to be fixed at:

Shakespeare: 198, Monkeys: 0

They plead for more time, for just one more extension. And then another. We are all familiar with their public-service announcements on television in which they make these irritating appeals.

Perhaps the goal has been set too high. Let us then leave the Bard for a moment and look at some even more disturbing numbers, from UNESCO's ten-year world survey (1994–2004) of not very good plays written in blank verse, and not very good sonnets, villanelles, sestinas, elegies, and odes. The result:

Not very good blank verse plays, sonnets, etc.: 219,656

That figure was widely reported and has not been seriously disputed. Less well known—hardly known at all—is this tidbit, which was buried deep in the appendix of the thick UNESCO volume:

Not very good odes, blank verse plays, etc., composed by monkeys: 0

* * *

So again, nothing, no blip of art from random pecking, good or bad, nor even of proto-art, unless one counts the humming, haunting, and hypnotic page of *z*'s which turned up last year in Paris. Never much taken with Shakespeare themselves, the French await the appearance and reappearance of their own Francophone glories. They wait for art to happen. Their central clearing house has been established in Marseilles, at the international headquarters of Peckers Without Borders.

As for the recent American commotion over the DeWitt Sheets affair, it has largely and mercifully subsided. Young Sheets, the *Blade* reader will recall, is the Memphis tyke, four years of age and illiterate, who was said to have pecked out with his tiny tapered fingers, uncoached, on a personal computer, this complete line from one of the three weird sisters in the tragedy of *Macbeth*: "And, like a rat without a tail, I'll do, I'll do, and I'll do."

* * *

It was complete even to Shakespeare's rather excessive punctuation. The Sheets woman, mother of DeWitt, later made a full, weeping confession to the fraud. Later still, alleging coercion, she recanted. She insists once again that DeWitt alone hit on the rat line. The woman is currently reported to be traveling about the country in a small car with young Sheets. She presents him on stage in his little professor's rig—gown, mortarboard—at state fairs and rock concerts, where he recites selected passages from time-honored soliloquies.

Now, without more ado, we come to the amazing new enterprise out on Warehouse Road, near the Loopdale Cutoff, where organized ape-pecking has finally arrived in our town—with bells on! In a *Blade* exclusive, I can take *Blade* readers inside the strange writing factory, to which I gained immediate entry with a flourish of my *Blade* press card. The "line chief," a sort of superintendent, was favorably impressed by the card, stupefied even, by the legal-looking scrollwork and the sunburst seal, which seems to radiate some terrifying powers of the state. He granted me full floor privileges.

I spoke there on Tuesday with some of the monkeys. Row upon row, they were ranged about at their pecking stands, in a high, open, oblong room, something like a gymnasium. The first one I approached, actually a surly mandrill, said, "Beat it. Can't you see I'm pecking?" The line chief came scuttling over to suggest that I put off all interviews until the mid-morning break.

I wandered around in my socks. This shoeless, padding-about policy had to do with preserving quiet, rather than from any Oriental sense of delicacy. Eavesdropping is a big part of my trade (I hold a master's degree in tale-bearing from one of the better Ivy League schools), but I saw no opportunities here. All was pecking with this crew, or a furious clicking.

White placards were posted along the walls exhorting the monkeys to STAY IN YOUR SEATS! PLEASE! At the upper end of the long room, on a dais, a string quartet was playing, softly, a medley of Sousa marches. Above the musicians, high on the wall, there was an oil portrait of the

poet and billionaire widow herself, Mrs. Hazel Perkins Jenkins, in her signature white turban. She smiles down on her workshop monkeys.

Mrs. Perkins Jenkins is, of course, their patroness. All of these
Pecking Centers—thirty-seven, to date, nationwide—are lavishly funded
by the Hazel Perkins Jenkins Foundation for the Arts, in Seattle. She is
a widow many times over. Of her five husbands, all rich and all now dead,
only one, Jenkins, professed any love for—or even the slightest interest
in—poetry. After his death she was saddened to learn, on flipping
through his diaries, that Jenkins himself had been faking the passion all
along. "I don't get it," he had confessed, in a number of entries. "But
then men were deceivers ever," she said, taking the disappointment in
stride. "Poor Jenkins, yes, it now seems that he too had a tin ear, but he
was only trying to please me. He had his quirks, as we all know." This
was a vague reference to the declining days of Jenkins, when he annoyed
ladies on city buses as he roamed aimlessly around Seattle.

There, in the drizzle of Puget Sound, atop the Foundation's south
tower, is the famous Shakespeare Countdown Clock, some thirty feet in
diameter. The minute hand stands, or appears to be standing, at eight
minutes before midnight—and The New Day. A few veteran observers
say they can perceive constant, unbroken movement of the hand, though
conceding it to be slight.

As it happened, I was looking at my own watch when, at 10:15 sharp,
the musicians stopped their scraping abruptly in mid-passage, and there
came two blasts from a Klaxon horn. I gave a start and an involuntary
and embarrassing little chirp of alarm. It was the morning break. The
peckers rose as one and stepped away from their stations. Heads thrown
back, mouths agape, they squirted soothing drops of balm into their eyes.
They flexed their simian fingers and twisted their necks about. They performed a few side-straddle hops in unison.

Trolley carts appeared, laden with bananas, grapes, and assorted
nuts, less than fifty percent peanuts. There were small club sandwiches,
crustless and elegant, and pitchers of organic fruit juices.

These monkeys were, for the most part, good-natured little fellows,
proud of their work and eager to talk about it. They are paid, I learned,
by the "swatch," this being a standard print-out sheet densely spattered
with letters of the alphabet, numerals, and the various punctuation sym-
bols. The peckers are penalized (token fine) for leaving spaces between

the characters, and rewarded (token bonus) when one of their swatches, seen from a little distance, gives the appearance of a near-solid block of ink, similar to *The Congressional Record.*

Their work is transmitted instantly to Seattle, where it is given intense scrutiny, line by line. And there is a redundancy arrangement to insure that nothing pecked is ever quite lost, into the void. For backup swatches are also printed out in the local Pecking Centers, then gathered, compressed, and bound into bales, like cotton. These monstrous, cubic haikus are shipped out weekly, air freight, to the Foundation's 2A Clearing House, which is a hangar leased from the Boeing company.

It is there that the American pecking harvest undergoes a final scanning, in the search for words and coherent snatches of language. A long white banner hangs across the cavernous work bay, reading, THE WIND BLOWETH WHERE IT LISTETH. The scanners, known as "swatch auditors," are 720 elderly men in baseball caps. They work in three shifts around the clock. They are paid well and seated comfortably on inflated doughnut cushions.

During breaks the auditors play harmless pranks on one another. These antics once caught the indulgent eye of Mrs. Perkins Jenkins, who was looking on from an observation gallery, and thereby hangs the tale of how her most celebrated poem, and by far her shortest one, "just popped into my head." It was not, that is, fabricated. The two stanzas simply came to her, suddenly and all of a piece, complete with title, "The Levity of Old Men." She dictated the words to her secretary at once, before they could evaporate. Such was the origin of this gem of the modern anthologies, and thus the grand old lady's unwavering trust in her muse.

My interviews went well enough until I came upon another touchy mandrill, Red Kilgore by name, as I could see by the prism nameplate on his pecking stand. He had been watching me, glowering.

"So," he said. "What is this thing you have about monkeys?"

"Well, I do, you know, associate monkeys with chattering and gibbering and shrieking."

"You don't approve of chattering?"

"I approve of chatting."

"Cute distinction. Do you find me gibbering now?"

"Not at all, no. But there on your screen, just a minute ago, I did see something that appeared to be, excuse me, gibberish."

"How many of our swatches have you actually read?"

"Some. A few. I extrapolate freely, of course. Like poll takers. It's an accepted practice."

"I suppose you think all that stuff you churn out at your paper is a lot better than the stuff we churn out here."

"Well, it is better, yes. But then we still use typewriters at the *Blade*."

"Say what?"

"Manual typewriters. They don't hum at you like the electric ones. And the ribbons are cheaper."

"But *typewriters*."

"They give you black words fixed hard on white paper."

"And that's good in some way?"

"Good enough. There are critics who say that things written with quivering cathode rays on greenish luminescent tubes have a different tone altogether. A loose, thin, garrulous feel."

"Tone. Feel. You seem to be saying to me that all those old Smith-Coronas in your office are so many Stradivaris."

"We use Underwoods and Royals."

"When will this report of yours be in the paper?"

"Tomorrow, with any luck."

"Will my name be in it?"

"Yes."

"On what page?"

"I don't know."

"What will the headline say? So I don't have to wade through all the other junk."

"Again, not my department. Probably something like 'Monkey Business.'"

"Look here, I know I'm wasting my breath, but let me try to explain something. Are you familiar with the law of large numbers?"

"That law, no, it doesn't ring a bell."

"Well, the idea is that a great many little uncertainties—a long series of coin-flippings, say—will miraculously add up to one big certainty. You will get half heads and half tails."

"How does that apply?"

"Order from disorder, you see. The moving finger of grace, unseen."

"Then you are in the disorder business here."

"We are in the volume business, sir. Moving product. And allow me to tell you this, that a certain brute quantity can attain a special quality all its own. We are not the least bit interested in your old elitist notion of writing as some sort of algebra."

"But Red, listen to yourself. Here you are speaking to me in that algebra."

"Not for long. Vamoose."

My article—this article—was much longer. Two editors slashed away on it, turn and turn about. But it was not spiked. What remained, now somewhat garbled, was actually set in type and scheduled to appear in the Sunday feature section. I was delighted. On Friday, however, the *Blade* went broke and out of business. There was no Sunday edition. Neither was there any money left for our final salary checks, let alone severance pay.

The closing out was poorly managed, overall. A scrap-iron dealer hauled away our typewriters. They were flung into his dump truck from a third-floor window of the city room. Even some of our clothes were seized, with the lawyers for the bank declaring them to be "workplace specific apparel, i.e., company uniforms, and as such, *Blade* assets." Can you imagine—making off with the old coats and ties and *shoes* of newspaper people? Frankie retaliated by stealing the blue Gremlin and keeping it hidden under a tarpaulin in some woods until the legal dust had settled. It was the pick of the litter. The blue one still had two or three hubcaps. It had come to this pass then, with the *Blade*'s ancient flotilla of Gremlins, once so jaunty, and always great favorites of the crowd when they cruised down Main Street in attack formation with the floats and fire trucks of city parades. Frankie picks me up every weekday morning at 7:40 in that blue car. She gives five or six impatient toots of the horn, when one light toot would do. We are both working now as peckers, level three, at the Pecking Center on Warehouse Road, not far from the Loopdale Cutoff, and happily so, I may say. The sheer abandon of it all. A revelation. I had no idea. The joy of writing in torrents. In swatches! By the bale! My master of arts degree means nothing at all to these monkeys and I have come to share their indifference. Red Kilgore was on to something. There is much to be said as well for the largesse of Mrs. Hazel Perkins Jenkins.

At odd moments, Frankie and I will pause in our work and look each other full in the face, then break out laughing again, over our old non-sense of writing by design. All that misplaced striving. We laugh till our eyes water up. Ever bold, Frankie said her formal goodbye to artifice some weeks ago, and this, today, is mine. We may have another little an-nouncement quite soon.

Oxford American, Winter 2005

Four

MEMOIR

Combinations of Jacksons

I made my first experiments in breathing underwater at the age of nine, in 1943. It was something I needed to learn in life so as to be ready to give my pursuing enemies the slip. At that time they were Nazi spies and Japanese saboteurs.

The trick looked simple enough in the movie serials, which pulled me along from one Saturday to the next with such chapter titles as "Fangs of Doom!" and "In the Scorpion's Lair!" First you cut a reed. You put one end of the reed in your mouth and lay face up, very still, on the bottom of a shallow stream. The other end was projected above the surface of the stream, and through this hollow shaft, as you lay buried alive in water, you *breathed*.

Agents of the Axis Powers were never far behind me. I could slow them a little with pinecone grenades, but I couldn't stop them. They came crashing through the woods firing their Lugers at me as I raced barefooted for the reed beds of Beech Creek, a last hope. If I could get there in time to make my arrangements, then the agents in their stupid fury would overlook the life-giving reed, one among so many, and, with their boots splashing down eight inches away from my rigid underwater body, go stupidly on their way downstream.

My attempts to bring this off took place in Cypress Creek and Smackover Creek, too—"smackover" being an Arkansas rendering of "chemin couvert," covered path, or road. These and Beech Creek were the swimming streams nearest to my home town, at the time, of Mount Holly, in Union County, Arkansas, which adjoins Union Parish, Louisiana. The name dates from the territorial days of the 1820s, when "Union" had a pleasing ring to it in the Jacksonian South, where the many sons of Jack came to settle and multiply.

Reeds grew here in abundance, in ponds and swamps and along creek banks, or what I took to be reeds, but they were the wrong kind of reeds, if in fact they were reeds. The green ones weren't hollow. The brown ones, the dead and withered stalks, were somewhat hollow but too thin to carry much air, not even enough to sustain a gasping kind of life in a skinny little boy. They also tended to collapse, like wet paper drinking straws, with the first sharp intake of breath. In or out of the water, you couldn't breathe through our reeds.

Our quicksand was a bust too, or I would have lured those running men to their deaths in the slough near Cypress Creek. Not Cypress Slough or the Slough of Despond or of anything else. That dark marsh wasn't big enough or distinctive enough to have a proper name; it was just "the slew." When I had led the men there and they were stuck fast in the gray mud, I would have looked on from a hump of firm ground, deaf to their pleas, refusing to hold out a pole to them, waiting—will these spies never sink?—until the earth had swallowed them whole. It couldn't have worked out that way though, because our quicksand, or quickmud, while quivering nicely underfoot, had no lethal depth, and may even have been slightly buoyant, and therapeutic to boot. I could never manage to sink more than about knee-deep in it.

Bamboo ("cane," we called it) was more promising than reeds, and we had plenty of that in the canebrakes. These woody shafts were thicker and stronger than reeds, and almost hollow, if not quite. Inside, at each circular joint, there was a partial blockage of some white pithy matter. With a long rattail file and a good deal of poking and blowing, it took me about five minutes to clear the pith. This was more like it. Now I had a sturdy and serious breathing tube, made on the spot from the materials at hand. I was man, the toolmaker.

Still, questions remained. My knife would be there, ready, in my pocket (or one of a series of knives, two-blade Barlows mostly, which I kept losing)—ready for cutting reeds and cane, for carving crude, non-returning boomerangs, for slicing two neat little drainage Xs across snake-bite punctures, for cutting off the sputtering ends of fuses leading to well-marked kegs of BLASTING POWDER planted in the bowels of hydroelectric dams, for cutting loose the ropes from any female reporters I might come across who had been left bound and gagged in remote cabins—ready for any wartime emergency. My Barlow was at the service of the nation. So much for the knife.

But was it likely that I would have a rattail file handy? Or—with a pack of killers at my heels, led by a tall man who ran with his monocle in place—the necessary five minutes, undisturbed, for all that reaming and poking of pith? Making every allowance for that, would my bamboo breathing tube, standing stark upright in the shallows of Smackover Creek, really fool anyone? It looked just like a breathing tube.

The war was much on my mind in those days, and it was almost entirely the one being fought on movie screens and in the pulp pages of "funny books," known as comic books in other parts of the country. Both names were misleading for the kind I liked, the ones featuring costumed vigilantes who made violent swoops on spy rings and gang hideouts, with no Miranda palaver. Along with Superman and Batman, there were many others, now largely forgotten, such as Bulletman, Plastic Man, The Sandman, Doll Man (a fighting homunculus about six inches tall, in a red cape), The Human Torch, Daredevil, Blue Beetle, Captain Marvel, Captain Midnight, and Captain America. Under any name the books were quite a bargain early on, at sixty-four pages in color for a dime. Or a kind of color. The palette was limited; Superman had blue hair. I never tired of the repetitive stories or the familiar scenes that were enacted over and over again.

> LOIS: But wait, Superman! What about my scoop?
> SUPERMAN: (Bounding skyward) No time for that now, Lois!
> I'm off to scramble some—YEGGS!!
> LOIS: (Tiny fists on hips) Well, of all th—!!??
> * * *

The course of events in the early part of the war, the real war, was much too confusing for me to follow. My picture of the fighting in Europe, vivid if false, was of two great armies, and only two, facing each other at some one fixed place. Like many generals, I was fighting the last war. The armies were locked in constant battle, night and day, winter and summer. The din never ceased, and there was a lot of smoke. I may have picked up the smoke from a popular country song of the time, which still chimes out in my head every two or three years, as though from a long tape loop.

There'll be smoke on the water
On the land and the sea

When our armee and navee
Overtake the enemee.

The only movement was a certain ponderous wavering of the battle line. One side would at last falter and give way altogether, and that would be the end. I knew we would win. A great-uncle by the name of Satterfield Fielding had assured me of that.

I was only eight years old but I remember the day well, early in 1942, when he told me the war would be over in ninety days—that we would sink the Japanese fleet in no time, just as we had taken care of the Spanish fleet at Manila Bay in 1898, the work of a few hours. He also told me that if I would dip a brand of snuff called Garrett Scotch, I would never get TB, but that Garrett Sweet was no good and I would do well to leave it alone.

Uncle Sat shot deer the year round, like Robin Hood, in season and out, as the whim or the need moved him, and he may well have been the last man in America who without being facetious called food "vittles" ("victuals," a perfectly good word, and correctly pronounced "vittles," but for some reason thought to be countrified and comical). He was a strong and fluent talker with far-ranging opinions. Attention wandered in the family as he ran on, except when he spoke from experience. There would be bits of hunting lore ("A real turkey could never win a turkey-calling contest") and tips on growing unfashionable corn (nonhybrid) and bumblebee cotton (hill cotton—stunted, unfluffy bolls) and on the best ways of dynamiting fish ("dinnamite," he called it) in the Saline River and Hurricane Creek.

There was some sort of family gathering on that day at his farm, small but his own, in the backwoods of Grant County, Arkansas, and everyone was scoffing and laughing at his notions about the war. Always impatient with him, groaning and rolling her eyes, his sister Emma (my grandmother) could be counted on to check him in his longer flights with "Oh, why don't you just hush, Sat. All you know is what you read in *The Sheridan Headlight*." Wounding indeed, if true.

He came out onto the back porch alone, already angry, and caught me dropping feathers into his water well. I was hanging over the upper framework of the well, dropping chicken feathers and guinea feathers one by one, to watch how they floated about on the surface of the still round pool down there. He gave me a shaking for feathering his drinking water, and then took me into his kitchen and showed me some blurred newspaper maps, perhaps from the *Headlight*.

They were scale maps of Japan and the United States, comparison maps, side by side. Here were the Japanese home islands, a little ragged chain of fragments, mere bits of flotsam. Over here, all of a piece, was the great continental mass that was the United States of America. A revelation. No one had told me about this. Uncle Sat watched me closely to see if I alone out of all these dense Fieldings, Waddells, and Portises could grasp his strategic point. It was clear enough to me: a small country had foolishly attacked a big one. It was fangs of doom. There was nothing more to worry about.

And yet I did worry. The war went on and on. Enemy agents with the faces of rats and hogs appeared to be gaining the upper hand in the funny books I read so greedily. These busy men were all around us, wrecking trains, scattering tacks on our highways, stealing the plans for our Boeing P-26 and our Brewster Buffalo, pouring deadly poisons into our city reservoirs, always from a "vial" or some curiously small bottle. They tempted us to waste gasoline and whispered that we need not save cooking fats for the munitions industry if we didn't feel like it. They changed some of our most brilliant scientists into morons with a colorless and odorless moron gas, pumped into the scientists' laboratories by way of a hand-bellows rig and a piece of rubber tubing.

* * *

It was possible to lose, as I was reminded whenever I saw my great-grandfather, Alexander Waddell, usually at family reunions, where he would be seated on display in the parlor of a great-aunt in Pine Bluff, holding a walking stick between his knees with his purplish hands. "Uncle Alec," as he was known generally, in and out of the family, was born in 1847, the same year as Jesse James, and, like Jesse, had fought for the Confederate States of America as a boy soldier, though not as a regular.

I don't know how zealous he was for the cause—enough, at least, to take up arms in defense of Jefferson County and the rest of southern Arkansas. The blood was up, at varying degrees of heat, out of a vast agricultural tedium from East Texas to Virginia, and the (white) boys walking behind mules and middlebuster ploughs rallied to repel what they saw as the invader of their new sovereign nation. President Lincoln had called out his troops to put down what he saw as an insurrection, "by combinations of Jacksons too powerful to be suppressed by the ordinary course of judicial proceedings." I think he wrote "combinations of Jacksons" in that momentous proclamation, but I quote from memory.

The southern boys responded to such recruiting notices as this one, placed in a Memphis newspaper, *The Appeal*, by Nathan Bedford Forrest, the rich slave trader and legendary cavalry commander, who was to have twenty-nine horses shot from under him:

200 Recruits Wanted!

I will receive 200 able-bodied men if they will present themselves at my headquarters by the first of June with good horse and gun. I wish none but those who desire to be actively engaged. My headquarters for the present is at Corinth, Miss. Come on, boys, if you want a heap of fun and to kill some Yankees.

N. B. Forrest
Colonel, Commanding
Forrest's Regiment

I suspect that the first part of that was written or edited by a meddlesome young staff officer, chewing on a pencil. ("Can't have *wish* here twice in a row, so I'll make it, what—*desire*, yes—the second time around.") The last sentence, shifting into the imperative mood, is Forrest himself, forthright as a pirate.

Uncle Alec had been a county and probate judge, and he still had his wits about him in 1943—no mismated shoes, no long hesitations in speech, groping for a name or some common noun. But his memories of the Civil War, or the ones he saw fit to recall in mixed company, ran mostly to jocular anecdotes, at least in my hearing. I didn't have sense enough or interest enough to ask him questions, and I was further impaired by lockjaw in the presence of very old people. Apart from the comic stories, three things that he said about the war have stuck in my head.

1. That his duties as a young private, and a small one at that, were, for the most part, watering and saddling the horses, and riding off here and there at a gallop on a partly blooded horse, a fast horse, with messages.

(A great drama must have a young messenger appearing briefly onstage, to bring some piece of devastating news and move the story along.)

2. How a heavy bank of fog settled low over the battleground at Jenkins' Ferry on April 30, 1864, and how the steady Yankees from Wisconsin and Iowa, backed up there against the flooding Saline River but not lacking for ammunition, stopped one frontal assault after another by firing blindly but effectively in volleys, through the fog and under it. The Arkansas troops made a try, and then the Missouri and Texas troops, 6,000 men all told. All were cut down or sent reeling back. In a matter of hours they took a thousand casualties. (Missouri, a slave state, didn't secede, despite the efforts of the governor, a Democrat named Claiborne Jackson. Nor did Kentucky, another slave state. But they did provide the southern armies with many fine soldiers—many more wore blue—and the eleven-state Confederacy did claim them as part of the new federation. Thus the auspicious—it was vainly hoped—thirteen stars on the battle flag, in this "second war for independence.")

3. How, after that fight, and after the Union soldiers had made their escape across the river on a shaky "India-rubber" pontoon bridge, hundreds of abandoned mules were running loose in the canebrakes, big 1,200-pound U.S. Army mules—which is to say free tractors for the destitute local farmers, or such few as were left, and them mostly old men, women, and children.

That Federal army of 12,000 men, commanded by Major General Frederick Steele, had set out from occupied Little Rock on March 23 for Shreveport, where it was to meet another Union Army column, escorted by a naval armada of sixty-two gunboats and transports with a brigade of U.S. Marines aboard, coming up the Red River in Louisiana. Neither force made it to Shreveport. The trans-Mississippi South, much neglected by Richmond, still had a few kicks left.

Steele was stopped in southern Arkansas at Camden, eighteen miles from Mount Holly. In a series of battles, culminating with the one at Jenkins' Ferry, the Federals were driven all the way back to Little Rock, on short rations and in cold rain and mud. Steele lost 2,750 men on the expedition, along with 635 wagons, 2,500 mules, and "enough horses to mount a brigade of cavalry," and counted himself fortunate. A fast-moving Stonewall Jackson, had one been present, would have cut him off in the rear and bagged the entire lot.

Steele almost had one more casualty in Wild Bill Hickok, a Union scout, who rode into Camden ahead of the army, put on a gray uniform, and did some spying. Something of a regional celebrity even then, he was soon recognized and had to make a run for it, "a bold dash" across the battle lines at Prairie d'Ane, on his horse, Black Nell. One account has him shooting two pursuing Confederate officers as Nell made "a mighty leap" over "an obstruction" (log? rail fence? ditch?). That is, Hickok twisted about in the saddle or stood in the stirrups and turned, cocked and fired his single-action revolver at least twice, and picked off two closing riders on the fly, all this while Nell was airborne. Well, maybe. In any case, it was a bold escape, and "a shout of triumph from the ten thousand troops in line greeted him, and he was the hero of the day."

In the fight at Poison Spring there were some scalpings, when a C.S.A. brigade of Choctaw cavalry clashed with a Federal regiment of black troops, the 1st Kansas (Colored), which had been operating, and plundering, on Choctaw lands in the Indian Territory, later to become Oklahoma. (The "poison spring," now in a state park, was misnamed through a misunderstanding. It still flows and still bears that name, but the unremarkable water isn't toxic or even bad-tasting.)

A white cavalry regiment, the 29th Texas, also carried a grudge against the 1st Kansas troops, who had driven it from the field in an earlier fight at Honey Springs, in the Territory. When the two met again, here at Poison Spring, in Arkansas, the Texans shouted across the lines that they would give no quarter. This time they won, and they gave no quarter. The Texans, the Arkansans, the Choctaws, and the Missourians shot some prisoners and finished off some of the wounded with bayonets and scalping knives. Not for the faint of heart, these late, bitter engagements. Murder and brutalities on both sides were common enough in this remote corner of the war, where it was waged, as the military historian Edwin C. Bearss writes, "with a savagery unheard of in the East." Little was made of it. To those eastern gentlemen in Richmond and Washington, the trans-Mississippi theater of operations wasn't so much a theater as some dim thunder offstage.

* * *

It may be that by 1943 Uncle Alec was just bored with all that, as with many other things, all cold potatoes now, but the memories hadn't evaporated. Long after his death I heard a few things he had told the men

in the family, now a little garbled in the retelling by second and third parties. One said that he had joined a Jefferson County militia unit at the
age of sixteen or seventeen, after his brother Joseph was killed fighting in
Georgia, and that he remained with that unit until the war ended.
Another one said no, that was only partly true, that he and another boy
had later left the militia to ride with what Uncle Alec called "a company"
(troop) of partisan cavalry, raised and commanded by a shadowy Captain
Jonas (or Jonus) Webb, from Pine Bluff (Jefferson County).

This Webb, all business, not much in the chivalry line, carried on
a rough and semi-private little campaign of his own across southern
Arkansas. He did on occasion, at his own convenience, work with the
official C.S.A. command, as at Jenkins' Ferry. A Confederate soldier
named Fine Gordon, in a reminiscence after the war, mentioned Webb
in passing, and darkly enough, as "a mean captain of the Southern
Army at Camden."

Webb's troop and similar bands roamed freely in that last, lawless
year of the war, and were something of a nuisance to both armies, to
say nothing of the local farmers, who were being bled white by foraging
parties demanding food, fodder, livestock, and whatever else they fan-
cied, at gunpoint. Brigadier General Joseph O. (Jo) Shelby, commanding a C.S.A. brigade (and sometimes a division) of Missouri cavalry
in Arkansas, regarded the guerrillas as little better than slackers and
highwaymen, and became so furious with them as to publish a general
warning: "I will enlist you in the Confederate army; or I will drive you
into the Federal ranks. You shall not remain idle spectators of a drama
enacted before your eyes." Here again, I think, we see the hand of a
literary adjutant.

The general did, however, have a soft spot for Quantrill's bush-
whackers, and for one in particular, Frank James, who had saved Shelby
from capture earlier in the war at the Battle of Prairie Grove, Arkansas.
Some twenty years later, in August of 1883, Jo Shelby appeared as a defense witness for Frank, at his murder trial in Gallatin, Missouri. The
charge was that in July of 1881, while robbing a Chicago, Rock Island
and Pacific train with four other men, Alexander Franklin James had
shot and killed a passenger named Frank McMillan. One of the bandits,
Dick Liddil, characterized by the prosecutor as "the least depraved"
member of the James Gang, identified Frank in court as the killer. Perhaps

he was, or it may have been his brother Jesse who did the deed; it was almost certainly Jesse who shot and killed the conductor of the train, one William Westfall. But in 1883 Jesse James was beyond the grasp of the court, having been murdered himself the year before—shot in the back of the head by Bob Ford, of ballad infamy.

It was Robert Ford, that dirty little coward,
I wonder how he does feel,
For he ate of Jesse's bread and he slept in Jesse's bed,
Then he laid Jesse James in the grave.

Frank was found not guilty, and there followed an uproar in Republican newspapers over what was seen as a scandalous verdict. It isn't clear how much influence General Shelby had on the jury, if any. Not that it mattered. The defense attorneys, in connivance with the sheriff, had packed the jury with twelve Democrats. And Jo Shelby wasn't at his best on that day. He—who had refused to surrender in 1865 and rode to Mexico City on horseback with his brigade, fighting his way through bandits and Juaristas, to offer his saber, in the service of another lost cause, to Maximilian, the young Hapsburg Emperor of Mexico—came to the Missouri courtroom a little drunk and unsteady on his feet.

He had to be guided to the witness chair, and, once seated, had some trouble locating the judge and jury. Twisting about in his seat, he tried to address first one and then the other. He argued with the lawyers and abused Dick Liddil. "God bless you, old fellow," he said to Frank, catching sight of him at the defense table. The judge wasn't amused. He found the general in contempt for coming to court "in a condition unfit to testify" and fined him $10.

That was more punishment than Frank got, or was to get the next year, when he was tried in Huntsville, Alabama, for the 1881 robbery of a Federal paymaster. Once again, a jury with Confederate sympathies found him not guilty.

Other charges against him here and there, such as the one in Hot Springs, Arkansas, near which he and Jesse and the Younger brothers had robbed a stagecoach in January of 1874, were dropped or simply not pressed. (All the coach passengers were robbed. One, a G. R.

Crump, of Memphis, got his watch and money back when Cole Younger learned that he had been a Confederate soldier—or so one story has it.) The State of Minnesota might also have made a claim on him, for the Northfield bank raid in September of 1876, but didn't bother to pursue it.

The law, for all practical purposes, was now finished with Frank. An old friend advised him to go back home to the farm in Missouri, to keep his head down and stay away from low company and fast horses. He had already surrendered his cartridge belt and his Remington .44 revolver. That was the end of the James Gang, and in a sense, in a kind of inglorious coda, the end of the end of the war, too, at long last. Or, no, that sounds pretty good, "coda," almost convincing, but it's wrong. The real end of the war came twenty years later, in 1904, in the very heart of the country, far from Fort Sumter, at a reunion of Quantrill's guerrillas in Independence, Missouri. There, in that election year, Frank brazenly announced that his choice for President was the sitting one, Theodore Roosevelt—*the New York Republican*. This didn't go down well, and he almost came to blows with his old hard-riding comrades. Unseemly spectacle, coots flailing away.

Unless there was another, better ending still later. For more than a century now, at intervals of about five years, southern editorial writers have been seeing portents in the night skies and proclaiming The End of the War, at Long Last, and the blessed if somewhat tardy arrival of The New South. By that they seem to mean something the same as, culturally identical with, at one with, the rest of the country, and this time they may be on to something, what with our declining numbers of Gaylons, Coys, and Virgils, and the disappearance of Clabber Girl Baking Powder signs from our highways, and of mules, standing alone in pastures. Then there is the new and alien splendor to be seen all about us, in cities with tall, dark, and featureless glass towers, though I'm told that deep currents are flowing here, far beyond the ken of editorial wretches in their cluttered cubicles. A little underground newsletter informs me that these peculiar glass structures are designed with care, by sociologists and architects working hand in glove with the CIA, as dark and forbidding boxes, in which combinations of Jacksons are thought least likely to gather, combine further, smoke cigarettes, brood, conspire, and break loose again out of a long lull.

Unlike the border ruffians Jesse (who sometimes called himself J. T. Jackson) and his brother Frank, Uncle Alec taught school for a while after the war, in cahoots with a carpetbagger from Indiana, one of the dumber ones, come south with his roomy bag to get in on the political plunder, to make his fortune in impoverished and all but depopulated Grant County, Arkansas. They were a pair of unlikely pedagogues. Uncle Alec could read and write and do his sums, which is all you need to know, but he was a very young man. The carpetbagger was older but illiterate. Uncle Alec, then, did the teaching, probably of a more basic and effective nature than is common today in public schools, and the carpetbagger did nothing except collect the monthly salary, of something like $20, which they split down the middle. The victor's spoils came to around thirty cents a day.

It was the carpetbaggers, of course, who named the county—a new one, formed largely from the western end of Jefferson County—for General Grant. Rubbing a little more salt in the open wound, they called the county seat Sheridan. That postbellum movement into the South of all the pale cranks in the Midwest, similar to one of those sudden squirrel migrations in the woods, has been overlooked, I think, as a source of some of the weirdness to be met with in our region.

I never knew my paternal great-grandfather, Colonel John W. Portis, who was a much older man (1818–1902) than Uncle Alec. He commanded an infantry regiment, the 42nd Alabama, was wounded in the Battle of Corinth, and was starved out in the siege of Vicksburg. I have the surrender parole he signed there on July 10, 1863 (the garrison had actually surrendered on the fourth), in which he gave his "solemn parole under oath that I will not take up arms again against the United States… until duly exchanged."

Some Uncle Sat of the day, looking up from his maps, could have told him and President Davis (shouted it, more likely) that with the fall of this city fortress on the bluffs of the Mississippi, and the simultaneous disaster at Gettysburg, in distant Pennsylvania, President Lincoln's re-election was pretty well assured, and the war lost. They wouldn't have listened. One more good push or two and the weary Yankees—"Those people," General Lee called them (graceless humanoids?)—must lose heart, flinch, and cut their losses. *Enough of these Jacksons! Great God almighty! Let them go and be done with them!* Such were the hopes. The next summer, duly exchanged, Colonel Portis was back in the field, at the Battle of Atlanta, and he didn't sign his final surrender parole until June 2, 1865, at Citronelle, Alabama, some two months after General Lee's surrender at Appomattox. This parole document gives a physical description: six feet tall, gray eyes, white hair. In three years of war he had gone white.

* * *

My Alabama grandmother wasn't pleased when her youngest son (a seventh son, my father) told her of his plans to marry an Arkansas girl. She kindly explained to him that the unfortunate women living west of the Mississippi River had, among other defects, feet at least one size bigger than those of their dainty little sisters to the east. No Cinderella to be found in the Bear State. Any mention of that old slander, even a teasing one fifty years later, could still make my placid mother bristle and blaze up a little. In any kind of refined-foot contest, she said, she would pit her Waddell-Fielding-Arkansas feet against all comers with Portis-Poole-Alabama feet.

My father was a dutiful son, but he defied his mother in this matter and married Alice, the Arkansas girl. So, a new family, a mingling of blood, a new combination of Jacksons, so to speak. We fetched up in southern Arkansas, at Mount Holly, where at dusk ("dusk-dark," it was called there) flying squirrels glided across our front yard, from oak to oak. I haven't seen one since.

Now a not quite deserted village, Mount Holly then had two cotton gins, a sawmill, two schools (white and black), a bank, a post office, a café, a barbershop, an ice house, three general stores and a sawmill commissary, a few moonshiners and bootleggers, one auto mechanic, one blacksmith, who was also the constable, and one known white Republican. My father pointed him out to me. (Now in much of the South it is the white Democrat to be pointed out with a whisper, as for a sighting of the ivory-billed woodpecker.) Some blacks still voted, when not deterred by the poll tax or some courthouse chicanery, for the Grand Old Party of Lincoln and Theodore Roosevelt, but by that time, the early 1940s, most had switched their allegiance to Franklin Roosevelt if not to the local "lily white" Democratic Party groups. They had also begun to christen their baby boys with his Dutch surname.

What was a bit odd, on two counts, Mount Holly proper had only one church, and that the true church of the elect, Presbyterian. The nor-

mal ratio at that time and place was about two Baptist churches or one
Methodist church per gin. It usually took about three gins to support a
Presbyterian church, and a community with, say, four before you found
enough tepid idolaters to form an Episcopal congregation. There was always difficulty in getting a minister who pleased everyone. What the eld-
ers of the church kept looking for, my father said, and what was hard to
find in the 1940s, was a wise, saintly, hearty, scholarly, eloquent thirty-
five-year-old Confederate veteran, who would be content to live on a
small salary, in something pretty close to apostolic poverty.

On Saturdays we usually drove to El Dorado, the county seat and a
flourishing oil town then, with two refineries. One was owned by Lion
Oil, a palindrome. Black-market gasoline was readily available, outside
the rationing system, but my father, scrupulous in such things, refused
to buy it, and we made do on the four or five gallons a week he was al-
lotted by the B sticker on his windshield. (B was better than A; an A got
less.) There was little chocolate to be had. The schoolyard rumor was
that all the Clark bars were going to the Japanese-American internment
camps over at Rohwer and Jerome, in the Delta, and to the German prisoners of war (most of them from Rommel's Afrika Korps) up at Camp
Chaffee, in the hills. A patriot like me had to do without. (We schoolboys
would have been hard pressed to explain the difference between the two
classes of prisoners. I can't remember hearing anyone, adults included,
question or even discuss the need for "relocating" the Japanese-
Americans from California. President Roosevelt had sent them here, so
it must be all right.) We lived in a place where they sent prisoners; what
to make of that?

Gasoline and candy bars were much less important to me than movie
theaters, or, as we called them, picture shows. The tale unfolding on the
screen was a picture show, and the theater building itself was also a picture show. El Dorado had four. The Majestic was fairly noisy, and the
Ritz a little noisier. The shabby and disreputable old Star was very noisy
indeed, with the hubbub of a pack of unruly boys, much on the move.
At the Star you sometimes had to try two or three of the folding seats
before finding one that didn't pinch your leg, or tip you forward and
dump you. There were frequent delays, as the celluloid film itself, or an
image of it, turned brown, writhed, curled, and caught fire before our
eyes. The breakdown would be followed at once by piercing whistles and

animal howls of outrage, a performance in itself by little shriekers who
had been eagerly awaiting the cue to show their stuff. No rats, though,
in disgusting numbers, pattering about underfoot at the Star, as was
widely believed. The story was kept alive by my fastidious older sister
(Star = rats at play) and others like her who had never set foot in the
place. This isn't to say that an occasional rogue rat never darted down
an aisle there.

I made a round of these three picture shows (and how well I knew
that circuit, starting from the courthouse square), seeking out the best
program. Decisions came hard. A very good bill would have been a chapter of the Captain Marvel or Dick Tracy serial, a Spike Jones comedy
short, a Boston Blackie feature, and a Western with Tim McCoy, George
O'Brien, or Johnny Mack Brown, my favorite cowboys. And yet there
were so many things to consider before I committed myself irreversibly
to a twelve-cent ticket. For example, Bob Steele was better with his fists
than any of my favorites. Ken Maynard was a better rider. Ken—and even
I could sense that he wasn't much of an actor, perhaps to his credit—
vaulted over the rump of his horse in the fast-getaway mount with a light
swagger that always pleased me.

When I was younger and in her keeping, my sister sometimes took
me against my will to the fourth picture show, the quiet Rialto, where
an attentive and well-mannered audience remained seated, and where
the more ambitious pictures played. Even very fat people could settle in
at the Rialto without fear of being dumped and laughed at, or of having
their tender and spreading flanks nipped at by the seats. I didn't object
to the decorum or the comfort, just the pictures. The posters outside,
which I always carefully read ("Theirs was a passion not to be denied!"),
were enough to sink the hopes of a small boy. In these stories there would
be some strange men scheming against each other and beating each
other's brains out to see who got to marry Bette Davis, or it might be
Joan Crawford. The winning suitor would get to spend every minute of
the rest of his life in the company of a harridan. I was soon asleep.

* * *

Mount Holly had its own summer pleasures. We, the village boys,
swam like seals by day in the creeks and ponds, and at night, with our
carbide lamps, we ran trotlines—a series of fishing lines hanging from a
central support line that was strung across a stream. We swung from vines

in the bottomlands, trying to reproduce, and never bringing off anything remotely like, Tarzan's aerial glide across the jungle, leaping from one opportune vine to the next. That, I've since learned, was even more of a cheat than I suspected: it was all done with ropes. Ignorant of the laws of physics, I did know from experience that when you jumped from a swinging vine to one that was hanging dead still and vertical, you weren't going any farther, and could only be left looking foolish, dangling there at rest. I was also uneasy, not knowing exactly why, with Batman's practice of shooting a rope line from atop a tall building across to a lower building, and then swinging *down* to the lower building on that line, which somehow remained taut.

We made model airplanes, little replicas of warplanes built far away from Mount Holly in huge factories with such satisfying corporate names as Chance Vought and Consolidated Vultee. First, with the models, there was the fragile skeleton to be assembled, of balsa ribs and stringers, and droplets of glue; this was then covered with a thin skin of paper, and painted with a dope sealant that smelled of bananas. The delicate work tried my patience, and gave me an early appreciation of how it is that real aircraft, no matter how fierce in appearance, must be the tinny and flimsy shells that they are, in order to leave the ground. In my haste, and with twinges of guilt, I sometimes cut corners, leaving out a troublesome strut or spar, like some crooked defense contractor.

We rigged up our own fireworks, with carbide (granular calcium carbide, bought in cans; it fizzes and gives off a combustible gas when mixed with water) and with black powder we compounded ourselves. We burned our own charcoal, and bought the other ingredients, sulfur and saltpeter, in little paper cartons at Bailey's store, arrayed there on the patent-medicine shelf with the big bottles of liniments, violent purgatives, female tonics, chill tonics, croup tonics, cramp tonics, catarrh tonics, and nerve tonics. No need in those days of tonics to be put through the indignities of "a full battery of tests," at great expense, for every little sinking spell. I no longer see tonics on the shelves of country stores, that space now being given over to videocassettes. Catarrh, with its fine pair of purring rs, seems to have gone away too, whatever it was.

Our watermelons (not always lifted from a melon patch; you could buy one, preferably a long green Tom Watson, for about fifteen cents) we left floating in the creeks to cool as we swam, mostly in Swift Hole, on Beech Creek. The water in Swift Hole wasn't swift; moccasins swam calmly about on the surface, untroubled by the slight current. We—David Bailey, Max Lewis, Gerald Lewis, Francis Crumpler, Richie Bidwell, Buddy Portis—paid little heed to the snakes and soon scattered them with our noise and splashing and, low comedians all, with our strutting antics along the banks. No one, that I recall, was bitten there. But Swift Hole was a hole, deep enough that we could dive into it from a height of eight or nine feet and not crack our necks on the bottom.

A leaning tree shaded the pool, and from a high limb there hung a rope with a stick tied at the end. You grabbed the stick with both hands, ran down the sloping bank, took flight, and at the peak of the upswing let go, doing a back flip or a half gainer on the way down. Some unknown person had patiently spliced the long rope together from the separated strands of a thick oil-field hawser, and hung it there for our de-light. One day it was just there. With the ingratitude of children we ac-cepted it as part of the natural order of things, as no more than our due, and asked few questions.

Mount Holly was just outside the oil fields, but we did have one lone gas well, on Cypress Creek. A man would drive up a dirt lane to the un-attended wellhead in his 1928 Ford Model A roadster, or his 1939 Chevrolet Master Deluxe sedan, and look furtively about. He would see us, some boys with purple stripes on our faces (pokeberry juice), pulling a ragged seine through the creek. Unterrified by the war paint, he would dismiss us as a threat and proceed to drain off something called "casing head" from the well, which he then poured into his gasoline tank.

This was a liquid condensate that formed in gas lines, and although it burned a little rough in car engines, it did burn, and was unrationed and free for the taking. There must have been some kind of bleeder valve in that tangle of high-pressure gas pipes, but I've forgotten how it worked, if I ever knew. I do seem to remember a Stillson wrench, an adjustable pipe wrench, in the hands of one of those furtive casing-head thieves. I remember, too, that we once dredged up a curious snake in our seine, along that same stretch of Cypress Creek. It was a rusty-orange color with a thick body and what appeared to be a barbed stinger protruding from its tail. Zoologists, who should venture outdoors more often, say the stinging snake exists only in folklore, but we were there and saw that beast. We all agreed it was a stinging snake.

It was in Beech Creek, in the shoal water below Swift Hole, that I carried on most of my underwater contortions with breathing tubes. Reeds were out, and among other rejects was a copper pipe, which left a sharp taste in the mouth. Another one, tasting worse, was a black and smelly rubber hose, a piece of old fuel line from a car, with a spiral curl to it like that of a pig's tail. I had to expose a small but conspicuous hand above the surface of the water to keep this one upright.

I kept coming back to bamboo, the best of a poor lot, and soldiered on. There was always another obstacle. When I was underwater, clutch-ing a tree root, lying more or less supine, and took a deep draft of air through my mouth tube, an equal volume of water would come rushing in through my nose, with a strangling effect. The nose clip existed then and might have solved the problem, but I couldn't be seen with a nose clip. Only girls used nose clips. Far better to strangle. Couldn't I simply have pinched my nostrils shut with thumb and finger? Yes, nothing easier, except that both hands were already occupied, with the tube and the root. And as I lay there more or less supine on the creekbed, struggling to breathe and to hold my upper body down, then my telltale feet would rise. Feet unfettered float, for all their bones, and when toes break the surface and bob about, they will catch the eye of the dullest observer.

I never did get it all worked out to suit me, and when the war ended, in 1945, I lost interest in breathing tubes and model airplanes and black-powder bombs and cigarettes rolled with rabbit tobacco or corn silk. A spell was broken. The world had changed. I put all that juvenile dementia behind me. It was time to take on some serious responsibilities in life. I cut a coupon from the back of a funny book and bought a $1.98 money order at the Mount Holly post office and sent them off to a place in New Jersey for a home-study course in ventriloquism.

* * *

Uncle Alec didn't quite make it to a hundred, dying a year short, in 1946. He had lived to see the U.S. Army, still with plenty of ammunition, if not mules, on the winning end of another great war, and he was probably the last man who could remember seeing Jo Shelby riding at the head of his mounted column along the Ouachita River near Camden, or hearing another general, the portly Sterling Price, calling out for one more charge into the fog and powdersmoke at Jenkins' Ferry.

No peevish coot, he made a good showing toward the end, still jaunty, laughing quietly in his chair, and with no bits of food on his chin that I can remember. A better showing, in his dark suit, vest, watch chain, and polished leather shoes, than many of the old-timers I see today, men who went ashore at Tarawa and Anzio, now much reduced in their retirement costume of grotesque white athletic shoes, pastel resort rompers, and white baseball cap crammed down hard on the head, bending the ears. Their model seems to be The Golfer.

A coot now myself, slightly peevish, of three score and five, I recently saw a vision in broad daylight of The Ghost of Christmas Yet to Come. The apparition was an old man at the wheel of an old tan Pontiac station wagon. He had stopped next to my car at a traffic light here in Little Rock. The wagon was a long, sagging barge, packed inside to the roof with lumpy objects bundled in green-plastic tarpaulins and tied up with what looked like clothesline. But what objects? At a guess, all his goods, his assets, now luggage: bits of chain, rolls of duct tape, forgotten cans of soup, jumper cables tangled around a jack frozen with rust, encrusted bottles of Tabasco sauce, sacks of Indian arrowheads, sacks of silver dimes, sacks of cat food, an old owlhead .32 revolver with a wobbly cylinder and a pitted barrel, corroded flashlights, ivory, apes, peacocks, and bottles of saw-palmetto capsules to treat the sinister prostate gland. The old man was smirking. It was the gloat of a miser. Stiff gray hairs straggled out of the little relief hole at the back of his cap, above the adjustment strap. In short, another Jackson, and while not an ornament of our race, neither was he, I thought, the most depraved member of the gang. He might even have made some claim to being a gentleman, as defined by my *Concise Oxford Dictionary*: "n. Man entitled to bear arms but not included in the nobility…"

There I was in the flesh, a little more weathered, just a few years from now. The resemblance was close. I saw myself sunk low there under the wheel, even to the string bolo tie with its turquoise slide, and even to that complacent smirk, knowing that all my flashlights and other treasures were right behind me, safely stowed and well hidden from the defiling gaze of others. I could see myself all too clearly in that old butterscotch Pontiac, roaring flat out across the Mexican desert and laying down a streamer of smoke like a crop duster, with a goatherd to note my passing and (I flatter myself) to watch me until I was utterly gone, over a distant hill, and only then would he turn again with his stick to the straying flock. So be it.

Uncle Sat, who never got TB and who wouldn't let young government agents tell him how to prune his peach trees and cure his hams and who ate better food than a rich man can buy today and who never lost so much as a finger while fooling around with his detonator caps and his sticks of dinnamite, was eighty-eight when he died, in 1964. I saw him now and then over the years, talking away, as ever, but I can call up his face more clearly, his red farmer's face, from an earlier time, at that kitchen table, over the newspaper maps. I can see the winter stubble in his fields, too, on that dreary January day in 1942. Broken stalks and a few dirty white shreds of bumblebee cotton. Everyone who was there is dead and buried now except me.

The Atlantic, May 1999

Five

DRAMA

Delray's New Moon

A Play in Three Acts

The Arkansas Repertory Theatre produced Portis's only play to date as a workshop production, directed by Cliff Baker, on the company's Second-Stage, premiering it on April 18, 1996, with the following cast:

MR. PALFREY	Scott Edmonds
FERN	Judy Trice
LENORE	Natalie Canerday
TONYA	Danielle Rosenthal
MRS. VETCH	Jean Lind
MR. NIBLIS	John Stiritz
MR. MINGO	Michael Davis
DELRAY	Michael Henderson
DUVALL	Graham Gordy
MARGUERITE	Stacy Breeding
KATE	Angel Bailey
MAE BUTTRESS	Rhonda Atwood
POLICE DETECTIVE	Tom Kagy

There is only one stage set. It is the dining room of an old hotel in Arkansas, formerly Miss Eula's Sunnyside Hotel, now being changed over to a dance hall called Delray's New Moon. The hotel is a two-story wooden structure situated just off the highway—Interstate 30—about halfway between Little Rock and Texarkana. There is a front door, with a large window beside it, that opens on to the parking area outside. There are restaurant tables and chairs, plain and inexpensive. There is a short bar of padded plastic, with four or five high stools standing before it. On top of the bar there is a small television set (facing away from the audience) and boxes of cocktail glasses. Behind the bar there is a sink with water taps, and behind that a swinging door leading to the kitchen. There are signs of renovation—a stepladder, a wooden tray of carpenter's tools, paint buckets. A stairway leads to the second floor, but only the first flight of stairs, to a landing, is visible to the audience. Near the bottom of the stairs is the opening of a hallway leading to the rear.

An outdoor sign, not yet hung, leans against an inside wall. It reads, DINE AND DANCE AT DELRAY'S NEW MOON. *Under the words there is painted a tilted champagne glass, with bubbles rising from it. There is a life-size cardboard cutout of a male and female dancer in black silhouette. The dancers are in formal dress and have a 1930s look. The man is holding the woman as she leans over backward in a dramatic pose. A silver crescent moon (cardboard wrapped in aluminum foil) hangs from the ceiling and twists slowly about.*

Cast of Characters

MR. PALFREY. *An old man in nondescript gray trousers, wide suspenders, and plaid shirt buttoned all the way to the top. He wears an old felt hat with a narrow brim, and uses a walking stick, an unpainted cane of white wood.*

FERN. *Mr. Palfrey's older daughter, who is about fifty years old. Her clothes are neat and plain.*

LENORE. *Mr. Palfrey's younger daughter, who is about thirty-five years old. She has a lot of upswept hair, big earrings, jangling bracelets. Her clothes are flashy.*

TONYA. *Lenore's daughter, a girl six or seven years old.*

MRS. VETCH. *An old woman, very ladylike, wearing her Sunday best—hat, purse and gloves.*

MR. NIBLIS. *A skinny old man wearing mismatched suit coat and trousers, white shirt and short, wide necktie. He has a sack of tobacco in his shirt pocket, and keeps his cigarette papers and his matches (big kitchen matches) in the hatband of his felt hat. He rolls and smokes cigarettes throughout the play. One lens of his eyeglasses is dark. He wears a hearing-aid, with big conspicuous wires running down from his ear to his clothing.*

MR. MINGO. *A dapper old man in a seersucker suit, polka-dot bow tie, straw boater hat and two-tone shoes, black and white. He uses two malacca canes.*

DELRAY. *The new owner, is about forty years old, wears a white guayabera, short white slacks, soft white loafers, gold necklace. He carries a ring of keys on his belt.*

DUVALL. *(Pronounced DOO-vall.) He is Delray's assistant, a young man about twenty years old. He has a reddish ponytail, tied with a ribbon, and wears jeans and T-shirt.*

MARGUERITE. *A slender little girl about nine years old, with stringy blonde hair. She wears old white tennis shoes with no laces, and a shiny blue-green dress with shoulder straps. One strap keeps falling off. She sells pecan rolls from a paper shopping bag.*

KATE. *The waitress, a girl in her mid-twenties. Hard and tense.*

MAE BUTTRESS. *A fat young woman about thirty years old. She wears glasses and a dark blue tailored suit, white blouse, bow tie, all suggestive of a uniform.*

POLICE DETECTIVE. *A stocky young man in plain clothes.*

HOUSE PAINTER. *An old drunk in white overalls, white shirt and heavy black shoes.*

Act I

The only occupant of the room is Mr. Niblis. He is seated at a table surrounded by luggage and pasteboard boxes tied up with string. He is smoking one of his hand-rolled cigarettes and is reading from scraps of paper that he takes from various pockets.

Enter Fern and her father, Mr. Palfrey, through the front door. She carries two suitcases and leads the way. He follows, rocking from side to side on his walking stick.

FERN. Well, we beat the rain anyway. (*She sets the bags down beside a vacant table and looks about*) I wish you would look. They've sure changed the old Sunnyside all up.

MR. PALFREY. (*Looking at sign*) Dine and dance. Dine and dance. Everybody wants to dine and dance.

FERN. (*Getting him settled in at a table*) Now just sit down there, Daddy, and be still. Don't stare at people and don't act ugly to people.

MR. PALFREY. (*Not listening. Pawing over his things*) You forgot my pillow.

FERN. I'm going after it now. Just stay right there.

She starts to go, comes back, removes the hat from his head, combs his tousled hair. She leaves. Mr. Palfrey and Mr. Niblis stare at one another, look away, stare again.

Enter Kate, the waitress, from the kitchen. She goes first to the front window and peers outside, looking left and right. Then she goes to Mr. Palfrey's table and gives him a menu. He puts on his glasses and looks it over.

MR. PALFREY. These are just dime-store glasses. That's all I ever needed. I haven't been to a doctor in twenty-one years. And don't plan to go any time soon, thank you.

He waits for her to marvel at this but she doesn't respond. He peers at the name tag on her uniform.

MR. PALFREY. "Kate," is it?

KATE. Yes.

MR. PALFREY. Well, Kate, tell me this. What time do the good-looking women come on?

KATE. *(In no mood for this banter)* Much later. What do you want?

MR. PALFREY. Can I still get breakfast?

KATE. *(Looks at watch)* Till ten-thirty, yes.

Mr. Palfrey, humming and tapping his fingers, continues his leisurely study of the menu.

KATE. *(Impatient)* If you don't know what you want, I can come back.

MR. PALFREY. Oh, I know what I want. I just don't see it here. What I want is a fat yearling coon roasted with some sweet potatoes. What I want, young lady, is some salt-cured ham that's been hanging in the smokehouse for about two years, along with five or six big cat-head biscuits, and some country butter and ribbon cane surrup [syrup]. But I can't get that, can I?

KATE. You can't get it here.

MR. PALFREY. You can't get it anywhere. Not any more. Them days are gone. It's a different country. Way too many new people to suit me. *(Resumes study of menu)* All right. Let me have this Number One. With bacon and grits. These biscuits—are they canned?

KATE. Yes.

MR. PALFREY. Then let me have toast. Are the grits soupy?

KATE. I don't know. They're just instant grits.

MR. PALFREY. I like my grits to stand up. Tell the cook. But not lumpy either. And I want tomato juice instead of grapefruit juice.

KATE. *(Points to warning words in menu)* "No Substitutions."

MR. PALFREY. Yeah, I know, they all say that, but what difference does it make?

KATE. I don't know. That's the rule. I just work here. How do you want your eggs?

MR. PALFREY. *(Sulking)* I can't have what I want.

KATE. You can have your eggs the way you want them.

MR. PALFREY. No, I can't either. Not here. Not in this place.

KATE. Fried, scrambled, what?

MR. PALFREY. Nobody can have anything the way they want it here. The customer is always wrong.

KATE. Over easy then?

MR. PALFREY. I don't have no say in the matter. Bring me whatever you want me to have.

Kate shrugs and leaves with order.

MR. PALFREY. *(Calling after her)* Wait. Here's my old man card. I get ten percent off.
KATE. You don't need a card. *(Exits to kitchen)*

Fern returns with his special pillow.

FERN. For just once in her life I wish Lenore could be on time someplace. "Ten o'clock," she said. "Tonya and I will be there waiting for you." I should know better by now.
MR. PALFREY. She'll be here. Don't worry. Just go on back to Texarkana. I'll be all right.
FERN. No, I'm not going to leave you here by yourself. You could be sitting here all day waiting for Lenore.
MR. PALFREY. She probably got caught in the rain and had to slow down some.
FERN. Then she should have made allowances for the rain. You always make excuses for her, Daddy.
MR. PALFREY. Well, she is my baby daughter, after all.
FERN. A pretty old baby, if you ask me.
MR. PALFREY. *(Looking over his things. Speaks up suddenly)* Where's my police scanner?
FERN. Didn't you put it in the trunk?
MR. PALFREY. It was on the kitchen table. You were supposed to load it.
FERN. Well, let me go look. *(She leaves)*
MR. PALFREY. *(Calling after her)* And my umbrella! And my big flashlight!

Enter Marguerite, the little girl. She is lugging a paper shopping bag that contains candy logs—big pecan logs. She approaches Mr. Palfrey and looks at him.

MARGUERITE. Are you a cripple old man?
MR. PALFREY. No, I'm not.

MARGUERITE. You have a walking stick.

MR. PALFREY. It's not a walking stick, it's just a stick I have to poke things with. I point at things with it and I knock down pears and apples out of trees with it. You don't see me creeping around, do you, and grabbing aholt of chairs when I cross a room?

MARGUERITE. (Brings out big bar of candy wrapped in cellophane) These are real good pecan logs and they only cost five dollars.

MR. PALFREY. (Fondling his stick) Look how pretty the wood is. That's holly. The whitest wood there is. I cut it and turned it myself. (Whacks it across his palm) And sometimes I use it to correct my chirren [children] with.

MARGUERITE. (Presses candy on him) They call this the family size. The money goes for our new band uniforms. We're going to have brand new scarlet and gold uniforms.

MR. PALFREY. (Puts on glasses, looks over candy) It looks like a ear of corn. A big roasting ear. (Reads label) I never heard of this outfit. Just some post office box in Memphis.

MARGUERITE. (Hanging over his shoulder, pointing to label) No, see, it says "Made of the finest ingredients." And look how many pecans you get for just five dollars.

MR. PALFREY. (Pushing her back) Here, get away so I can see for myself.

MARGUERITE. They can't sell these in stores because they're too big and they have too many pecans. Mrs. Vetch has been eating on hers for more than a week.

MR. PALFREY. (Pitches candy into shopping bag) No, I can't use it. But I tell you what I will do. If you can make me laugh I'll give you <u>ten</u> dollars.

MARGUERITE. (Thinks it over) I can dance some. (Twirls about and curves her arms up in Spanish dancer pose) Next year I'm going to take tap lessons at Irene's House of Dance.

MR. PALFREY. Dancing? How would that make me laugh?

MARGUERITE. They're going to have dancing here pretty soon and I'm going to be right in the middle of it. With sequins in my hair.

MR. PALFREY. No, you're not. This place is turning into a honky tonk. They're not going to let you come into a honky tonk.

MARGUERITE. Delray said I could come as a performer. He said he would introduce me as "the radiant Miss Annabel." When I do my scarf dance.

MR. PALFREY. You're Annabel?

MARGUERITE. That's only my dancing name. My real name is Marguerite, which means "pearl." You know what though? *(Hands on hips)* My birthstone is the beautiful blue sapphire! But my favorite color is cerise!

MR. PALFREY. "Annabel." *(Savoring the name)* "Annabel." That's not bad. "Blanche" is a good name too. If I had another little baby girl I would name her Blanche.

MARGUERITE. No, I like "Annabel" better. I read this real real good book, see, called "The Radiant Miss Annabel Lee," about a poor orphan girl with long auburn hair. It was her crowning glory. It was so long she could sit on it but the boss made her cut it off when she went to work at the fish canning factory. But she didn't let it get her down. She always made the best of everything. She nursed injured animals back to health and she threaded needles for old ladies. She cheered up people with broken hearts. She wrote love letters for people who couldn't write very good love letters. Annabel loved children too and she wrote tiny poems in green ink on their little fat hands. She took them out blackberry picking and when the little ones got tired and cried and dropped their buckets she showed them how to do the chicken walk and soon turned their tears to bubbling and infectious laughter. And everywhere she went everybody just loved Annabel so much because she helped them out with their problems. And they all said the same thing about her. They all said, "How fortunate we are to have Annabel here with us! How radiant she is!" And that's how I got my dancing name.

MR. PALFREY. Well, I don't care nothing about your boogie-woogie or your rock and roll or your nut logs. My deal is this. You make me laugh and I'll give you a ten-dollar bill.

Enter Kate with coffee and food. Marguerite lingers by the table and watches Mr. Palfrey salt and pepper his fried eggs, heavily, with both hands.

MARGUERITE. Oooooo! I hate grits!

MR. PALFREY. You don't know what's good, girl. I eat grits every day. They keep my coat glossy.

MARGUERITE. *(Speaking up, just as he is about to attack his eggs with knife and fork)* We say the blessing at our house before we eat.

MR. PALFREY. We do too, but when you're out on the road you don't always have time for that. (*Trails off as he is made to feel the lameness of
the excuse*) All right then. (*Drops his head a bit and mumbles the prayer
rapidly and mechanically*) Bless this food to the nourishment of our
bodies and consecrate our lives to thy service in Jesus name amen.
(*He falls on the eggs with knife and fork, with furious criss-cross chopping
moves. Marguerite, startled by the clatter of cutlery on china, jumps back*)

*Enter Delray from the rear hall. He comes striding in to investigate the noise
and looks at Mr. Palfrey with disgust.*

DELRAY. What the devil! Kate! Duvall! Where is everybody? Kate!
KATE. (*Sticks her head out kitchen door*) What? What is it now?
DELRAY. (*Pointing to Mr. Palfrey*) There! That's what! We're not sup-
posed to be open!
KATE. Why not?
DELRAY. Didn't Duvall tell you? Everything was to be shut down last night.
KATE. Nobody told me anything. Sammy came on as usual. He's back
here in the kitchen.
DELRAY. Well, tell him to shut it down right now and get everything
cleaned up. I want it all ready for a complete inventory. No, forget
it, I'll tell him myself. That's the only way I can get anything done
around here. (*Exits through kitchen door, pushing Kate aside*)
MARGUERITE. (*To Mr. Palfrey*) Wait! I know! I've got something at
home to show you! It'll make you laugh out loud! It's worth ten dollars easy! Watch my sack for me!

*She takes off at a run and exits through front door. There are noises of people
on stairs. Duvall, Delray's young assistant, enters on the stairway with two
old people, Mrs. Vetch and Mr. Mingo. He helps them along and settles them
in at a table near Mr. Niblis, where their luggage is gathered.*

DUVALL. There we go. All set, are we?
MRS. VETCH. (*Looking about*) Where is Ruth Buttress?
DUVALL. She's on the way. You'll be off to Avalon in no time, and you
know, I'm tempted to go with you. (*Reads from brochure*) "The days
are full at Avalon and before you know it, it's bedtime!"

MR. NIBLIS. *(Speaking for the first time)* What was that? What did Duvall say?

MRS. VETCH. He said the days are full at Avalon!

DUVALL. Are they ever! *(Runs finger down Avalon brochure, reads from it)* Bingo, bridge tournaments, sand modeling, singalongs, paper folding, balloon twisting, sack race, bottle race, wheelchair race, aerobics, soap sculpture, piñata smashing, tug-of-war—the eighties versus the nineties on Tuesdays—

MR. MINGO. Yes, we've read all that, Duvall.

DUVALL. Well then, let's get into the spirit of the thing. Why don't we give a cheer? "We're off to Avalon!" Okay? All together now. With me. You too, Mr. Niblis. *(Raises hands in manner of song leader)* WE'RE OFF TO AVALON! *(But no one joins in)* All right then, how about some coffee?

MR. MINGO. Yes, please.

MRS. VETCH. A cherry Coke for me, Duvall. In a glass, please, not a plastic cup.

DUVALL. Hey, you got it! Coming up!

Duvall exits to kitchen. Mr. Palfrey stares at the other old people. They steal glances at him. Finally, Mr. Mingo speaks to Mr. Palfrey.

MR. MINGO. Haven't I seen you here before?

MR. PALFREY. Who are you?

MR. MINGO. I am Mr. Mingo.

MR. PALFREY. How old are you, Mr. Mingo?

MR. MINGO. I am carrying ninety-nine years on my back, sir. I am at death's door.

MR. PALFREY. You look old but you don't look that old.

MRS. VETCH. He's really only about eighty-six.

MR. MINGO. Life plus ninety-nine years. That was my sentence.

MR. PALFREY. I knew he didn't look that old.

MR. MINGO. The terms to run concurrently.

MRS. VETCH. Eighty-seven, I think, or eighty-eight.

MR. MINGO. Could be. Maybe so. I wouldn't be surprised. Something like that.

MR. PALFREY. He looks all broke down and wore out but I knew he didn't look that old.

MR. MINGO. I've seen you here more than once.

MR. PALFREY. Well, we've been stopping off here for two or three years now. Fern likes the lemon ice box pie. They always set a good table here at the Sunnyside. Sometimes we stop here and sometimes we stop at that barbecue joint down the road.

MRS. VETCH. You can forget about the lemon pie.

MR. MINGO. They no longer set a good table here. Miss Eula's gone, you know. She sold out to Delray and we're being evicted. Mrs. Vetch and I are the last of the old residents. And Mr. Niblis there. He likes to keep to himself.

MR. NIBLIS. Only when I'm reflecting on things. Naturally I don't like being disturbed when I'm reviewing my life.

MR. PALFREY. I thought he was deaf and dumb.

MR. MINGO. Oh, he can hear well enough. That's a dummy hearing-aid. There's no battery in it. He only wears it to discourage conversation.

MRS. VETCH. They're hauling us off in a dump truck today. They're going to dump us at the Grim Hotel in Texarkana.

Duvall re-enters with tray of refreshments.

DUVALL. I don't know why you keep saying that, Mrs. Vetch. You know very well it's Avalon you're going to, over in the beautiful Chinkypin Forest.

MRS. VETCH. Same thing.

DUVALL. Not at all. No comparison. Night and day. And you're not going away in a truck. Ruth Buttress is coming to pick you up in a nice air-conditioned van with captains' chairs.

MRS. VETCH. But I'm just so worried, Duvall. They came over and signed us up so fast. I'm just so afraid of what we're getting into.

DUVALL. Listen to me. You're going to make a lot of new friends at Avalon and have loads of fun. You won't have time to mope, with all your leathercraft classes and your essay writing contests and your field trips to paper mills and bakeries. *(Takes brochure from hip pocket)* And look here, when the weather is nice there'll be folk dancing on the lawn and some of the great old games you played as a child. Pop the Whip, Piggy Wants a Motion, Red Rover. Yes, you'll join hands and roar out your challenge to the opposing team—"Red Rover, Red

Rover, let—" *(He looks about)* "—let Mr. Niblis come over!" And he'll
hurl himself at your line, trying to crash through. Then a good supper,
and a nice visit with your new friends, and then maybe a thrilling love
story on television, and before you know it—it's bedtime.

MRS. VETCH. But what about my privacy?

DUVALL. Oh…you'll have a certain amount.

MRS. VETCH. Can I take my small traveling iron? Some of my things I
just don't trust anybody else to press. I asked Delray about it and he
didn't know.

DUVALL. <u>Iron</u>. That is a puzzler. Let me make a note of that. *(Takes pen
and notebook from shirt pocket and writes slowly, speaking aloud the words)*
Memo…Mrs. Vetch…For Ruth Buttress…a request…to keep…
one…small…personal…portable…traveling…heating…and pressing…appliance. *(Claps notebook shut and puts it away with a smile)*
There. Leave it to me. It's in my hands now. *(Goes to bar, begins un-
packing cocktail glasses from box)*

MR. MINGO. *(To Mr. Palfrey)* Don't you live in Texarkana?

MR. PALFREY. Well, I do and I don't, Mr. Mingo. I stay there part of
the time with my daughter Fern—she's out there fooling around in
the car—and then I stay for a while with my baby daughter Lenore
in Little Rock. They trade me off, you see. I meet myself coming and
going. It used to be a year at each place. Then it was six months.
Now it's down to three. Right here is where they trade me off, at the
halfway point. Here or down there at the barbecue joint.

MR. MINGO. And you are—

MR. PALFREY. Mr. Palfrey.

MR. MINGO. Palfrey, yes. Now I have it. I've heard Mr. Ramp speak of you.

MR. PALFREY. *(Looking about)* Where is Ramp?

MR. MINGO. Oh, he's been gone for several months now. When was it?

MRS. VETCH. About the same time Miss Eula left.

MR. NIBLIS. Ramp is on the run. He's traveling incognito.

MR. MINGO. He signed up for Avalon with us and then he just disappeared. We don't know where he is. Somebody said they carried him
off to a ranch in Oklahoma.

MR. PALFREY. An old man like that? I've heard of boys' ranches where
they take in these bad boys. I've heard of dude ranches. I never heard
of an old timer ranch.

MR. MINGO. Maybe I got it wrong. Maybe it was a camp or a farm.

MR. PALFREY. Well, tell me this, Mr. Mingo. What happened to the
old Sunnyside? It used to be a nice clean family place to eat. Now
it's what, some kind of honky tonk?

MR. MINGO. The county went wet, that's what happened. They voted
in liquor by the drink and Miss Eula sold out to this dancing fellow,
Delray.

MR. NIBLIS. Delray has thousands of dollars.

MR. PALFREY. Everybody wants to dine and dance.

MR. NIBLIS. And if you leave 'em alone for more than ten minutes
they'll be dancing around the golden calf.

MR. MINGO. I can't really blame Miss Eula. She's no spring chicken,
you know, and good help is hard to get. So yes, now it's a roadhouse.

MRS. VETCH. And Delray has kicked us out. They're coming today to
haul us off in a dump truck.

MR. PALFREY. Don't you have any chirren [children] to look after you?

MR. MINGO. I've got a son who has retired from the post office but his
wife won't have me in the house. His small birdlike wife. She says I
make her nervous.

MRS. VETCH. My son was killed years ago in Korea. He was a brave
and handsome captain in the paratroopers. He died on the field of
honor. His daughter Jeannie is married to a clown in Shreveport.
She's a sweet girl, too, and she keeps after me to stay with her but I
couldn't possibly live under the same roof with that fat clown she's
married to.

MR. PALFREY. What about—

MRS. VETCH. You don't know what it is to outlive your only child.

MR. PALFREY. (Nodding at Mr. Niblis) What about him?

MR. MINGO. Mr. Niblis? Oh no, he's an old bachelor. He has no family.

MR. NIBLIS. No, I've never been blessed with a wife. My mother was
one of eleven children and my father was the youngest of seven
brothers, and here I am a barren old man with neither chick nor
child. One day I'll have to answer for that. One day real soon now.

MR. MINGO. Not that he didn't make the effort. He tells me he pro-
posed marriage to three or four women along the way.

MR. NIBLIS. More than that.

MR. MINGO. He just couldn't get very far with them.

MR. NIBLIS. I couldn't get anywhere with them. One summer in Nashville I was rebuffed by five women in a row. Some of those women were wearing hats and carrying purses—like Mrs. Vetch here—and some were not. Every one of them found me unpleasant and rejected me out of hand.

MRS. VETCH. Can you wonder?

MR. NIBLIS. Still, it left me more time for my work. Women will take up a lot of your time. And then there's the money. I've heard it takes a good deal of money to keep them fed and amused.

MR. MINGO. He claims to be a prophet. That was his work.

MRS. VETCH. He tried to kiss some of those ladies.

MR. NIBLIS. Not after I saw how much it alarmed them.

MR. MINGO. "Things are not what they seem." That was his prophetic message.

MR. NIBLIS. Things are not at all what they seem.

MR. MINGO. You may be right at that.

MR. PALFREY. What did Ramp say when they came and got him?

MR. MINGO. I don't know that he had any parting words. There was no formal leave-taking. Nothing in the way of a valedictory address. No one saw him go. He was just here one day and gone the next.

MRS. VETCH. Good riddance, in any case. That very disturbing smile! And his old baggy clothes, my goodness! It was like somebody else had dressed him.

MR. MINGO. Yes, as though he had been dressed hastily by employees of the state. He sneaked around a lot, too. You never knew what door he might pop out of next.

MR. NIBLIS. Look who's talking about sneaks.

MR. MINGO. He would come out of his room every morning with that knowing smile on his face. I think he had something hidden away in there, perhaps some rare animal that would surprise us all if we knew what it was. Some small animal with a pounding heart. I had a good look around his room after he left, hoping to find some droppings. I intended to send them off for analysis and identification. But I found nothing.

MR. NIBLIS. We'll never know now. What he was up to.

MRS. VETCH. And yet Miss Eula thought he was so clever and so handsome.

MR. PALFREY. I wonder if we're talking about the same Ramp. The Ramp I know is a retired barber, a hard little pine-knot of a man. He has sharp features. He looks exactly like a fox.

MR. MINGO. Yes, that's our Mr. Ramp.

MR. PALFREY. He smells something like a fox too. Gives off a strong musky fox odor.

MRS. VETCH. That's the very same man.

Fern returns with a big flashlight and an umbrella.

FERN. Well, I looked everywhere. That scanner is just not in the car.

MR. PALFREY. *(Stunned)* You didn't load my scanner?

FERN. You had it last. It was there on the kitchen table with the cord wrapped around it.

MR. PALFREY. What am I going to do in Little Rock at night without my police scanner?

FERN. I'll send it up to you on the bus tomorrow.

MR. PALFREY. That won't do me any good tonight.

FERN. You can watch TV with Boyce and them tonight. I just called up there. No answer.

MR. PALFREY. She's on the way, that's why. How could Lenore answer the phone if she's on the road?

FERN. If she is on the road. Look, it's already after eleven.

DUVALL. *(Overhearing the remark)* Eleven! *(Drops his work with glasses and goes to small television set at other end of bar. Turns it on. The screen faces away from the audience, and only the murmuring sound of a football broadcast is heard)*

MR. PALFREY. Folks, I'd like you to meet Fern, my oldest daughter and the biggest worry wart in southwest Arkansas. Fern, this is Mrs. Vetch and this is Mr. Mingo. That's Mr. Niblis over there.

Exchange of greetings.

MR. PALFREY. Listen to this, Fern. Mrs. Vetch's daughter married a circus clown down in Shreveport.

MRS. VETCH. No, it's my grand-daughter, and her husband is not a circus clown, he's just a big coarse—buffoon.

MR. PALFREY. They've been living here at the Sunnyside and now they're being kicked out so these new people can have their honky tonk here.

FERN. Well, I declare. That's awful. Where will you go?

MRS. VETCH. They're hauling us off today in a dump truck. To the city dump.

MR. MINGO. It's actually Avalon we're going to.

FERN. Avalon? That's the place they advertise on TV so much.

MR. MINGO. Yes, Dr. Lloyd Mole's new place.

FERN. (Quoting from ad) "The days are full at Avalon and before you know it, it's bedtime!"

MR. MINGO. That's it, yes. Delray put the Avalon people on to us and they came over and signed us all up for the Special Value Package. One flat fee up front and no more worries.

MRS. VETCH. We signed up in a weak moment. It just sounded so good. One big payment and then no more worries. That's the Special Value Package.

MR. NIBLIS. They didn't sign me up for the Special Value Package.

MR. MINGO. No, somebody else paid Mr. Niblis's fee. Some secret admirer.

MR. NIBLIS. Without asking me.

MRS. VETCH. You didn't have any place else to go. You ought to be grateful. Nobody but Miss Eula would put you up for that little bitty Social Security check you get.

FERN. But why can't you stay on here?

MRS. VETCH. I don't know. Delray wants us out. And it's just so hard to bear at my age. I kept my little room here so neat and clean. The food was so good. I had my pots of begonias on the window sill. I had all my mother's beautiful things around me.

MR. PALFREY. (Calling out to Duvall across the room) Hey! You! Booger Red! Shut that thing off! Nobody wants to hear that TV racket at this time of day! Your paying customers are over here trying to visit!

DUVALL. You'll want to hear this. It's the Arkansas-Texas game. It's the early game today.

MR. PALFREY. Naw, we don't want to hear that either. It's way too early in the day for that. Just keep it down over there. (Then to others) They won't let you have the kind of juice you want and then they try to run you off with all their TV racket.

MR. MINGO. I hope the Razorbacks can win, but you know, I prefer a good high school game. The boys seem to show more spirit.

MR. PALFREY. Don't get me wrong. I like football myself and I want our boys to stomp the devil out of Texas any time they can, but there's a time and a place for things. A time and a place, Mr. Mingo.

MR. MINGO. I love the fall of the year.

MR. PALFREY. That's me too. I've always said that. Give me the fall of the year, when the crops are laid by, with nice cold mornings, and football and hunting coming in.

MR. MINGO. Don't they hunt turkeys in the spring?

MR. PALFREY. Yes, but I don't hunt gobblers. Never cared for it. Sitting real still on wet dirt under a bush all day. I stand up like a man when I hunt. I do all my hunting in the fall and winter when the trees are bare. With nothing green but the pines and cedars.

MRS. VETCH. The magnolia stays green around the year.

MR. MINGO. The holly, the cypress.

MR. NIBLIS. The live oak.

FERN. Mistletoe. The privet hedge. Various ornamental shrubs.

MR. PALFREY. Yes, I could have named all those and more, too, but pines and cedars are what you mostly see. And the truth is, I don't hunt any more at all. The government won't let you kill but one or two ducks now and my loving daughters made me sell off all my dogs.

FERN. Now don't start in on that again. You could have kept your dogs at Texarkana and you know it. It was Lenore who put her foot down on the dogs.

MR. PALFREY. But that wasn't none of her doing. It's the city of Little Rock that won't let you keep dogs. Oh, two or three maybe, but they won't let you keep a pack of dogs. I'll tell you another thing. They'll steal your dog in Little Rock. You have to watch him ever minute. They made off with Blanche one night. That was my last dog, Mrs. Vetch. Poor old Blanche.

FERN. Lenore said she was stolen anyway.

MR. PALFREY. (Notices Mr. Mingo flexing his fingers) What's wrong, Mr. Mingo? That old "arthuritis" acting up on you?

MR. MINGO. I don't know what it is. My hands don't hurt anymore, they're just cold and numb. My feet too. Ice cold extremities. It seems all my blood vessels are silted up. When I walk my hip joints crackle like green sticks in a fire, and when I sit down my legs go to sleep. I couldn't stand up right now if the house was on fire. And when I lie down I get throat spasms and my throat wants to close.

MR. PALFREY. It sounds to me like you're about two-thirds dead, Mr. Mingo.

MR. MINGO. About half dead, Mr. Palfrey, but you weren't far off. I also have gravel in my kidneys.

MR. PALFREY. *(Flexing his own fingers)* Look at that. Look how limber they are. I still tie my own necktie ever Sunday morning.

Marguerite comes flying back in. She has a small color photograph.

MR. PALFREY. Well, look here. It's little Miss Prissy again.

MARGUERITE. Here! This will give you a good laugh! *(She looks at photo, laughs, then gives it to Mr. Palfrey)* It's worth ten dollars, easy. See. That's my fat bulldog, Norris, and my fluffy black cat, Doris. They're wearing cute party hats with rubber bands under their little chins, and look how they're sitting at the table with the teacups. It's a tea party. Norris and Doris, you see.

MR. PALFREY. Yes, I see that, but I don't like the look out of this dog's eye. I know dogs. I have a sure hand with dogs. One of these days this dog will tear that cat's head off.

MARGUERITE. Oh no! Norris just loves Doris! They play together and they lap up their milk out of the same bowl. Sometimes we all dance together in the back of the new truck. I twirl my long red scarf around and around. They try to catch at it and we all get dizzy. And Daddy comes out on the front porch and says, "Hey, no dancing in the back of the new truck!" But we act like we don't hear him and just keep dancing away like nobody's business. *(She whirls about, flinging her arms)* WE'VE GONE CRAZY AND WE CAN'T STOP DANCING!

MR. PALFREY. Here now. That's enough. *(Grabs her arm)*

MARGUERITE. You said you would give me ten dollars.

MR. PALFREY. *(Holds out photo)* Not for this.

FERN. What did he tell you, hon?

MARGUERITE. He said he would give me a ten-dollar bill if I could make him laugh.

FERN. *(To Mr. Palfrey)* Well. Pay her. She showed you a funny picture.

MR. PALFREY. It's not funny enough.

FERN. Give her the money, Daddy.

MR. PALFREY. *(Takes bill from snap-top coin purse and pays her. Taps finger on photo)* Better not take this Norris to Little Rock. They'll steal him up there before you can turn around good. Pen him up is my advice. Put a muzzle on him. He's a bad boy, I'm telling you.

MARGUERITE. *(Skips off with money, photo and shopping bag. Pauses in doorway)* Norris is not a bad boy! Norris just loves Doris! *(Sticks out her tongue at Mr. Palfrey and exits)*

FERN. *(To Mrs. Vetch)* But I don't see why you can't keep your rooms upstairs and let them have their dance hall down here. What will they use the hotel rooms for?

MRS. VETCH. I don't know. Mr. Delray Scantling doesn't confide in me. I have my own dark suspicions. Which I will keep to myself.

A pause, as they all think this over.

MR. PALFREY. I take it you are a Christian lady, Mrs. Vetch.

MRS. VETCH. Yes, and one of the most severe kind if you were thinking of taking some liberty.

MR. PALFREY. I was only going to say—

MRS. VETCH. *(Raising hand)* No, Mr. Palfrey, not another word on that, if you please. Shame on me for putting thoughts in your head.

FERN. *(Rising, with purse)* Is the ladies' room still back there?

MRS. VETCH. Yes, it's in the same place off the hall, but it doesn't say "Ladies" anymore. Delray has painted a lady's slipper on the door. With high heel and a big silver buckle.

Fern exits through rear hallway.

MR. MINGO. And he's painted a top hat on the door of the men's room. A black top hat, with stick and white gloves.

MR. NIBLIS. *(Low grunts, murmuring)*

MR. PALFREY. What was that?

MR. MINGO. Murmurs. He murmurs when he's reviewing his life.

DUVALL. *(Calls out across the room)* Hogs on the thirty and driving! *(Gets no response)* The Texas thirty! *(Still no response)*

MR. MINGO. (*Looking at Avalon brochure*) Avalon. That's where they
    carried King Arthur, you know.
MR. PALFREY. Who?
MR. MINGO. King Arthur. He was wounded in battle. A terrible head
    wound. Ruth Buttress came by in her van and took him away to a
    place called Avalon. We hear nothing more of him after that.
DUVALL. (*Claps both hands to his head*) I can't believe it! Another fumble!

Fern enters.

FERN. The strangest thing! There's a man lying on a bed!
MR. PALFREY. Where? What bed?
FERN. Back there off the hall. There's a kind of dark alcove with a bed
    in it. He's lying there like a dead man with his mouth open.
MR. PALFREY. A dead man!
FERN. I didn't say he <u>was</u> dead, I just said he <u>looked</u> dead. A man in
    white clothes. I didn't want to touch him.
MRS. VETCH. In the alcove, you say. I don't remember a bed back there.
    Do you mean a day bed or a couch?
FERN. No, it's an ordinary double bed. An iron bedstead with a bare
    striped mattress on it.
MRS. VETCH. But I don't understand. A man sleeping in a public place
    like that.
MR. PALFREY. You don't reckon it's Ramp, do you? Barbers wear white.
    Maybe they didn't carry him off to that death ranch after all.
MR. MINGO. I don't see how he could have been lying there all this time.
MR. PALFREY. Unless he <u>is</u> dead and nobody noticed him. (*To Fern*) Is
    it a little old man with a sharp nose?
FERN. His mouth is open. I don't know about his nose. It's dark back
    there.
MR. MINGO. Wait. I know. It might be Kate's boyfriend. Yes, it might
    very well be Prentice. Having a nap.
MR. NIBLIS. Prentice is a gangster.
MR. MINGO. A criminal anyway.
MR. NIBLIS. Prentice is a scoundrel.
MR. MINGO. A thief anyway. (*To Fern*) Is he wearing white jail coveralls?
FERN. White something. And heavy black shoes.

MRS. VETCH. Wearing his shoes on the bed?

MR. MINGO. I'll bet it's Prentice. Kate must be hiding him here.

FERN. Her boyfriend is a criminal?

MR. MINGO. Yes, and it's hard to keep him in custody. He was in jail at Hot Springs until two or three days ago, when he climbed over the fence in the exercise yard.

MRS. VETCH. Kate says he's not really a crook.

MR. NIBLIS. Barbers don't wear heavy black shoes. They wear these soft white leather shoes with a lot of little air holes in them.

MR. MINGO. Prentice steals equipment from unguarded construction sites, with his low-boy trailer. He steals backhoes and front-loaders— these ungainly machines that creep about scraping the face of the earth.

MRS. VETCH. Now you don't know that to be true, Mr. Mingo. Kate says it's his brother-in-law that does all the stealing. He takes the low-boy trailer out at night without Prentice's permission. She says the state police have had it in for Prentice for a long time.

MR. PALFREY. It still could be Ramp, you know. He's not cutting hair anymore and he might have gone over to a heavier, darker shoe.

MR. MINGO. Unknown man on bed. Who could it be? That's the question we need to address.

MRS. VETCH. We could get Duvall to look into it.

MR. MINGO. Yes, I think that might be the thing to do.

A pause. They all look at Duvall across the room but do and say nothing.

MR. PALFREY. If you could ever tear him away from his ball game. Well, what can you expect, Mr. Mingo, it's a different country. These new people don't want to work, not like you and me had to work, from daylight to dark, six days a week, rain or shine. Dine and dance, that's all they want to do. When they're not watching their TV shows. You and Mr. Niblis and me might cash in tomorrow. The last yellow-jacket of the season might sting us to death. We might check out next month, with the first killing frost, but it won't matter much, and you know why? Because we've seen the best of this country.

MR. MINGO. But you know, I never really did any hard work. I managed to escape all that. Nobody in the Mingo family ever put himself out much.

FERN. How did you make a living?

MR. MINGO. I spread panic for a living. I worked here and there for different newspapers.

FERN. You mean you wrote things in newspapers?

MR. MINGO. I'm afraid so, yes. The Mingos have traditionally gone into undemanding fields like that—journalism, government service, pharmacy, photography, usury. Mingos have been beekeepers, and night clerks in motels. They have operated small ferry boats at remote crossings on narrow streams. It was my curious fate to become a writer of newspaper editorials.

FERN. Really? That must have been interesting. It never occurred to me that—

MR. MINGO. No, you don't think of them as being composed by anything human. It's a dead form, like opera. It was dead when I started too, but that didn't discourage me. Day after day I gave political advice, economic advice, military advice, agricultural advice. Lapidary comment for all occasions. I gave freely of myself.

MR. NIBLIS. Vain labor. All those idle words.

MR. MINGO. I offered artistic advice, engineering advice, cooking advice. I gave moral instruction. No one paid the least bit of attention to anything I wrote. I knew that, of course, but then a change came over me. I came to believe that people were after all, listening to me, acting on my counsel, heeding my lightest word. It was a crushing responsibility.

MR. NIBLIS. One day real soon now, Mingo, you'll have to answer for every last one of those idle words.

MR. MINGO. I spoke to my publisher about this feeling and he had me put away in a hospital. Quite a well known clinic, specializing in the treatment of journalists and their delusions. Journalists and other bystanders, onlookers, eavesdroppers and talebearers. It wasn't a bad place. The doctors said I was suffering from intrusive thoughts. They put me on some dope and told me to eat a lot of bananas. I soon recovered. I was soon back at work, if you can call it that, and I did well enough for a time.

MR. NIBLIS. Spewing out more vain words.

MR. MINGO. No doubt, but they didn't seem vain to me at the time. I was conscientious in my work. I was never afraid to be dull, for instance. To drone a bit.

MR. NIBLIS. Nobody will dispute that.

MR. MINGO. I did well enough for a time and then a darker change came over me. It was slowly revealed to me that my words were withering the grass and turning everything brown. I felt personally responsible for extensive crop failures. So you can understand why I had to stop writing.

MR. NIBLIS. And how the readers must have cheered, Mingo, when you laid down your busy pen.

MR. PALFREY. But I don't know why you had to stop writing. Things like that happen. I once give a man some mortgage advice and he lost his house. That didn't stop me from talking.

MRS. VETCH. But I don't see—I mean—surely yours were printed words, Mr. Mingo. It's not as though you were speaking on the radio and spewing out your poison words willy nilly into the air. Where they could then waft across the countryside and settle on the flowering crops.

MR. MINGO. Don't ask me to explain the mechanics of it, Mrs. Vetch. I suspect the contaminants were not airborne, but something more in the nature of a malignant radiation. I can only tell you that I saw the blighted fields for myself, and how those fields were perfectly congruent with the circulation area of my newspaper. And how those same fields quickened and greened up when my articles no longer appeared in the paper.

MRS. VETCH. Nobody would want to turn the earth brown with his words. No decent person.

MR. MINGO. No, indeed, and I saw then what I had to do. It was the only honorable thing I could do—take early disability retirement.

FERN. (Musing) "Intrustive thoughts." I didn't realize they could put you away for that.

MR. PALFREY. It's amazing what the government can do these days. What these federal judges take on themselves. It's a different country, Fern.

MR. MINGO. I was a middle-aged man when I received my first disability check. Young middle-age, really. My face had not yet dropped, from gravitational stresses. My nose and ears were still of modest size. That was many years ago and I haven't done a lick of work since that day.

MR. NIBLIS. *(Shouting)* Look, the van is here! It's Ruth Buttress! Time to go, everybody! All aboard for Avalon!

MRS. VETCH. *(Reaching for her things)* Oh my goodness! Already?

MR. NIBLIS. Time to go! Ruth Buttress is here with all the latest news from Hell! All aboard! It's roundup time! On to the slaughter house!

MRS. VETCH. But I'm just not ready yet!

MR. MINGO. No, wait. Mr. Palfrey, your legs are better than mine. Would you mind taking a look out the window? To see if—

FERN. Here, I'll go. *(Goes to front window)* There's no van. Just that tan car with a man sitting in it.

MR. MINGO. I suspected as much. One of Mr. Niblis's childish jokes. When he's not brooding he's making a nuisance of himself, crying out false news bulletins.

MR. NIBLIS. *(Shrugs, rolls another cigarette)* Well, it's something to do.

MRS. VETCH. He claims to be some kind of prophet.

MR. MINGO. One of the very minor prophets.

MRS. VETCH. He's some kind of outdoor preacher. He's not really ordained.

MR. NIBLIS. Correction. Ordained, but not ordained by man or by any corrupt institution of man. I am fully ordained in the Invisible Church, which is the only true church. We know who we are.

MRS. VETCH. That may be so, Mr. Niblis, but I would not feel at all easy in my mind, going away on my honeymoon, if you had conducted the marriage service.

MR. PALFREY. But where is this Avalon anyway? I see that old fat gal on TV talking about it all the time.

FERN. "There's always room for you—at Avalon." That's what she keeps saying.

MRS. VETCH. Yes, that's Ruth Buttress. She's the Matron of Avalon.

MR. NIBLIS. She's a front for Dr. Lloyd Mole. A so-called doctor.

MRS. VETCH. "No waiting list ever," she says. "On the Special Value Package."

FERN. I wonder how they manage that.

MR. PALFREY. But just where is the place?

MR. MINGO. It's somewhere over there in the Chinkypin National Forest, deep in the woods. In that great swamp called the Chinkypin Bottoms.

MR. NIBLIS. On Chinkypin Bayou [Pronounced "Bye-O"]. Far from prying eyes. They say it's so dark in those woods that the owls fly in the daytime there, and the bats flit.

MR. MINGO. And the nighthawk, with his fine white throat.

MRS. VETCH. It used to be a Boy Scout camp. Camp Chinkypin.

MR. NIBLIS. It was too rough for the Scouts. The Scouts couldn't take it, so they're shipping us over there.

FERN. Is it a nursing home or a retirement village or what?

MR. MINGO. A little of both, I think. An internment center, in any case. Some sort of terminal warehouse for old people. A place to languish and die.

MRS. VETCH. Duvall told me that some of the ladies are put up in their own little rose-bowered cottages at Avalon. But I wonder if that can apply to me, being on the Special Value Package.

MR. NIBLIS. Duvall doesn't know the first thing about Avalon.

MR. PALFREY. There's a lot of snakes in the Chinkypin Bottoms. I drove down there one time to buy some steel drums off a fellow and ever where you stepped there was another snake. Spreadin' adders, coachwhips, copperheads, canebrake rattlers, blue racers, big rusty moccasins—ever kind of snake in the world. I stayed the night at that fellow's house and you couldn't sleep for the squirrels barking and the hogs bumping up against the floor. It come a shower of rain in the night and these big pine rooter hogs, don't you know, got up under the house and snorted and made a big hog commotion.

FERN. Wasn't there something in the paper about Dr. Mole?

MR. MINGO. Oh yes, he's been in and out of the news for years. You may be thinking about that business in Florida. His red vinegar therapy and his controversial yeast injections.

MR. NIBLIS. The big Fungometrics scandal. That's when they run him out of Florida.

MR. MINGO. I think he sold babies at one time too.

MR. NIBLIS. Little newborn babies, still red and puckered-up.

MR. PALFREY. The well water at that fellow's house was brown. It had a sulfur smell to it and it tasted like alum. And the mosquitoes drove me crazy. I cleared out of there before daylight.

MR. NIBLIS. Without your steel drums?

MR. PALFREY. My drums was already loaded and tied down, Mr. Niblis.

MR. NIBLIS. That's what Ramp did too. He cleared out early. Before Ruth Buttress could get aholt of him.

MR. PALFREY. Maybe he's already over there at Avalon.

MR. NIBLIS. Not him. He's too smart. He got out while the getting was good. Ramp was smarter than us.

MRS. VETCH. *(Sighing)* It's just so hard, making a change like this at my age.

MR. PALFREY. Well, I guess you'll just have to make the best of it, won't you? I don't have to worry about that myself. You'll never catch me in a place like Avalon. I raised my chirren up right and I have two loving homes to go to.

Pause.

MR. MINGO. You know, I've never told anyone this before, but he's gone now and I can't see that it will do any real harm. *(Looking about, lowering voice in confidential manner)* <u>Mr. Ramp took food to his room.</u>

MRS. VETCH. But we all took food to our rooms, Mr. Mingo!

MR. MINGO. Some more than others. Your little cans of red sockeye salmon did not escape my notice, Mrs. Vetch.

MRS. VETCH. But Miss Eula didn't really mind! She never enforced that rule, as you well know! She winked at her own rule! My goodness, everybody did it! You could hear munching and smacking in every room! Even with the doors shut!

MR. MINGO. One night I saw Mr. Ramp ducking into his room with a plate of finely chopped nuts. The kernels had been chopped to a uniform fineness. He tried to conceal that plate from me. I'm convinced he was keeping some small animal in his room.

MR. NIBLIS. Mingo thinks Ramp had a roomful of canary birds.

FERN. Wouldn't you have heard them cheeping and warbling?

MR. MINGO. One or two birds, I suggested. I never said a roomful. I never said an aviary.

MR. NIBLIS. More likely it was just some pet mouse or spider or lizard, like these prisoners keep in their cells. Trying to teach a roach, you know, to sit up and beg.

MR. MINGO. I was particularly watchful of Mr. Ramp in those last days. I was on stakeout, you might say. Another week or two and I would have gotten to the bottom of that mystery.

MR. NIBLIS. Ramp was too clever for you.

Sound of thunder, followed by rain beating against glass. Fern goes to the front window and looks out, her hand shading her eyes.

FERN. Well, here it comes.

MR. PALFREY. Did you roll the windows up?

FERN. Yes…Still no sign of Lenore…That tan car is still out there.

MR. MINGO. With two men in it?

FERN. It looks like just one.

MR. MINGO. A state police detective. They come and go.

DUVALL. It's a new one out there today.

MR. PALFREY: Keeping an eye on this honky tonk.

MR. MINGO. No, it's not that. They're waiting for Prentice. It's another stakeout. They know he'll turn up sooner or later to see Kate. Where the nectar is, there will be the bee also. The first principle of the manhunt.

FERN. *(Musing)* Betrayed by their own love for each other.

MR. PALFREY. *(Musing)* He knew it was dumb but he just couldn't stay away from his honky tonk sweetheart.

Enter Delray, with his Daily Planner, a memorandum book. He marches directly to Mr. Palfrey.

DELRAY. This is <u>not</u>, repeat <u>not</u>, a honky tonk. Will you people please stop using that term? Is that too much to ask?

MR. PALFREY. What is it then?

DELRAY. Delray's New Moon is going to be a very smart supper club, sir, with a strict dress code, and a slender white candle on each table. How many times do I have to go through this? We're not going to have louts in here clumping around in boots and hats, drinking beer out of cans. And we're not going to have a disgusting mob of kids dancing to their stupid music. Everybody has the wrong idea.

FERN. I wouldn't think there would be enough people around here to support a—

DELRAY. Excuse me, M'am, you're thinking local. My vision is national. Right out there, a mile away, is Interstate Thirty, one of the very busiest of cross-country thoroughfares. It's the new Broadway of America. My highly select guests will be coming from far and wide. In one year's time this place will be as famous as that drugstore in South Dakota that tourists flock to. Thousands of people—civilized people—will plan their trips around an evening of dining and dancing at Delray's New Moon. You're going to see night club history made here. (*Looking about proudly*) I'm having it all done up in an oyster shade.

MR. NIBLIS. What was all that? What did Delray say?

MRS. VETCH. (*Raising her voice*) An oyster shade! He's having it all done up in an oyster shade!

MR. MINGO. There's an unknown man back there on the bed, Delray.

DELRAY. (*Not listening, goes to Mrs. Vetch, takes her hand*) Well, now, look at you! Don't you look nice today, Mrs. Vetch! I just know you're going to be crowned queen of hearts at Avalon!

MR. NIBLIS. The van is late, Delray.

DELRAY. What is this, Mr. Niblis? Drooping spirits? On the day of your big adventure?

MR. NIBLIS. Where is Ruth Buttress?

DELRAY. Ruth Buttress is on the way. She'll be here any minute now.

FERN. There's a strange man back there lying on a bed. I didn't want to touch him.

DELRAY. What bed?

MR. MINGO. In that alcove off the hall.

DELRAY. (*Not listening, looking at his Daily Planner*) I don't know what you're talking about.

MR. PALFREY. We can't get Booger Red over there to look into it. He's all wrapped up in his ball game.

DELRAY. Sir, there is no one named Booger Red employed at Delray's New Moon, and there never will be.

Delray goes to the bar, where Duvall is intently watching the television game.

DELRAY. No, no, no. These stemmed glasses don't go under the bar, they hang from the overhead rack. Nothing is where it should be. Duvall? Duvall? Do you hear what I'm saying?

DUVALL. *(Raises hand for silence)* Wait. Field goal. *(Leans and goes into bodily contortions as ball is kicked, then slumps with disgust as try obviously fails)*

DELRAY. Sammy and Kate opened up as usual this morning. I told you last night the place was to be closed. That kitchen should have been shut down and ready for my inspection.

DUVALL. I'll see about it at halftime.

DELRAY. *(Pulls plug on television set)* No. Now. *(Opens memorandum book)* Turn to "Saturday" in your Daily Planner. "Things to do today." Look. Not one of them has been done. Every day we're falling further and further—where's your Daily Planner?

DUVALL. I lost it somewhere.

DELRAY. You lost your Daily Planner? And you said nothing to me about it? What if it should fall into the hands of my competitors?

DUVALL. I'm using this notebook now. *(Flips through it, stops to read)* Mrs. Vetch wants to know if she can take her iron to Avalon. It's a small—

DELRAY. I don't want to hear one more word about Mrs. Vetch's small iron. I want to see some work going forward here. I'm beginning to wonder about your dedication, Duvall. You said share in my vision and help me whip this place into shape. Isn't that what you told me? No, don't write that down! You keep writing things down but nothing ever gets done. Why is that?

DUVALL. I can't do everything. I need a helper.

DELRAY. No, Duvall, you <u>are</u> the helper. Your job is to help <u>me</u>. You are a management trainee.

DUVALL. If I'm in management why don't I have any keys?

DELRAY. *(Jiggles ring of keys on belt)* Keys come later.

DUVALL. But I can never look forward to having a helper? I thought this was America, Delray.

DELRAY. How can I get through to you? Don't you realize how fortunate you are? To be permitted to share in my dreams? Of transforming this old derelict hotel into a little wayside jewel?

DUVALL. Everything takes so long. I thought we would be open by now, and I would be in my maroon dinner jacket. You said I would carry

off-white menus two feet high cradled in my arm. That I would greet
the guests and assume a grave manner—frown even—as I checked
their names against our reservations book.

DELRAY. Do you know what your fitness grade is at this moment? It's
unsatisfactory.

DUVALL. I do my job. I have a pleasant word for everybody.

DELRAY. But you don't do your job, that's just it. Do you know what an
executive does? He executes. He sees things through to completion.
(Shakes finger at him) And what do you do? You start something and
then drift away.

DUVALL. *(Goes rigid, distant, almost menacing)* No, don't point your finger at me, Delray. Nobody points their finger at me.

Pause. The mood gradually passes, Duvall returns to normal.

DUVALL. Maybe I should go back to college full time and get my psychology degree.

DELRAY. Maybe you should. That might be the best place for you.
Maybe you should go back to the campus and hang around for thirty
or forty years.

DUVALL. But then I couldn't make my car payments.

DELRAY. *(Solemn, pushes face into Duvall's face)* Listen to me. Put your
right hand on my shoulder. Give me your full attention. Do you dare
to win, Duvall?

DUVALL. *(Taken aback. Then becomes solemn himself)* Yes…I do.

DELRAY. I didn't quite hear that.

DUVALL. I do dare to win.

DELRAY. Do you dare to lead?

DUVALL. I do dare to lead, Delray.

DELRAY. Say "I can."

DUVALL. I can.

DELRAY. From your heart.

DUVALL. I can!

DELRAY. "I will."

DUVALL. I will!

DELRAY. Once more.

DUVALL. I can! I will!

DELRAY. Good boy. *(Claps him on the back)* That's more like it. A fresh start. Now sort these glasses out and let's get on with it. *(Looks at watch)* What's keeping that van? Where is Ruth Buttress? I want these old people out of here. They frighten me. They disgust me. Why aren't they wearing their Avalon caps?

DUVALL. I'll see to it. Those caps are around here somewhere.

DELRAY. And let's get a sign in the window. "Closed for Remodeling."

DUVALL. Leave it to me.

DELRAY. Tell Kate and Sammy to clean up back there and then clear out.

DUVALL. Leave it to me.

DELRAY. Good boy.

Delray exits. Duvall remains seated, plugs in television set, resumes watching game. Attention shifts back to old people, whose conversation now becomes audible.

MRS. VETCH. How much longer do they expect us to sit around here waiting? Why don't they just tie us up in towsacks [pronounced toe-sacks] with some brickbats and drown us like kittens? Get it over with, I say. I'm ready. Why don't they just wring our old necks like chickens and watch us flop around on the floor? I'm tired of waiting for Ruth Buttress. I'm ready to go.

MR. MINGO. The van will be here all too soon, I'm afraid.

Muttering from Mr. Niblis.

MR. PALFREY. How far along do you reckon he is?

MR. MINGO. He never tells us.

MRS. VETCH. Sometimes he blows froth and bubbles when he's reviewing his life.

FERN. Look, he's smiling. It may be that he's lingering over his happy boyhood days.

MR. MINGO. He tells us nothing about his boyhood.

MRS. VETCH. *(Beats at cigarette ashes smoldering on Mr. Niblis's clothes)* Now you've set yourself on fire again!

MR. NIBLIS. *(Coming around)* What?

MRS. VETCH. *(Pours Coke on burning spot)* You're burning another hole in your clothes!

MR. PALFREY. Where had you got to, Mr. Niblis? In raking over your life?

MR. MINGO. He won't say. He reveals nothing. I've always been open about such things myself. I share with one and all. The long farce of my own life.

MRS. VETCH. It's just so hard, ending up like this. A woman's life is so—strange. I don't know where it all went. Or my mother's things. She had so many beautiful things and now they're scattered to the four winds. (She touches boxes) Of course I still have a few odds and ends. I have my scrapbooks. But not my linens or my silver or my china. There's a big grinning ape in Shreveport eating off my mother's Wedgwood dinner service.

Sounds of a car driving up. The engine is raced, then shut off. Heads turn, apprehensive looks at front door.

MR. MINGO. Ah. Here she is. We're off at last. To the vale of Avalon.

MRS. VETCH. (Flustered, gathering at her things) Oh my! So soon? And in the rain too! I hadn't counted on leaving in the rain!

MR. NIBLIS. What is it? What's going on?

MR. MINGO. Time to go. Our time has come to be put away. Ruth Buttress is here.

MR. NIBLIS. (Stubs out cigarette, reaches for bag) Well, that's it then. The jig is up.

MRS. VETCH. But I still don't understand why we can't stay on here at the Sunnyside, Mr. Mingo. It was never properly explained to me. Don't they owe us a better explanation? I'm just not ready to go yet.

MR. MINGO. I know, but we have a firm appointment.

Act II

The scene is the same, moments later.

FERN. *(Who has gone to the window)* No, it's not the van. It's Lenore and Tonya. About time, too.

Lenore, Fern's much younger sister, enters hastily out of the rain, with her daughter Tonya, a girl six or seven years old. There are greetings.

MR. PALFREY. *(Still seated, holding his arms out to Tonya)* There she is! There's my baby! Come here this minute and give Granddaddy some sugar!

Tonya goes to him, submits to being hugged, and kissed on both cheeks. Then she backs away and wipes her face with her arm.

MR. PALFREY. Hey, don't you wipe my sugar off! Would you look at that? That girl is wiping off my sugar!

LENORE. I had trouble getting the car started. I don't know what's wrong with it. Then we got caught in the rain.

FERN. One excuse is enough. Do you know how long we've been waiting here?

MR. PALFREY. Aw, it don't matter. We was having a nice visit here with these folks. Here, Lenore, I want you to meet—

LENORE. No, we don't have time for that, Daddy. Let's get your things loaded. Boyce wants to talk to you about something important. Let's go. Let's get your things loaded. I hate driving in the rain. All those big trucks throwing up slop on your windshield.

MR. PALFREY. Well...all right then...

Bustle of departure, farewells. Fern is the last to leave. She stops at front door, then comes back to Mrs. Vetch. Takes her hand and pats it.

FERN. You'll make some new friends there. Avalon won't be so bad.

MR. NIBLIS. It will be the abomination of desolation.

FERN. Well...goodbye...

She leaves. There is only the sound of the rain and the television ball game. The three old people sit staring, vacant, motionless. Outside there are sounds of car doors closing. One car is started. Then come the feeble grinding noises of the starter on the second car. The engine doesn't catch. The starter noises become weaker. More slamming of car doors. Mr. Palfrey, his two daughters and Tonya troop back in and return to their table.

MR. PALFREY. Just go on, Fern. Go on back to Texarkana. No use in you waiting around here. It's nothing much. We'll get it fixed.

FERN. On Saturday? You can't get a car fixed on Saturday. I don't like to leave you stranded.

LENORE. And that's just what we are! We're stranded travelers! I'll have to call Boyce to come get us! Where's the phone?

FERN. The pay phone is just outside there.

LENORE. *(Looks in purse for change, starts for door)* Always something!

TONYA. *(Calling after her)* But Daddy's not at home! He's gone to the gun, knife and coin show!

LENORE. I forgot! *(Claps forehead)* Now what? Now we really are stranded!

MR. PALFREY. Don't take on about it so. It's nothing much. *(Calls to Duvall)* Hey! You! Booger Red! You want to make twenty dollars real fast!

DUVALL. Doing what?

MR. PALFREY. We need a jump start on that green car out there. But I want you to brush off the battery terminals first. Can you do that?

DUVALL. I can do anything I take a notion to do.

MR. PALFREY. A jump from the blue car to the green car, that's all. You get it started and I got a twenty-dollar bill for you. But I don't want you messing with it if you don't know what you're doing.

DUVALL. Aren't you a little bit out of touch with things, sir? You don't know much about the youth of America today, do you?

MR. PALFREY. I don't know nothing about you.

DUVALL. You should read *Parade* magazine in your Sunday paper sometime. You might learn a thing or two about all the brilliant young achievers of my generation. We have new ideas and new values. We have a new spirit.

MR. PALFREY. *(Holds up $20 bill)* Five minute's work. Twenty dollars.

DUVALL. We are your artists and your explorers of tomorrow. We are your group therapists and your guidance counselors and your committee chairmen.

MR. PALFREY. There's a steel brush and some jumper cables in the trunk of that blue car.

DUVALL. As soon as I get my psychology degree I'm going into clinical work. Disturbed people will come to me and pay me good money to listen to all their personal stuff. People who have lost their way in the world and don't know what to do.

MR. PALFREY. A little more far [fire] to the starter of that green car, that's all it needs. It won't take long. If you know what you're doing.

Pause.

DUVALL. You're not daring me to start that car, are you?

MR. PALFREY. I dare you and I double-dog dare you.

DUVALL. *(Strides across room)* Let me have the keys.

MR. PALFREY. The keys are in the cars.

DUVALL. And the money.

MR. PALFREY. After it's started.

DUVALL. *(Snatches bill from Mr. Palfrey's hand)* I get paid up front.

MR. PALFREY. That's one of your new ideas?

DUVALL. I've made my commitment. The car will be started.

Duvall goes to the front door, where he is intercepted by Delray, who comes in shaking rainwater from his arms and fingers.

DELRAY. All the glasses in place?

DUVALL. Not yet. I got to get that old guy's car started.

DELRAY. That's nothing to do with us!

DUVALL. It's a matter of personal honor. I've been challenged, Delray.

DELRAY. We don't have time for that!

DUVALL. Look, I'm putting those people back on the road. You don't want them hanging around here all day, do you?

DELRAY. *(Looks at Mr. Palfrey. Exasperated sigh)* All right, but don't waste a lot of time on it. Are the painters working upstairs?

DUVALL. Not today. Not on Saturday.

DELRAY. Then who's up there?

DUVALL. Nobody. The painters won't be back till Monday. I made a sweep this morning and all the rooms are clear. The last of the old nesters are down. Vetch, Mingo, Niblis. There was no trouble. Mr. Niblis was down early. I was afraid we might have to gas him out.

DELRAY. You tell me you made a sweep and all the rooms are clear. Well, all the rooms are not clear. I was outside just now and I saw some people in that corner room at the back. Room Six, I think it is. The faces of four or five morons, all crowded together at the window, peering down at me.

DUVALL. Literally morons?

DELRAY. Yes, watching my every move.

DUVALL. Grinning and making faces at you?

DELRAY. No, just watching me steadily like—I don't know—a family of cats. When I moved my hand—slowly, like this—their heads turned and they followed the movement with their eyes.

DUVALL. It sounds like we've got some window peepers on our hands.

DELRAY. Window peepers peep into windows, not out of windows.

DUVALL. Probably just some kids. They like to play in empty hotels. I pray to God they're not playing with matches up there.

DELRAY. Kids like to play in empty hotels? What, pretending to be little traveling salesmen?

DUVALL. Well, you know, they like to prowl around in empty buildings.

DELRAY. Where is Ruth Buttress?

DUVALL. No sign of her.

DELRAY. No late word from Avalon?

DUVALL. Nothing. (*Pointing up stairs*) You need some help with the intruders?

DELRAY. No, just get that old man and his family on their way.

DUVALL. Try to gauge their level of understanding, Delray, before you explain what you want them to do.

DELRAY. What?

DUVALL. The morons. You need to establish the level of their listening skills and their interactive social skills. Go slow with them. Appeal to their self-esteem. That's the approach I would take. Gain their confidence before you—

DELRAY. I can handle the morons in Room Six. You just take care of that car business and get back to your work pronto.

DUVALL. Check.

They exit, Duvall outside, Delray up the stairs.

MR. PALFREY. *(To Tonya)* How do you like your new school, baby?

TONYA. Fine.

MR. PALFREY. Do you like your new teacher?

TONYA. I like her fine.

MR. PALFREY. What have you been doing in school?

TONYA. Dressing up like different animals and different vegetables.

LENORE. She didn't make the honor roll.

MR. PALFREY. That's all right, she'll make it next time. *(Then back to Tonya)* Now tell me this, baby. Here's what I want to know. Who do you love best—Papaw Gibbet or Grand-daddy Palfrey?

TONYA. I love you best, Grand-daddy.

MR. PALFREY. *(Gives her a dollar bill)* See how crafty she is, Mr. Mingo? She gets that from me. That's her Palfrey blood. She's a sharp little thing and her breath is sweet enough but look how big and red and flat her feet are. *(To Tonya)* Show him, hon.

Tonya holds up a sandaled foot.

MR. PALFREY. See? Flat as a pancake. But all the Palfreys have small feet with fine high arches. That's a Gibbet foot, Mr. Mingo, not a Palfrey foot. Let Boyce Gibbet marry into your family and that's the kind of feet you'll get ever time.

Tonya walks back toward corridor.

MR. PALFREY. *(Claps hands together)* No, don't go back there, baby. You stay up here with us. There's a dead man back there on a bed, or a sick man. He might have something bad wrong with him. We don't know what's going on in this honky tonk.

TONYA. But I need to go to the bathroom, Grand-daddy.

MR. PALFREY. Well here, Lenore, take her on back there and let her do her job, but keep aholt of her hand and come straight back. We don't know what's going on around here. It used to be a nice place to stop off for pie.

Lenore and Tonya exit. Enter Duvall, furious, wet, dirty.

DUVALL. There's fire getting to the starter but it's dragging. I can't do any more. I'm through fooling with it.

MR. PALFREY. Wait, you haven't done anything yet. That plunger thing must be stuck in the solenoid. Get a rock and tap on it. Two or three smart taps will break it loose.

DUVALL. *(Drying hands on towel behind bar)* Tapped, you say? You want it tapped? *(Goes to carpenter's tool tray and picks up claw hammer)* I'll give it two or three smart taps!

MR. PALFREY. Not too hard now.

Duvall exits. Fern goes to window to watch him.

FERN. *(Peering through glass)* What is he doing? *(Sudden alarm)* No, not that car! Not the blue car! There's nothing wrong with my car!

She dashes outside. Four or five rapid hammer blows are heard, steel on steel. Duvall re-enters, puts hammer away, washes again at sink, resumes watching ball game. Fern re-enters, agitated.

FERN. Now he's messed up <u>my</u> car! Now <u>it</u> won't start!

MR. PALFREY. What did you do, Booger? Did you bust the solenoid? On the wrong car?

DUVALL. *(Speaking over his shoulder)* Me no savvy solenoid. Leave me alone. Don't talk to me anymore.

MR. PALFREY. What's wrong with that fellow?

MRS. VETCH. It's better not to upset Duvall.

MR. MINGO. It's best not to arouse Duvall. I suspect the green and blue confused him.

FERN. Now we <u>are</u> stuck. Well, I'll just have to call Garland and tell him to come get us.

Fern exits to make telephone call. Enter Lenore and Tonya.

LENORE. Where's the waitress? I want a piece of lemon ice box pie.

MR. PALFREY. I warn you, that girl is snippy.

MRS. VETCH. Hon, they haven't had lemon pie here since Miss Eula left. Or banana pudding either.

LENORE. *(Looking around)* What's going on? Are they closing up the Sunnyside?

MR. PALFREY. The old woman sold out. These new people are turning the place into a dance hall.

LENORE. *(Looking at Niblis, Vetch, Mingo)* Those people are running a dance hall?

MR. PALFREY. No, not <u>them</u>. They were living here and now they've been kicked out of their nice little rooms.

MR. MINGO. Evicted. Delray is showing us the door.

MRS. VETCH. We're waiting for Ruth Buttress.

MR. MINGO. You are seated in the grand ballroom. Right here is where the dancers will glide about. The hypothetical elegant dancers.

MR. PALFREY. A van is coming to haul them off to Avalon.

LENORE. Avalon! Of all things! That's just what Boyce wants to talk to you about, Daddy. He sent off and got some literature. *(Rummages in purse, finds brochure, gives it to Mr. Palfrey)* See? "Avalon. A New Concept in Twilight Care."

MR. PALFREY. *(Holding brochure loosely)* What do I want with this?

LENORE. It won't hurt you to look it over. *(Points to brochure again)* See? "The days are full at Avalon and before you know it, it's bedtime." Boyce thinks you might enjoy going to a place like that.

MR. PALFREY. *(Crumples brochure, drops it on floor)* Boyce can think again.

There is a sudden outburst from Duvall.

DUVALL. That guy was way out of bounds! With both feet! How can we ever hope to win against crooked crap like that!

The others look up but don't respond. Fern enters.

FERN. Well, Garland said he would get up here as soon as he can. He's got two or three errands to run first.

LENORE. I've just been talking to Daddy about a new arrangement, Fern. Boyce thinks he might want to cut his visits a little shorter. Back to a month, say. (To Mr. Palfrey) He thinks you might like it better, Daddy, not staying in one place so long.

MR. PALFREY. A month? Move twelve times a year?

LENORE. He thinks—

MR. PALFREY. Boyce has been thinking way too much.

LENORE. He's thinking about what's best for you.

MR. PALFREY. Boyce is thinking about Boyce.

LENORE. So if you don't like the idea of the shorter stay, then Boyce thinks maybe we ought to look into this Avalon place. We can get you right in. There's never any waiting.

FERN. I wonder how they manage that.

LENORE. There's just one lump payment and then no more worries.

MRS. VETCH. On the Special Value Package. That's what we're on.

FERN. I wonder how they do it at the price.

MR. NIBLIS. Fast turnaround, that's how. Accelerated disposal. When we check in the front door they're dragging corpses out the back door. Out the door, into the dumpster and off the books.

MR. MINGO. And not much lamented.

FERN. Oh come on. Who would do such a thing?

MR. NIBLIS. A foul lump of grease named Lloyd Mole, that's who. It's the vital organs racket. They're bootlegging vital organs out of Avalon. Dr. Mole and his accomplice Ruth Buttress.

MR. MINGO. You signed up for it.

MR. NIBLIS. I never signed up for anything. It was you, Mingo, who got sold a bill of goods. And now they've got your earnest money.

MRS. VETCH. Mr. Niblis thinks they're going to cut out our vital organs and sell them to rich people. Sick rich people.

MR. MINGO. I'm afraid he flatters us there. They don't even want our vital organs, so called.

MR. NIBLIS. That's how much you know, Mingo. Mole is going to rip out our hearts and our kidneys and our big flopping brown livers.

MR. MINGO. No, you're dramatizing yourself again. What would they want with our petrified livers? What would anybody want with an old heart like mine? An old sloshing and leaking bag of blood.

MR. NIBLIS. An old cankered bag of pride and fear and deceit, you mean. Nobody is interested in your opinions. *(Points to Mr. Mingo's two-tone shoes)* Look at those shoes. Nobody wants to hear the opinions of a man wearing ludicrous shoes like that.

MR. MINGO. At one time they listened.

MR. NIBLIS. Pitiful shoes, just crying out for attention. A man your age should be done with all those little vanities.

MRS. VETCH. I just hope the place is clean.

MR. MINGO. They heeded my every word. I was a prophet too in my own way.

MR. NIBLIS. Here's a prophecy for you, Mingo. In three months time we'll be gone. We'll be off Mole's books. Mark my words.

MRS. VETCH. I hope the linens are clean. I hope the towels are soft. I hope they don't have roaches at Avalon. I hope the bathroom floors are not wet. I hope they have large-print books. I hope they're not cross with us. I hope they don't scold us a lot. I've heard some bad things about that home called Gathering Shade. They hang a placard from your neck if you misbehave, and you must wear it in shame for a week. "I Spread Rumors." Things like that. "I Talked Back to Staff." "I Am a TV Hog."

MR. MINGO. But we have to be realistic, Mrs. Vetch, and expect some indignities. Certain brutal familiarities.

MRS. VETCH. Do you think Ruth Buttress will be kind? I hope so. I hope they don't have little spiders in the beds.

MR. NIBLIS. All vain hopes.

MRS. VETCH. I hope they don't interfere with us. Those people at Avalon.

MR. NIBLIS. What do you mean?

MRS. VETCH. You know—interfere with us.

MR. NIBLIS. Tamper with us in some way? Mess with us?

MR. MINGO. Meddle with us? Annoy us?

MRS. VETCH. Interfere with us—you know.

MR. MINGO. No, I don't know what you're getting at, but the people at Sinking Embers, I'm told, do meddle with you. They sometimes wake you in the night. They rouse you from your deepest slumber. Some orderly on the night shift. Some young fellow like Duvall there. He sits by your bed in the dark and asks difficult questions in a soft voice.

MRS. VETCH. Difficult questions! Oh dear! Not that too! Not hard questions on top of everything else! I know I won't be able to answer them properly!

MR. NIBLIS. That won't be anything new to me. Indignities, mockery, scorn, hard questions, hunger—I've seen it all. Privations of every kind. You get used to that, living in apostolic poverty.

MR. MINGO. You exaggerate, as usual. You go too far, Mr. Niblis, in your comparison. Not one of the twelve apostles, as far as we know, was ever caught sneaking a bowl of banana pudding into his room at night. Or any other creamy yellow custard. Hardly a spiritual exercise. *(Raising hand)* No, please. No embarrassing denials. I'm not blind. I've seen you at your little pudding game too many times.

MR. NIBLIS. Where were you hiding, Mingo? You might as well tell us. It can't make any difference now. Where was your peephole?

MR. MINGO. *(Soft laughter)* I had more than one.

MRS. VETCH. We did have some awfully good puddings and pies here at the Sunnyside. We must count our blessings.

MR. PALFREY. I think Mr. Niblis may be on to something. They do bootleg these kidneys and things, you know. I saw a show about it on TV.

MR. MINGO. Yes, but not in terms of old people. That's nonsense. I don't know where Mr. Niblis gets such bizarre ideas. There's no real money to be made out of the tripes of an old man like me. They don't even want our blood anymore.

MRS. VETCH. I was once a member of the Five Gallon Club.

MR. NIBLIS. You wait. Mole won't be satisfied till he's wet his hands good in our blood.

MR. MINGO. No, it will be bad enough but it won't be that bad. We'll just be sitting around all day in a big room. That's all. Day after day we'll sit there in Asiatic resignation.

MR. PALFREY. With your mouths open. Gone all slack-jawed.

MR. MINGO. Chapfallen, yes. Our poets have a word for everything. We'll sit there slumped and gaping as we're being methodically dried out.

FERN. Dried out?

MR. MINGO. Or dried up. You must have noticed—all these old folks homes have giant evaporators in their basements. You can hear the turbines roaring under the floors. Avalon will be no different. They'll draw all the moisture out of our bodies, all the volatile components, until we're reduced to living mummies. Little stick figures, just bits of bone and hair and leather. Until we're not much bigger than spider monkeys. That's how those places work. They dry old people up, by painless degrees. Death by slow desiccation. It's virtually odorless, they say.

Pause. They think this over.

FERN. *(To Lenore)* And you would put your own father away in a place like that. But you don't care, do you, Lenore? Whether they dry Daddy up or not.

LENORE. You're so hateful to me. I love my Daddy. I don't want to see my old Daddy dried up any more than you do, but it's just not fair, the way things are now. You have a lot more room in your house and yet you only keep him half the time. A new arrangement is all I'm talking about.

FERN. But you're only keeping him three months at a time now.

LENORE. Boyce thinks a month of Daddy is plenty.

FERN. It's not Boyce's Daddy.

LENORE. But we have to face facts. We have to plan ahead. Boyce thinks we'll never find a better deal than this Avalon deal. There's just one payment up front and no more worries.

MRS. VETCH. On the Special Value Package.

LENORE. *(Recovers crumpled brochure from floor, smoothes it out, offers it again to Mr. Palfrey)* It won't hurt you to look it over, Daddy. Nobody's going to mistreat you at Avalon. I wouldn't stand for it a minute.

MR. PALFREY. *(Knocks brochure from her hand with his stick)* I ain't going to no nursing home, Lenore! Get that through your head! I'd rather sleep in a corncrib with the rats. I'd rather sleep in a dumpster with the garbage.

MR. MINGO. I wonder. We say such things but I wonder if we would really prefer to sleep rough like that, on ketchup bottles and eggshells and rotting produce.

FERN. You think she cares? Lenore doesn't care whether Daddy has to sleep on wet garbage or not.

LENORE. You're so mean and spiteful to me. Because I'm still young and attractive and you're not.

Enter Delray. He comes down the stairs in anger.

DELRAY. *(Muttering)* Daddy this and Daddy that. *(Goes to Duvall and unplugs television set again)* Do you know who's up there, Duvall? In those rooms you said were clear? It's those painters you said weren't working today. The many sons of that alcoholic painter.

DUVALL. Working on Saturday?

DELRAY. No, they're not working. They're looking for their drunk Daddy. He didn't come home last night. They've lost their Daddy. They won't leave until they've found their Daddy. Where is Kate? Kate!

Enter Kate, from kitchen through swinging door. She has changed from her uniform into street clothes. She carries a small travel bag and is brushing her hair.

KATE. What?

DELRAY. *(Noting change of clothes, bag)* What is all this?

KATE. You told us to clear out. We're clearing out.

DELRAY. Right. Is the painter back there?

KATE. What painter?

DELRAY. What painter, she says! Is the kitchen ready for my inspection?

KATE. I guess so. Anyway, Sammy's gone. He carried off all the frozen steaks. And that big microwave oven too. Maybe some other things. Do you have my money?

DELRAY. All my steaks! I suppose you just stood by and watched him!

KATE. I was in the bathroom changing clothes. When I came out he was gone. I think he poked some rags or something down the drains too. All the sinks are stopped up.

DELRAY. I'll put him behind bars! That microwave is not even paid for!

DUVALL. He may not be so easy to catch, Delray. A raging fry cook on the lam.

KATE. Can I have my money now?

DELRAY. You'll get your check at the end of the month. Leave an address with Duvall. Is the painter back there?

KATE. Who?

DELRAY. The painter! The old man who paints! The Daddy of that family of painters!

KATE. Nobody's back there. Look, Delray, I don't know where I'll be. I'm leaving town. I need my money now.

DUVALL. Off to meet a certain fugitive, are we?

KATE. None of your business.

DUVALL. A little rendezvous at some Pakistani motel? And then what? Off in the truck and the low-boy trailer?

KATE. Mind your own business.

DUVALL. Off on a five- or six-state crime spree?

KATE. Don't mess with me, Duvall. You say another word about Prentice and I'll slap you off that stool.

DUVALL. *(Mock alarm, raises fists)* Hey, I better put up my dukes then!

DELRAY. *(Suddenly noticing, with a start, the continued presence of the old people and the Palfreys)* No! Look! They're all still here! There seems to be even more of them! Where is that van? What's keeping Ruth Buttress?

KATE. Let me have a hundred, Delray, and we'll call it even.

DELRAY. I'll mail the check to your mother in due course.

KATE. All right, but twenty now, so I can buy a tank of gas.

DELRAY. No! I don't do business that way. Now stop bothering me.

MR. NIBLIS. *(Speaking up from across the room)* Delray has thousands of dollars. And he won't even pay his help.

DELRAY. This doesn't concern you, Mr. Niblis.

MR. NIBLIS. He's well connected. All the big banks in Little Rock are behind him.

DELRAY. Banks? What banks? Are you crazy? No bank in the world will lend money to a night club. For your information, Miss Eula herself is carrying the note for Delray's New Moon.

MR. PALFREY. Better not take your dog to Little Rock. If you care anything about him. You'll never see him again.

DELRAY. *(Struck by an idea)* Is that policeman still out there?

MR. PALFREY. That's what I told that little Annabel girl too. Better leave Norris at home.

DELRAY. *(Goes to window, peers through glass, down which water is streaming)* Good, he's still waiting. I'll have him put out the alarm on Sammy.

Delray exits through front door. Duvall plugs in television set, resumes watching game. Kate goes to window, peers out.

MR. MINGO. Yes, now is your chance, Kate, to beat it out the back way. While the detective is occupied.

MRS. VETCH. But have you thought this through, Kate? I mean, don't sell yourself short. I just know an attractive girl like you can find someone more suitable than Prentice. You really don't have to keep low company, you know. You could take a business course by mail and learn how to—

Kate, not listening, walks across room, jerks down silver crescent moon, breaks it across her knee, then tramps on it. Kicks over cardboard dancers.

MRS. VETCH. —these business lessons by mail, you see, and learn how to—

KATE. Bye, y'all.

MRS. VETCH. —and learn how to—

MR. MINGO. A waste of breath, Mrs. Vetch.

MRS. VETCH. I just hope Prentice is kind to her.

MR. NIBLIS. If he knows what's good for him he'll be kind to her.

MRS. VETCH. Well, you can't tell girls anything. But you never know. It might even work out.

MR. NIBLIS. You think so? Here's another prophecy for you. In three months time Kate will fling a skillet full of hot grease into Prentice's face.

Pause.

MRS. VETCH. She might just squirt some hair spray in his eyes and walk out on him.

MR. MINGO. Or, as he sleeps, drive a ball-peen hammer deep into his skull.

FERN. Did you tip that girl, Daddy?

MR. PALFREY. What for? I didn't get what I wanted.

MR. MINGO. What's the score, Duvall?

DUVALL. (*Slow, grudging reply*) We're a little behind but there's still plenty of time. The Hogs are driving.

MRS. VETCH. Poor Kate hasn't been gone two minutes and already we're putting her out of our minds. Already we've gone on to ball games and other things.

Delray enters from the rain.

DELRAY: The dragnet is out, you'll all be pleased to know. Sammy will soon be in custody.

MR. NIBLIS. Like us. Put away.

DELRAY: *(Sees broken moon on floor)* What! Who pulled down my new moon? Who did this, Duvall? And look! My life-size cardboard dancers!

DUVALL. *(Intent on game)* I didn't notice anything was down.

MR. MINGO: Strictly speaking, Delray, that is a near new moon early in the first quarter. The new moon is invisible.

DELRAY. And look! Walked on it! Or stomped on it! This is criminal!

MR. MINGO. Or danced on it.

DELRAY. No dancer would dance on my beautiful moon!

MR. MINGO. There are jigs of contempt too, Delray.

DELRAY. Did Kate do this?

He gets no answer. Sounds of a vehicle driving up. There are reflections from a revolving emergency light. Sounds of a slammed door, then of the vehicle departing. Mae Buttress enters, disheveled, with wet hair and smudges on her face. She carries a shoulder bag and clipboard. She is running her fingers through her hair.

DELRAY. Thank God! Ruth Buttress! At long last! The old folks are all packed up and ready to go! *(Notices her condition)* What's wrong? What are you doing?

MAE. I'm shaking broken glass from my hair. I've just escaped from a terrible accident on the Interstate.

DELRAY. What!

MAE. Jerry was driving too fast in the rain and the van skidded into a bridge railing. My heart is still pounding. I saw my life pass before my eyes.

DELRAY. Are you hurt? Shouldn't you—

MAE. No, I'm all right. The ambulance let me out here and is taking Jerry on to the hospital. I told him over and over again he was driving too fast.

DELRAY. Then—there's no van! No Avalon van!

MAE. Another one is on the way, don't worry. I've already called Mom. She was really steamed too. Mom will make Jerry wish he had died on that bridge.

DELRAY. No van! More delays!

MAE. A short delay, that's all. Let's get on with it. (*Takes pencil and begins to check items on clipboard*) All four of these pickups are ambulatory, I take it.

DELRAY. More or less.

MAE. Good. Any facial hair on these people?

DELRAY. Some.

MAE. Any fleshy growths?

DELRAY. Growths. No, I don't think so.

MAE. Can dress and feed and relieve themselves without assistance?

DELRAY. Yes.

MAE. Any incontinence?

DELRAY. I have no idea.

MAE. How about blockages then? Any big blockages?

DELRAY. Again, I don't know.

MAE. Any morbid obesity?

DELRAY. No.

MAE. No bad bloating? No big big tummies?

DELRAY. No.

MAE. Impaired speech?

DELRAY. Not at all. Far from it.

MAE. Any purulent discharge from their ears?

DELRAY. Any what?

MAE. Drainage. From their ears.

DELRAY. I know nothing about their ears.

MAE. Nothing?

DELRAY. Next to nothing.

MAE. Any hallucinations, visual or auditory?

DELRAY. Not that I know of.

MAE. Frequent falls? Frequent fractured femurs?

DELRAY. No broken bones since I've been here.

MAE. Any prosthetic devices?

DELRAY. Just the usual ones, I believe. The odd pin or screw in the hip. One glass eye, royal blue. Mr. Niblis.

MAE. Any signs of senile dementia, or any signs or suggestions or symptoms of onset of senile dementia?

DELRAY. No, I wouldn't go that far.

MAE. Sudden fits of weeping?

DELRAY. No.

MAE. Confused? Addled?

DELRAY. I wouldn't quite say that, no.

MAE. Mood?

DELRAY. Despair.

MAE. Any whimpering?

DELRAY. Let's say fretting.

MAE. Mom won't tolerate whimpering.

DELRAY. Well, they are, naturally, apprehensive.

MAE. But just the usual feelings of distress and terror?

DELAY. Yes.

MAE. Heaving long sighs?

DELRAY. Sometimes.

MAE. But not given to throwing fits?

DELRAY. No.

MAE. No restraint straps or injections indicated?

DELRAY. No. But did I hear you say "four"? Actually there are only three of them.

MAE. Well, let's just see what we have here on the manifest. *(Reads)* "Delray's New Moon, formerly the Sunnyside Hotel. One female, three males. Vetch, Ramp, Niblis, Mingo." I make that four.

DELRAY. Yes, but you can scratch Mr. Ramp off your manifest. He's been gone for some time now.

MAE. You refuse to produce Ramp?

DELRAY. I am unable to produce Ramp. He's gone, I tell you.

MAE. Gone where? Expired? Wandered away? What?

DELRAY. I don't know. He just left suddenly. It must be two months ago now.

MAE. To another care unit? He's been snatched out from under us? Not by Sinking Embers! Those people are little better than gangsters! And they're going to find themselves in some very hot water if they keep making these false and defamatory statements about Dad! But they'll never crush his spirit! Never! Dad thrives on odium!

DELRAY. I can tell you nothing more about Mr. Ramp.

MAE. Then you refuse to surrender Ramp.

DELRAY. I would gladly surrender Ramp if I could. I tell you I don't know where he is.

MAE. Ramp at large. Yipes. Now I'll have to run a tracer on him. You wouldn't believe the paperwork. *(Looks at old people across the room)* But look, there are four. One old female and three old males.

DELRAY. Yes, but the old fellow with the white stick is not one of the Avalon party.

MAE. Well, I can't just "scratch Ramp off," as you put it. It's not that simple. I'll need some hard documentation to account for him. Mom is not going to like this one bit.

DELRAY. You keep saying "Mom."

MAE. My Mom, yes. Ruth Buttress. The Matron of Avalon.

DELRAY. But I thought <u>you</u> were Ruth Buttress.

MAE. *(Laughing)* No, no, no. I am <u>Mae</u> Buttress, the daughter of Ruth Buttress. Mom doesn't do pickups. What an idea! And certainly not on the Special Value Package. I am Mae Buttress, from Receiving and Interrogation.

DELRAY. I beg your pardon then.

MAE. No, it's quite all right. A common mistake. We do look alike, you know. We're both full-figured women and we dress alike too. Mom just loves it when people take us for sisters. When we're out on the town together in our matching orange pantsuits. We've always been great pals.

DELRAY. *(Goes to bar, takes three manila envelopes from shelf beneath)* Here we are. Everything in order. Releases, Medicare forms, biography sheets. All complete, I believe.

MAE. *(Looks over papers)* Signed and notarized? Check. SS numbers? Check. Okay. Good enough, as far as they go. Still no Ramp, I see. Ramp at bay. But not for long. Bio sheets? Check. Dad likes to look these over first thing. He likes to have a little one-on-one chat with each new guest. About their allergies, you know, and their medication and their unencumbered assets. He likes to point out the great advantages of giving him power of attorney and of having all their checks deposited directly to the Avalon account. His little power of attorney pow-wows, he calls them. You know Dad and his gentle humor.

DELRAY. No, I don't even know who Dad is.

MAE. Why, Dr. Lloyd Mole, of course! I thought you knew! There's no secret about that. The paternity has never been seriously questioned! I am the love child of Dr. Lloyd Mole and Ruth Buttress, his longtime associate!

DELRAY. I had no idea.

MAE. Oh, it was the talk of the medical community at one time—their tempestuous love story. So young they were then, and so dedicated to the healing arts. Thrown together night after night, working long hours, fighting against their desires in the night lab, with the sacrificial white rats gibbering away in their cages and twitching their whiskers.

DELRAY. That's an interesting story.

MAE. It's a modern Cinderella story. Mom was Keeper of the Rats at that time, and let me tell you something, she never pampered her rats either, the way some of those silly girls did. Her rats got just what was coming to them. Mom was all business, even then. The lab girls laughed at her and made jokes behind her back. They thought they were so cute in their little white outfits, the skinny little twits!

DELRAY. A wonderful story.

MAE. Wait, you haven't heard the best part. When Dad came in as lab chief, all the girls of course fell in love with him. He was a short young man, round and dark, Mole by name, and somewhat Moleish in appearance, with his tiny close-set eyes, and a kind of burrowing sleekness about his head and shoulders. He was quiet, oh so quiet, but everyone could see how brilliant he was. They knew he was going places. He was just seething with hidden fires and bold new marketing concepts. He was a catch. Now, out of all those lab cuties, who do you think it was that captured Dad's heart? It was Ruth Buttress, the drudge, the frump, he chose, over all the silly girls! The prince, you see, Lloyd Mole, had found his Cinderella!

DELRAY. Well then, there you are. Is there any more paperwork? Are you through with me?

MAE. Will you please do me the courtesy of allowing me to finish?

DELRAY. I'm sorry.

MAE. At that time it was unheard of for a lab chief to carry on with his rodent control officer, but Dad didn't care. He snaps his fingers at all these silly social conventions. And besides, what else could he do? Mom had fairly bowled him over with her brisk air of command and her firm hand with the rats.

DELRAY. So. Mose is your father.

MAE. Mom was everything he had dreamed of. She believes it was her stout calves that first caught his eye.

DELRAY. So. Mose is your father. And yet you introduce yourself as Buttress.

MAE. Mole, not Mose. His name is Mole.

DELRAY. But you prefer the name of Buttress.

MAE. Oh, he tells me not to call him Dad, but he's only teasing. That's just his way. No one seriously questions the paternity.

DELRAY. He seems to shy away from the honor.

MAE. But that's only Dad and his gentle humor. You don't know him. He has such a playful nature, really, but it doesn't come through when he's in the courtroom or on television news. His merry twinkle. Make no mistake, I am his natural daughter, his love child, and I love who I am. I am Mae Buttress, American, fleshy and sensual, a glowing compound of Mole and Buttress, and I glory in it. How do you like that, Mr. New Moon?

DELRAY. I'll have to think about it. I don't know what to make of it.

MAE. I love my work, too. I live for my work.

DELRAY. Well then, am I all clear? Anything for me to sign? I will sign anything you have on that clipboard. I know nothing more about Mr. Ramp. You might ask Mrs. Vetch and or Mr. Mingo over there.

MAE. (Turns to look at them) Surely they don't expect to take all that stuff with them. They must be dreaming. One bag with a few personal effects—that's all they'll need on the Special Value Package.

DELRAY. Mrs. Vetch would like to take her electric iron. A travel iron. Is that permitted? She's a nice lady.

MAE. Not possible, I'm afraid. Small personal treasures like that can only arouse envy, which can only lead to discord. No special pillows either. I see one over there. And that cigarette smoking will stop at once.

DELRAY. It's just a small travel iron. She's a nice lady. Maybe you could bend the rule.

MAE. Of course she's a nice lady. Why do you keep harping on that?

They're all nice people. What are you suggesting—that we at Avalon are somehow not very nice? Let me assure you that this Vetch woman will continue to be treated as a lady—as long as we get prompt and cheerful obedience from her. Mom insists on that. (*Looking at them again*) Where are their balloons and their ID tags? Why aren't they wearing their Avalon caps?

DELRAY. The caps, yes. And the balloons. We have them here somewhere. Duvall!

MAE. And their gifts. Do they have their gifts?

DELRAY. Now what gifts are those?

MAE. For Dad. He expects a little gift from each new guest. Didn't you read our booklet?

DELRAY. I only dipped into it.

MAE. Nothing very expensive, you understand—shaving kit or a pocket knife. Just some little token of love for him. Dad is hurt when he doesn't get a gift. And it must be properly wrapped, and tied up with a ribbon. (*Suddenly she staggers, grasps back of chair for support*) Oh! Mercy!

DELRAY. What is it?

MAE. My head went light there for a moment.

DELRAY. Delayed shock, perhaps, from your accident.

MAE. Yes, or a light concussion. If I could have something cold to drink—

DELRAY. Certainly. Duvall! A Coke over here for Miss Buttress! Pronto!

DUVALL. Small Coke?

MAE. Big Coke. Not too much ice.

DUVALL. Hey, you got it! Coming up!

Duvall brings Coke. Mae drinks.

DELRAY. Better now?

MAE. Yes, thank you.

DELRAY. You'll be all right?

MAE. It's nothing. A passing dizzy spell.

DELRAY. Good. That's great news. I have to run now. There are so many demands on my time. Please give my warm regards to Dr. Moles. He provides a wonderful service.

MAE. Mole, not Moles. Where do you get Moles?

DELRAY. Right, Mole, no "s." I've got it down now. I'll leave you here in the ballroom with my— (*Looks about, transported for a moment*) How I love my New Moon ballroom! Not very big but it's coming along nicely, don't you think? (*Then back to business*) Yes, well, I'll leave you here with my executive assistant, Duvall. He will introduce you to your clients. Here, Duvall, I want you to meet Miss Buttress, who has just had a hair-raising escape from a car wreck. She is the Matron of Avalon.

MAE. No, no, that's my Mom.

DELRAY. I thought your mom was Ruth Buttress.

MAE. So she is. She is Ruth Buttress, and she is the Matron of Avalon, not me. Weren't you listening? I don't know how I can make it any plainer. I am Mae Buttress, the love child of Dr. Lloyd Mole and his longtime associate, Ruth Buttress. I am in Receiving and Interrogation. It's my Mom, Ruth Buttress, R.N., who is the Matron of Avalon.

DELRAY. Right, I think I've got it now. (*Then to Duvall*) Miss Buttress is here to pick up Mrs. Vetch and the others. She hasn't met them yet. Will you do the honors?

DUVALL. Be glad to. My pleasure.

DELRAY. And see about their caps and their balloons.

MAE. And their shipping tags.

DUVALL. Hey, you got it. Right this way, Miss Buttress.

Delray exits upstairs.

MAE. (*Miffed, as she watches him go*) I like that! Demands on his time! Who does he think he is anyway? I mean, really, trifling about with our names in that disrespectful way! Is he quite right in the head? What was all that stuff about his ballroom?

DUVALL. Sorry, but that's confidential material. I can't discuss Delray's dream with outsiders.

MAE. Then don't discuss it! I don't give a hoot about his dream! Let's get on with this!

They set off across the room. Mae lightly and accidentally brushes against Duvall. He stops, goes rigid, looks off into space.

DUVALL. Don't do that again.

MAE. What? Do what?

DUVALL. Bump up against me like that. Don't do it again. I don't like being jostled.

MAE. I didn't jostle you! A slight brush, that's all! Why on earth would I want to jostle you? *(Shakes more glass out of her hair)* What a day!

They resume their advance on the old people. Before Duvall can make the introductions, Mae goes wobbly again. She drops her Coke and clipboard and collapses into his arms. He is unable to support her weight and lets her down with a thump in front of the old people. She lies there unconscious, face up.

PALFREY. What happened?

DUVALL. I don't know. She just passed out. Delray said she was in a car wreck out on the highway.

MRS. VETCH. A wreck on the highway! Oh, I hope it wasn't a school bus with some little children hurt!

MR. PALFREY. "I heard the wreck on the highway." Roy Acuff used to sing that song a lot. Nothing but blood and glass and brains ever where you looked.

FERN. Who is she?

MR. PALFREY. Who is that old fat gal anyway?

MR. MINGO. *(Poking her arm with his finger)* No so much fat as gelatinous. Look how her flesh gleams and trembles.

MRS. VETCH. *(Poking Mae lightly with the toe of her shoe)* Really? I wonder what she's been feeding on?

MR. MINGO. Gorging on, I would say.

MR. NIBLIS. Who is it? Is it that man that was on the bed?

MRS. VETCH. Are you blind? That's not a man!

MR. MINGO. An easy enough distinction to make, I would think. We don't need a magnifying glass for her, do we?

MR. NIBLIS. What?

MR. MINGO. Some people need to get their eyes examined.

MR. NIBLIS. Who is Mingo talking to now?

MR. MINGO. To whom it may concern. I name no names.

LENORE. But who is she? That's what we want to know.

MR. MINGO. It's that woman from Avalon. Ruth Buttress.

MRS. VETCH. *(Bending over to take a closer look)* Ruth Buttress! But she
    looks so much older on television.
FERN. Ruth Buttress. Well, my goodness.
MR. MINGO. *(Touching her again with his finger)* So, we meet at Phillippi,
    Ruth, and you flat on your back. If I could lift my icy feet, I would
    plant one on your chest.
MR. NIBLIS. Who? Who did he say it was?
MRS. VETCH. Ruth Buttress! The Matron of Avalon!
MR. NIBLIS. *(Poking her with his umbrella)* You'd think they would send
    somebody in better health to pick us up.
MR. MINGO. Instead of a stretcher case.
MRS. VETCH. She's worse off than we are.

*Mr. Mingo, still seated, begins to drum his feet feebly up and down in clip-clop
fashion.*

MRS. VETCH. What are you doing? Will you please stop that? You're
    getting on everybody's nerves!
MR. MINGO. Bear with me…little victory dance…a bit more…not
    much longer now…another step or two…this ballroom dancing will
    take it out of you…*(Steps falter and stop)* There. I'm done.
MR. PALFREY. *(To Duvall)* Well, don't just stand there. Do something,
    Booger. Prop up her feet so the blood can drain back into her head.

Duvall, grudgingly, drops to his knees and begins resuscitation work on Mae.

MR. MINGO. Don't let her choke. Make sure her tongue is clear. Just
    reach in there with your finger and flip it clear.
FERN. Check her pulse. Pat her skin. I don't like her color. See if her
    skin is clammy. Her color is not good at all.
LENORE. I wonder if her color ever was real good.
MR. PALFREY. Take off her glasses. Get her arms and legs straightened out.
    Undo her bow tie. Unbutton her. Unlace her. Unlace Ruth Buttress.
DUVALL. *(Stops work)* What do you mean? What are you talking about?
    Is she laced up in some way?
MR. PALFREY. I don't know. Sometimes they are. Underneath, you
    know. Or buckled up.

DUVALL. *(Resumes works with distaste. Places hands on her warily)* I don't like any part of this.

MR. PALFREY. Be careful. Easy now.

DUVALL. *(Exasperated)* Careful of what?

MR. PALFREY. I think she's under compression. Easy does it—when you find those catches under there. Gently! Watch it! Watch it now! Just release those catches one at a time or she'll go off in your face like an air bag!

Duvall, alarmed, jerks his hands clear and draws back. He stops work altogether and stands up, looking down at Mae. The others also look at her, in silence, for a time.

MRS. VETCH. *(Sighing)* It seems so long since we had anything to eat.

MR. NIBLIS. We never got our lunch, that's why. Much less our breakfast.

MRS. VETCH. Nothing like this ever happened when Miss Eula was running things.

MR. MINGO. Nothing even remotely like this.

MR. PALFREY. More and more people are fainting these days. Have you noticed that? Left and right, all over the country. The least little bit of bad news and they keel over like possums, with their paws up in the air. I never passed out in my life.

LENORE. Can't we even get a sandwich? A nice chicken salad sandwich on toast?

DUVALL. The kitchen is closed. Delray's orders.

MR. PALFREY. These new people will serve you a rat salad sandwich on toast if they feel like it, Lenore. The paying customer don't have any say in the matter.

MRS. VETCH. I'll bet Kate could find us a little snack.

MR. NIBLIS. Kate has run off with Prentice. You saw her go yourself.

MRS. VETCH. Oh yes, I forgot. I hope he's kind to her. Is Sammy back there?

DUVALL. He's gone too, with all our prime K.C. steaks.

MRS. VETCH. Where is Delray?

DUVALL. Upstairs, dealing with some morons in Room Six.

MRS. VETCH. Morons? What do they want here?

DUVALL. We don't know yet. I think some cruel mother was driving through on the Interstate and just dumped them off here.

MR. MINGO. Maybe you could make a run down to the barbecue joint for us, Duvall.

DUVALL. I can't do everything!

LENORE. Can you do anything? You sure can't fix a car.

DUVALL. I'm not the handyman around here. I wasn't hired to do all this menial work. I should be back in college working on my psychology degree.

MR. PALFREY. You'd be better off dead, son.

FERN. (*Holding the backs of her fingers to Mae's forehead*) But what about Ruth Buttress? We really ought to do something. She doesn't seem to be coming around. Her color is not good at all.

DUVALL. I'll put her on the bed back there. Then I'm through. That's all I intend to do. I'm not unlacing Ruth Buttress.

Duvall takes Mae by the wrists and begins dragging her away.

MRS. VETCH. (*Scandalized*) Not on the same bed with the strange man! Wearing the heavy shoes!

Duvall says nothing. He continues to drag Mae in a rough manner. One of her shoes comes off.

LENORE. Shouldn't he put her on rollers or something?

Duvall drags Mae offstage. There is a flash of lightning, followed by a clap of thunder. The hotel lights flicker and go off, leaving the room dim.

MR. NIBLIS. (*Gleeful*) There it goes! There went the transformer! That's it! Lights out! Sweet dreams, everybody!

Act III

A bit later. The room is now dimly lighted by candles. Mrs. Vetch, Mr. Niblis and Mr. Mingo are seated as before, but are now holding Avalon balloons on strings, and wearing Avalon caps, which are baseball caps with very long bills. Conspicuous yellow shipping tags are wired to their lapels. Mr. Palfrey and his daughters are seated as before. Lenore is eating a pecan log. Marguerite, Delray and Duvall are absent.

MR. MINGO. What was I saying? Someone broke my concentration there. Where was I? Someone broke my stride.

MRS. VETCH. Still air.

FERN. How the still air in here reminded you of your boyhood home.

MR. PALFREY. I thought he said <u>stale</u> air.

LENORE. *(Putting aside the pecan log, licking her fingers)* Where is that Duvall boy with our barbecue sandwiches? We can't live off these big nut logs. They're way too sweet and sticky.

MR. PALFREY. People don't know what stale air is until they've been in an old folks home.

MRS. VETCH. Miss Eula loved fresh air. How she loved throwing the windows up with a bang every morning! No still air for her!

MR. PALFREY. <u>Stale</u> air was what I thought Mr. Mingo said.

MR. NIBLIS. Or a veterans' hospital. Talk about your stale air. Try that and see how you like it. A good long whiff of that and your knees will buckle, Mr. Palfrey.

MR. PALFREY. It's all them bathrobes.

MRS. VETCH. Bathrobe fumes. Yes, you may be right. And those flannel pajamas. Reeking pajamas.

MR. PALFREY. It's all them bathrobe vapors is what it is.

MR. MINGO. <u>Still</u> air was what I said, but—

MR. NIBLIS. Can you wear shorty pajamas at Avalon?

FERN. Not out in the lobby, no, I wouldn't think so.

MRS. VETCH. Certainly not! Did you expect to lounge about in the parlor and receive guests in your shorty pajamas, Mr. Niblis? What very strange notions of propriety you have!

MR. PALFREY. Is he so proud of his shanks? Why would he want to show his old shanks to all the guests?

MRS. VETCH. Two white sticks.

MR. NIBLIS. I wasn't thinking of guests. I've never had a guest.

MRS. VETCH. And you a preacher, too. You might have made some friends, you know, if you had attended to your pastoral duties instead of just hollering at people on street corners.

MR. NIBLIS. I wasn't called to do social work. I wasn't called to offer cheap comfort. I was called to preach the living Word, not to clap people on the back.

MRS. VETCH. I think I'd rather die myself than go out and address strangers in public like that. Didn't smart-alecks come up and make fun of you and try to provoke you?

MR. NIBLIS. (*Snort of laughter*) Tried to is right! The harder they pressed me, Mrs. Vetch, the better I liked it. I made mincemeat out of those hecklers. I got the best of every argument.

MRS. VETCH. Watch out—spiritual pride.

MR. NIBLIS. I blistered their hide good. All they could do was sputter for a little bit and then slink away.

MRS. VETCH. That sounds like boasting and pride to me.

MR. NIBLIS. Maybe so, but I ripped 'em up one side and down the other. My street corner was only a street corner to you, Mrs. Vetch, but it was Mount Carmel to me and I was Elijah the Tishbite facing down the eight-hundred-and-fifty prophets of Baal and Asherah. I had the devil on the run there for a little while. You look at me now and wonder, but I was a lot better man back then.

FERN. (*To Mrs. Vetch*) But you don't mean Miss Eula would throw the windows up when it was raining, do you?

MRS. VETCH. No, no, weather permitting. I thought that would be understood. How we miss her! Such a good country cook, and such a good woman too, always so cheerful and understanding! (*Sighing*) But her loving presence is no longer felt here.

MR. NIBLIS. You could feel it for a few days after she left.

MRS. VETCH. There was a brief afterglow, yes. (*Looking about*) Now all quite gone from these rooms.

MR. MINGO. Still air was what I said, but Mr. Palfrey was right when he—

MR. NIBLIS. I can't say we miss Ramp. We don't feel his absence.

MRS. VETCH. But did we ever feel his presence much?

MR. NIBLIS. Still, he was smarter than us.

MRS. VETCH. I miss my son too. My gallant son. At least he was spared all this. He won't be like us. They can't put him away. He'll always be twenty-six years old.

Pause.

MR. PALFREY. Bus station air is pretty bad air.
MR. NIBLIS. Bus station air is sweet air compared to the air in your flophouse hotel across the street from your bus station. The Hotel Central, the Commercial Hotel, the City Hotel, the Terminal Hotel, the Vagrants Hotel. I know those places. Your one-sheet hotels, your no-sheet hotels, your gray-sheet hotels. Talk about sharp air! It would make your eyes water! It would turn your knees to jelly, Mr. Palfrey.
MR. MINGO. Still air was what I said, but—
MR. NIBLIS. Like Belshazzar's quivering knees. When he was at his profane feast and he saw those burning words on the wall. (*Quoting, grave delivery*) "So that the joints of his loins were loosed, and his knees smote one against another."
MR. MINGO. Still air was what I said, but you were right, Mr. Palfrey, the air in our house was stale too, quite dead. All our windows were nailed shut and my mother stuffed rags under the doors to keep out drafts. That stagnant air stunted our development in so many ways. I believe it accounts for our dull Mingo eyes. The dead air, the perpetual gloom. We had red curtains that were never parted or drawn. We lived in that twilight, about like it is here now, except that ours had more of a reddish, infernal tone.
MRS. VETCH. Why do we have to wear these fool caps?
MR. NIBLIS. Duvall said we couldn't take them off till we get to Avalon.
MRS. VETCH. We look like a bunch of cancer patients.
MR. MINGO. Not that there weren't signs of life. There was murmuring around our dinner table as we aired our grievances. We didn't look directly at one another, you understand. Our eyes seldom met, and then only for a moment. Just a darting glance to identify the speaker, then quickly back to the business of ripping and tearing our food. Mingos have teeth like dogs. We gobbled our food and muttered away, making our halting points in Mingo family debate. Nothing dramatic, no raised voices, just smoldering family quarrels that went

on for years, unresolved. There wasn't enough oxygen in our house to feed a real blaze.

MR. NIBLIS. A little of the Mingo family goes a long way with me.

MR. PALFREY. How big is your cancer, Mrs. Vetch, and where is it?

MRS. VETCH. I don't have a cancer, thank you.

MR. MINGO. Did I mention the long tradition of defeat in the Mingo family? It's a miracle the line is not extinct. In the survival of the Mingos you see Darwin's theory exploded. Mingos lose heart easily. I remember one night—

MR. NIBLIS. What is he off on now? More Mingo stuff?

MR. MINGO. It was a Thursday night—sandwich night. We were sitting around the table holding our sandwiches with both hands before our face. Like this, before our downcast faces. (*Mimes holding of sandwich, chewing*) So there we were, our faces in partial eclipse, our Mingo eyes—the glaucous eyes of cavefish—rolling sluggishly about over the tops of our sandwiches—when my sister Neva suddenly spoke up and said she had an important announcement to make.

MR. NIBLIS. Can't somebody break his stride again?

MRS. VETCH. His stride? Mr. Mingo striding? Why, it takes him ten minutes to get up the stairs!

LENORE. I think that Duvall boy has run off with our sandwich money. That boy with the blue ribbon in his hair.

MR. NIBLIS. Where is that delivery van? I'm starving to death. At least they'll have to feed us at Avalon. I'm ready to be put away. Let Mole do his worst.

MRS. VETCH. The van turned over! Didn't you hear about that bad wreck on the highway? That was the Avalon van!

MR. NIBLIS. Somebody said it was a school bus. With a lot of little children killed.

MRS. VETCH. No! Can't you pay attention for one minute! That heavy woman who took a tumble right here before your eyes! That was Ruth Buttress! She was driving the van!

MR. PALFREY. (*Quoting*) "That thing was as big as a pumpkin but we think we got it all." That's what these cancer doctors say to you after they've cut some great big tumor out of your guts. Then you go back for a check-up and they say, "Well, it looks like we didn't get it all, after all. It looks like we missed a right smart of it. Here's some dope pills for you and some BC powders. Go on back home and go to bed. You're just all eat up with cancer and your days are real short now."

MRS. VETCH. I don't have a cancer, thank you.

MR. MINGO. Well, of course, we all stopped eating and looked at Neva. We were holding our sandwiches up with both hands, like this. Like so many mouth harps. Yes, like mouth organs. If some sly Gypsy or some skulking tramp had peered through a crack in our curtains he might well have thought he had stumbled on to a harmonica academy. We were stunned. I mean, Neva speaking up like that, with such urgency, on sandwich night. What was she going to announce? What could it possibly be?

MR. NIBLIS. I've got a bellyful of the Mingo family.

LENORE. One thing we know—it's not going to be sandwich night here. That Duvall boy has run off with our money.

Enter Marguerite.

MARGUERITE. No, he hasn't. I saw him down at the barbecue joint. The lights are back on down there. Duvall said he would be back directly.

She squeezes into a chair with Tonya—a wooden chair with arms. She tickles Tonya in the ribs and makes her laugh.

MR. MINGO. So, when Neva spoke up again, out of that expectant hush—

MRS. VETCH. I must say, Mr. Mingo—you don't paint a very pretty picture of your family circle on sandwich night.

MR. MINGO. *(Dismissive wave)* That was nothing. That was a lovely dinner party. You should have dined with us on soup night, Mrs. Vetch. The noise alone was enough to—

FERN. But what was it that Neva announced?

LENORE. That she was pregnant, Fern, what else? I could see that coming a mile away.

MR. MINGO. Not at all. She announced that she was going away to jewelry school, to improve her skills. My father, you see, had told Neva more than once to stay away from art, but she wouldn't stop making bracelets. She spent all her time in her room making bracelets, at her little workbench.

Pause.

FERN. Well, we're waiting. What happened? Did she go off to jewelry school?

MR. MINGO. Oh yes. Or at least she made the effort. She packed a grip and went down to the Missouri-Pacific depot and got a daycoach seat on the northbound Eagle. When she arrived at the site of the jewelry school she found nothing but wet ashes. The school had burned down the night before. Neva lost heart and came back home, on the southbound Eagle. Her flight was brief.

MR. NIBLIS. We've had more than enough of the Mingos at their food. My attention is flagging again. You're all talk, Mingo. Just one idle word after another. Look at us. We're sheep waiting for the slaughter. We sit here talking nonsense all day while Ramp is running around out there free as a bird. Traveling incognito and incommunicado.

FERN. So did Neva go on making bracelets against her father's wishes?

MR. MINGO. Yes, she did. He lost heart too, you see, and gave up. But I don't know that Neva ever sharpened her workbench skills very much.

MRS. VETCH. But why would Mr. Ramp travel incognito? I don't see the point. Hardly anybody knew who he was anyway. They wouldn't even know him as Mr. Ramp.

MR. MINGO. An obscure man seeking a deeper darkness.

MR. NIBLIS. Don't sell him short.

MR. MINGO. With every passing day I lose a little more interest in Mr. Ramp.

MR. NIBLIS. He was a lot smarter than you. All you do is run your mouth, Mingo. Ramp was a man of action. He cleared out before Ruth Buttress could lay her hands on him.

MR. PALFREY. (*Turning to Marguerite and Tonya*) What are y'all doing over there? Putting red paint on your fingernails?

TONYA. No sir. She's just drawing a little green bird on my hand.

MRS. VETCH. I wonder how she's doing.

MR. PALFREY. Who? How who's doing?

MRS. VETCH. You know. Back there on the bed. Ruth Buttress.

MR. MINGO. Has Ruth rallied then?

FERN. I hope she's resting comfortably.

Enter Delray, coming down the stairs with a flashlight.

DELRAY. I hope she's all doubled up with cramps in her belly. Don't talk to me about Ruth Buttress. She comes here out of the rain with broken glass in her hair. She drinks a big Coke. The second van is on the way, she tells me. Then she goes to bed. All right, where is this second van? I never even saw the first one. So where are all these phantom vans from Avalon?

MARGUERITE. Look at us, Delray.

DELRAY. What, two girls in one chair? I've seen everything now. Where has Duvall got off to? Have you seen Duvall?

MARGUERITE. He's down at the barbecue joint eating parched peanuts and watching the football game. The lights are back on down there.

DELRAY. The lights are on everywhere in America except at Delray's New Moon. Which has just paid an enormous deposit to the Arkansas Power and Light Company. *(His flashlight flickers and goes out. He shakes it)* And now they've shut off my flashlight. *(He gives Marguerite a quarter)* Here, Marguerite, go to the barbecue joint just as fast as your little legs will carry you. Tell Duvall the roof is leaking in Room Three. I want him back here pronto. Tell him those people upstairs have scattered and I need his help in rounding them up. Tell him I am deeply disappointed in him.

MARGUERITE. I can't remember all that.

DELRAY. Just tell him I said to get back here on the double. And tell him…tell him…tell him that until he learns steady application to his work he can never expect to…no, that's enough. Go!

Marguerite runs for the door.

DELRAY. No, wait! Tell him not to come back! Do you hear? Tell Duvall he's all done at Delray's New Moon! Tell him he's out! Tell him I never want to see his face again! Tell him he is no longer a part of Delray's dream!

She starts again.

MR. MINGO. Find out the score, Marguerite.

MARGUERITE. Duvall wouldn't tell me the score, Mr. Mingo, but he said the Hogs are driving again.

DELRAY. Go! Go! Tell him he's useless! Tell him he's worthless! Tell him he's hopeless!

She starts again.

MRS. VETCH. Marguerite! Wait! Will you please see about our sandwiches while you're at it?

MARGUERITE. I'll bring 'em back myself, Mrs. Vetch! As soon as I tell Duvall he's all done here at the New Moon! I won't be long!

DELRAY. You have your instructions! Go!

She starts again.

TONYA. *(Calling after her)* You said you would show me how to do the chicken walk!

MARGUERITE. As soon as I get back! Stay right there! Don't try any dancing steps till I show you just what to do!

DELRAY. Go!

Marguerite goes out, then pops her head back in the doorway for a parting shot.

MARGUERITE. O-U-T spells out goes me!

She leaves. Delray exits to the rear.

MRS. VETCH. Marguerite is such a good girl.

MR. NIBLIS. Little Marguerite is a fine girl.

MRS. VETCH. She's a sweet girl.

MR. MINGO. Marguerite is a frisky girl. I wonder if she will remember anything at all about us when she too has been abandoned in some old folks home.

MRS. VETCH. Oh really now, Mr. Mingo!

MR. MINGO. Sitting there despondent with a hump on her back. Chewing her cud day after day, smacking her lips. All lost in some dim and tangled dream.

MRS. VETCH. Why must you dwell on such unpleasant things? How can you be so cruel? Why couldn't you just let us think of her as an innocent little girl with a tender heart?

MR. NIBLIS. Because that's not his nature. That wouldn't be Mingo. It was thoughts like that that got him put away the first time. The doctors turned him loose way too soon if you ask me.

MRS. VETCH. I hope she doesn't take up with some sorry scamp. When her time comes to marry.

MR. NIBLIS. Mingo lost all his shame in that newspaper racket. The man hasn't blushed in sixty-five years.

MRS. VETCH. I do hope Marguerite will find some nice boy that is worthy of her. Some fine young gentleman.

MR. NIBLIS. What are her chances of that?

MR. MINGO. No, I don't think she'll remember us at all. When her time comes to be put away. Childhood amnesia will see to that. We'll be utterly gone from human memory.

MRS. VETCH. (*Cocking her head, raising her hand*) Hush. What's that? Listen. I hear somebody moving around upstairs.

Pause.

MR. NIBLIS. You don't reckon it's Ramp come back, do you?

MRS. VETCH. I feel in my bones that Mr. Ramp has gone for good. I can't imagine who it could be. Unless…(*Sudden illumination*) Unless it's Delray's women! Yes, it is! It's Delray's cheap and tacky women from New Orleans! They're here! Strutting around up there in their boots!

Enter Delray with two empty plastic buckets, heading for the stairs.

DELRAY. What was that? What are you saying about me now?

MRS. VETCH. He's already shipped his women in! We're not even out the door yet and Delray has already installed his women in our rooms!

MR. MINGO. Delray doesn't do things by halves.

MRS. VETCH. He stops at nothing, Mr. Mingo!

MR. NIBLIS. Delray has thousands of dollars.

MRS. VETCH. He's capable of anything!

MR. PALFREY. Way too many new people moving in around here.

DELRAY. Do you sit there and accuse me of transporting women across state lines, Mrs. Vetch?

MRS. VETCH. You couldn't wait one more day! You couldn't even wait till they had hauled me off like trash before you put some old red-headed hussy in my room!

MR. NIBLIS. It sounds like Ramp to me. Those little stops and starts. I think Ramp must have slipped back into his room.

MR. MINGO. With his No Admittance sign hanging from the door-knob? I doubt it.

DELRAY. No, Mr. Ramp is not back in his room, and there is not one woman upstairs, tacky or otherwise. What you hear are the footsteps of the painter's sons. Their father is missing and for some reason they're trying to find him.

MR. MINGO. I hear measured steps, I don't hear troubled steps. In a search for a lost father you expect to hear a more agitated tread.

DELRAY. Whatever they may sound like, those are the steps of the painter's four or five sons. They're looking under beds and in dark closets for their drunk Daddy.

MR. PALFREY. Listen to that, Lenore. Them old boys are trying to find their Daddy and you're down here trying to lose yours.

LENORE. I am not. All I said was—

FERN. We heard what you said. We're not deaf.

MR. PALFREY. Them old boys love their Daddy. They're looking high and low for him and you're down here trying to get shed of yours.

LENORE. I am not. I just happen to mention Avalon and everybody jumps all over me. What's wrong with Avalon? It's a nice place out in the woods. You like the woods, Daddy. You like to talk. You could talk and visit out there all day long with people your own age. They feed you good. They wait on you hand and foot. The days are full at Avalon. I wish I could go to a nice place like that and just mess around with arts and crafts all day. Boyce thinks that Special Value Package is the best deal we'll ever get. And the thing is, it's a limited offer.

FERN. She wants to put you away, Daddy. She wants to put you down just like she had Blanche put down.

MR. PALFREY. Blanche? No. It was some dog thief in Little Rock that made off with poor Blanche.

FERN. That's what they told you.

LENORE. Blanche was old.

Pause.

MR. PALFREY. (*Stunned*) Then Blanche has been dead all this time.

LENORE. She was old and blind and sick, Daddy. It was her time to be put away.

FERN. She wasn't that sick. She dragged one leg, that's all.

MR. PALFREY. Poor old Blanche. I was hoping she had found a good home with a dry bed to sleep in.

LENORE. She was all wore out, Daddy. Her time had come. We have to face up to these things.

FERN. She wasn't all that sick. She wasn't any trouble. Blanche was just a little house dog who never bothered anybody.

LENORE. She bothered Boyce. He said she looked like a monkey.

Enter Marguerite, lugging two brown paper sacks from the barbecue joint. She is greeted with delight. There follows a bustle, with much chattering, as the sandwiches are sorted, distributed and eaten.

MARGUERITE. The pork sandwiches have one toothpick and the beefs have two. The real hot hot sauce is in the cup with the X on top.

Marguerite takes a sandwich to Tonya, who is still sitting in the wooden chair. Tonya eats and laughs as Marguerite begins to demonstrate the chicken walk, bobbing her head and throwing her feet out in stiff, measured steps. Mr. Palfrey looks at her and laughs, for the first time.

There are sudden noises in the corridor at the rear—raised voices, scuffling, a shriek, squeaking bedsprings. Mrs. Vetch and the others stop eating and turn their heads in alarm. Marguerite stops dancing.

FERN. My stars!

LENORE. What on earth!

MRS. VETCH. Are we to be spared nothing?

Enter young police detective from rear corridor, with the drunk painter and Mae Buttress in tow. She and the old painter are handcuffed together. They are dazed and stumbling. A trickle of blood runs down from Mae's scalp, and there is blood on the knuckles of one hand. Blood is also running from the detective's swollen lip.

DETECTIVE. *(Dabbing at lip with handkerchief)* Everyone stay calm. I'm with the state police. It's all over. I've got Prentice and I've got his woman too.

MRS. VETCH. But that's not Prentice! Look how old he is!

MR. MINGO. Isn't that the missing house painter?

MR. PALFREY. It's a police bust going down in this honky tonk!

DETECTIVE. Stay in your seats, please. Don't interfere. Everything is under control. *(Takes cellular telephone from belt and punches up a number. Speak into phone)* Yeah, it's me again at the New Moon. It's all wrapped up. I've got Prentice in custody. He was here all the time. She was hiding him in the back. I caught 'em in bed. That sap is still wearing his jail whites.

MR. MINGO. I believe those are painters' whites.

DETECTIVE. Stay out of this, sir. You're perfectly safe now.

MR. MINGO. We know that but—

DETECTIVE. *(Ignores him, resumes speaking into phone)* Yeah, and Prentice is drunk too, or sick. He looks a lot older than his picture. I don't know what these women see in him. I don't know how he ever climbed over that fence. What?…Some resistance, yeah, but from her, not him. I had to pop her one and I'm bringing her in too. This Kate is a lot bigger woman than they told me. They didn't tell me to look for a blue barrel….Right. On the way. 'Bye. Out. *(Puts phone away)*

MRS. VETCH. But that's not Prentice's woman! That's not Kate! You've got the wrong people! That's Ruth Buttress! You can't arrest Ruth Buttress!

DETECTIVE. Just keep calm, M'am. There's no danger now.

MRS. VETCH. Yes, we know that, but—

MAE. *(Groggy)* Not Ruth Buttress. I am Mae Buttress…

DETECTIVE. *(Gives sharp yank to handcuffs)* And no more out of you!

Enter Delray, coming down stairs.

DELRAY. Who is this? What's going on now?

MRS. VETCH. That man has just arrested Ruth Buttress and her elderly lover!

DELRAY. For what? *(Tugs at detective's sleeve)* Wait! There's some mistake! You're not taking Ruth Buttress away, are you?

DETECTIVE. Stand back, you! Don't you ever get between me and my prisoners! You so much as touch my clothes again and I'll haul you in too, for battery!

DELRAY. But look, you don't understand! This is Ruth Buttress, from Avalon. She's here to carry these people off to an old folks home. Regrettable, yes, but what can you do? A regrettable necessity. They got old, okay? Is that my fault? And this old fellow here is my painter. Ask him. He can tell you. I'm having the place done up in an oyster shade.

DETECTIVE. Out of my way, pal.

MRS. VETCH. But you must have seen her on television! You can't just come in here and arrest the Matron of Avalon!

LENORE. Look, Ruth's knuckles are bloody.

MR. NIBLIS. Who did he say it was?

MRS. VETCH. It's Ruth Buttress! Can't you see? He's put Ruth Buttress in handcuffs!

MR. NIBLIS. *(Peering at them across the room)* And Mole too? This is better and better.

FERN. I don't think that's Dr. Mole.

MRS. VETCH. Well, of course it isn't! Dr. Mole would never make a house call in white overalls like that!

MAE. *(Groggy)* Ruth Buttress is my Mom, I tell you. I am Mae Buttress, from Receiving and—

DETECTIVE. *(Yanks handcuffs again and holds a blackjack under nose)* You want some more of this?

MAE. No...I don't.

DETECTIVE. Better keep your trap shut then. You said you were subdued back there. Now are you subdued or not? *(Shaking blackjack)* Just let me know, Kate.

MAE. I'm subdued.

MRS. VETCH. But why does he keep calling her Kate? When we all know that Kate has gone away to her secret rendezvous?
MAE. (*Licks blood on knuckles. Whispers*) What a day!

The detective goes out the front door with his two prisoners. Delray follows, still protesting. Outside there are raised voices, then sounds of blows and grunts. Marguerite runs to the window to see what is happening.

MARGUERITE. (*Her face at the window*) Oh no, he's hitting Delray!...This is terrible!...Oh y'all, somebody do something!...This is awful!...Now he's knocked him down!...He's got him down on the ground!...He's got Delray laid out like a starfish in the handicap parking space and he's beating the daylights out of him!

She dashes outside to intervene. Fern goes to join her. The fighting noises stop. Voices are heard, followed by the slamming of car doors, and then the sound of a car driving away. Delray re-enters, beaten and bloody, his clothes torn. Fern and Marguerite assist him to the sink behind the bar. They wipe at his face with damp cloths.
Sounds of a car driving up.

MARGUERITE. Oh no, it's that policeman again! He's coming back to get Delray!
FERN. (*Looks at watch*) No, I don't think so. This must be Garland. It's got to be him. (*Calls over to Mr. Palfrey*) Are you ready, Daddy? It's Garland. We're going home.
MR. PALFREY. What, back to Texarkana? You mean to stay?
FERN. Yes.
MR. PALFREY. But when will I get to see Tonya?
FERN. Lenore and Boyce can bring her down to visit sometime. If they can ever find the time.
LENORE. You're so mean to me.
MR. PALFREY. I don't know about this. What will Garland say?
FERN. Garland will do the right thing.
LENORE. And Boyce won't?
FERN. It's not in him, Lenore. Garland could teach you both some manners.
MR. MINGO. Unless it's the second van. It might be that second van from Avalon.

MRS. VETCH. Oh my, I had forgotten all about that! There's always another van!

Fern and Marguerite go to window and look out. Marguerite gives a yelp of recognition and dashes outside.

FERN. Well, shoot, it's <u>not</u> Garland.
MRS. VETCH. Who then? Don't say a van.
FERN. No, it's some big rusty looking car. I don't know who it is. They're not getting out.

Marguerite returns breathless.

MARGUERITE. You know what? You'll never guess! Miss Eula is back, in her old Shivalay [Chevrolet]!
MRS. VETCH. Miss Eula!
MARGUERITE. She's with Mr. Ramp! They ran off and got married and have just got back from their honeymoon in Antlers, Oklahoma!
MRS. VETCH. What! No!
Mr. NIBLIS. What is Marguerite talking about?
MRS. VETCH. Can't you let me catch my breath? She has the most distressing news! Can't you let me collect my wits before you start in with all your questions?
MARGUERITE. I've got to run home and tell Mama this.
MR. MINGO. No, wait.
MRS. VETCH. She has a sister living in Antlers but I don't understand this at all! I mean, why would she want to marry Mr. Ramp? I mean, surely you can go visit your sister in Antlers, Oklahoma, without having to marry Mr. Ramp!
MR. NIBLIS. Ramp? Have they caught Ramp? How far did he get?
MR. MINGO. Tell them to come on in, Marguerite, so we can offer our congratulations.
MARGUERITE. Miss Eula won't get out of the car. She's afraid y'all will laugh at 'em and make fun of 'em for getting married when they're so old like that.
MRS. VETCH. We wouldn't dream of laughing!

MR. MINGO. Oh, we'll laugh a little bit. They have to expect that. A December bride has to expect some teasing.

MRS. VETCH. No, we won't laugh either. Go back to Miss Eula, Marguerite, and tell her to come out of that car this instant! I want to hear all about this very strange elopement!

Marguerite goes out. Returns.

MARGUERITE. Miss Eula says let her think about it for a minute. She says Mr. Ramp is a mature man.

MR. MINGO. We can't argue with that.

MARGUERITE. She says Mr. Ramp is a wonderful companion.

MR. MINGO. What does Mr. Ramp say?

MARGUERITE. He's taking a nap in the back seat.

MR. MINGO. Ah. Already he's gone to bed and turned his face to the wall. Is he clutching some small animal to his breast?

MARGUERITE. I don't know. He's kind of all bunched up back there.

MRS. VETCH. Tell Eula we all love her and we've missed her so much, and we want to see her. Nobody's going to laugh.

MR. MINGO. You have my promise.

Marguerite goes out. Returns.

MARGUERITE. Miss Eula says Mr. Ramp is a wonderful companion but he can't see to drive good anymore and she had to do all the driving to Antlers and back.

MR. MINGO. Yes, but are they coming in or not?

MARGUERITE. I don't know. She's trying to wake Mr. Ramp up.

MR. MINGO. Well, go help her. And then bring them in. Don't take no for an answer. Drag them in if you have to.

MRS. VETCH. How does Miss Eula look?

MARGUERITE. Her cheeks are red with real thick rouge.

MR. NIBLIS. Tell her people are starving to death in here on cold barbecue. We never got our lunch, much less our breakfast.

Marguerite goes out.

MRS. VETCH. The very idea! Mr. Ramp! A suitor! Of all people! And that sly courtship was going on right under our noses!

MR. PALFREY. I told you he was a fox. Didn't I tell you he smelled just like a fox? He married that old woman for her car.

FERN. For that car?

MR. PALFREY. There ain't no two ways about it.

MR. NIBLIS. For her hotel, you mean. Delray has already got himself a nice car.

MRS. VETCH. Not Delray! She didn't marry Delray, for goodness sakes! It's bad enough as it is!

MR. MINGO. Not all that bad. She is not the bride of Satan, Mrs. Vetch.

MR. PALFREY. All these new people drive around in fine new automobiles that they can't afford. I know that sorry crowd too well.

MR. NIBLIS. He doesn't need another car. Delray has already got himself a nice car.

DELRAY. (Slumped behind bar, holding wet cloth to head) I have a car, Mr. Niblis. I do not have a nice car.

Marguerite returns.

MR. MINGO. Well?

MARGUERITE. Miss Eula says don't rush her. She says Delray is two months behind in his payments.

DELRAY. Oh? And what else does Miss Eula have to say?

MARGUERITE. She wants her money, Delray, but she says you have one month to catch up.

Pause.

DELRAY. (Doesn't reply to Marguerite. Looks about room, muses) The dance floor isn't nearly big enough. I knew that all along.

MR. MINGO. Would you like to know where you went wrong, Delray?

DELRAY. No.

MR. MINGO. There was a moment—just a few weeks back—when you over-reached yourself.

DELRAY. I'd rather not hear about it.

MR. MINGO. It was a critical moment. Perhaps I should have spoken up at the time. Shall I tell you now about that pivotal moment?

DELRAY. No.

MR. MINGO. Then just let me review some of your policies—some of your more dubious policies—leading up to that fatal moment.

DELRAY. No, please don't bother, Mr. Mingo.

MARGUERITE. Miss Eula wants her money, Delray, or she wants the Sunnyside back. But she says you can have one more month to catch up.

DELRAY. The money has run out. There is no more money, and no prospects. I am defaulting. Tell her I accept foreclosure. I relinquish all claims.

MARGUERITE. Tell her what?

DELRAY. (*Takes ring of keys from belt*) Here. Give her these. Tell her the New Moon didn't work out.

Marguerite goes out with keys. The hotel lights flicker and flare up. The television set resumes its murmur.

MRS. VETCH. The lights are back! Will you look! Miss Eula returns and the lights come on again! Don't tell me that's an accident! It's the miracle of the lights at the Sunnyside Hotel!

MR. NIBLIS. (*Takes off Avalon cap. Rolls another cigarette*) I don't know about that. A reprieve anyway.

MR. MINGO. Executive clemency, Mr. Niblis. And not to be scorned. A brief reprieve is all anybody ever had.

MRS. VETCH. It's a little period of grace! That's what we've been granted! Let us make the most of it!

MR. MINGO. Is the game still on, Delray?

DELRAY. (*Glances up at television screen*) Yes. Or another one.

MR. MINGO. Maybe you could find out the—

Delray unplugs the television set.

MR. MINGO. —the score.

FERN. (*Places hat on Mr. Palfrey's head*) Ready? Don't forget your flashlight now. Garland will be here any minute.

MR. PALFREY. You should have told him to stop off at NAPA and pick
up a new solenoid.

LENORE. But what about the Special Value Package?

FERN. Are you still going on about that? After all you've heard here
about Dr. Mole and his devilish machines that are sucking all the
juices out of our retired people?

LENORE. I wasn't talking to you.

FERN. Who have worked so hard all their lives?

LENORE. I wasn't talking to you, I was talking to Daddy. So what do I
tell Boyce about Avalon, Daddy?

MR. PALFREY. Tell him I'd rather live in a crawdad hole, Lenore. Tell
Boyce to mind his own business for a change and leave other people's
dogs alone. Come here, Tonya, and give Granddaddy some sugar.

Marguerite bursts through the doorway.

MARGUERITE. He's up! Mr. Ramp is up! *(She holds the front door open
with one foot)* Get ready! Here they come! No, wait! Miss Eula is
tucking Mr. Ramp's shirt-tail in! Now she's taken his arm! She's got
all her keys in the other hand!

MRS. VETCH. How does she look, Marguerite? Is she radiant?

MARGUERITE. Little gray curls are hanging off her head! She's wearing
her galoshes! Her cheeks are rosy! Mr. Ramp's face is red, too!

MR. MINGO. Already they're beginning to look alike!

MRS. VETCH. Oh, I wish we had some—well, no, orange blossoms are
out of the question! But something! Some pale pink roses for her!
Or even a handful of daisies!

MARGUERITE. Here they come, everybody! Here they are! Mr. and
Mrs. Ramp!

*Marguerite begins to clap her hands. Mr. Niblis touches cigarette to his Avalon
balloon and pops it. He and the others—except for Delray, who is holding his
head—join Marguerite in ragged applause. Before Miss Eula and Mr. Ramp enter,*

The curtain falls.

Epilogue

INTERVIEW

Gazette Project Interview
with Charles Portis

The *Gazette* Project, undertaken by the University of Arkansas in Fayetteville, collected interviews with staff members from the last fifty years of the *Arkansas Gazette*, which was founded in 1819 and whose assets were taken over by the rival *Arkansas Democrat* in 1991 after a bitter newspaper war. The *Gazette*, under the leadership of Harry Ashmore, won two Pulitzer Prizes in 1958 for its editorials on and news coverage of the integration crisis at Little Rock Central High School.

    This interview was conducted in Little Rock by Roy Reed, a reporter who had worked with Portis at the *Gazette* and who went on to a career at the *New York Times* and as a journalism professor in Fayetteville. Reed, author of a biography of former Arkansas governor Orval Faubus, a collection of essays (*Looking for Hogeye*) and most recently a memoir titled *Beware of Limbo Dancers*, edited a book of the interviews, *Looking Back at the Arkansas Gazette*, published by the University of Arkansas Press in 2009. This is the full transcript of the interview that was excerpted there.

    ROY REED: All right. This is Charles Portis with Roy Reed, May 31, 2001. Just to back up what's on this piece of paper here, we have your permission to record this interview and turn it over to the University, is that right?

    CHARLES PORTIS: Yes, yes.

    REED: What led you to go to work at the *Gazette*? What were you doing before?

PORTIS: I got out of college in May of 1958 and went to work for *The Commercial Appeal* in Memphis, where I stayed for the rest of that year. But I really wanted to work for Harry Ashmore's *Gazette*, so I came over to Little Rock one weekend and asked Mr. Nelson about a job. He gave me a job.

REED: What I'm doing is writing down all the names that are mentioned, so the transcriber can get them right.

PORTIS: Yes, A. R. Nelson, the managing editor. I think he used initials because his name was Arla. I was on the night police beat for a while and then became a general assignment reporter. This was January or February of 1959. The tail-end of all that desegregation business at Central High. The schools were still closed that year.

REED: In 1959?

PORTIS: Yes.

REED: What kind of stories did you cover on general assignment?

PORTIS: Well, a lot of Citizens Council meetings—Amis Guthridge, Jim Johnson. The pro-segregationist people. And meetings of the other side—Daisy Bates, Everett Tucker. But there were other things, as well. Life went on. State Fair stories. Murders, ice storms.

REED: Amis Guthridge. He represented that cast of characters?

PORTIS: To me, he did, yes. He was always available. A lot of people on that side refused to talk to the *Gazette*, but Amis didn't mind. He would talk freely and at great length.

REED: Were you at my house at a party one night when Pat Owens got drunk and called Amis Guthridge on the phone?

PORTIS: Probably. Pat was a great one for that. At some point in the evening he would go for the telephone.

REED: How did they go? What kind of...?

PORTIS: Well, you know, put-ons. Pretending to be some earnest but slightly insane person with some questions to ask. Spinning it out. Pretending not to understand the meaning of simple words. The game being not to laugh and to keep the other party on the line as long as possible.

REED: Owens would enjoy putting on the persona of a revivalist preacher.

PORTIS: Yes, but we turned the tables on him once. Do you remember a guy on the copy desk named Don—something or other?

REED: Yes.

PORTIS: Out of California, I think. A heavy drinker. He slept on Pat's couch a lot when he couldn't remember where he lived. Anyway, he left, went back to California or Oregon. Then Jim Bailey and I wrote a letter to Pat, purporting to come from Don, saying he had married a woman with three or four kids, and they were making their way back across the country, in an old car, staying with friends along the way. That they were now in Beaumont, Texas, getting the car repaired, and were looking forward to a good long stay in Little Rock, at Pat's house. We arranged to have the letter mailed in Beaumont. I think Paul Johnson knew someone there. We let Pat sweat it out for a week or so, after he got the letter. Waiting for Don.

REED: That guy, Don. I think I can see his face.

PORTIS: He squinted up at you through glasses. He would come sidling up to you in a spooky way and say, "What's your read on De Gaulle?" A smart guy, good at his work, but a little strange, in some California way.

REED: Was he the model for the guy in *Dog of the South*?

PORTIS: Oh, no. I hadn't thought of Don in years. Until you mentioned Pat.

REED: I had it in my mind that it was a particular copy editor.

PORTIS: Oh, no.

REED: Well, I've been telling people for years that it was this Don what's-his-name. Whatever became of Don?

PORTIS: Who knows. One of those copy desk drifters. They could always get work. The good ones. Like Deacon. He once showed me four W-2 slips—representing jobs at four different newspapers in one calendar year. What about Pat? Is he still in Montana?

REED: He's still in Montana. He had that awful stroke years ago, and it kind of changed him.

PORTIS: The last I heard, he was writing some sex book. It sounded...I don't know...

REED: Yes, I read it.

PORTIS: I never saw a copy.

REED: Did you ever hear him talk about his politics growing up in Montana? You know, he identified with all those old lefties.

PORTIS: Yes, the Wobblies, the IWW. I knew he came out of that school.

REED: Then he ended up at the *Detroit Free Press*. He was the labor reporter up there for a long time. Knew all those guys. Who were some of the other people in the *Gazette* newsroom at that time?

PORTIS: Well, you, of course, and Bill Lewis, Ken Parker, Charlie Allbright, Matilda Tuohey. I remember asking Matilda, when Pat came to work there, if she would like to meet him. She said no, not just yet. Maybe in three or four months, if he still happened to be there. Otherwise, the introduction would have been all for nothing, wasted, on a transient.

REED: What was it about Matilda? She had that tough air about her.

PORTIS: Yes, maybe from being the only female in the newsroom.

REED: Later on, I found out that she would befriend young reporters. Take them home with her and give them cookies and things.

PORTIS: I've heard that. I don't think Pat got any cookies. I did know she was a devout Catholic, for all her gruff manner. And she was a great promoter of the Strunk and White writer's manual, which was big at the time. E. B. White telling us to cut out all our blather.

REED: Frank Peters? You remember him?

PORTIS: Yes, the best educated person on the staff. Ashmore included. You went to Frank if you wanted to know who Plotinus was. But for broad worldly knowledge you went to Leland DuVall. Leland could explain to you in detail just how a certain banking swindle is worked. Or the workings of some intricate piece of farm machinery. You couldn't stump him.

REED: What happened to Frank?

PORTIS: Well, he left the *Gazette* to become editor of the *Rome Daily American*, an English-language paper there. It seems to me that he succeeded Ray Moseley in that job.

REED: Yes, he did.

PORTIS: I was already in New York, and I remember seeing Frank off there on a west side pier. He was taking a ship to Europe. And later he was the music critic—is that right?—for the *St. Louis Post-Dispatch*. I believe he won a Pulitzer Prize for his work there.

REED: I think that's right. You mentioned Bill Lewis. What do you remember about him?

PORTIS: Bill and Pat were the most productive reporters on the paper. They could cover anything—get the stuff and bring it in quickly, with a minimum of fuss and grumbling. Not that they were alike in any other way.

REED: A very fast writer.

PORTIS: Yes, and always solid stuff. Just the kind of reporter that editors are always looking for.

REED: Ken Parker—I guess he was state editor at that time.

PORTIS: Yes, he and Pat Carrithers ran the state desk. And they didn't get along very well. I liked them both, but things were always a little tense over there. One morning, early, they had a big blow-up.

REED: I never knew about that.

PORTIS: Yes.

REED: I guess it was before I got to work. Charlie Allbright—did you take over the "Our Town" column from him?

PORTIS: Yes. Charlie went to work for—Winthrop Rockefeller, I think—and Mr. Nelson gave me the job. I thought I would do it well, but I could never—I don't know—get into a stride. Clumsy, half-baked stuff. It was a grind. I had to do five of those things each week, plus a long Sunday piece—an expanded feature story with pictures. And when you find yourself trying to fill space, you're in trouble.

REED: Do you remember any particular columns you did?

PORTIS: No. Bits and pieces. All that is mostly a blank. Well, I do remember a Sunday piece on a big cock-fighting meet in Garland County. Pat Carrithers and I drove down there. All these high-rollers in dusty Cadillacs with Texas and Louisiana plates. With their fighting chickens. Flashing their thick wads of cash.

REED: Let me remind you of one column. You had a friend, you said, whose hobby was collecting old Christmas cards, and that he'd appreciate it if you could mail them to him. Do you remember that?

PORTIS: [Laughs] No.

REED: Where did you live then?

PORTIS: Out on 21st or 22nd Street, off Main, near the old VA Hospital. We had to double up then, on what we were paid. There were four of us in a little furnished house—Jack Meriwether, me, Ronnie Farrar and a guy named—Hawkins, I think it was. The house of abandoned neckties. Jack was an assistant city manager, and Ronnie was a reporter for the *Democrat*. I don't know what Hawkins did. I'm not sure we even knew who Hawkins was, but he slept there and paid his share of the rent.

Our landlord was John Yancey, the much-decorated Marine, one of Colonel Carlson's Raiders. He owned a liquor store nearby, on Roosevelt Road. We made a point of paying our rent on time. One look at Yancey and armed robbers fled the store. Or at least one did. I asked John about the holdup guy, and he said, "Well, his sporting blood turned to horse piss, that's all." Some previous tenant of that house had left a lot of very wide and garish neckties hanging in a closet. I like to think he had turned his back forever on 21st Street and his old life of wide ties. I wore one to work one day—a big orange tie with a horse's head on it, with rhinestone eyes. Mr. Nelson came over and said, "I don't know, Buddy, that tie—don't you think—I mean, meeting the public—A tie like that..."

REED: But we did wear coats and ties.

PORTIS: Oh, yes, such as they were. There was something about that in the style book at *The Commercial Appeal* in Memphis. Those little booklets, you know, telling you how things were done there—spelling quirks, that sort of thing. At the beginning of this one there was a general edict that went something like this: "The employees of *The Commercial Appeal* will dress and conduct themselves as ladies and gentlemen at all times." Well, yes, a good policy, all very Southern, I approved, but it was hard to dress as a gentleman on $57 a week. Even then.

REED: Newsrooms look different now. I mean the people.

PORTIS: Yes, they're pretty sad places. Quiet, lifeless. No big Underwood typewriters clacking away. No milling about, no chatting, no laughing, no smoking. That old loose, collegial air is long gone from the newsrooms. "A locker room air," I suppose, would be the negative description. We wore coats and ties, and the reporters now wear jeans, and yet they're the grim ones. This isn't to say we were loose in our work.

REED: That's exactly right. Something's been lost.

PORTIS: But our coats and ties and trousers didn't always match.

REED: Now that thing about the Christmas cards—I don't mean to wear that out, but it seems to me you got more than one column out of it.

PORTIS: I probably milked everything.

REED: Poor Meriwether ended up getting hundreds of those cards in the mail. I ran into him a few months after that and asked how he felt about it. He said, "Indignant." But I guess he was a good sport about it, and it was actually the kind of thing Meriwether would have done if he had been writing the column.

PORTIS: Yes, that sounds more like something in Meriwether's line than mine. A bad influence.

REED: You mentioned Ray Moseley a while ago. What kind of guy was he?

PORTIS: Well, he was leaving the *Gazette* just as I came, so it was hello and goodbye. There had been some scrap in the office. Ray and someone came to blows.

REED: Tom Swint.

PORTIS: Yes. But I never really knew Ray. I did run into him again somewhere—New York, maybe. I think he's been with the *Chicago Tribune* for some time now.

REED: Yes, he's their London guy. What about Bill Shelton? What do you remember about him?

PORTIS: Well, his integrity. Seeing to it that we got things right, in big matters and small. No slack. No excuses. He communicated with notes, you remember. He didn't like talking. He would type out a note and put it in your mailbox—those little pigeon holes across from the city desk. Something he could have spoken to you in three or four seconds.

REED: Was he a teacher in regards to language and news reporting, that sort of thing?

PORTIS: Yes, but not in any systematic way, as I recall. He would deal with your errors as they came up. I used the word "afterwards" in a story once, and he lopped off the "s," saying it was unnecessary. I still prefer the "s," but he was usually right. I don't remember any—program of instruction. It was assumed that you knew your job, more or less.

REED: I didn't realize till twenty or thirty years later, but it was Bill Shelton who taught me sequence of tenses. Does that ring a bell with you?

PORTIS: No, I don't remember getting into that.

REED: He was very strict on sequence of verb tenses.

PORTIS: "...to care for him who shall have borne the battle..." Lincoln's nice use of the future perfect tense.

REED: Turns out there was an exact way to do it, and Shelton knew what it was. How long were you at the *Gazette*?

PORTIS: A little under two years.

REED: You mentioned something about notes from Shelton, and it reminded me of the bulletin board. Do you remember any of the notes that appeared there?

PORTIS: Yes, those fake announcements and directives. Well, I don't remember any specific ones. Office humor. Some were pretty good.

REED: I think your brother Richard was behind some of that. When he came to the paper later.

PORTIS: I'm sure he was.

REED: Bob Douglas remembers Richard as being one of the best copy editors he had there.

PORTIS: Yes, he and Jonathan were both good editors. Good writers, too, but they no longer bother with it. Richard came to his senses and went to medical school. I never worked on a copy desk. There was a rule at *The Commercial Appeal* that new reporters had to put in a few months on that duty, to get the feel of things. But the rule was waived—a shortage of reporters or something—when I went there.

REED: What do you remember about Harry Ashmore?

PORTIS: Well, you think of the editor of a newspaper as being some remote figure in a back office, going home at four in the afternoon. But Ashmore was out and about in the city room, checking on things, at all hours. He would sit on the corner of your desk and have you fill him in on just what Governor Faubus said, and how he said it, and who was there. He would grill you and make suggestions. More like a managing editor. A very open and genial boss to deal with.

REED: Did you ever go out drinking with him?

PORTIS: No. Or once or twice in a group. We weren't pals.

REED: He was much more than just the editor of the editorial page?

PORTIS: Yes, indeed. He was interested in everything. He would look over the photographs and make selections.

REED: What about Douglas? What do you remember about Bob Douglas?

PORTIS: Bob, yes. I don't remember exactly what he was then— copy editor, news editor—but I know he had more authority than the title suggested. He didn't need the rank. He had a natural authority that everyone recognized. Even his bosses deferred to him.

REED: He seems never to have forgotten a detail of his history.

PORTIS: No, and that was part of it. He knew things.

REED: Wasn't he also the guy you once referred to in your column as the funniest man in Arkansas?

PORTIS: Yes, that was from a story he told me once about a funeral in a country church, up around Kensett. It was an ordinary church with the two aisles—pews on the left and right and in the middle. The service had already started. The coffin was on a platform, a bier, beneath the pulpit. An old man came in late, making his way down the left aisle, when he caught his foot on a sprung board or something. He went into a stumbling trot, trying to regain his balance, and appeared to be making for the coffin—making a headlong assault on the coffin. Everyone froze. But at the last moment he managed to veer off to the right, short of the coffin, and continue his run down the right-hand aisle. I can't remember now whether his momentum carried him on out the door, or whether he just plumped down into a pew at the rear.

REED: You remember Joe Wirges?

PORTIS: Oh yes, Joe broke me in on the night police beat there. He was the day man, the police reporter. He had been doing it for so long, you know, that he was almost one of the cops himself. That's one way of doing it, and he did it very well. I tried to keep a little more distance— not so much stuff off the record—but that way you get frozen out of things. You can make a case for either approach. There was no police information officer then. You had to get the stuff, as best you could, from individual cops and detectives.

REED: He was kind of a legendary figure.

PORTIS: Yes, indeed, maybe senior to everyone except Mr. Heiskell. Joe had seen it all—lynchings, electrocutions, shootouts. There was a radio show in the 1940s and 1950s, "The Pall Mall Big Story" or "Front Page," something like that. Dramatized stories about crime reporters. One of Joe's adventures was on that show. He told me he got $500 for it.

REED: It seems to me that he died on the same day Mr. Heiskell died.

PORTIS: I don't remember that.

REED: What do you remember about Mr. Heiskell? J. N. Heiskell?

PORTIS: Well, you know, he was in his nineties then, but still fairly active. He would come through the newsroom now and then, usually with a galley proof in his hand, and some questions. I remember doing a story about the river. The Corps of Engineers had told me that the Arkansas River would soon run blue through Little Rock, when all these new locks and dams were in place. Mr. Heiskell came by to ask me about that. The muddy, reddish old Arkansas out there flowing blue? Was I quite sure of that? "Blue, Mr. Portis?" I said I was sure the claim had been made. He went away shaking his head, over the absurd claim or my gullibility, or both. But the engineers were right, you know. The river is blue at times. Jerry Neil told me that Mr. Heiskell stopped him once in the hall and said, "Mr. Neil, have you ever stopped to consider just how different things might be if General Lee had had just one scouting airplane at the Battle of Gettysburg?" Jerry said he hadn't. But, yes, Mr. Heiskell was there every day. He knew what was going on.

REED: Did you ever write any of those stories—those ideas of Mr. Heiskell that got passed along?

PORTIS: Yes, a "Mr. Heiskell must," something like that. I don't remember any offhand but certainly did some. But, remember, we couldn't use the word "story." It smacked of fiction. Mr. Heiskell said the proper word for a news account was "article." And we couldn't use "evacuate" as of a building or a city being evacuated. He thought it might remind readers of a bodily function. I don't know what softer word we used. There can't be many synonyms for "evacuate." And no photographs of snakes or other vermin, with those same sensitive readers in mind. And we spelled "Tokyo" with an "i" instead of a "y." But I sort of liked those quirks.

REED: JNH.

PORTIS: Yes, that was it. That was the note for those must-do things.

REED: I had a box full of JNH's when I left. Gave them back to Bill Shelton, and he was not amused.

PORTIS: Bill was hard to amuse. I ignored notes, too—just kept putting things off till they were forgotten or dead. But maybe not the JNH ones. I think I did act on those.

REED: You had worked at the *Arkansas Traveler* at the University. Was that your only other newspaper experience?

PORTIS: Well, no, I worked at the *Northwest Arkansas Times*, too. The last year or so I was in Fayetteville. I did the courthouse beat, the sheriff's office, the jail, Judge Ptak's municipal court. A weird judge, to say the least. Justice was swift there. And I edited the country correspondence from these lady stringers in Goshen and Elkins, those places. I had to type it up. They wrote with hard-lead pencils on tablet paper or notebook paper, but their handwriting was good and clear. Much better than mine. Their writing, too, for that matter. From those who weren't self-conscious about it. Those who hadn't taken some writing course. My job was to edit out all the life and charm from these homely reports. Some fine old country expression, or a nice turn of phrase—out they went. We probably thought we were doing the readers a favor. Ted Wylie was the editor.

REED: You worked there a year?

PORTIS: Or a little more, yes.

REED: While you were a student?

PORTIS: I was a student, yes. It was very early in the morning [when] I'd go down to the *Times* office. In my 1950 Chevrolet convertible, with the vertical radio in the dash and the leaking top. The Chevrolets of that period had a gearshift linkage that was always locking up, usually in second gear. I would have to stop at least once on the way to work—raise the hood and pop it loose by hand.

REED: That was when the Fulbrights still owned the paper?

PORTIS: Yes. The publisher was—Gearhart?

REED: Sam Gearhart—does that sound right?

PORTIS: Yes, and there was another executive—I can't recall the name.

REED: Was Mrs. Fulbright still there? Roberta Fulbright?

PORTIS: She was still alive, but I don't recall seeing her there in the office. Maybe she came by later in the day.

REED: Did the Senator himself ever show up?

PORTIS: I don't remember seeing him there, either.

REED: But you did a whole range of work at the paper?

PORTIS: Within a limited range, yes.

REED: How did you happen to go to work there?

PORTIS: I think I just went down and asked for a job. I was in journalism at the university, and Mr. Thalheimer may have put in a word for me. One of my teachers there. But I don't remember the details. I was just suddenly working there.

REED: What did you do at the *Traveler*?

PORTIS: I'm not sure I ever worked for the *Traveler*, in any formal way. I wrote a few columns, sort of comic pieces, but I don't believe I was on the staff. Ronnie Farrar was the editor at that time. Then Sammy Smith and Kenny Danforth. Or maybe the other way around.

REED: You wrote a particular piece that was reprinted in the *Gazette*. It had to do with—it was during the Central High crisis. You remember that?

PORTIS: Vaguely. Something about…

REED: About *Time* magazine?

PORTIS: *Time* magazine, yes, yes. I remember that. But not much about the thing itself.

REED: How'd you come to do that?

PORTIS: I don't know. You get an idea, and you start fooling around on a typewriter.

REED: They had Faubus on the cover, as I remember, and then it had this cover story about him, which was pretty denigrating of not only Faubus but the state of Arkansas.

PORTIS: Yes, I think that was probably the provocative thing. The smartass stuff about Arkansas.

REED: You remember how that piece ended up?

PORTIS: No.

REED: I happened to see it not long ago. A suggestion that they ought to plow up Manhattan and plant it in turnip greens.

PORTIS: So, my smartass response. But I don't remember that part.

REED: What got you interested in journalism to start with?

PORTIS: Oh, I don't know. I got to be something of a reader in the service. Paperback books, whatever came to hand. I got out of the Marines in May of 1955 and went back to Hamburg. A friend of mine there, Billy Rodgers, had just gotten out of the Air Force, and he had a car. So we drove up to Fayetteville and enrolled for the summer semester at the university. An all-day drive, then. I think Hamburg is actually closer to LSU and Ole Miss than Fayetteville. Anyway, we registered, and you could do that then, just show up with a high school diploma and $50, or whatever the tuition fee was, and you were in. You had to choose a major, so I put down journalism. I must have thought it would be fun and not very hard, something like barber college. Not to offend the barbers. They probably provide a more useful service. But, remember, Footsie Britt had been in Hill Hall, too, and we could claim him. Surely the only journalism major ever to win a Medal of Honor. Maybe the only one named Maurice. But the degree was in liberal arts, and the journalism courses were only a small part of that, thirty hours or so.

REED: Were you always good at English?

PORTIS: Well, adequate, I suppose. I didn't have much trouble with it in school. Diagramming sentences, that kind of thing. If you mean the mechanics of it. Although Bill Whitworth, for—what, thirty-odd years now—has been trying to drum into my head the difference between "which" and "that." I go pretty much by feel. People who know more about grammar than we know, well, aren't they pedants?

REED: When I was twelve or thirteen, I had begun to read pretty much, and I liked fiction and decided to write novels, and somebody came along and said, "Well, first you have to make a living and one way to do that is to work for newspapers."

PORTIS: Yes, it was probably something along those lines. It was a writing job. They would pay you to write things.

REED: But I never got back to novels, and you did. Were both your parents in education?

PORTIS: No, only my father. He was from Alabama, a graduate of Birmingham Southern College. His brother, my Uncle Cecil, was a lawyer, and he came over to south Arkansas during the oil boom of the 1920s, trading in leases and options. He got my father a teaching job in Norphlet.

REED: Little oil town.

PORTIS: Yes, between El Dorado and Smackover. And my father got to be the school superintendent there in short order. The job paid well—the school district had all that oil money. He was a very young man. I have the idea he made more real money there than he was ever to make again. He later got a master's degree at Fayetteville. But, no, my mother didn't go to college. She liked writing and had a gift for it, but never the time to work at it much. Fits and starts. A good poet with a good ear. But neither of them were wide readers. Again, maybe, because they didn't have the time. And, anyway, the Portises were talkers rather than readers or writers. A lot of cigar smoke and laughing when my father and his brothers got together. Long anecdotes. The spoken word. But he was something of a Bible scholar. And he read *The Congressional Record*, of all things. He had a taste for politics, local, national, all the ins and outs of the game. I didn't get that gene. I've often thought how much he would have enjoyed all this political stuff on cable television, the debates and hearings, all that.

REED: What was his name?

PORTIS: Samuel Palmer Portis.

REED: And your mother's name?

PORTIS: Alice Waddell. He met her in Norphlet. She was the daughter of a Methodist minister there. One of eleven children. None of them left now.

REED: There are three of you boys and one girl, right?

PORTIS: Yes, my sister was the oldest. I was two years younger. She died in 1958.

REED: What was her name?

PORTIS: Alice Kate, which she didn't like. She preferred "Aleece," spelled A-L-I-E-C-E. But I think that was partly to prevent confusion with my mother, who was also Alice.

REED: She died of what?

PORTIS: A cerebral hemorrhage. She was just twenty-eight. Married and with two small sons.

REED: I had a sister who died at 29. It's...

PORTIS: Yes, and my father never really got over it. She was his favorite. She had a very quick intelligence.

REED: I had a call the other day from your sister's son's wife.

PORTIS: Sam Sawyer or Paul Sawyer?

REED: Sawyer, yes. Nathania.

PORTIS: Nathania, yes, Paul's wife. She's writing a thesis on Harry Ashmore. She called me about that.

REED: I felt like she was right on top of it.

PORTIS: Oh, yes, she would be. Diligent and well organized. She'll get it done.

REED: Well, Buddy, you have now worked for two newspapers that are no longer alive. Is there something about those papers that—did they have things in common?

PORTIS: Well, the *Gazette* and the *Herald Tribune*, they were both good places to work.

REED: You mean, good people to be around?

PORTIS: Yes, that's it, good company, and a pleasant atmosphere. I've been in other newsrooms where you could feel the gloom and fear hanging about. People who hated their work and their bosses.

REED: Who were some of your favorite people at the *Trib*?

PORTIS: Well, my favorite boss was my immediate boss, Buddy Weiss, the city editor. Murray Weiss, that is. Demanding, but always very good to me. He later went to Paris as editor of the European edition of the paper. His wife was from Snyder, Arkansas—he met her when he was in the Air Force, I think. He didn't believe me when I told him I knew Snyder well. He had never found anyone, even from Arkansas, who had ever heard of Snyder. But it's not far from Hamburg, in Ashley County. There was a succession of managing editors— Fendall Yerxa, Jim Bellows, Dick Wald—and they all treated me well, too. Better than I deserved.

REED: Who hired you?

PORTIS: Dick West, a Yankee gentleman. He was the city editor before Buddy Weiss. I had sent him some clippings from the *Gazette* and asked about a job. He wrote back to say come by and see him when I was in New York. Not a firm offer. But I gave notice at the *Gazette* and went to New York, and he hired me. A little later he took a job at Grolier Encyclopedia. I remember those first few days at work. I would go over and ask Bob Poteete, the assistant city editor, for permission to call Chicago, Miami, wherever, having to do with some story I was working on. Bob had worked for the *Gazette*, too. He was from Perryville. Finally, he said, "Why do you keep asking me this?" I said, "Well, at the *Gazette* you had to get permission to make long-distance calls." He laughed, at my bush-league ways, and said, "Hell, call whoever you please."

REED: Maybe that's why they went out of business. Yes, at the *Gazette* we not only had to get permission to make a long-distance call, we didn't even have our own phones. Remember, you and I shared a phone for a long time.

PORTIS: Yes, I do remember. But Bob and I weren't the only *Gazette* hands on the paper. There was Inky Blackmon on the re-write bank. The legendary *Herald Tribune* re-write bank. But its glory days had faded by then. And later there was Bill Whitworth and Pat Crow. We had quite a few Southerners there. Fulbright?

REED: Newton Fulbright?

PORTIS: Newt Fulbright, yes, from Texas. And Phil Carter, Hodding Carter's son, from Greenville, Mississippi. I remember once there was a call from Mayor Wagner's office. One of his aides had some statement to give us. Bob Poteete took the call, and he relayed it to Newt, who re-layed it to Phil, who said he was tied up, too—a likely story—and he passed it on to me. The City Hall guy was mad over being pushed around like this, and by all these alien voices, and he said, "This is *The New York*

Herald Tribune, isn't it?" I said it sure was. He mimicked my accent and said, "I thought maybe I had the bleeping *Birmingham Herald Tribune.*"

REED: Well, it was pretty much the same with *The New York Times* in those days. *The Times* was a better paper for it, I always suspected.

PORTIS: Yes, probably so. Still, you know, we like to think we were hired and promoted strictly on merit, but I've since wondered if there wasn't a certain amount of affirmative action going on then, favoring Southern boys. Hiring guys like us. I hope it wasn't because we worked cheap. I remember this copy desk fellow one night in Bleeck's bar, in the rear of the *Tribune* building. Across from the old Metropolitan Opera. He was usually a very reserved fellow, but on this night he was drunk and raging. He had been passed over for promotion to, I think, assistant copy editor, and he said, "Well, I've learned one damned thing for sure. You're not going anywhere on this paper unless you went to Yale or you're from below the bleeping Mason-Dixon Line."

REED: Wonder who that was?

PORTIS: I can't—I can see him now, but I can't call the name. It'll come to me.

REED: Was that the one you had the arm-wrestling contest with?

PORTIS: Oh no, that—how did you know about that? That was down in the Village.

REED: You want to tell about that?

PORTIS: There wasn't much to it. It was late one night in some joint down in Greenwich Village. The guy was from *The Times,* I believe.

REED: As I heard it, yes.

PORTIS: We were sitting at the table, a few of us from the *Tribune.* Dennis Duggan, me, Warren Berry, I think. Maybe Penny Brown. And this fellow from *The Times,* who was a stranger to me. He wanted to arm-wrestle, and as I recall, he kept challenging me. So we went at it, and there was a pop. His arm broke. Very strange. He went into a kind of swoon, and it was Dennis, I think, who took him off to a hospital, somewhere down there near Sheridan Square.

REED: I heard he was a big husky guy.

PORTIS: No, no, nothing like that. Just average size.

REED: Well, the story's been improved.

PORTIS: It certainly has. I didn't know it was a story.

REED: Not twice as big as you and that kind of thing?

PORTIS: No, that would have made it a story, but no. It was just a freakish thing. A weak bone or something.

REED: All right. This is the second tape if I can get it to stand up. We were talking about life at the *Arkansas Gazette*. I just thought of something that Tom Wolfe said about you in print one time, having to do with Malcolm X. Do you remember that interview?

PORTIS: Yes, in a studio at some radio station in New York. I can't imagine what I was doing there. Malcolm X and two or three reporters, including me. I was asking him about the "X" business. About why he would abandon the hated Anglo name of—"Little," was it? "Malcolm Little?"—and yet keep the "Malcolm" part, not a very African name. He said the difference was that some slave-owners had imposed the surname on his family, but his mother had given him the name of Malcolm. Good point. A sharp fellow. He treated me with a little less contempt because I said something about Marcus Garvey and the back-to-Africa move-ment. How it went nowhere. He treated the other reporters with slightly more contempt, I mean, because they were just asking topical questions that he was used to dealing with. I think he later changed his name again, to something Arabic. He had a presence.

REED: Tom Wolfe, in this essay, said you addressed him throughout the interview as "Mr. X."

PORTIS: Yes, I probably did. But what can you do? To call him "Malcolm" would have been a little familiar, wouldn't it? And, yes, Tom came to us from the *Washington Post*. He was polite enough not to roll his eyes when I asked if he might be related to the other Thomas Wolfe. He said he wasn't, but it must have been a tiresome question for him then. I wonder if it comes up at all now. Speaking of the other Wolfe, I remember that an old brig rat from Phenix City, Alabama, gave me a copy of *Look Homeward, Angel* at Camp Lejeune, North Carolina, in 1954. An old corporal who had been promoted and busted a lot. More ribbons and hash marks than stripes. He said his girlfriend had read this entire book to him, and it wasn't bad stuff to listen to. Do barmaids still do that? It must have taken weeks. She worked in a bar in Jacksonville. Or maybe she was the only one who ever did it. I had never heard of Thomas Wolfe. It was a revelation. Chesty Puller, by the way, the leg-endary Chesty, was our commanding officer. Anyway, Tom, yes, he and Lewis Lapham were our better writers. Good writers are not always good newspaper reporters, but they were. Lewis came from the *San Francisco Chronicle*. Or was the *Express*? I said, "San Francisco must be a good town for reporters," and he said, yes, it was okay, but out there you were always dealing with the branch managers of things. New York was the place. We were in the right place. Tom was a quiet and easy going fellow, one of the crew. The white suit was the only flamboyant thing about him. He raised the tone of things in the newsroom a bit. Probably not enough. We were general assignment reporters, and we sat there in a clump— Lewis, me, Edward Silberfarb, Tom. And Terry Smith, Jim Clarity, Phil Carter, Phil Cook.

REED: You remember Breslin?

PORTIS: Jimmy Breslin, yes. He came later. Wrote a very popular column. I met him but didn't really know him. I think I must have gone to London not long after he came.

REED: I had to cover a story opposite him one time in Hayneville, Alabama, one of those Ku Klux trials down there, and Claude Sitton, my national editor, was on me because Breslin, you know, was a colorful writer, and Sitton wanted more of that in my copy. I treasure the day when I was able to call Sitton and say, "Did you see that long quote in Breslin's column today? Leroy Moton saying so and so?" I said, "It's all made up." Son of a bitch didn't say it. Even had it wrong. I mean he had been trying to badger—

PORTIS: Not well fabricated?

REED: No, not well fabricated. So I took great joy in being able to point that out. That was the last I heard from Sitton on that subject.

PORTIS: Well, you know, Claude and I worked together on all that civil rights turmoil in the South. The early sixties. Or rather we worked against each other. He with the *Times* and me with the *Tribune*.

REED: Did you spend much time down there?

PORTIS: Quite a bit, yes. I didn't care much for beat reporting, covering the same thing day after day—short attention span—but I went where I was sent. First to Albany, Georgia, where Dr. King was in jail for—I think it was "parading without a permit." Then to Birmingham and that all-night riot there. Then to Mississippi and then back to Alabama, with Governor Wallace "standing in the schoolhouse door." I may have the sequence wrong. Those things have all run together in my head.

REED: Oh, you were at Tuscaloosa for that?

PORTIS: Yes, I was there. It was a staged event, more or less. The outcome wasn't in doubt. Those black students were going to be admitted to the University of Alabama. Wallace had been meeting with Robert Kennedy and Nicholas Katzenbach, and he wanted a big show of federal force there, a lot of marshals, when he made his defiant speech—which reminds me of Leander Perez, that segregationist boss down in Plaquemines Parish, Louisiana. Earl Long said to him, "What you gonna do now, Leander? Da Feds have got da H-bomb." Some of it was the Civil War being replayed as farce.

REED: Inky Blackmon. Wasn't he an old *Gazette* man?

PORTIS: Yes, in the 1930s. He must have gone to the *Herald Tribune* in the early 1940s. Maybe the first Arkie there, unless you count Henry Stanley in the 1870s. The reporter who found Dr. Livingstone in Africa. Stanley grew up on a plantation down around Pine Bluff. Something Bayou. Plum Bayou? He worked for the old *Herald*, which merged with the *Tribune* in the 1920s.

REED: I forget Inky's first name.

PORTIS: Marion, I think. M. C. Blackmon. He wrote some stories for *The New Yorker*, and I think that's how he gave his name. I probably shouldn't call him an Arkie. He set me straight on that point. "I'm from Louisiana, not Arkansas," he said to me. "I only worked in Arkansas for a time." But he retired to Little Rock, not Louisiana. He stood apart from everybody at the bar in Bleeck's and drank spritzers—those white wine and soda things. Not much of a talker. He did tell me once that he was proud of the work he had done at the *Gazette* in putting together a historical supplement in 1936. A big statehood centennial thing. Mostly a one-man project, I gathered.

REED: One of Mr. Heiskell's ideas.

PORTIS: I'm sure it was. And a good one. Inky, I believe, was the very last of the old veterans on the *Herald Tribune* rewrite bank. Much celebrated in its day.

REED: Those old rewrite men—they were under-appreciated heroes.

PORTIS: Yes, they were. And we still had a version of that system—of "leg men" and "rewrite men." The leg men were these mystery voices from out there in the police stations and courts and boroughs. You never saw those people. They would get the stuff and call it in. The rewrite

men would type it all up, very fast, into coherent accounts. All neatly
tailored to fit the exact space available—two paragraphs, five, a dozen.
Great short-order cooks. They were facile writers, and I don't mean that
in a slighting way. They could bat it out. Harry Ashmore could do that,
you remember? He wrote fast about as well as he wrote slow. The news
magazines adopted that system—the hunter/gatherers out in the field
and the writers in the office.

REED: You said you and Tom Wolfe worked on rewrite.

PORTIS: Yes, and Lewis, too. Inky didn't approve of our banter and
laughing during the lulls—unseemly conduct on the rewrite bank. We
were all pressed into that duty at one time or another, particularly in the
summers, when people were on vacation. Shanghaied into it. I could do
it, after a fashion, but I wasn't comfortable working with a pile of facts
gathered by someone else. They weren't quite real to me. And every reporter, no matter how senior, had to write obituaries now and then. A
good policy. They were regarded as news stories and were to be written,
not just dashed off. Of course, we didn't have to report every death in
the city either. I'm forgetting Sanche here. He was working rewrite one
night and won a Pulitzer Prize. Sanche De Gramont. It was in that cat-
egory of reporting under deadline pressure. Some Metropolitan Opera
star had collapsed and died during a performance. I think it was Leonard
Warren. The Met was nearby and Sanche raced over there on foot and
got the stuff. Then he ran back and knocked out a full account of it in
just a few minutes, right on deadline.

REED: De Gramont?

PORTIS: Sanche De Gramont, yes. A French count. Ancient family.
Not that he traded on that. In fact, Sanche later became an American
citizen and changed his name to Ted Morgan.

REED: That's Ted Morgan?

PORTIS: Yes. He wrote a good book on Africa, about the Niger
River, and a biography of Somerset Maugham. Among others.

REED: It seems to me that Homer Bigart was on the rewrite desk at
the *Times* after the *Trib* folded. Did you know Bigart?

PORTIS: I knew who he was, certainly, his reputation, and I think
I did meet him once somewhere. But I didn't know him.

REED: He might have been off covering some war.

PORTIS: He could have been. Like Marguerite Higgins. She wasn't working for the *Tribune* then, but she came through the newsroom now and then. Our celebrity people were mostly in sports: Red Smith, Terry's father, and Stanley Woodward—"Coach," we called him. But then later, Jimmy Breslin and Tom Wolfe. When Tom began doing those pieces for the Sunday magazine.

REED: Do you know if that story is true about Bigart or Marguerite Higgins? I guess it was well known that they despised each other, and when she got pregnant and Homer found out about it, he stuttered, "Oh, oh, oh, oh, really? Who, who, who, who's the mother?"

PORTIS: Tough old gal, yes.

REED: The University of Arkansas Press reprinted a bunch of his foreign correspondence, war coverage, five or six years ago. Pretty good reading, even now.

PORTIS: Holds up, does it?

REED: Yes. You were at the *Trib* how long?

PORTIS: Let's see. Four years–1960 through 1964. Three years in New York and one in London.

REED: How did you like London?

PORTIS: I liked it, but it was hard staying on top of the job. It was a juggling act. I was bureau chief, meaning administrative duties, and I was also the only reporter. So I wasn't chief of much. One reporter, down from, I don't know, a dozen or more, during World War II. In New York they had told me not to bother duplicating the wire service stuff. I was to do longer, leisurely things. But, of course, they wanted both, the breaking news and the longer pieces.

REED: That's a familiar story.

PORTIS: Yes, and then running the office, too. We had other people there—John Crosby, who wrote a culture column, and Seymour Freidin, our Cold War man, who was usually off in the Balkans somewhere, but I was the only day-by-day reporter. Joseph Alsop would come through town, and I would have to send someone to his hotel to pick up his copy. He expected a lot of service and deference.

REED: Another familiar story.

PORTIS: Yes, and we had Telex operators and a secretary and an advertising office. Stringers calling in from Scotland, book reviewers. There were cranks and complaints to deal with. Here's one. There were a lot of freeloaders in London who claimed to work for the *Herald Tribune*. The paper was known there from the international edition published in Paris. These scammers would wangle free airline tickets and free meals at expensive restaurants, saying they were travel writers, critics, whatever. I finally nabbed one. The manager of a theater up around Piccadilly called to ask if so-and-so, who wanted some free tickets to the opening of a play, was a reviewer for the paper. I said, "No, but tell him to come pick up the tickets at a certain time." I would be there to deal with him. He showed, and we had some words there in the theater lobby. He insisted that he had done some reviewing for the *Tribune*. I took him back to the office and called New York. Someone in the arts section said, well, yes, he had written a single review for them, some years back, but wasn't authorized now to say he represented the paper. My one pitiful bust. I had to let him go on a technicality, with a warning not to try this again. All pretty silly, but we were getting a lot complaints from angry PR people and businessmen. They were flying the scammers, gratis, to Majorca, feeding them, entertaining them, but never saw anything in the paper about it. No reviews, no mentions, nothing. What was going on? The point being that I kept getting dragged away from reporting into these management comedies.

REED: Where were you?

PORTIS: Not on Fleet Street. Our offices were in the Adelphi Building, just off the Strand, near the Savoy Hotel. It was a big fixed expense, that bureau, and probably should have been shut down at that stage of things. Hard to do, I suppose, for prestige reasons, but it really was a white elephant by that time. The *Tribune* should have just kept a couple of correspondents in London, working unencumbered, out of their apartments. Or in some little cubicle on Fleet Street with a desk and a telephone. Sending the stuff back by commercial cable. We could have called it a bureau. This was the time, you remember, of "Swinging London." Not that all that many swingers were doing all that much actual swinging. Or no more than usual. Some journalist professes to see a pattern, and he gives it a name that catches on. Others take it up and inflate it. Then your editor wants a "Swinging London" story, so you go out and find some swingers. Tom Lambert told me what I was in for. A good man. I replaced Tom there, and he stayed on for a couple of weeks to show me the ropes and introduce me around. David Bruce was the U.S. Ambassador. Archie Roosevelt was the CIA station chief, though, of course, he wasn't called that. It was a busy station then. A grandson of Theodore. I bought Camel cigarettes through a Marine gunnery sergeant at the embassy. The prime minister was Sir Alec Douglas-Home. He gave us—a handful of American correspondents—one or two off-the-record interviews and spoke of Lyndon Johnson as, "your, uh, rather racy president." Referring, I suppose, to Johnson's barnyard humor. I had Karl Marx's old job there, you know. He was the London correspondent for Horace Greeley's *New York Tribune* in the 1850s. Dick Wald was my New York boss, and I told him once that the *Tribune* might have saved us all a lot of grief if it had only paid Marx a little better. Dick didn't take the hint. Well, a small joke. I was paid well enough.

REED: Did you have trouble, too, with the telephones in London?

PORTIS: Oh, yes, all the time. Those strange clicks and wrong numbers. Broken connections. Tom said some of the clicks were taps, the crude wiretaps of the day. He said the British intelligence services had taps on all the phones in foreign news bureaus. But sometimes it was worse when the phones did work. Randolph Churchill called one day, drunk and rambling on. Something about his son's forthcoming wedding. It was around four in the afternoon, our early deadline, a bad time. I was knocking out a last-minute piece, so I was a little impatient with him, trying to keep him to the point, whatever it was. Impossible—he wouldn't listen. Our chief Telex operator was a little, round old fellow, a cockney worrywart named Frankie Williams, and he was hovering and checking his watch and chirping away at me. "Oh, Charlie, Charlie, you really must work faster. New York wants this copy now." New York was a fearful place to him. And to Frankie I was one of those hapless Japanese embassy clerks in Washington, trying to peck out a long declaration of war in an alien language. I waved him off and told Churchill we were pretty busy here and that it would help if he could maybe give me the gist of all this. He said, "Perhaps if you would stop interrupting me, I could tell you!" And that his good friend, Jock Whitney, would be hearing very soon about my "brusque manner" with him. Randolph Churchill, wounded by bad manners. I told him to call back when he was more or less sober. I never heard anything from Mr. Whitney, on that score. That's John Hay Whitney, who owned the paper.

REED: And how long were you in London?

PORTIS: A year. As I say, the *Tribune* people had always treated me very well, but I wanted to try my hand at fiction, so I gave notice and went home. On a ship this time, the *Mauretania*, a Cunard liner. I went second class, which was called "cabin class." Meant to sound less offensive. But I did have a cabin to myself, and there were so few passengers, as it turned out, that we were all lumped together with the first-class group for dining and such things. Everyone was solicitous—the stewards, the officers. Was I quite comfortable? Would I like another cabin? A tour of the ship? A complimentary drink or two? I was assigned to the purser's table for meals. One afternoon I was out on deck alone, enjoying the bleak North Atlantic. This was November of 1964. It was a cold crossing and a fairly rough one. The purser joined me there at the rail for a chat. Then he began hemming and hawing, trying to ask me something that was embarrassing to him. Finally I got the drift of it. Put bluntly, his questions would have been: Just who are you? Should we know you? If you are so important, why are you traveling cabin class? The Cunard office, he said, had marked me down on the passenger list as one of the notables, to be shown special attention. I laughed and said, well, I couldn't explain it. Some mix up there. I was no VIP and no mystery figure, only a newspaper reporter, and an unemployed one at that. I said they had obviously mixed me up with some very distinguished passenger, who was now being snubbed by everybody and shut out of all the shipboard fun. But it was okay with me if they would like to continue these courtesies. Later that day it came to me, what must have happened. This had to be the work of Frankie Williams. He must have called the Cunard people about my passage, telling them Lord knows what. Or more likely he wrote them in some very formal way on a *Herald Tribune* letterhead. Frankie was still taking care of me and the dignity of the bureau. This was one of the *Mauretania*'s last runs—if not the last—on that regular service from Southampton to New York. Too bad. The apple green *Mauretania*. Big jet planes had taken away the business.

REED: Let me just fill in a couple of small gaps. When and where were you born?

PORTIS: December 28, 1933, in El Dorado, Arkansas.

REED: Oh, you're just a kid.

PORTIS: A few weeks ago I had to dig out that birth certificate. An ominous Dr. Slaughter delivered me.

REED: Born in El Dorado and lived in…?

PORTIS: Well, let's see. Norphlet, El Dorado, Mount Holly and Hamburg. All roughly on a line along the Louisiana border.

REED: And went to school in all those places?

PORTIS: Yes, except for Norphlet. I was too young there. I went to the first two grades in El Dorado, at Hugh Goodwin School, then to Mount Holly, and then to Hamburg for the eighth through twelfth grades.

REED: I remember you once wrote a letter to the editor of the *Gazette*, denying that you were from El Dorado. I don't know how you put it, but…

PORTIS: I think that was about some reference in the paper, saying I was from El Dorado, period. I was setting things straight. A quibble. I must not have had much to do that day.

REED: Right, okay. Since the newspaper days you've been in the novel writing business.

PORTIS: Yes.

REED: You have written six?

PORTIS: Five.

REED: And occasional non-fiction?

PORTIS: Now and then, yes. Keeping my hand in.

REED: Was the most recent one for *The Atlantic*? For Bill Whitworth?

PORTIS: Yes, I believe it was.

REED: Buddy, can you think of anything we haven't covered about the *Gazette*, or anything else?

PORTIS: No, that pretty well does it.

REED: Okay, if I think of something else, I'll call you. Thanks very much.

PORTIS: You're welcome.

Appendix

TRIBUTES

Comedy in Earnest

By Roy Blount Jr.

Roy Blount Jr. is the author of twenty-three books, covering subjects from the Pittsburgh Steelers to Robert E. Lee to the Marx Brothers' film *Duck Soup*. He is a regular panelist on NPR's *Wait, Wait...Don't Tell Me!* and is a member of the American Heritage Dictionary Usage Panel. Born in Indianapolis and raised in Decatur, Georgia, Blount now lives in western Massachusetts with his wife, the painter Joan Griswold.

The risk you take on Charles Portis, of course, is that you may sound like Dr. Reo Symes on the author John Selmer Dix. According to Symes, Dix wrote his masterpiece, *Wings as Eagles*, while riding back and forth from Dallas to Los Angeles on the (noon out of Dallas) bus for a whole year. "He was a broken man all right," says Symes, "but by God the work got done. He wrecked his health so that we might have *Wings as Eagles*"—compared to which, according to Symes, all other writing is just "foul grunting."

Symes (a character in Portis's *The Dog of the South* who, incidentally, has "long meaty ears") is going overboard. But it's hard to shrug off his opinion, because *Wings as Eagles* is a book of tips for salesmen, and Symes "had sold hi-lo shag carpet remnants and velvet paintings from the back of a truck in California. He had sold wide shoes by mail, shoes that must have been almost round, at widths up to EEEEEE. He had sold gladiola bulbs and vitamins for men and fat-melting pills and all-purpose books and hail-damaged pears. He had picked up small fees counseling veterans on how to fake chest pains so as to gain immediate admission to V.A.

hospitals and a free week in bed. He had sold ranchettes in Colorado and unregistered securities in Arkansas."

I can't help thinking that Portis has in his travels met people who sold each of these things. But Portis never seems to be selling anything himself. His fiction is the funniest I know, but the last thing in the world his characters have in mind is putting themselves across as comical. They are taking on the world in earnest. Hershel Remley, Lucky Ned Pepper, Sidney Hen: their perfect names never seem made up. Lesser comic writers drag their characters onstage and shout, "Get a load of this guy!" Portis's characters just show up.

Take Squanto, the talking bluejay in Portis's craziest novel, *Masters of Atlantis*. Any ordinary writer would wring no end of hilarious chatter out of an articulate bluejay. You know how bluejays in nature can get carried away. The single thing Portis directly quotes from Squanto is *"Welcome June. To Mystery Ranch. Welcome June. To Mystery Ranch."* The italics, Portis's, are not I think for emphasis but to suggest how any talking bluejay would sound. Yet Squanto is a vivid character, who also affords the author, and the reader, considerable narrative mileage.

Squanto—a gift from an admirer—is a sign that his master, Austin Popper, a subordinate crank in the international order of Gnomons, is getting ideas of his own. Squanto helps to propel, though not in the direction Popper has in mind, an extraordinary sequence in which the June whom Squanto addresses is fecklessly—by Popper, that is—wooed. And as Squanto ages, and evinces an inner life ("Popper fed a glazed cherry to Squanto. The jaybird was getting old. One wing drooped and he no longer talked much in an outright way. During the night he muttered") and dies, we realize that our story, however delusional and even inconsequential it might seem to the casual observer, is moving briskly along.

Ray Midge, the narrator of *The Dog of the South*, is another dead-serious bird. He is not upset when somebody calls him "rat face," because "it was old stuff to me, being compared to a rat. In fact, I look more like a predatory bird than a rat but any person with small sharp features that are bunched in the center of his face can expect to be called a rat about three times a year."

Midge is tracking his runaway wife, Norma, and her paramour, Guy Dupree, by following the trail of receipts from his credit card, which they stole along with his car. A Mexican hotel owner apologizes for booking

Midge into the same room that Norma and Guy stayed in when they came through. Midge says it doesn't matter. "Then there was a disturbance in the kitchen and he went to investigate. When he came back, he said, 'It was nothing, the mop caught fire. All my employees are fools.'"

The mop caught fire! Midge himself is less combustible. *The Dog of the South* is, in this sense, willful: Portis purposely undertook to write a novel with a boring narrator. But that doesn't mean Midge lacks feeling. He recalls the unsuitable houses he looked at to buy with Norma, when they were still together:

"The last one had been a little chocolate-brown cottage, with a shed of the same rich color in the back yard. The real-estate fellow showed us around and he talked about the rent-like payments. In the shed we came across an old man lying on a cot. He was eating nuts from a can and watching a daytime television show. His pearly shins were exposed above his socks. A piece of cotton covered one eye.

"'That's Mr. Proctor,' said the real-estate bird. 'He pays fifty a month for the shed and you can apply that, see, on your note.' I didn't want an old man living in my back yard and the real-estate bird said, 'Well, tell him to hit the road then,' but I didn't want to do that either, to Mr. Proctor."

Uncanny the radiance that "eating nuts from a can" takes on, in this context.

Midge at twenty-six is a prematurely old man himself, and afraid of getting older. ("Think about this," someone tells him. "All the little animals of your youth are long dead.") But he is unbowed. In engineering school, which he didn't finish, Strength of Materials was his favorite subject. "Everybody else hated it because of all the tables we had to memorize but I loved it, the sheared beam. I had once tried to explain to Dupree how things fell apart from being pulled and compressed and twisted and bent and sheared but he wouldn't listen….He would always say—*boast*, the way those people do—that he had no head for figures and couldn't do things with his hands, slyly suggesting the presence of finer qualities."

Portis's characters are insensitive and narrow in ways often held against men. But the characters have tensile strength. This applies not only to Rooster Cogburn, the male protagonist of *True Grit*, but also to the narrator and female lead, Mattie Ross, a tough little nut. The love story, buddy story, loyalty story, whatever you want to call it, of those two is all the more poignant for its utter lack of romance, sex, or even outright affection.

As for rat-faced Midge, he staunchly persists in not being a rat to anybody, even to such a conscienceless rat as Dr. Symes, who while his own mother is dying (or so it appears, but she rallies) is angling to get his hooks into the little island off Ferriday, Louisiana, that she does not want him to turn into something profitable like a Christian boys' ranch or a theme park called Jefferson Davis Land. ("Every afternoon at three Lee would take off his grey coat and wrestle an alligator in a mud hole.")

When the mother Symes presses Midge to express an opinion on the afterlife, he says, "It's just so odd to think that people are walking around in Heaven and Hell."

"Yes," says Mrs. Symes, "but it's odd to find ourselves walking around here too, isn't it?"

If a religion should organize itself around that principle, I'm in.

Like Cormac McCarthy, but Funny

By Ed Park

Ed Park is the author of the novel *Personal Days* (2008), which was a finalist for the PEN/Hemingway Foundation Award. He is a founding editor of *The Believer*, where this essay originally appeared in March 2003, and a former editor of the *Voice Literary Supplement*. He is currently the literary fiction editor at Amazon Publishing's New York City imprint.

CHARLES PORTIS, AUTHOR OF *TRUE GRIT*, GOT JOHN WAYNE HIS ONLY OSCAR. HE ONCE HAD KARL MARX'S OLD GIG (AS THE LONDON BUREAU CHIEF FOR THE *NEW YORK HERALD TRIBUNE*). HE'S WRITTEN FOUR OTHER NOVELS, THREE OF THEM MASTERPIECES, THOUGH WHICH THREE IS UP FOR DEBATE. HERE'S 7,000 WORDS ABOUT A GUY YOU'VE NEVER HEARD OF, BUT SHOULD, WE SAY.

DISCUSSED: *Dr. Slaughter*, Gringos, The Dog of the South, *Turnip Greens, a Japanese Napkin-Folding Club, Ink-Stained Wretchdom, Gore,* True Grit, *the Old Testament, Glen Campbell, the Covered Path, Occult Mischief, Ambidextrous Romanians, Pure Nitro.*

I. AMONG THE JOURNALIST ANTS

In 1964, in the midst of so-called Swinging London, Charles McColl Portis had Karl Marx's old job. Portis (who turns seventy this year) was thirty at the time, not yet a novelist, just a newspaperman seemingly blessed by that guild's gods. His situational Marxism would have been hard to predict. Delivered into this world by the "ominous Dr. Slaughter" in El Dorado, Arkansas, in 1933, Charles Portis—sometimes "Charlie" or "Buddy"—had grown up in towns along the Arkla border, enlisted in the Marines after high school and fought in the Korean War. Upon his discharge in 1955, he majored in journalism at the University of Arkansas (imagining it might be "fun and not very hard, something like barber college"), and after graduation worked at the appealingly named Memphis *Commercial Appeal*. He soon returned to his native state, writing for the *Arkansas Gazette* in Little Rock.

He left for New York in 1960, and became a general assignment reporter at the now defunct *New York Herald Tribune*, working out of what has to be one of the more formidable newsroom incubators in history— his comrades included Tom Wolfe (who would later dub him the "original laconic cutup") and future *Harper*'s editor Lewis Lapham. *Norwood*'s titular ex-Marine, after a fruitless few days in Gotham, saw it as "the hateful town," and Portis himself had once suggested (in response to an aspersion against Arkansas in the pages of *Time*), that Manhattan be buried in turnip greens; still, he stayed for three years. He apparently thrived, for he was tapped as the *Trib*'s London bureau chief and reporter—the latter post held in the 1850s by the author of *The Communist Manifesto* (1848). (More specifically, his predecessor had been a London correspondent for the pre-merger *New York Herald*.) Recently, in a rare interview for the *Gazette* Project at the University of Arkansas, Portis recalls telling his boss that the paper "might have saved us all a lot of grief if it had only paid Marx a little better."[1]

Indeed, as Portis notes in his second novel, the bestselling *True Grit* (1968), "You will sometimes let money interfere with your notions of what is right." If Marx had decided to loosen up, Portis wouldn't have gone to Korea, to serve in that first war waged over communism, and (in the relentless logic of these things) wouldn't have put together his first protagonist, taciturn Korea vet Norwood Pratt, in quite the same way. Perhaps the well would have run dry—fast. Instead of writing five remarkable, deeply entertaining novels (three of them surely masterpieces, though which three is up for debate), Portis could be in England still, grinding out copy by the column inch, saying "cheers" when replacing the phone.

In any event, Portis left not only England but ink-stained wretchdom itself—"quit cold," as Wolfe writes in "The Birth of the New Journalism:

An Eyewitness Report" (1972), later the introduction to the 1973 an-
thology *The New Journalism*. After sailing back to the States on "one of
the *Mauretania*'s last runs," he reportedly holed up in his version of
Proust's cork-lined study—a fishing shack back in Arkansas—to try his
hand at fiction.

These journalists work pretty fast, and the slim picaresque *Norwood*
appeared in 1966, to favorable notice. Portis's signature drollery and itin-
erant protagonist (Norwood Pratt, auto mechanic and aspiring country
singer, ranges from Ralph, Texas, to New York City and back, initially to
recover seventy dollars loaned to a service buddy) are already in place.
The supporting cast includes a midget, a loaf-groping bread deliveryman
and a sapient chicken, and a looser hand might have plunged the tale into
mere chaos or grotesquerie. But Portis's sense of proportion is flawless, and
the resulting panorama, clocking in at under 200 pages, stays snapshot-
sharp throughout—a road novel as indispensable as *On the Road* itself.[2]

With reportorial precision, and without condescension, *Norwood* captures all manner of reflex babble, the extravagant grammar of commercial
appeal—stray words bathed in the exhaust of a Trailways bus. This om-
nivorous little book has a high metabolism, digesting everything from
homemade store signs ("I Do Not Loan Tools") and military-base graffiti
to actuarial come-ons and mail-order ads for discount diamonds.
Appropriately enough, the characters are constantly chowing down. On
one leg of the journey, Edmund B. Ratner (formerly the "world's smallest
perfect man," before he porked out) and Norwood's new sweetheart, Rita
Lee Chipman, are described as having eaten their way through the Great
Smoky Mountains. Norwood's decidedly humble (call it American) menu
nails the country's midcentury gastronomy with a precision that today
takes on near archaeological value: canned peaches, marshmallows,
Vienna sausages, cottage cheese with salt and pepper, a barbecue sandwich washed down with NuGrape, a potted meat sandwich with mustard,
butter on ham sandwiches, biscuit and Br'er Rabbit Syrup sandwiches, an
Automat hot dog on a dish of baked beans, Cokes and corn chips and
Nabs crackers, a Clark bar, peanuts fizzing in Pepsi, a frozen Milky Way.

* * *

No bloat for Portis, and no sophomore slump, either: In 1968 *The
Saturday Evening Post* serialized *True Grit*, a western that both satisfies
and subverts the genre. (The only title of his to have remained almost

continuously in print, *True Grit* has just been republished by Overlook, joining that press's recent paperback reissues of the author's four other books.) The novel, published later that year by Simon & Schuster, could hardly seem more out of step with the countercultural spirit of '68.[3] Writing in 1928 (i.e., on the eve of the Great Depression), a spinster banker named Mattie Ross revisits the central chapter in her life: the winter of 1873, when, as a fourteen-year-old from Yell County, Arkansas, she hunted down her father's killer, Tom Chaney, with the help of a tough U.S. marshal that she hires (the "old one-eyed jasper" Rooster Cogburn) and a young Texas Ranger (the cowlicked LaBoeuf).

"Thank God for the Harrison Narcotics Law," Mattie declares, in what might have read as a sort of antediluvian rebuke to the era of one-pill-makes-you-listen-to-Jefferson-Airplane. "Also the Volstead Act." Mattie never minces words or judgments—she's not from Yell County for nothing—and the poles of wrong and right are firmly fixed. Unlike Huck Finn, to whose narrative hers is sometimes compared, Mattie knows the Bible back to front, handily settling spiritual debates by citing chapter and verse. To those men of the cloth, for example, who might conceivably take issue with her belief that there's something sinister about swine, she says: "Preacher, go to your Bible and read Luke 8:26–33."[4] (Portis's father was a Scripture-studying schoolteacher, and his mother—whose name he gives to the steamer *Alice Waddell*—was the daughter of a Methodist minister.) Her steadfast, unsentimental voice—Portis's sublime ventriloquism—maintains such purity of purpose that the prose seems engraved rather than merely writ.

When Roy Blount, Jr., says that Portis "could be Cormac McCarthy if he wanted to, but he'd rather be funny," he may be both remembering and forgetting *True Grit*, which for all its high spirits is organized along a blood meridian, fraught with ominous slaughter. Blood literally stains the book's first and last sentences, and Rooster, though admirable in his tenacity and his paternal protectiveness of Mattie, has a half-hidden history of trigger-happy law enforcement and less defensible acts of carnage. Indeed, the Overlook reprint provides a necessary corrective for latter-day Portis enthusiasts, a prism for the acts of violence in his other books: the cathartic fistfight punctuating *Norwood*'s homecoming and *Gringos*' startlingly gory if swift climax. (The latter novel's narrator, Jimmy Burns, is also a Korean War vet, and Norwood reveals to Rita Lee that he killed two men "that I know of" in that conflict.) Portis's current reputation as a keen comedian of human quirks, though well-deserved, is limiting. Put another way: After cars, Portis is most familiar with the classification and care of guns. (Even Ray Midge, the ever-observant milquetoast who tells his story in 1979's *The Dog of the South*, knows his firearms.)

Not that True Grit stints on comedy—in one of the funniest set pieces to be found in all of Portisland, Rooster, LaBoeuf, and a Choctaw policeman suddenly break into an escalating marksmanship contest, pitching corn dodgers two at a time and trying to hit both, eventually depleting a third of their rations. Mattie's precocious capacity for hard-bargain-driving (selling back ponies to the beleaguered livestock trader Stonehill) is revealed in expertly structured repartee, and her rock-ribbed responses to distasteful situations amuse with their catechism cadences. (When Rooster, in his cups, offers sick Mattie a spoonful of booze, she intones, "I would not put a thief in my mouth to steal my brains"). But Mattie also re-creates, poignantly and despite herself, her stark discovery of a world gone suddenly wrong, and what had to be done to set it right. Old Testament resonances are always close at hand: Her father's killer bears a powder mark on his face, a Cain figure to say the least, and not to be pitied, and her own taste for frontier justice will lead her into a pit of terror, biblically populated by snakes. The price that Mattie pays may be greater than she knows.

True Grit's fame, of course, extends well beyond the book itself. The phrase has lodged in the culture, somewhere below *catch-22* and above *nymphet*. And Henry Hathaway's enjoyable if foreshortened film version (1969) firmly yokes the story to John Wayne, who at sixty-two won his only Oscar for his portrayal of Rooster. Alas, the movie (which also stars Kim Darby as Mattie and Glen Campbell as LaBoeuf) doesn't capture the retrospective quality of Mattie's voice, as she fixes on the events over the widening gulf of years ("Time just gets away from us," she writes, in the book's penultimate and heartbreaking line). Wayne, in a full-bodied performance, draws the focus away from his employer/charge, so that the title refers far more to Rooster than Mattie.[5]

Some see the book as Portis's albatross. Ron Rosenbaum, whose enthusiasm for the novelist's lesser-known works was instrumental in their republication, found it necessary (in a 1998 *Esquire* piece) to distance Portis from his most famous creation ("too popular for its own good"), in order to make his case for the *true* gems of the Portis canon. But the novel occupies a position similar to that of *Lolita* in relation to Nabokov's works: Though it might not be your personal favorite, it cannot be subtracted from the oeuvre; nor can his other writings fall outside its shadow.[6] If Portis's subsequent novels—*The Dog of the South, Masters of Atlantis, Gringos*—have as a shared theme the seriocomic echo of lost, irretrievable greatness,[7] it's possible that *True Grit* is the genuine article—a book so strong that it reads as myth. As Wolfe notes of Portis's enviable success: "He made a fortune....A *fishing* shack! In *Arkansas*! It was too goddamned perfect to be true, and yet there it was." And here it is—here it is, again.

* * *

In *The New Journalism*, Wolfe invokes the original laconic cutup, who happened to sit one desk behind him at the *Trib* office south of Times Square, as stubborn proof that the dream of the Novel—with its fortune-changing, culture-denting potential—never really died, even at a time when journalists were discovering new narrative ranges, fiction-trumping special effects. There was only one trophy worth typing for, one white whale worth the by-line and fishing wire, the Great, or even just the Pretty Good, American Novel, and Charlie Portis was going to try and snag it.

Or maybe the scoopmonger's life just bugged him. In "Your Action Line," a two-page lark published in *The New Yorker* at the end of 1977 (still in the eleven-year no-novel zone between *True Grit* and *The Dog of the South*), Portis addressed such pressing queries as "Can you put me in touch with a Japanese napkin-folding club?" (If a similar peep had emerged from Camp Salinger, it would scan as Zen koan.) The exchange ends with encyclopedia-caliber dope on a heretofore obscure insect:

> Q—My science teacher told me to write a paper on the "detective ants" of Ceylon, and I can't find anything about these ants. Don't tell me to go to the library, because I've already been there.
>
> A—There are no ants in Ceylon. Your teacher may be thinking of the "journalist ants" of central Burma. These bright-red insects grow to a maximum length of one-quarter inch, and they are tireless workers, scurrying about on the forest floor and gathering tiny facts, which they store in their abdominal sacs. When the sacs are filled, they coat

these facts with a kind of nacreous glaze and exchange them for bits of yellow wax manufactured by the smaller and slower "wax ants." The journalist ants burrow extensive tunnels and galleries beneath Burmese villages, and the villagers, reclining at night on their straw mats, can often hear a steady hum from the earth. This hum is believed to be the ants sifting fine particles of information with their feelers in the dark. Diminutive grunts can sometimes be heard, too, but these are thought to come not from the journalist ants but from their albino slaves, the "butting dwarf ants," who spend their entire lives tamping wax into tiny storage chambers with their heads.

If Portis had long since escaped the formicary, his books nevertheless continued to draw on his previous work environment. Here and there, fixed in amber, his former fellow ants appear.

Heading the London bureau, Portis kept getting entangled in "management comedies," expending too much precious time trying to stamp out unscrupulous freeloaders; he describes (for the *Gazette* Project) setting up a small sting operation to nab a writer who was using a tenuous *Trib* association—a single review, written years prior—to score theater tickets gratis. But Portis's fictional portraits of the less-upstanding members of the trade are not without a certain affection. The rogues are legion: Norwood breaks bread in Manhattan with Heineman, a freelance travel writer (supposedly on deadline for a *Trib* piece) who writes articles on Peru from his Eleventh Street digs and frankly aspires to the freeloading condition. (Laziness, he confesses, holds him back.) In *Masters of Atlantis*, hack extraordinaire Dub Polton, commissioned to compose the biography of Gnomon Society head Lamar Jimmerson, has a formidable reputation ("He wrote *So This Is Omaha!* in a single afternoon," says one awed Gnomon), and is so confident in his vision for *Hoosier Wizard* that he doesn't take down a single note. The master of this subspecies of charlatan might be overweening travel writer Chick Jardine. In Portis's jaunty 1992 story for *The Atlantic*, "Nights Can Turn Cool in Viborra," the consummate insider confesses to his readers, "I seldom reveal my identity to ordinary people," while taking pains to mention his "trademark turquoise jacket"—perhaps a gentle dig at the dapper Wolfe. Chick has also devised a product called the Adjective Wheel, which he sells to his fellow (well, lesser) travel writers at $24.95 a pop.[8]

More abusive than even writers, of course, are editors. In the *Gazette* Project interview, Portis mentions a job in college for a regional paper, where he edited the country correspondence:

> ...from these lady stringers in Goshen and Elkins, those places. I had to type it up. They wrote with hard-lead pencils on tablet paper or notebook paper, but their handwriting was good and clear. Much better than mine. Their writing, too, for that matter. From those who weren't self-conscious about it. Those who hadn't taken some writing course. My job was to edit out all the life and charm from these homely reports. Some fine old country expression, or a nice turn of phrase— out they went.

Perhaps as penance for these early deletions, he created Mattie Ross, whose idiosyncratic style is most immediately identifiable by her liberal, seemingly arbitrary use of "quotation marks"—as if to let a phrase "stand alone" was to risk having it "fall by the wayside" at the whim of some "blue pencil." (A brief list of Mattie's punctuated preferences would include "Lone Star State," "scrap," "that good part," "moonshiners," "dope-heads," "Wild West," "land of Nod," "pickle," and "night hoss.") The punctuation not only highlights the phrases in question—some of them perhaps "old country expressions" of the time—but also comes to reflect her thriftiness. If *True Grit* is Mattie's true account, meant for publication, then the quote marks act as preservatives—insurance that her hard work will not be weeded out by some editorial know-it-all. Quotation marks mean the thing is true—to the degree that someone said it, or that it had some currency then.[9]

For Mattie has, apparently, tried her hand at the freelance game. An earlier experience with the magazine world came to grief. She has written a "good historical article," based mostly on her firsthand observation of a Fort Smith trial, prior to meeting Rooster Cogburn. Though the piece has a rather vivid (or as she would say, "graphic") title—*"You will now listen to the sentence of the law, Odus Wharton, which is that you be hanged by the neck until you are dead, dead, dead! May God, whose laws you have broken and before whose dread tribunal you must appear, have mercy upon your soul. Being a personal recollection of Isaac C. Parker, the famous Border Judge"*—the magazine world "would rather print trash."

As for newspapers, the cheapskate editors "are great ones for reaping where they do not sow"—always hoping to short-change contributors, or else sending reporters around to get an interview gratis. Ever the banker, Mattie means for her story to make money—which *True Grit* went ahead and did.

* * *

Totting up his fee sheets, a struggling Rooster opines that unschooled men like himself have a raw deal. "No matter if he has got sand in his craw, others will push him aside, little thin fellows that have won spelling bees back home." A century hence, this orthographical ace might be Raymond E. Midge, the twenty-six-year-old ex–copy editor and perpetual college student who narrates *The Dog of the South* (1979). That Portis effortlessly makes Midge, a nitpicking, book-burrowing cuckold, as indelible and appealing as the battle-scarred man of action (or strong-willed girl revenger) is ample proof of his scope and skill.

Thanks to a few wizards of international fiction, the proofreader has had some pivotal roles—Hugh Person in Nabokov's *Transparent Things* (1972), Raimundo Silva in José Saramago's *The History of the Siege of Lisbon* (1996). Denizens of the copy desk have not enjoyed a similar literary profile. Though the professions bear some resemblance, the latter's task is more Sisyphean and perhaps more conducive to despair—sweating the details on something as disposable as a newspaper, in most cases gone inside a week, if not a day. No novel captures the occupation's particular brand of virtues and neuroses as well as *The Dog of the South*; it's the perfect job (or former job) for a character so constitutionally driven to remark on deviations from the norm. (At twenty-six, he's lived as many years as there are letters in the alphabet.) Ray Midge sets out for British Honduras to recover his car and perhaps Norma, his wife[10]—both stolen by his former co-worker, the misanthropic Guy Dupree. Dupree's errant behavior—he's finally investigated for writing hostile letters to the president—and burgeoning anarcho-communist tendencies reflect a harsh if hysterical world view possibly aggravated by his days in the newspaper office: "He hardly spoke at all except to mutter 'Crap' or 'What crap' as he processed news matter, affecting a contempt for all events on earth and for the written accounts of those events."[11]

Midge, conversely, pays enormous attention to all events on earth, and *The Dog of the South*, his written account of them, allows the reader to share his pleasure. "In South Texas I saw three interesting things," he writes, and then lists them. Indeed, he's inordinately proud of his better-than-average vision, noting that he can "see stars down to the seventh magnitude." Perhaps it is something to boast about, but in compensation for his assorted failings, he seems to have attributed to his eyesight super-hypnotic powers:

> I watched the windows for Norma, for flitting shadows. I was always good at catching roach movement or mouse movement from the corner of my eye. Small or large, any object in my presence had only to change its position slightly, by no more than a centimeter, and my head would snap about and the thing would be instantly trapped by my gaze.

* * *

A military history buff with "sixty-six lineal feet" of books on the topic (he would know the exact dimensions), Midge sees himself on a mission, and in his hilarious, unconscious self-inflation, he makes vermin sound like Panzer units trying some new formation.

Freed from copy editing, then, Midge proceeds to read the world at large, the way any good Portis protagonist would—but his job training means his observations are that much more acute. He contemplates spelling errors (a strange man hands him a card that reads, inscrutably, "adios AMIGO and watch out for the FLORR!"), the abysmal Spanish-language skills of his traveling companion, Dr. Reo Symes, and the bizarrely mangled locutions of the chummy Father Jackie (e.g., *wanter* instead of *water*). Encountering an emergency flood relief effort, Midge fervently pitches in, but is nevertheless distracted when a British officer reprimands someone "to stay away from his vehicles 'in future'—rather than 'in the future.'" It's funny enough the first time; when a similar omission occurs twelve pages later, after Midge discovers Norma in the hospital ("I would have to take that up with doctor—not 'with the doctor'"), the repetition alleviates, if just for an instant, the unspoken sadness that's dawning on him.

In British Honduras, Midge meets Melba, the friend of Dr. Symes's mother. At Symes's insistence, he reads two of her stories, and like an amateur Don Foster *[the professor who identified the anonymous author of the novel* Primary Colors *by analyzing sentence structure and diction—Ed.]*, he notes certain compositional tendencies:

Melba had broken the transition problem wide open by starting every paragraph with "Moreover." She freely used "the former" and "the latter" and every time I ran into one of them I had to backtrack to see whom she was talking about. She was also fond of "inasmuch" and "crestfallen."

Like all good copy editors, Midge is something of a pedant; nevertheless he seems more to relish than disdain such human details. He may debate, at length, some nicety of Civil War lore, but he rarely passes judgment on the people he meets, even when they forget his name: Dr. Symes calls him Speed; an addled Dupree mistakes him for Burke (yet another copy editor); for some reason, Father Jackie thinks his name is Brad. But names are important, as a character asserts in *Masters of Atlantis*. Midge notes the nominal errors with exclamation points, but no real outrage, until the end of his quest, when a dazed Norma calls him by Dupree's first name—not just once, but repeatedly. It's the only slip that really hurts.

"I was interested in everything," Midge confesses early on, and in the book's final paragraph, right before his quietly devastating revelation which colors all that has come before, Midge notes that upon his return to Little Rock he finally received his BA, and is contemplating graduate work in plate tectonics. He wants to literally read the world, to study its layers and its lives.

II. THE BALLOONIST

At age nine, a daydreaming Portis conducted underwater breathing experiments at Smackover Creek—a life-saving measure, rehearsed in the eventuality of pursuit by Axis nasties. The toponym, he explains in "Combinations of Jacksons" (published in the May 1999 *Atlantic*), is "an Arkansas rendering of 'chemin couvert,' covered path, or road.'"

Few could have predicted that after the brisk gestation of *Norwood* and *True Grit*, eleven years would pass before *The Dog of the South* emerged, a period that constitutes a *chemin couvert* of sorts. Silence, with side orders of cunning and exile, can lend luster to a writer's work. Deep processes are afoot, some calculus of genius or madness, penury or plenty. Given the Central American trail of *Dog* and *Gringos*, and the occult mischief of *Masters*, one imagines Portis hitting the road, unearthing pre-

Columbian glazeware, eavesdropping in hotel bars—and reading, reading, reading: Ignatius Donnelly's *Atlantis* and Colonel James Churchward's *Lost Continent of Mu*, special-interest magazines like the ufological *Gamma Bulletin*, dense books "with footnotes longer than the text proper," to say nothing of the whole of Romanian fiction, which contains "not a single novel with a coherent plot."

That earlier Portisian lag, alas, is now officially smaller than the one between 1991's *Gringos* and whatever he's currently working on. In Portis's last book to date, Jimmy Burns observes of a fellow expat:

> Frank didn't write anything, or at least he didn't publish any-
> thing....The Olmecs didn't like to show their art around either. They
> buried it twenty-five feet deep in the earth and came back with spades
> to check up on it every ten years or so, to make sure it was still there,
> unviolated. Then they covered it up again.

Is a new cycle of Portisian activity on the horizon, at the end of a decade-and-change? The recent magazine appearances of "Combinations of Jacksons" (1999) and "Motel Life, Lower Reaches" (2003), memoiristic pieces that bookend the Overlook reprint project, is enough to make one wonder whether (or if you're me, pray that) Portis is writing at length about his life.

Maybe he'll fill in the blanks, reveal what he's been up to all these years, though if anyone understands the character of silence, the value of secrets, it's Charles Portis. *The Dog of the South* contains its own Portis doppelgänger—its own commentary on authorial mystique—in the fig-ure of John Selmer Dix, MA, the elusive writer of *With Wings as Eagles*, which he penned entirely on a bus, a board across his lap, traveling from Dallas to L.A. and back again for a year. His whereabouts remain a mys-tery; assorted reported sightings, like those of Bigfoot or Nessie, cannot be taken at face value. Dr. Reo Symes, the most vigorous, wildly comic jabberjaw in all of Portisland, is *Wings*'s unlikely champion ("pure nitro," he calls it)—a huckster on the skids who maintains an unlikely reverence for what appears to be nothing more than a salesman's primer and its reticent creator.

Symes's limitless patter circles the indissoluble truths contained in this criminally overlooked document, and his earnest-rabid claims for

With Wings as Eagles sound not unlike those of Portis fanatics to the uninitiated: "Read it, then read it again....The Three T's. The Five Don'ts. The Seven Elements. Stoking the fires of the U.S.S. Reality. Making the Pep Squad and staying on it." All else in the world of letters is "foul grunting." When Midge modestly counters that Shakespeare is considered the greatest writer who ever lived, the doctor responds without hesitation, "Dix puts William Shakespeare in the shithouse." Midge, "still on the alert for chance messages," reads a few pages of Symes's copy of *Wings*, but finds its dialectical materialism a touch opaque:

> He said you must save your money but you must not be afraid to spend it either, and at the same time you must give no thought to money. A lot of his stuff was formulated in this way. You must do this and that, two contrary things, and you must also be careful to do neither.

As important to Symes as the visible text is what happened after its publication, the story behind the story, during the time when Dix "repudiated all his early stuff, said *Wings* was nothing but trash, and didn't write another line, they say, for twelve years." Symes has an alternate theory: He believes Dix continued writing, at greater length and with even more intense insight, but "for some reason that we can't understand yet he wanted to hold it all back from the reading public, let them squeal how they may." Thousands of pages repose in Dix's large tin trunk—which, of course, is nowhere to be found.

* * *

Portis's trunk resurfaces, after a fashion, in his next book, *Masters of Atlantis* (1985), which sustains its seemingly one-joke premise through tireless comic invention and an ever-shifting narrative focus. At once the oddest ball among his works and a full-vent treatment of themes common to *Dog* and *Gringos*, a clearinghouse of obscurantist scribblings and a satire that skewers without malice, Portis's sprawling third novel loosely follows the life of Lamar Jimmerson, whose eventual sedentary existence is in perverse contrast to the typical Portis rambler. Jimmerson's destiny crystallizes after the First World War, when a grateful derelict gives him a booklet crammed with Greek and triangles—an Nth-generation copy of the Codex Pappus, containing the wisdom of lost Atlantis. Portis's inspired tweaking of subterranean belief systems touches on alchemy, lost-continent lore, and reams of secret-society mumbo-jumbo. The original codex, written untold millennia ago, survived its civilization's destruction in an ivory casket, which eventually washed ashore in Egypt, to be decoded after much effort by none other than Hermes Trismegistus (the mythical figure deified by the Egyptians as Thoth, the Greeks as Hermes, and the Romans as Mercury). Hermes became the first modern master of the Gnomon Society, which counts among its elite ranks Pythagoras, Cagliostro, and, as it happens, Lamar Jimmerson of Gary, Indiana.

That the document is bunk is the obvious joke, but Portis wraps it in antic bolts of faith and failure. Indeed, *Masters of Atlantis* works as a thoughtful, whimsical companion to Frances A. Yates's *Giordano Bruno and the Hermetic Tradition* (1964), a study of the magical and occult reaches of Renaissance thought. Yates lays her cards on the table, explaining that the "returning movement of the Renaissance with which this book will be concerned, the return to a pure golden age of magic [i.e., the supposed era of ancient Egyptian wisdom], was based on a radical error of dating....This huge historical error was to have amazing results."

The amazing result in *Masters* is an alternately deadpan and high-flying pageant of secret sharers, unreadable tracts,[12] and highly dubious theories, determining the rise and fall—and rise?—of an institution insulated from the American century unfolding outside by nothing more than the unshakeable belief of its adherents. The adepti cultivate their secrecy and self-regard by maintaining rules against dissemination to outsiders, or "Perfect Strangers," a code as strict as it is arbitrary. For instance, the Romanian-born alchemist Golescu, a caretaker at the Naval Observatory, would seem a shoo-in for Gnomonic acceptance. His achievements read like a variation on Symes's catalogue of Dixian wisdom:

> Through Golescuvian analysis he had been able to make positive identification of the Third Murderer in Macbeth and of the Fourth Man in Nebuchadnezzar's fiery furnace. He had found the Lost Word of Freemasonry and uttered it more than once, into the air, the Incommunicable Word of the Cabalists, the Verbum Ineffabile. The enigmatic quatrains of Nostradamus were an open book to him. He had a pretty good idea of what the Oracle of Ammon had told Alexander.

But Golescu doesn't make the cut. He knows too much—or at least says too much. His strident claims betray an insufficiently covered path. The point of the Verbum Ineffabile—the unspeakable word—is that you don't say it.

Most mortals, it seems, are doomed to remain Perfect Strangers, but at least there's the possibility of writing something oneself, a validating work of comprehensive greatness. In *Gringos*, freelance bounty hunter and former antiquities dealer Jimmy Burns journeys to the Inaccessible City of Dawn, bringing along his friend Doc Flandin, an ailing Mexico hand. Doc is ever on the lookout for the Mayan equivalent of Dix's tin trunk or the Hermetically unsealed casket—a fabled cache of lost *libros* that would provide further pieces to the puzzle of that vast and vanished civilization. Burns doubts any such books even exist. In any case, Doc claims to be nearly finished with his own "grand synthesis" of Mexican history, a scholarly tour de force explaining the truth behind myths and answering ancient riddles; among other things, Doc's book would "tell us who the Olmecs really were, appearing suddenly out of the darkness, and why they carved those colossal heads that looked like Fernando Valenzuela of the Los Angeles Dodgers."

Somewhere in limbo, apart from or behind the printed ephemera— confession magazines and pre-1960 detective novels and something called *Fun with Magnets*—that crop up in Portis's novels more frequently than any work of high literature, is a dream library stocked entirely with vanished books and unwritten ones, impossible genius texts that tantalize from across the void. Chances are that Doc's unfinished manuscript will join the rest of those ghostly titles. But time doesn't always run out, and at least once the dream becomes manifest. Mattie Ross waits half a century to write *True Grit*, and during those years the factual grit of her life story at last forms a pearl. Though Portis's compositional timeframe isn't quite as long as Mattie's, his periodic absences from the thrum of publication help give each one of his books what those Burmese journalist ants call a "nacreous glaze," a shimmering coat of perfect strangeness.

* * *

Portis has published a single work of fiction since *Gringos*—"I Don't Talk Service No More," a spare, haunting short story that appeared in the May 1996 *Atlantic*. *[The short story "The Wind Bloweth Where It Listeth," page 170, appeared in the* Oxford American *in 2004 under the column*

"Writers on Writing," though it is a work of fiction.—Ed.] The unnamed narrator, an institutionalized Korean War veteran, sneaks into the hospital library every night to make long-distance calls to his fellow squad members, participants in something called the Fox Company Raid. He remembers their names, though some other details have grown hazy. At the end of this call, his fellow raider "asked me how it was here. He wanted to know how it was in this place and I told him it wasn't so bad. It's not so bad here if you have the keys. For a long time I didn't have the keys."

Instead of closure, the last sentence casts a pall over the story, and the mention of keys conjures the great locked enigmas drifting through Portis's last three books.

In *Dog*, Symes disputes an alleged Dix sighting, musing, "*Where were all his keys?*" (According to Dixian lore, the great author, wise with answers, never went anywhere without a jumbo key ring on his belt.)

The "Service" narrator's resounding isolation connects with the loneliness found in so many Portis characters. Norwood Pratt and Jimmy Burns, wry loners capable of brute force, wind up married and in more or less optimistic situations. But happiness eludes the other protagonists. Lamar Jimmerson and most of the Gnomons in *Masters of Atlantis* can't form mature emotional attachments; Jimmerson barely notices as his wife leaves him and his son avoids him. And how is it that *The Dog of the South*, Portis's finest comic achievement, subtly shades into melancholy? When Midge finds Norma, by chance, in the hospital, he calls it a "concentrated place of misery"; his earlier angst-free, even chipper take on his cuckoldry suddenly shifts, in her presence, to a terrible feeling of rejection. The mere fact of his being strikes her as wearisome:

> "I don't feel like talking right now."
> "We don't have to talk. I'll get a chair and just sit here."
> "Yes, but I'll know you're there."

Dog's last two lines erase miles of cheer that have come before. *True Grit*'s matter-of-fact final sentence ("This ends my true account of how I avenged Frank Ross's blood over in the Choctaw Nation when snow was on the ground") harbors a more cosmic sadness; as pathetic fallacy, it feels like an American cousin to the faintly falling snow that closes Joyce's "The Dead." Portis carries over this precipitous finish to his own life in "Combinations of Jacksons." A "peevish old coot" himself now, he peers back over the years to when his Uncle Sat showed him scale maps of tiny Japan and the immense U.S., to dispel his boyhood fears of a protracted war. The last lines run: "I can see the winter stubble in his fields, too, on that dreary January day in 1942. Broken stalks and a few dirty white shreds of bumblebee cotton. Everyone who was there is dead and buried now except me."

Portis is careful to keep the tears at bay with laughter; to borrow the impromptu skeet targets from Rooster and company, he's a literary corn dodger. In *Dog*, Dr. Symes's mother, a missionary, periodically grills Midge on his knowledge of the Bible, a knowledge he repeatedly professes not to have. "Think about this," she says, pointedly fixing his thoughts to the matter of last things. "All the little animals of your youth are long dead." Her companion Melba promptly emends the truism: "Except for turtles."

The statement, at once hilariously random but completely realistic, neutralizes the threat of gloom; it's the sort of bull's-eye silliness that pitches Portis's reality a few feet above that of his fellow page-blackeners. Significantly, he gives Lamar Jimmerson some experience with skyey matters: *Masters of Atlantis* opens with the young man in France during the First World War, "serving first with the Balloon Section, stumbling about in open fields holding one end of a long rope."

The truth is up there—well, maybe. (*Gringos*, among its other virtues, navigates UFO culture with more than cursory knowledge and without easy condescension.) Of all the moments when Portis's prose turns lighter than air, my personal favorite involves the aforementioned Golescu, whose chaotic turn in *Masters of Atlantis* gives the book an early-inning jolt. In addition to claiming membership in various sub rosa brotherhoods, some of them seemingly contradictory, Golescu possesses the talents of a "multiple mental marvel," to borrow magician Ricky Jay's term. Asking for "two shits of pepper," he takes pencils in hands and demonstrates for a bemused Lamar Jimmerson his ambidexterity and capacity for cerebral acrobatics, in a rapid-fire paragraph of undiluted laughing gas. It's what Dr. Symes would have called pure nitro.

> "See, not only is Golescu writing with both hands but he is also looking at you and conversing with you at the same time in a most natural way. Hello, good morning, how are you? Good morning, Captain,

how are you today, very fine, thank you. And here is Golescu still writing and at the same time having his joke on the telephone. Hello, yes, good morning, this is the Naval Observatory but no, I am very sorry, I do not know the time. Nine-thirty, ten, who knows? Good morning, that is a beautiful dog, sir, can I know his name, please? Good morning to you, madam, the capital of Delaware is Dover. In America the seat of government is not always the first city. I give you Washington for another. And now if you would like to speak to me a sequence of random numbers, numbers of two digits, I will not only continue to look at you and converse with you in this easy way but I will write the numbers as given with one hand and reversed with the other hand while I am at the same time adding the numbers and giving you running totals of both columns, how do you like that? Faster, please, more numbers, for Golescu this is nothing…"

Read it, then read it again—at a spittle-flecked rush, with a mild Lugosi accent—and observe how everything turns into nothing, how all that is solid melts into air.

Endnotes

1. Many of the biographical details about Portis in this piece have been gleaned from a leisurely interview, conducted by Roy Reed on May 31, 2001 (page 285).

2. Whereas Kerouac was said to have been more passenger than driver, Portis knows his cars inside out, and his oeuvre overflows with automotive asides. Even the *Gazette* interview is graced with these vehicular discursions: Speaking of his stint at the *Northwest Arkansas Times*, Portis conjures up the vehicle he drove to work in, a 1950 Chevrolet convertible, "with the vertical radio in the dash and the leaking top," and notes the species-wide "gearshift linkage that was always locking up, especially in second gear."

3. The new *Portable Sixties Reader*, ed. Ann Charters (Penguin, 2003), does not mention Portis at all.

4. Mattie also has strong opinions on particular political matters, but the issues could not be at a more distant remove for the general reader in 1968 (or today), lending an air of comedy and verisimilitude. On Grover Cleveland: "He brought a good deal of misery to the land in the Panic of '93 but I am not ashamed to own that my family supported him and has stayed with the Democrats right on through, up to and including Governor Alfred Smith, and not only because of Joe Robinson."

5. If the film of *True Grit* somewhat revises the book, the less-known screen adaptation of *Norwood* (Jack Haley, Jr., 1970), also scripted by Marguerite Roberts, scrambles both *Norwood* and *True Grit*. Glen Campbell (*Grit*'s LaBoeuf) here plays Norwood, and Kim Darby (Mattie) is Rita Lee Chipman; Mattie's unacknowledged teenage longing for LaBoeuf ("If he is still alive and should happen to read these pages, I will be happy to hear from him," Mattie writes at the novel's close) becomes consummated in *Norwood*, or just about. Roberts's *Grit* script shunted Mattie in favor of the bigger-than-life Rooster; for this film the screenwriter dilutes some of *Norwood*'s cool by revealing that Rita Lee has been made pregnant by another man before they meet—a significant, possibly feminist tweak of the original plot. (Incidentally, the contra-hippie theme that runs through Portis, made more explicit in *Gringos*, is elaborated in this film, most notably when Campbell-as-Norwood takes the stage after a numbing sitar exhibition. He sings a good-timey country number presciently called "Repo Man" to the uncomprehending, wigged-out crowd, until a more lysergically inclined combo unseats him.) As it's unlikely I'll ever have the chance to write about this film again, let it be noted that the date of *Norwood*'s theatrical release, a year after *Midnight Cowboy* won the Academy Award for Best Picture, lends Campbell-as-Norwood a certain Voightian frisson during the scenes in New York, where he sticks out like a Stetsoned sore thumb. Which makes the bit in *Cowboy* where Voight regards himself in the mirror and says approvingly, "John Wayne," a sort of anticipatory gloss on Wayne co-star Campbell's future appearance in Gotham. (The celluloid *True Grit* also spawned a 1975 sequel, *Rooster Cogburn*, starring Wayne and Katharine Hepburn.)

6. Toward the end of *Norwood*, a conversational non sequitur seems to anticipate *True Grit*'s heroine. Someone mentions a Welsh doctor to the British-born midget Ratner: "Cousin Mattie corresponded with him for quite a long time. Lord, he may be dead now. That was about 1912."

7. In books and in blood, as in this analysis from *Masters*: "One's father was invariably a better man than oneself, and one's grandfather better still."

8. Travel writers, not to say homo britannicus, get ribbed by Portis again in "Motel Life, Lower Reaches," part of the *Oxford American*'s relaunch issue (January-February 2003). Describing a cheap motel in New Mexico, he notes a small population of "British journalists named Clive, Colin, or Fiona, scribbling notes and getting things wrong for their journey books about the real America, that old and elusive theme."

9. Portis is well aware of the seemingly disproportionate effects of punctuational caprice. In *Masters of Atlantis*, Whit and Adele Gluters' suitcase bears their surname in caps and quotes, leading to this flight of fancy: "Babcock wondered about the quotation marks. Decorative strokes? Mere flourishes? Perhaps

theirs was a stage name. Wasn't Whit an actor? The bag did have a kind of back-stage look to it. Or a pen name. Or perhaps this was just a handy way of setting themselves apart from ordinary Gluters, a way of saying that in all of Gluterdom they were the Gluters, or perhaps the enclosure was to emphasize the team as-pect, to indicate that 'THE GLUTERS' were not quite the same thing as the Gluters, that together they were an entity different from, and greater than the raw sum of Whit and Adele, or it might be that the name was a professional tag expressive of their work, a new word they had coined, a new infinitive, to gluter, or to glute, descriptive of some new social malady they had defined or some new clinical technique they had pioneered, as in their mass Glutering sessions or their breakthrough treatment of Glutered wives or their controversial Glute therapy. The Gluters were only too ready to discuss their personal affairs and no doubt would have been happy to explain the significance off the quotation marks, had they been asked, but Babcock said nothing. He was not one to pry."

10. Midge himself, with his rules against record playing after nine p.m. and aversion to dancing, is a deviation from the norm, or from Norma—at least in the eyes of his mother-in-law, who calls him a "pill."

11. At a small museum in Mexico, Midge finds Dupree's comments in the guestbook: "A big gyp. Most boring exhibition in North America."

12. Many years after the publication of *Gnomonism Today*, a sharp-eyed dis-ciple discovers that the printers have omitted every other page.

Our Least-Known Great Novelist

By Ron Rosenbaum

Ron Rosenbaum graduated from Yale with a degree in English literature and then dropped out of Yale Graduate School to write full time. He is the author of seven books, most recently *Explaining Hitler*, *The Secret Parts of Fortune*, *The Shakespeare Wars,* and *How the End Begins*. He once met Charles Portis at a Waffle House near the Little Rock airport.

When this essay was first published in 1998 in *Esquire*, four of Portis's five novels were out of print. His championing of Portis's non–*True Grit* oeuvre spurred Overlook Press to acquire the rights to republish the unavailable books in paperback, and now all Portis's novels, including *True Grit*, are available in editions from Overlook.

L isten, I bow to no one when it comes to expertise on the myth and reality of secret societies in America, in distinguishing the dark nimbus of paranoia and conspiracy theory surrounding them from the peculiar human truths at their heart.

As the author of the still-definitive study of America's ultimate secret society, Skull and Bones, I have been shown the much-whispered-about photos that the all-woman break-in team took of the interior of the Skull and Bones "Tomb"—complete with its candid shots of that sanctum sanctorum of America's clandestine ruling-class cult: the Room with the License Plates of Many States. I could tell you the secret Skull and Bones nicknames of the class year of D_{154}, in the coded Skull and Bones calendar of the years. (Let's give a shout out to good old J. B. "Magog" Speed, for instance.)

I say I bow to no one, but that's not true. When it comes to knowing and limning the heart of the heart of the secret-society-esoteric-knowledge-weird-nickname-ancient-mysteries-of-the-East racket, I bow—*we should all bow*—to one man, one novelist. Not Pynchon or DeLillo or any of the other usual suspects on the secret-society subject, but a maddeningly under-appreciated American writer who in a brilliant and shockingly little-known novel has somehow captured more of the truth about this aspect of America, about the longing for Hidden Secrets, the seductions of secret societies, than all the shelves of conspiracy-theory literature. The only man to penetrate the true heart of dimness. I'm speaking of Charles Portis and his now-almost-impossible-to-find novel (suppressed by You Know Who?), *Masters of Atlantis*.

It's an indictment of the dimness of our culture that the film *Conspiracy Theory* made millions while *Masters of Atlantis* languishes in the recesses of secondhand-bookstores, out of print, not even in paperback, and Portis gets neither the popular nor the literary-world acclaim that he deserves. In a way, Portis has not helped matters; he lives off the beaten path down in Arkansas with an unlisted phone number, doesn't do publicity, has never networked, and refused, politely but firmly, to talk to me for this piece.

Who is this man Portis? His is not a Salinger-like antisocial reclusiveness, more a kind of publicity-shy modesty. And we do have a few clues about his past. We know he grew up in a tiny town near the Arkansas-Mississippi border. We can guess from a recent short story he published in *The Atlantic Monthly* that he served as a marine in the Korean War. We know that he was a rising star at the legendary writers' newspaper *The New York Herald Tribune*, eventually heading its London bureau, and that he departed abruptly in the mid-sixties to return to Arkansas to start turning out a remarkable series of novels, beginning with *Norwood* in 1966.

Meanwhile, Portis has become the subject of a kind of secret society, a small but fanatic group of admirers among other writers who consider him perhaps the least-known great writer alive in America. Perhaps the most original, indescribable *sui generis* talent overlooked by literary culture in America. A writer who—if there's any justice in literary history as opposed to literary celebrity—will come to be regarded as the author of classics on the order of a twentieth-century Mark Twain, a writer who captures the soul of America, the true timbre of the dream-intoxicated voices of this country, in a way that no writers-workshop fictionalist has done or is likely to do, who captures the secret soul of twentieth-century America with the clarity, the melancholy, and the laughter with which Gogol captured the soul of nineteenth-century Russia in *Dead Souls*.

Tom Wolfe once spoke about the way city-born creative-writing types go directly from East Coast hothouse venues to places like Iowa City, where "they rent a house out in the countryside, and after about their fifth conversation with a plumber named Lud, they feel that they know the rural psyche."

Charles Portis is the real thing to which these grad-school simulacra can only aspire in their wildest dreams. He is a wild dreamer of a writer, and I don't want you misled by the references to Mark Twain into thinking he is some kind of regionalist or humorist. Nora Ephron, one of the founding members of the Portis Society (as I've come to think of the circle of devotees), compares him in scope, sophistication, and originality to Gabriel Garcia Marquez. "He thinks things no one else thinks," she says.

For some members of the Portis Society, an appreciation of his work is a matter of life-and-death urgency. Roy Blount, Jr., has written of Portis's third novel, *The Dog of the South*, "No one should die without having read it." And that's not even his favorite (although it is mine). He's partial to *Norwood* and speaks of those for whom Portis is a kind of life-and-death test of human beings. How a fellow Portis Society member couldn't decide whether to marry the woman he loved until she read *Norwood*.

It's funny: Before I spoke with Blount and learned of his "Don't die until you've read *The Dog of the South*" pronouncement, I'd used the rhetoric of imminent death in my appeal to Portis for an interview. I'd tried to explain in a letter to him how much his work mattered to me by telling him that if I had to choose any one section of any one novel to be read aloud to me on my deathbed in the hours before expiring, to remind me of the pleasures that reading had brought me during my lifetime, it would probably be certain passages in *The Dog of the South* involving one of Portis's inimitable, seedy-but-grandiose con men, Dr. Reo Symes.

I'll try to explain why those passages in particular fascinate me, but first I need to discuss the initiation rite to the Portis Society, the barrier you literary sophisticates must be able to get past (or limbo beneath) if you are to show yourselves worthy of Portis's genius. A kind of test of true—as opposed to surface, image-conscious—literary sophistication.

The test is a novel Portis wrote before *The Dog of the South*, *Masters of Atlantis*, and *Gringos*, his great dreams-of-secret-knowledge trilogy. A novel that was—I hesitate to use the word, it's so deeply shaming in literary terms—too *popular* for its own good. A novel whose title I almost dare not utter to the uninitiated, because it may completely throw you off the scent of Portis's greatness. (Not because there's anything wrong with it in itself, but because of its image.) A novel whose title I'm therefore going to disguise and not utter for the moment. Or maybe I'll give it a more inoffensive (at least in this context), substitute title, say, *Necrophilic Whores of Gomorrah*.

Well, admit it, you'd probably be more receptive to my case for Portis's greatness if he'd written some Burroughsian necrophilia novel rather than the all-too-fatally popular novel he *did* write, whose title is, I blush to say, *True Grit*. Yes, he's *that guy*, and they made a movie out of it that won John Wayne his only Oscar. Now, get over it and let me get back to Dr. Reo Symes. He's the greatest in a great gallery of Portisian talkers: brilliant and garrulous con artists, deliriously gifted fabricators, delusional mountebanks, disbarred lawyers, defrocked doctors, disgruntled inventors, dispossessed cranks, and disgraced dreamers who crawl out of the cracks and crevices of Trailways America with confident claims that they have the Philosopher's Stone, the key to all mysteries. Or, more often, that they had it and lost it, or had it stolen from them but are close to getting it back.

This Dr. Symes is quite a character himself. No longer a doctor—he lost his medical license over some trouble with a miracle arthritis cure he was peddling called "the Brewster Method." ("You don't hear much about it anymore but for my money it's never been discredited," Symes says.) Lately, he's been involved in a scheme to manufacture tungsten-steel dentures in Tijuana (the "El Tigre model," he calls it), and he seems to be on the run from some scam involving "a directory called *Stouthearted Men*, which was to be a collection of photographs and capsule biographies of all the county supervisors in Texas." Somehow, the money collected from the stouthearted supervisors is missing, although Symes insists, "It was a straight enough deal."

But when he runs across Portis's narrator, Ray Midge, an Arkansas guy who's retracing the steps of his runaway wife by using credit-card receipts, all Dr. Symes can talk about is the mysterious, elusive John Selmer Dix, a writer of inspirational books for salesmen. Symes is obsessed with Dix's greatness, with the idea that in his last days Dix had somehow broken through to some new level of ultimate revelation that tragically was lost to the world with his death, when the trunk in which he carried his papers disappeared.

"Find the missing trunk and you've found the key to his so-called 'silent years,'" Symes tells Ray Midge. Symes is fixated on what might be false sightings of Dix and what seems to be a proliferation of Dix impostors. He knows of only one man who claims to have seen Dix "in the flesh...in the public library in Odessa, Texas, reading a newspaper on a stick."

"Now the question is, was that stranger really Dix? If it was Dix answer me this. *Where were all his keys?*" (The keys to his trunk of ultimate secrets, of course.) "There are plenty of fakers going around....You've probably heard of the fellow out in Barstow who claims to this day that he *is* Dix....He says the man who died in Tulsa was just some old retired fart from the oil fields who was trading off a similar name. He makes a lot of the closed coffin and the hasty funeral in Ardmore. He makes a lot of the missing trunk....There's another faker, in Florida, who claims he is Dix's half brother....They ran a picture of him and his little Dix museum in *Trailer Review*."

Dr. Symes's delirium rises to a pitch of inspired madness tinged with an element of Oliver Stone paranoia ("the hasty funeral in Ardmore"), a poetic desperation that makes you intuit that it's not the reality of Dix that obsesses him but the *idea* of Dix—of someone somewhere who Had It All Figured Out but who disappeared in a Trailways haze. What Portis is getting at is the deep longing, the profound, wistful desperation in the American collective unconscious, to believe that somehow things do make *some* kind of sense, that life is not all chaotic horror and random acts of cruelty by fate, that there is an Answer, even if it's locked in a trunk somewhere and we've *lost the keys*.

The search for the lost keys is at the heart of Portis's subsequent two novels as well. In *Masters of Atlantis*, a secret society founded by a con artist and his gullible dupe comes to be a source of genuine meaning and faith for half a century of devotees (with the suggestion that all secret societies pretending to esoteric knowledge, from Skull and Bones to the

Masons to the CIA, are the products of collective self-delusions). In *Gringos*, a beautiful, intense, comic-phantasmagoric novel, it's the search for the Inaccessible Lost City of Dawn somewhere in the Mayan rain forests that draws, like a magnet, all the lonely and dispossessed, the mad romantics and con artists of the States, to seek out what is missing from their lives by going Below the Border to search for the indecipherable truths encoded in the Mayan hieroglyphics.

Rereading Portis is one of the great pure pleasures—both visceral and cerebral—available in modern American literature. Except it's really *not* available to those who aren't Portis Society initiates (who have squirreled away multiple copies of *Masters of Atlantis* in locked trunks to ensure a lifetime supply). It is a crime and a scandal, it's virtually clinically *insane*, that Portis's last three books are out of print and not in paperback—almost as inaccessible as the lost works of John Selmer Dix. Some smart publisher will earn an honored place in literary history and the hearts of his countrymen by bringing out a complete and accessible edition soon—now.

Meanwhile, I can't stop thinking about Dr. Symes and Dix. What *is* it with all those Dix impostors, those shadowy half brothers with their little Dix museums in *Trailer Review*? Are they real or figures of Symes's Dix delirium? Is the proliferation of Dixes a way of expressing the notion that we're all, in some way, Dixes, hauling around locked trunks containing the inaccessible, unimaginable secrets we hide from one another? Perhaps Portis could tell, but Portis isn't talking, at least not to me.

On *True Grit*

By Donna Tartt

Donna Tartt is the author of the novels *The Secret History* (1992) and *The Little Friend* (2002).

It's commonplace to say that we "love" a book, but when we say it, we really mean all sorts of things. Sometimes we mean only that we have read a book once and enjoyed it; sometimes we mean that a book was important to us in our youth, though we haven't picked it up in years; sometimes what we "love" is an impressionistic idea glimpsed from afar (Combray…madeleines…Tante Leonie…) as opposed to the experience of wallowing and plowing through an actual text, and all too often people claim to love books they haven't read at all. Then there are the books we love so much that we read them every year or two, and know passages of them by heart; that cheer us when we are sick or sad and never fail to amuse us when we take them up at random; that we press on all our friends and acquaintances; and to which we return again and again with undimmed enthusiasm over the course of a lifetime. I think it goes without saying that most books that engage readers on this very high level are masterpieces; and this is why I believe that *True Grit* by Charles Portis is a masterpiece.

Not only have I loved *True Grit* since I was a child; it is a book loved passionately by my entire family. I cannot think of another novel—any novel—which is so delightful to so many disparate age groups and literary tastes. Four generations of us fell for it in a swift *coup de foudre*—starting with my mother's grandmother, then in her early eighties, who borrowed it from the library and adored it and passed it along to my mother. My mother—her eldest granddaughter—was suspicious. There wasn't much overlap in their reading matter: my gentle great-grandmother—born in 1890—was the product of an extremely sheltered life, and a more innocent creature in many respects than are most six-year-olds today; whereas my mother (in her twenties then) kept books like *The Boston Strangler* on her bedside table. Purely from a sense of duty, she gave *True Grit* a try—and was so crazy about it that when she finished it, she turned back to the first page and read it all over again. My own middle-aged grandmother (whose reading habits were rather severe, running to politics and science and history) was smitten by *True Grit*, too, which was even more remarkable since—apart from the classics of her childhood, and what she called "the great books"—she didn't even care all that much for fiction. I think she might have been the person who suggested that it be given to me to read. And I was only about ten, but I loved it too, and I've loved it ever since.

The plot of *True Grit* is uncomplicated, and as pure in its way as one of the *Canterbury Tales*. The opening paragraph sets up the premise of the novel elegantly and economically:

> People do not give it credence that a fourteen-year-old girl could leave home and go off in the wintertime to avenge her father's blood but it did not seem so strange then, although I will say it did not happen every day. I was just fourteen years of age when a coward going by the name of Tom Chaney shot my father down in Fort Smith, Arkansas, and robbed him of his life and his horse and $150 in cash money plus two California gold pieces that he carried in his trouser band.

The speaker is Mattie Ross, from Yell County near Dardanelle, Arkansas, and the time is the 1870s, shortly after the Civil War. Mattie leaves her grief-stricken mother at home with her younger siblings and sets out after Tom Chaney, the hired man who has killed her father. ("Chaney said he was from Louisiana. He was a short man with cruel features. I will tell more about his face later.") But Chaney has joined up with a band of outlaws—the Lucky Ned Pepper gang—and ridden out into the Indian territory, which is under the jurisdiction of U.S. Marshals. Mattie wants someone to go after him; and she wants someone who will shoot first and ask questions later. So she asks the sheriff in Fort Smith for the name of the best marshal he knows:

> The sheriff thought on it a minute. He said: "I would have to weigh that proposition. There is near about two hundred of them. I reckon William Waters is the best tracker. He is a half-breed Comanche and it is something to see, watching him cut for sign. The meanest one is Rooster Cogburn. He is a pitiless man, double-tough, and fear don't enter into his thinking. He loves to pull a cork. Now L.T. Quinn, he brings his prisoners in alive. He may let one get by now and then but he believes even the worst of men is entitled to a fair shake. Also the court does not pay any fees for dead men. Quinn is a good peace officer and a lay preacher to boot. He will not plant evidence or abuse a prisoner. He is straight as a string. Yes, I will say that Quinn is about the best they have."
>
> I said, "Where can I find this Rooster?"

Movie fans will call to mind the aging John Wayne, who famously portrayed Rooster Cogburn on the screen, but the Rooster of the novel is somewhat younger, in his late forties: a fat, one-eyed character with walrus mustaches, unwashed, malarial, drunk much of the time. He is a veteran of the Confederate Army; and, more particularly, of William Clarke Quantrill's bloody border gang, notorious in American history for the massacre at Lawrence, Kansas, and also for launching the careers of the teenaged Frank and Jesse James. Mattie runs Rooster to ground in his squalid rented room at the back of a Chinese grocery store. "Men will live like billy goats if they are let alone," she remarks, disapprovingly, and he's happy enough to take Mattie's money to ride out after her father's killer—but not to let Mattie come along.

> He sat up in the bed. "Wait," he said. "Hold up. You are not going."
>
> "That is part of it," said I.
>
> "It cannot be done."
>
> "And why not? You have misjudged me if you think I am silly enough to give you a hundred dollars and watch you ride away. No, I will see the thing done myself."

Mattie is not the only party after Tom Chaney; so is a vain, good-looking Texas Ranger named LaBoeuf who has already tracked Chaney over several states. LaBoeuf (whose name is pronounced "La Beef," and who is somewhat overly proud of his membership in the Rangers) wants to team up with Rooster to bring Chaney back alive and collect the bounty. But the dandy LaBoeuf, clanking along in his "great brutal spurs" and "Texas trappings," is no more interested than Rooster in allowing a fourteen-year-old girl to tag along on a manhunt; moreover, LaBoeuf's intent is to bring Chaney back to Texas to hang for shooting a Texas state senator in a dispute over a bird dog, a claim which Mattie hotly disputes:

> "Haw, haw," said LaBoeuf. "It is not important where he hangs, is it?"
> "It is to me. Is it to you?"
> "It means a good deal of money to me. Would not a hanging in Texas serve as well as a hanging in Arkansas?"
> "No. You said yourself they might turn him loose down there. This judge will do his duty."
> "If they don't hang him we will shoot him. I can give you my word as a Ranger on that."
> "I want Chaney to pay for killing my father and not some Texas bird dog."
> "It will not be for the dog, it will be for the senator, and your father too. He will be just as dead that way, you see, and pay for all his crimes at once."
> "No, I do not see. That is not the way I look at it."

Not surprisingly, Rooster and LaBoeuf contrive to slip away from Fort Smith without Mattie. But she strikes out after them; and as hard as they ride, they cannot lose her. ("What a foolish plan, pitting horses so heavily loaded with men and hardware against a pony so lightly burdened as Blackie!") Finally, when they cannot get Mattie to turn back, they accept her: first, in anger, as a worrisome tag-along; then, grudgingly, as a mascot and equal of sorts; and at last—as she stands among them and proves herself—a relentless force in her own right.

Like *Huckleberry Finn* (or *The Catcher in the Rye*, or even the Bertie and Jeeves stories for that matter) *True Grit* is a monologue, and the great, abiding pleasure of it that compels the reader to return to it again and again is Mattie's voice. No living Southern writer captures the spoken idioms of the South as artfully as Portis does; but though in all his novels (including those set in the current day) Portis shows his deep understanding of place, *True Grit* also masters the more complicated subtleties of time. Mattie, having survived her youthful adventure, is recounting her story as an old woman, and Portis is such a genius of a literary mimic that the book reads less like a novel than a firsthand account: the Wild West of the 1870s, as recollected in a spinster's memory and filtered through the sedate sepia tones of the early 1900s. Mattie's narrative tone is naive, didactic, hardheaded, and completely lacking in self-consciousness—and, at times, unintentionally hilarious, rather in the manner of Daisy Ashford's *The Young Visiters*. And like *The Young Visiters* (which is largely delightful because it views the most absurd Victorian crotchets as obvious common sense), a great part of *True Grit*'s charm is in Mattie's blasé view of frontier America. Shootings, stabbings, and public hangings are recounted frankly and flatly, and often with rather less warmth than the political and personal opinions upon which Mattie digresses. She quotes scripture; she explains and gives advice to the reader; her observations are often overlaid with a decorative glaze of Sunday School piety. And her own very distinctive voice (blunt, unsentimental, yet salted with parlor platitudes) echoes throughout the reported speech of all the other characters—lawmen and outlaws alike—to richly comic effect, as when Rooster remarks austerely of a young prisoner he has brought back alive to stand trial: "I should have put a ball in that boy's head instead of his collarbone. I was thinking about my fee. You will sometimes let money interfere with your notion of what is right."

Mattie is often compared to her literary ancestor, Huckleberry Finn; but though the two of them share some obvious similarities, in most respects Mattie is a much harder customer than careless, sweet-tempered Huck. Where Huck is barefoot and "uncivilized," living happily in his hogshead barrel, Mattie is a pure product of civilization as a Sunday school teacher in nineteenth-century Arkansas might define it; she is a straitlaced Presbyterian, prim as a poker. "I would not put a thief in my mouth to steal my brains," she says coolly to the drunken Rooster; tidy, industrious, frugal, with a head for figures and a shrewd business sense. Her deadpan manner is reminiscent of Buster Keaton: Mattie, too, is a Great Stone Face; she never cracks a smile when recounting the undignified and ridiculous situations in which she finds herself; and even predicaments of great danger fail to draw violent emotion from her. But this deadpan flatness serves a double purpose in the novel, for if Mattie is humorless, she is also completely lacking in qualities like pity and self-doubt, and her implacable stoniness—while very, very funny—is formidable, too, in a manner reminiscent of old tintypes and *cartes des visites* of Confederate soldier boys: dead-eye killers with rumpled hair and serious angel faces. One cannot picture Huckleberry Finn in the same light; for while Huck is an adventuresome spirit, duty and discipline are wholly foreign to him; conscripted by any army, any cause, he would desert in short order, slipping away the first chance he got to his easy riverbank life. Mattie on the other hand is the perfect soldier, despite her sex. She is as tireless as a gun dog; and while we laugh at her single-mindedness, we also stand in awe of it. In her Old Testament morality, in her legalistic and exacting turn of mind, in the thunderous blackness of her wrath— "What a waste!…I would not rest easy until that Louisiana cur was roasting and screaming in hell!"—she is less Huck Finn's little sister than Captain Ahab's.

True Grit is an adventure story, and though the two books in most respects could not be more different, Mattie's quest in some ways reflects Dorothy Gale's in *The Wizard of Oz*. Practical Dorothy, throughout all her trials, is really only working her way back home to Kansas; while practical Mattie, with her own mission and her own brace of unlikely travelling companions, is riding in the historical shadow of a very different Kansas: the mythical outlaw territory of Quantrill and his Confederate raiders. While Quantrill—a brilliant tactician—was romanticized in some quarters as an outlaw chieftain á la Alexandre Dumas, the massacre he led at the abolitionist town of Lawrence, Kansas, is considered the worst atrocity of the American civil war, and history has tended to view Quantrill as a cold-blooded killer. One man—shot five times when he tried to surrender—was left for dead by his assailant with the parting advice: "Tell old God that the last man you saw on earth was Quantrill." Rooster, presumably, has come by some of his famous meanness under Quantrill's tutelage; the incident with Odus Wharton and the bodies in the fire does seem to have some parallels with unpleasant incidents in historical accounts of raids at Lawrence and Centralia; and certainly he has picked up Quantrill's reputed habit of riding against his enemy with the reins of his horse between his teeth and a revolver in each hand. And yet it is scoundrelly old Rooster who—like Huck Finn, revolting instinctively against the accepted brutality of his day—rises unexpectedly to *True Grit*'s moments of justice and nobility. He does this in a number of minor comical respects (as in his satisfying encounter with the two "wicked boys" who are tormenting the mule on the riverbank) not to mention the novel's extraordinary climax. But perhaps the most gratifying moment in the entire book is when Rooster is jolted from his ambivalence about Mattie by the sight of LaBoeuf falling upon her with a switch:

> I began to cry, I could not help it, but more from anger and embarrassment than pain. I said to Rooster, "Are you going to let him do this?"
>
> He dropped his cigarette to the ground and said, "No, I don't believe I will. Put your switch away, LaBoeuf. She has got the best of us."
>
> "She has not got the best of me," replied the Ranger.
>
> Rooster said, "That will do, I said."
>
> LaBoeuf paid him no heed.
>
> Rooster raised his voice and said, "Put that switch down, LaBoeuf! Do you hear me talking to you?"
>
> LaBoeuf stopped and looked at him. Then he said, "I am going ahead with what I started."
>
> Rooster pulled his cedar-handled revolver and cocked it with his thumb and threw down on LaBoeuf. He said, "It will be the biggest mistake you ever made, you Texas brush-popper."

True Grit, in short, begins where chivalry meets the frontier—where the old Confederacy starts to merge and shade away into the Wild West. And without giving anything away, I can say that the book ends at a travelling Wild West show in Memphis in the early 1900s: which is to say, at once in the twentieth century and firmly enshrined in myth and legend.

True Grit was first published in 1968. When it came out, Roald Dahl wrote that it was the best novel to come his way in a long time. "I was going to say it was the best novel to come my way since…Then I stopped. Since what? What book has given me greater pleasure in the last five years? Or in the last twenty?" Certainly when I was growing up in the 1970s, *True Grit* was widely thought to be a classic; when I was about fourteen years old, it was read along with Walt Whitman and Nathaniel

Hawthorne and Edgar Allan Poe in the Honors English classes at my school. Yet (because, I believe, of the John Wayne film, which is good enough but which doesn't do the book justice), *True Grit* vanished from the public eye, and my mother and I, along with many other Portis fans, were reduced to scouring used bookstores and buying up whatever stock we could find because the copies we lent out so evangelically were never returned. (In one particularly dark moment, when my mother's last copy had disappeared and a new one was nowhere to be had, she borrowed the library's copy and then pretended that she had lost it.) Now—thankfully—the book is back in print, and I am delighted to have the honor of introducing Mattie Ross and Rooster Cogburn to a new generation of readers.

The Book That Changed My Life: *Gringos*

By Wells Tower

Wells Tower is the author of the short-story collection *Everything Ravaged, Everything Burned* (2009). This appreciation appeared in the June 2011 issue of *GQ* magazine as part of a feature in which he and other authors wrote about books that were important to them.

Sometime after my fifth reading of Charles Portis's *Gringos*, I stopped worrying so much about death, politics, and getting fat, and I started worrying about my car.

Gringos is a compact, hilarious meander in the life of Jimmy Burns, an amateur archaeologist, junk trader, and shade-tree mechanic eking out a transcendently unexamined life in Mexico's Yucatán peninsula. Burns's anxieties are more automotive than existential, a stacking of priorities that, as the book proceeds, begins to resemble a quietly heroic state of grace. These are the sorts of unassailable proverbs you get from Jimmy Burns: "You put things off and then one morning you wake up and say—today I will change the oil in my truck." Repeat this line a few times. It sticks in your head like the answer to a Buddhist koan.

I put Burnsisms into practice all the time. The other day, I was driving around with my lady friend when, out of nowhere, she yelled, "Look, dammit, there are some things going on between us we seriously need to discuss."

"Okay," I said, "but right now I need to listen to that thumping sound, which I think is a blown sway-bar bushing." I don't know what a sway-bar bushing is, but saying these words made everything get calm and quiet so that all I could hear was the soothing drone of the engine and the tranquil grinding of my sweetheart's molars.

Over the course of the novel, Burns's heroics range past the everyday and into more swashbuckling territory. At one point, he's compelled to blow out the brains of a homicidal hippie guru, but he doesn't let the killing ruffle his composure. "Shotgun blast or not at close range, I was still surprised at how fast and clean Dan had gone down," Burns reflects. "I wasn't used to seeing my will so little resisted, having been in sales for so long."

Most people know Charles Portis only as the author of *True Grit* (whose comic brilliance both the recent Coen brothers adaptation and the 1969 John Wayne film failed to fulfill), but for my money *Gringos* is his subtlest, funniest, and most valuable for its depth of inarguable wisdom: If your clutch plate doesn't rust to your flywheel and you get a fair price on that set of used tires, you've tasted as much of life's sweet fullness as anyone deserves.

Sources

I. SELECTED NEWSPAPER REPORTING AND WRITING

The stories on pages 3–8 are reprinted by permission of the *Commercial Appeal* in Memphis, Tennessee.

The stories from the *Arkansas Gazette* on pages 10–18 are reprinted by permission of the *Arkansas Democrat-Gazette* in Little Rock, Arkansas.

The stories on pages 19–66 from the *New York Herald Tribune* are reprinted by permission. © 1960–1964 *The New York Times*. All rights reserved. Used by permission and protected by the copyright laws of the United States. The printing, copying, redistribution, or retransmission of this content without express written permission is prohibited.

II. TRAVELS

"That New Sound from Nashville," *Saturday Evening Post*, February 12, 1966. © 1966 SEPS by Curtis Licensing, Indianapolis, Indiana. All rights reserved.

The following song lyrics quoted in the story are used by permission:

Page 72: "Mule Skinner Blues," by Jimmie Rodgers and Vaughn Horton © 1931, 1950 by Peer International Corporation. Copyright renewed. International copyright secured. Used by permission. All rights reserved.

Page 73: "A White Sport Coat (and a Pink Carnation)," words and music by Marty Robbins © 1957 (renewed 1985) Mariposa Music, Inc.

"An Auto Odyssey through Darkest Baja." *Los Angeles Times Home Magazine*, February 26, 1967.

"The Forgotten River." *Arkansas Times*, September 1991.

"Motel Life, Lower Reaches." *Oxford American*, January/February 2003.

III. SHORT STORIES

"Your Action Line." *The New Yorker*, December 12, 1977.

"Nights Can Turn Cool in Viborra." *The Atlantic*, December 1992.

"I Don't Talk Service No More." *The Atlantic*, May 1996.

"The Wind Bloweth Where It Listeth." *Oxford American*, Winter 2005.

IV. MEMOIR

"Combinations of Jacksons." *The Atlantic*, May 1999.

V. DRAMA

Delray's New Moon. Previously unpublished. First performed by the Arkansas Repertory Theatre, April 18, 1996.

EPILOGUE

"*Gazette* Project Interview with Charles Portis," conducted by Roy Reed on May 31, 2001, in Little Rock, Arkansas, for the David and Barbara Pryor Center for Arkansas Oral and Visual History at the University of Arkansas in Fayetteville. The interview has been previously available on-line at http://pryorcenter.uark.edu/projects/arkansasgazette/CPortis.pdf (accessed June 18, 2012). Reprinted here courtesy of Special Collections, University of Arkansas Libraries, Fayetteville, and the Pryor Center for Arkansas Oral and Visual History.

APPENDIX

"Comedy in Earnest," by Roy Blount Jr., was adapted for this collection from two essays that were originally published in the *Oxford American* ("True Lit," March–May 1999; later reprinted in his collection *Long Time Leaving*) and *Arkansas Life* ("Charles Portis," December 2010). Used here by permission of the author.

"Like Cormac McCarthy, but Funny," by Ed Park, originally appeared in *The Believer*, March 2003. Reprinted by permission of the author.

"Our Least-Known Great Novelist," by Ron Rosenbaum, originally appeared in *Esquire*, January 1998. The essay was reprinted in his collection *The Secret Parts of Fortune* (Random House, 2000) as "Charles Portis and the Locked Trunk Secret" and as an afterword to *The Dog of the South* (Overlook, 1999). Reprinted here by permission of the author.

"On *True Grit*," by Donna Tartt, originally appeared as the introduction to a paperback edition of the book published in the U.K. by Bloomsbury

Acknowledgements

First of all, I thank Charles Portis for allowing me to edit this collection, and Rod Lorenzen of Butler Center Books for making it happen. Even before it looked like there would ever be a book like this, Mike Reddy expressed his desire to work with me on anything Portis related, and his art is a wonderful complement to the words. Mr. Portis's agent, Lynn Nesbit, was supportive and helpful in bringing the project to fruition, and my own agent, Chris Parris-Lamb, went beyond the call of duty, as always. H. K. Stewart worked with some knotty obstacles to bring an elegant design to the interior of the book. Ali Welky saved me from making some embarrassing mistakes and gave the book a loving but exacting copyedit.

Eddie Dean, Portis fan extraordinaire, was crucial in narrowing down selections from the *Arkansas Gazette*. Margaret Schlankey of the Briscoe Center for American History at the University of Texas aided me in unearthing some hidden gems in the morgue of the *New York Herald Tribune*, and the entire staff there was very gracious during my days in Austin. Judy Trice, through Kathryn Pryor, was most generous in lending me her script of *Delray's New Moon*. Especially notable among those who helped research or grant permissions were Chris Peck of the *Commercial Appeal*, Frank Fellone of the *Arkansas Democrat-Gazette*, Gerald Braun of PARS International, Lindsey Millar of the *Arkansas Times*, Marc Smirnoff of the *Oxford American*, and David Jácome of Peer Music.

The authors of the appreciations in the appendix—Roy Blount Jr., Ed Park, Ron Rosenbaum, Donna Tartt, and Wells Tower—get great appreciation in turn from me for their eagerness to allow their work to be reprinted here. Along the way, Kathy Robbins and Arielle Asher in the Robbins Office and Amanda Urban and Shira Schindel at ICM greased the gears.

Providing moral, practical, and/or liquid support throughout the project were Jay Barth, Sheila Callaghan, Chuck Cliett, Graham Gordy, Walter Jennings, Michelle Kaemmerling, Annie Stricklin, David Stricklin, the entire Butler Center staff, and not least the crew at the Faded Rose—Rick Cobb, Sam Ulmer, Brian Poole, Mitch McCollum, Terry McCoy, Chess Green, and the late Mike Scott—all of whose "humorous sallies" deserve to be transcribed in Hester's Red Letter.